Praise for

Tori
Carrington

"A highly charged, sensual story laced with intense emotion,
humor and some of the sharpest dialogue ever written. The
sizzling tension between Mitch and Liz catapults this tale
into the stratosphere. Tori Carrington is definitely one of the
hottest writers to be included in the Temptation line."
—*Rendezvous* on *The P.I. Who Loved Her*

"Emotional dialogue, sizzling passion and powerful prose
combine to make this story the best yet of the...series.
Readers will be begging for the next book from this
exceptional author."
—*Rendezvous* on *For Her Eyes Only*

"Seduction has never been so good! Magnificent!"
—Karen L. Williams, Rhapsody Book Club

Dear Reader,

In September 2004 you got a chance to revisit the first McCoy in *Marry Me...Maybe?* Hold on to your socks because here come the next two brothers in *From McCoy, with Love*.

After one close call with matrimony, Mitch McCoy is a happily confirmed bachelor...until his long-lost bride breezes back into town wearing another wedding dress and red shoes! In *The P.I. Who Loved Her,* Mitch might not be "in love" with Liz anymore, but he's never stopped wanting to "make love" to her. But will Liz finally give Mitch the wedding night they never had? Or will her latest groom track her down first?

In the Holt Medallion winning story *For Her Eyes Only,* I.N.S. Agent Jake McCoy prides himself on being a loner. So how does sexy illegal alien Michelle Lambert steal her way into his heart—and his bed—so quickly? She won't go home without her child and Jake can't blame her. Unfortunately, he can't keep his hands off her, either. Torn between duty and desire, Jake never guesses he'll soon be a fugitive himself—and a married man! *From McCoy, with Love* leads into a brand new McCoy title next month, *A Real McCoy.* Stay tuned for this one because you'll never guess who's coming to dinner....

We'd love to hear from you. Write us at P.O. Box 12271, Toledo, Ohio 43612, or e-mail us at toricarrington@aol.com. Also, visit our Web site at www.toricarrington.com.

Wishing you happy—and hot!—reading,

Lori & Tony Karayianni
aka Tori Carrington

THE MAGNIFICENT MCCOY MEN miniseries
HARLEQUIN TEMPTATION

Signature Select™

MINISERIES

Tori Carrington

FROM McCOY, WITH LOVE

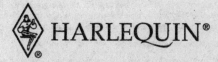

HARLEQUIN®

TORONTO • NEW YORK • LONDON
AMSTERDAM • PARIS • SYDNEY • HAMBURG
STOCKHOLM • ATHENS • TOKYO • MILAN • MADRID
PRAGUE • WARSAW • BUDAPEST • AUCKLAND

ISBN 0-373-21758-7

FROM McCOY, WITH LOVE

Copyright © 2005 by Harlequin Books S.A.

The publisher acknowledges the copyright holder
of the individual works as follows:

THE P.I. WHO LOVED HER
Copyright © 2000 by Lori and Tony Karayianni.

FOR HER EYES ONLY
Copyright © 2000 by Lori and Tony Karayianni.

Dear Reader,

The editors at Harlequin and Silhouette are thrilled to be able to bring you a brand-new featured author program beginning in 2005! Signature Select aims to single out outstanding stories, contemporary themes and oft-requested classics by some of your favorite series authors and present them to you in a variety of formats bound by truly striking covers.

You may notice a number of different colored bands on the spine of this book. Each color corresponds to a different type of reading experience in the new Signature Select program. The Spotlight books will offer a single "big read" by a talented series author, the Collections will present three novellas on a selected theme in one volume, the Sagas will contain sprawling, sometimes multi-generational family tales (often related to a favorite family first introduced in series) and the Miniseries will feature requested, previously published books, with two or, occasionally, three complete stories in one volume. The Signature Select program will offer one book in each of these categories per month, and fans of limited continuity series will also find these continuing stories under the Signature Select umbrella.

In addition, these volumes will bring you bonus features...different in every single book! You may learn more about the author in an extended interview, more about the setting or inspiration for the book, more about subjects related to the theme and, often, a bonus short read will be included.

Watch for new stories from Vicki Lewis Thompson, Lori Foster, Donna Kauffman, Marie Ferrarella, Merline Lovelace, Roberta Gellis, Suzanne Forster, Stephanie Bond and scores more of the brightest talents in romance fiction!

We have an exciting year ahead!

Warm wishes for happy reading,

Marsha Zinberg

Marsha Zinberg
Executive Editor
The Signature Select Program

THE P.I. WHO LOVED HER

CHAPTER ONE

"YOU KNOW, Mitch McCoy, you really need to get a life."

Mitch downshifted as he neared the outskirts of Manchester County, Virginia, then tugged at his tie. Only the pickup's headlights broke the inky darkness, his own voice broke the all-consuming silence. Still, he wouldn't be surprised if Sheriff Mathison waited on the other side of the next cornfield, ready to nab him for speeding. Next to him, Goliath stared at the closed passenger window, a patch of coffee-colored fur disturbed by the air conditioner blower. The dog—a mammoth, butt-ugly husky and shepherd mix—whined and turned mournful eyes on him.

"I know what you mean, sport. I know what you mean."

And he did know. In the past few months he'd come to know exactly what wanting an unnamed something meant. Waking up in the morning in a cold sweat, reaching for something—or someone—that wasn't there. Speaking thoughts and ideas aloud only to discover there was no one around to hear. Living with an intangible hole in the vicinity of his chest—a hole that wasn't going to be filled tonight by going home to an empty house.

The entire McCoy clan was still in Bedford, Maryland, celebrating his brother Marc's marriage to Melanie Weber, even though the miserably happy couple had already left for their honeymoon cruise to the U.S. Virgin Islands. *The Virgin Islands.* Marc had said something about it being romantic. Maybe it was Marc and Mel's idea of romance. A ship would be the last place he'd find romantic. All that…water. Garish tropical-print shirts. Food-laden buffet tables. Sunshine. Sex—

Mitch's foot slipped from the gas pedal. Where had *that* thought come from?

It wasn't that he begrudged his brother his happiness. It was a miracle Marc and Mel had finally sorted everything out, despite the drastic way in which they had. It was just that, of the five McCoy siblings, clueless Marc seemed like the last person who would stand at an altar, much less be the first.

Well, he hadn't exactly been the *first.* But he had been the first to actually make it to the nuptials part.

That was it—the reason he was so agitated. All this talk of weddings…of the L word…of making promises and sticking to them. It should have occurred to him when he'd had to squirm in that uncomfortable pew for an hour, forced to watch Marc and Melanie complete what he had never had. Forced to remember the day he'd been left at the altar as if it were yesterday.

But it hadn't been yesterday. He tugged at his tie again. It was seven years ago last month Liz Braden had left the town, and him, behind.

At any rate, his…restlessness hadn't developed overnight. No, it had been months—if not years—in the making. He'd grown listless in his role as P.I., just as years before he'd grown frustrated at the rigmarole as an FBI agent. While he still shared an office in D.C. with his two partners, Mike Schaffer and Renee Delancy, he'd passed most of his clients over to them, keeping only those to whom he felt personally obligated. Then he'd returned home to Manchester to pursue a dusty old dream—a dream he'd secretly harbored since his mother had told him about the Connor tradition of horse-breeding. He'd readily abandoned the fantasy at eighteen when he'd followed in the footsteps of every other McCoy male for the past four generations and entered the military, then later, law enforcement.

But rather than his frustration abating as a result of the recent changes in his life, it had quadrupled. The crappy thing was he knew exactly when that had happened: the night Marc had asked him about Liz Braden.

What was it his brother had asked? He couldn't remember the exact words, but he all too clearly remembered their meaning: Had he ever regretted not going after Liz?

If only Marc knew that he *had* gone after her. In a sense, anyway.

Goliath whined again, louder this time. Mitch frowned at him in the darkness. "What is it, G? Do you have to water the weeds?"

The mutt lumbered to an alert position, a line of slobber dropping from the side of his meaty mouth to his elephantine front paws, indented on the edge of the seat.

Mitch glanced in the rearview mirror to find the road behind him empty. He downshifted again and flicked on his high beams, illuminating the dark stretch of Route 28 in front of him.

Aw, who was he kidding? He was the last person to be applying armchair psychology to his life. In all likelihood, his agitated state was due to something far simpler. Say, lack of sex? It had been a long time since he'd buried himself in some prime, sleek, female flesh. Too long. He told himself that right now any female would do. But he knew that wasn't true. He simply figured that's how most men who hadn't had any in a while feel.

Fifty feet ahead on the opposite side of the two-lane road, a stopped car with its yellow hazard lights flashing stood out against the otherwise black June night.

Still, someone with a great smile and a fine pair of thighs would be nice. He squinted at the woman standing next to the car. Anyone but—

Liz.

Mitch tightly hauled the steering wheel to the left to stop the truck from catapulting over the embankment and into the ditch. He cursed, his heart rate leaping. Marc and his damn questions. He'd never have thought of Liz if it wasn't for his brother. Well, that wasn't entirely true, but he'd certainly never hallucinated seeing her before.

He was worse off than he thought.

A deep breath whistled from between his teeth as he stared at the brand-spanking-new Lexus gleaming in the twin beams of his headlights. In a town filled with pickups, a pricey automobile pulled off the side of the road at twelve-thirty in the morning was sure to raise some speculation. Goliath nudged his shoulder. Mitch ignored him as the bright beam of his headlights reflected off the woman kneeling next to the left rear tire.

His brakes quietly squealed as he stopped his truck even with the car. "Need some help, lady?"

The woman wrenched a crowbar up and down. Mitch's gaze followed the way her sweetly shaped bottom within her white dress swayed with each movement. Hmmm….

"Thanks, but no," she said. "I've changed tires before. One more isn't going to make much of a difference."

Mitch glanced at the digital clock on his dash, then back to her tempting backside. To hell with wanting someone with a great smile. He'd settle for a grade-A bottom like this one had.

It's a wedding dress.

He stared at the silky white material skimming the woman's lavish curves and nearly choked. Okay, that was it. He'd had enough of weddings, and anything associated with them, to last a lifetime.

Goliath pawed his denim-clad legs. Mitch held the dog back from where he strained toward the open window.

"What's up, G?" He hadn't seen him this animated in years. The tinny sound of music reached his ears. It wafted from the open door of the Lexus. Country, he guessed, grimacing. He scanned the lighted interior, finding the car empty. No air freshener hanging from the mirror, no purse on the seat, no sign of a suitcase or overnight bag. He glanced over the roof toward the dark ditch he knew paralleled the road. He found no sign of a shadowy figure waiting to ambush him.

"You're getting cynical in your old age," he muttered, then said to her, "Suit yourself."

He shifted the truck back into gear.

He'd moved thirty feet before he stepped on the brakes again. He tapped his side-view mirror until the woman in white was back in sight. *Damn.* He couldn't just leave her there. Despite his natural caution and the fact that the county crime rate was basically nil, Pops had taught him and his brothers better than to leave anyone—much less a woman—stranded on the road in the middle of the night.

Sighing, Mitch hooked a U-turn, bringing his truck back behind the Lexus and its Massachusetts license plate. Nothing to indicate it was a rental. Then again, most states had done away with marking rentals. He ground to a stop directly behind the car. He rolled up the window enough to prevent Goliath from jumping out, then climbed from the truck cab.

"Indulge me," he said, before she could protest. He hoisted the spare from the Lexus's trunk, then nudged her out of the way. "Neither of us is going to rest until you're safely back on the road." He jacked the car up a little higher, his muscles bunching under his shirt at the familiar scent of wild cherries. The music battled with the cadence of crickets in a nearby cornfield.

"Mitch?" the woman said over the sound of a twangy guitar. "Mitch McCoy, is that you?"

He stood up so quickly, he nearly tripped over the spare lying on the road behind him.

Holy... It *was* Liz.

WELL I'LL BE....

Liz dragged her gaze over the long, delicious length of man standing before her, from his shiny boots, to his tight, new jeans, then up to where a tie hung haphazardly around the collar of his crisp white shirt. She didn't know who was more shocked by the midnight encounter, her or Mitch. And she was definitely sure the fine specimen before her was Mitch. Years may have passed since she'd last seen him, but she'd recognize the tantalizing man anywhere. No one could fill out a pair of jeans quite the way Mitch could.

Liz ran the tip of her tongue along her suddenly dry lips. *Amazing.*

She finally looked up to his face and gave a short, impulsive laugh. No, she'd have to say *he* was the more surprised of the two by far. He looked like someone had just whacked him in the head with a two-by-four. She smiled. Imagine that. She had rendered Mitch McCoy speechless.

"You changed your hair color," he finally blurted, more than said.

She tucked a dark strand behind her ear, a small part of her flattered he'd noticed—which was majorly stupid. The last thing she should have been doing was blushing at a man's attentions. Even if that man was Mitch McCoy. "Yeah. I, um, didn't always have more fun as a blonde." Of course, she wasn't having that much fun as a brunette either, if her current predicament was any indication.

His gaze flicked rather than slid over her attire, lingering in certain places and causing a curious, sizzling warmth to meander through her bloodstream. Well, *that* certainly hadn't changed, had it? It had taken Richard Beschloss five dates to get to first base with her. One look from Mitch and…

Well, she didn't think it prudent to take that thought any further.

His gaze reached her breasts. The meandering heat quickened to a scamper and she found it suddenly impossible to breathe.

His gaze quickly lifted to her face. "Liz, is that blood on your dress? What kind of trouble have you gotten yourself into now?"

If anything was capable of reminding her of the mess she was currently in, *that* was. She glanced down at the dark stain on the bright white of her dress. Trust Mitch to immediately identify it correctly. Back in Jersey she'd gotten away with telling a gas station attendant she'd spilled chocolate syrup on herself.

She looked back at Mitch, whose gaze was riveted to her breasts.

"Are you hurt?" he asked.

"No…no, I'm fine," she said, feeling the ridiculous urge to laugh again. Now her ex-groom, on the other hand…. "Don't, um, worry, it's not mine. I'm as fit as the day I last saw you."

Mitch reached up and tugged almost violently on his tie, drawing her gaze to the base of his neck. All at once, her mind filled with the image of the two of them standing in the front room of Gran's house, him in his new suit, her standing in her bare feet staring at him proudly. It had been his first official day as an agent of the FBI. "Why, Mitch McCoy, you clean up real nice." She'd laid on her best southern drawl, forgetting how torn she was between wanting him to succeed in what he'd chosen to do, and needing him to be there for her.

How long had it taken her to break him of the habit of fussing with his tie? Two months? Three? How many times had she smoothed his collar, only to be sidetracked by the clean-smelling expanse of his skin there, just under his jaw?

She dragged her gaze up to his, watching her guardedly. She caught her bottom lip between her teeth.

"Somehow I knew you'd still be in Manchester," she said, her voice a little too breathless, a little too revealing. She reached for the crowbar and continued jacking up the car. "Small-town boy Mitch McCoy, who'll die in the same spot he was born."

She slid a glance over her shoulder, relieved to find him grimacing at the gibe. "What's *that* supposed to mean?"

She shrugged.

Oh, yeah, she'd known odds were she'd run into Mitch when she came back to Manchester. And she'd even admit to feeling a tingle of excitement at the prospect of coming face-to-face with him. The only problem was, she hadn't counted on running into him the instant she rolled over the county line. Hadn't expected to be reminded of how much she had missed him.

That was just one of those things about life: when it rained, it bloody well stormed.

She cleared her throat. "How's, um, your father?" she asked, acutely aware that he was watching her backside.

He jostled her out of the way then knelt in front of the tire. "Fine. He's fine."

"And your brothers?"

"They're fine, too." He sat back on his heels. "Look, Liz, I'm really not in the mood for a game of catch-up. It's been a really long day. I'd like nothing more than to get you on your way, then go home and crawl into bed." She watched him stiffen, then close his eyes and mutter a curse. He finished hoisting the car up and methodically removed the lug nuts from the flat. Her mind turned over all the possible reasons for his reaction, then she homed in on the most likely: the mention of bed and her in the same sentence.

The warmth that had spread through her veins earlier edged up a degree or two. She rode out a delicious shiver, and tried to remind herself of the long list of reasons she had *not* to play with the fire flickering in front of her in the shape of Mitch McCoy. First and foremost, the fact that she had been minutes away from marrying another man, oh, not twelve hours ago.

Still, not even that impetus was enough to stop her from wanting Mitch in much the same way she'd always wanted him, despite the number of years that separated then from now.

He glanced at her over a broad shoulder. "So what brings you back to Manchester, Liz? Last I heard, you were in Chicago."

She smiled. He might not want to play catch-up when it came to himself, but it appeared she was a whole different matter. "So you kept tabs on me. I'm impressed." She watched his frown deepen. "I do have to say I'm a little disappointed, though. I left Chicago a few years back."

"Let me guess. You left for Massachusetts."

"Um, actually no," she said quietly. "There were a couple of cities in between." She felt inexplicably uncomfortable. "But they don't matter. Not now."

The crowbar slipped from a lug nut and he nearly pierced the flat tire with the pointed end.

"What is it with the dress, Liz? Is your groom stashed in the trunk, or is this style one you've taken a liking to?"

She inwardly winced at the below-the-belt jab. "I don't know, Mitch. Did you see anyone in the trunk when you got the tire out?"

"Damn. Stepped right into that one, didn't I?" He continued working on the flat tire. "You never answered my question."

She stared at him blankly.

"What are you doing back in Manchester?"

Now that *was* a question. What was she doing back in Manchester? It was something she'd been asking herself ever since she realized a few hours ago that was where she was heading.

She shrugged. "I don't know. I was feeling a little nostalgic for the past, maybe?" She turned away from where he watched her a little too closely and drew in a deep breath of the damp, summer night air. "I'll be on my way as soon as some things settle down in Boston."

She hadn't realized he'd moved until he stood right next to her. "These things that need to settle down—they don't have anything to do with the blood on your dress, do they?"

She glanced at Mitch's profile in the darkness. For just an instant, she remembered that her favorite pastime had once been staring at him. Tracing the outline of his nose with her finger…running her tongue along the fine ridge of his jaw….

She cleared her throat. "No. Well, not exactly anyway."
She wiped at a smudge on her long skirt then turned her best
smile on him. "This stain really has you worked up, doesn't
it?"

He rubbed his long, slender fingers against his chin, making her fingers ache to do the same. "Yeah, well, you always
did have this way of getting under my skin."

"Yeah. Ditto," she said, eyeing his mouth. His wide, generous mouth she had once kissed for hours at a stretch. Dipping her tongue in and out of its hot wetness. Sucking on
his bottom lip then catching it between her teeth. "Guess
some things never change, no matter how much you want
them to."

"Yeah."

Her gaze slammed into his. What seemed like an eter-
nity of unanswered questions and unacknowledged truths
seemed to pass between them. Then Mitch drew away and
moved stiffly back to the car, a line of quiet oaths filling
his wake.

Liz straightened the strap of her dress and sighed. Truth
be told, she didn't know what she was doing back in
Manchester. One minute she was punching Richard in the
nose at the Beschloss estate, the next she was on her way to
Virginia with no clothes, no resources, and every reason to
think she wouldn't have access to either for a while. At least
not until Rich regained his cool. Of course, if she'd known
what was going to happen, she never would have sold her
apartment and moved all her things to Rich's place. Or
rushed out with little more than her car keys and the clothes
on her back, her plans not stretching beyond getting out of
the house *now*. Good thing she always kept her driver's license and a gas card in the car's glove compartment or she'd

never have made it out of Massachusetts. She'd also found a few dollars' worth of change in the car, but that was it.

She had suspected there was something inherently wrong with getting engaged to a spoiled bank vice president whose family just happened to own the financial institution he worked at and where she had all her accounts. And here she thought her misgivings had to do with all that blue blood that ran through his veins.

Then there was Mitch....

She watched him lower the car and tighten the lug nuts. He got up and held out the crowbar and jack.

"Here. Since you didn't want my help to begin with, I'm sure you won't mind cleaning up."

She accepted the items, then flicked a glance down the road. Mitch followed her line of vision.

"What's the matter? You expecting company?"

She laughed her response, then abruptly stopped. Was it naive to think that Rich wouldn't follow her?

The sound of a barking dog made her jump. Then she recognized the over-zealous, roaring bark of this particular dog. She stared at the truck behind the Lexus.

"That's not..." She met Mitch's exasperated gaze. "You still have Goliath?"

His silence was all the answer she needed. She thrust the jack and crowbar back at him, then lifted her skirts and hurried in the direction of the truck.

Mitch stood planted to the spot on the asphalt, clutching the tools. He felt as if someone had grabbed the edges of the invisible rug that constituted his life and given it a good yank, throwing everything into chaos. Funny, it was the same way he had always felt when around Liz Braden. Actually, it depended on the day. Years ago he'd described her as the

sunlight that had chased the shadows from the dark side of his soul. Tonight, she was definitely a rug-yanker.

He watched her open the truck door as enthusiastically as if she wore jeans and a T-shirt rather than a wedding dress. The aging brown-white-and-black dappled dog leapt out. If he didn't know better, he would think the mutt recognized the woman who had rescued him from life as a mangy farm dog. He lapped repeatedly at her face and ran around her with more energy than he'd shown for years. Remembering Goliath's whining in the truck before he'd even spotted the disabled car, he idly wondered if the dog had known what was coming all along.

Or maybe he was as much of a sucker for a pretty face as he was.

Mitch leaned against the bed of the truck, watching the two get reacquainted, Liz murmuring endearments and roughhousing with a dog he would have thought she'd forgotten by now. Forgotten much as she had forgotten him.

"God, how old is he?" she asked.

"Twelve." Mitch cast a glance down the dark road. What had she been looking for?

"Don't worry," she said, stepping beside him, a puppy-like Goliath at her heels. "I lost the car following me a couple hundred miles back."

"Car?" Mitch jerked toward her. "What car?"

"I'm joking. Like I said, there's nothing to worry about." He noted the teasing look in her eyes. "What are you doing out this late, anyway?"

"I…it's…" he started, then stopped, the irony of the situation just now hitting him. "I'm coming back from a wedding reception in Maryland." He tugged again at his tie. "Marc got married."

She nodded, the warm silence of the night pressing in around Mitch along with the pure scent of her. "And you?" she asked.

"Me what?"

She motioned toward his tie and dress attire. "Are you…married?"

He made a point of slowly gazing at her dress. The blood-stain was limited to the one area. No splatters, not a trace on the long, lacy skirt. "Yep. Five years. Three kids. Five cats. A goat. All complete with white picket fence."

Her eyes narrowed. He grinned.

"I'm joking," he said, echoing her words of moments before. Hey, two could play at this game, couldn't they? "Nope, I'm not married. One try at the altar was enough for me."

"Cute. Really cute, McCoy." She laughed. "Funny, I just realized the same thing about myself this morning. About one try at the altar, that is." Her hazel eyes twinkled in a way that made it impossible to look away.

In that moment, it was almost too easy to forget she had once run her hand lovingly down his chest only to rip his heart out. Her gaze said as much as it ever had…maybe even more. Her luscious mouth just as little.

Concentrate on the bloodstain, McCoy. The bloodstain.

"Well, I guess I'd better get back on the road," she said. "There's a lot I have to do before I call it a night."

Mitch squashed the urge to grasp her wrist, to ask her exactly what she had to do, where she had been, why she had changed the color of her hair…anything to make her stay a little longer.

His reaction surprised even him.

But rather than giving in to it, he pulled in a deep breath, then let loose a sharp whistle. Goliath loped back from the long grass at the side of the road. The dog burrowed his nose into Liz's wedding dress and whined, then bounded into the truck.

"You staying at your grandmother's place?" he asked, thinking of the old Victorian that hunkered at the edge of town. Though Old Man Peabody looked after it, no one had lived there since Liz's maternal grandmother had died, and Liz herself had left seven years ago for parts unknown.

"I was thinking about it."

He hiked an eyebrow. "Aren't you going in the wrong direction?"

She shivered visibly despite the warm air. "I...I thought I'd take a look around town and see what's changed first. You know, this being my first time back in so long."

He nodded as if the idea made perfect sense. It made none. What was she hoping to see at twelve-thirty in the morning? He looked back down the road. "Well, I probably won't be crossing paths with you again before you leave. Have a nice visit, won't you?"

Tucking her wayward white skirt around her legs, she climbed into the Lexus. He closed the door for her, but not before he caught a glimpse of her spike-heeled red shoes. He jammed his fingers through his hair.

"Goodbye, Mitch," she said through the open window.

"Right, 'bye."

He stepped back from the door to allow her to drive away. He should be getting into his truck, heading for the empty McCoy farmhouse a couple of miles away. But he stood stock-still, his gaze plastered to the rear end of the Lexus. He barely noticed the hazard lights were still flashing. His entire body pounded with lust. Lust remembered and re-ignited.

Liz was back.

LIZ MISSED the turnoff by half a car length, backed up, then pulled the Lexus onto the two ruts that served as her grandmother's driveway. She coasted rather than pulled to a stop, then put the car in Park.

She lay back against the buttery leather headrest, surprised to find herself feeling more than a bit…well, flighty. The sensation had begun the instant she realized she couldn't marry Richard and had climbed to dizzying proportions when she'd bumped into Mitch. If she were a believer in cosmic events, fate, she might even indulge in a little wagering that a higher being had masterminded the entire midnight meeting by guaranteeing that her tire would go flat at just the moment Mitch was passing by.

Except that she had noticed the tire was losing air somewhere back in Jersey. She had thought about changing it then, but once she'd realized where she was heading, she'd been in an all-fired hurry to get there. She'd stopped only for gas.

Still, the tire could have waited until she got to Gran's…..

Blaming her errant thoughts on lack of sleep and the sharp change of direction her life had taken, she automatically reached for a purse that wasn't there, then opened the car door. It wasn't until she was halfway to the back of the house that she noticed the hazard lights were still blinking. She didn't care. She was too busy reacquainting herself with the familiar structure in the dim beams of the headlights.

How many summers had she spent here when she was growing up? Ten? Twelve? Regardless of the number, it struck her that the old house was the singular constant in her life, a place that remained the same while the rest of her surroundings forever changed. This house and her grandmother had been an anchor in a world made topsy-turvy, first, by her mother's perpetual migrating from city to city, apartment to apartment, then, by her own almost vagabond existence. When she was younger, Liz had always known she could handle anything as long as she could share those brief, sweet summer months with Gran. It was the place she had run to now.

Her steps slowed the nearer she drew to the back door. Unlike years before, though, Gran wouldn't be there waiting for her, to hug her in that suffocating way that always made her smile, question her about her new haircut, or tell her those goofy stories to illuminate the reasons why she shouldn't grow up too soon.

Boy, could she really use a wise-up talk from Gran now.

But she had lost Minerva Braden seven years ago…she had inherited all that had been hers…become engaged to Mitch, then…

"That was all a long, long time ago, Lizzie," she said out loud, using the words she imagined her grandmother would have. "Before Mitch. Before that jerk Richard Beschloss. Before you found yourself on the road with no purse, no clothes, nowhere to go…."

Despite the dark, she knew exactly where to put her hand over the window molding to find the back-door key. She was glad Old Man Peabody hadn't moved it during his weekly checks and maintenance of the place. She remembered asking Gran once why she bothered even locking the door if everyone knew where the key was anyway. Her grandmother had told her that if someone was that determined to get in, let them do it in a way that wouldn't require repairs. Liz wrapped her fingers around the cool metal, then inserted the key in the lock, bombarded by memories of Gran's practical wisdom.

Assaulted, as well, by sexy memories of Mitch McCoy.

Yes, she admitted, she'd frequently revisited memories of her first love during her time away. Memories that had seen her through some particularly lonely stretches. Memories that had grown tattered with time, but, in one midnight meeting, had grown vividly…real all over again.

Before she'd even completely closed the door, she kicked off her red shoes in the mudroom, then she started stripping out of the constraining wedding dress. She sucked in her breath and yanked down the zipper as she made her way into the kitchen and across the room to where she knew a kerosene lamp was stored in the pantry. She pulled the top of the dress down over her camisole, and freed her arms, feeling around on the second shelf as she shimmied out of the dress. Taking the lamp down, its weight and the sloshing of the kerosene making her sigh in relief, she picked up the dress and strode toward the counter where she found matches in a top drawer.

Within moments the room was aglow with warm light…enough light for her to examine just how bad the stain on the front of the wedding dress was. She bit her bottom lip. It was much worse than she thought. No wonder Mitch had asked so many questions. She couldn't blame him for thinking she'd offed someone. It looked suspiciously as if she had.

Who'd have thought so much blood could gush out of a person's nose?

Once on the road, she had stopped at the first gas station, then gone into the bathroom to pour some water over the dress. Given that the mirror had been little more than a scratchy piece of metal, she hadn't been able to get a good look at the damage. What she could see now made her cringe to think what it would look like in daylight.

It was a shame really. She'd liked the dress. In fact, she'd

liked the dress more than she'd liked the man she had almost
married. But that revelation hadn't come until just before the
ceremony, when she realized she couldn't marry a man she
didn't love.

I should have just run out on him like I ran out on Mitch.

She poked the tip of her finger into a loop in the intricate
lace. The reason she had sought Richard out was she hadn't
wanted to do to another man what she had done to Mitch
McCoy.

Foot by foot, she piled the dress up onto the counter,
catching it twice when it would have slithered over the side,
then picked up the lamp and went in search of something to
wear.

Funny, the tricks the mind plays on a person. In her heart,
Mitch was still that dreamy-eyed, strapping twenty-five-
year-old. Who would have thought he would have…filled out
so nicely? Her stocking feet padding against the dusty wood
floor, she made her way up the stairs. His green eyes seemed
somehow more intense with the slight crinkles at the corners.
His hair was longer than the short cut he'd worn then, nearly
brushing the tops of his shoulders in a wild way that made
her remember back when they had played cowboys and In-
dians in Farmer Howard's bean fields. Mitch had always
played the Indian—a Mohawk more accurately, because he'd
always been the exacting type—while she had taken great joy
in wearing a gunbelt and squeezing off the caps trailing from
the toy metal gun.

But that part hadn't been the most fun. Oh, no, the best
part was when they sat down to hammer out the details of
their peace treaty, which ultimately led to playful romps on
the sun-warmed ground.

She caught herself smiling…again. She hadn't smiled

this much—genuinely smiled—in what seemed like forever. She and Mitch had been a whole eight and eleven then. Not that it mattered. For some reason, they'd always fit well. Even Gran had mentioned it…years later, right after she had tanned Liz's hide after a particularly explorative roll in Old Man Peabody's cornfields with Mitch that left her with her shirt unbuttoned, her budding, sensitive chest exposed to the hot summer sun.

At the top of the stairs, Liz stopped and leaned against the railing. She didn't think it odd that she was remembering all this now…and enjoying it. As far as her professional life was concerned—along with her personal life on top of that—she had just suffered one hell of a setback. If Richard froze her assets as he'd threatened, she was facing a major demotion. From top-paid business consultant to homeless person, overnight.

Talk about setbacks.

Still, she couldn't seem to make herself care one way or another right now. Though she did need to figure out a way to get her hands on some cash at some point soon.

She stumbled toward her old bedroom—once her mother's room, with little cabbage roses on the wallpaper and a canopy bed. She put the lamp on the side table and listlessly scavenged through the bureau drawers. She took her old pillow out, then opened the next one. The plastic covering the one item that lay at the bottom of the cavernous depths seemed to wink at her. She reached in and touched her old waitressing uniform. It seemed so very long ago when she'd worked at Bo and Ruth's Paradise Diner.

Smiling wistfully, she stripped the cover sheet from the bare mattress. Sleep. That's what she needed. She was too bushed to think about Rich and all the havoc he'd promised to wreak. Too exhausted to wonder about her meandering visits to the past, and her body-thrumming reaction to Mitch McCoy. Too tired to hunt for something else to wear, to take off her lingerie or to get linens from the hall closet. Tomorrow was soon enough to do all that and to try to make some kind of sense out of the mess that was her life.

CHAPTER TWO

MITCH HAD NO SOONER closed his eyes than they were wide open again. He rolled over…and nearly injured himself for life. Lying flat on his back, he groaned at his fully aroused state and tried to rid his mind of the images even now clinging to the edges of his consciousness. Provocative lips… tantalizing curves…the flick of a pink tongue. All belonging to one woman: Liz.

So much for getting any sleep.

He got up from the bed and yanked up his shade to find the sun peeking over the mist-shrouded horizon. He grimaced. Despite his exhausted state, he must have squeezed out a few hours of shut-eye, because it was morning already.

He headed for the bathroom, took a bracing, cold shower, dressed, then headed down to the kitchen. He stopped in the empty room. Where the hell was Pops?

He wasn't sure what he was looking for. A return to normalcy, maybe? A solid sign that his life hadn't completely gone to hell in a handbasket overnight? Perhaps he wanted to tell his father Liz had returned and get some of that advice Pops had been real good at doling out lately? It occurred to him that he hadn't heard Sean come in from Maryland last night.

He started the coffee, then headed toward the foot of the stairs. "Pops? Coffee's on!"

He glanced at his watch. It wasn't like his father not to be up yet. Sundays he usually beat the sun and had breakfast half fixed by the time Mitch even thought about crawling out of bed. It was the one morning they spent together by mutual, silent agreement, before Mitch headed out to tick off the next item on his list of things-to-be-done around the property and before Sean went off to…

He scratched his head, only then realizing he had no idea what his dad had been doing with his Sundays lately.

"Pops? You want eggs or pancakes for breakfast?"

"Eggs sound good."

Mitch swung around to face his father coming in from outside. He shrugged out of his suit coat. His *suit coat.* It suddenly dawned on him that he hadn't heard his dad come in last night because he never *had* come in.

"Hey, Mitch, I see you made it home all right."

Mitch watched him pour a cup of coffee. "Yeah, good thing one of us did."

Sean took a long sip, his face a little too…cheerful for Mitch's liking. "Yeah" was all he said, then grinned.

Mitch grimaced.

Okay, chances were that his dad had had one too many at Marc and Mel's wedding reception and had opted for a motel room rather than making the long ride home. Or…

He groaned. Or else Pops's sex life was a whole helluva lot more active than his.

He rubbed his forehead. He couldn't remember a time when he could link the words "Pops" and "sex" together. He wasn't sure how he felt about his ability to do so now. From what he remembered, and what others had to say in the small, everybody-knows-everybody-else's-business town, Pops had been blown away by his wife's unexpected death. While it didn't completely excuse some of the rougher periods Mitch and his brothers had gone through without a cohesive parental presence in their lives, it explained a lot. And, as Connor sometimes reminded them, Pops didn't drink *and* chase women. He merely drank.

Now the opposite was true: Pops no longer drank, he, um, chased women. Or at least one, if Mitch's suspicions were true.

Mitch tried to stretch the kinks from his neck. He really didn't need this heaped on top of everything else that had happened since last night.

"On second thought, I'm going to skip breakfast this morning," Sean said. "I think I'll go catch a quick shower instead."

"Yeah," Mitch said absently. "Why don't you do that."

Sean started to step from the room, coffee cup in hand. He halted near the door and eyed Mitch closely. Too closely. "Everything all right? Pardon the expression, but you look like you've just seen a ghost."

Mitch turned toward the counter. "The ghost of summers past, maybe," he said to himself. His intention that morning had been to unload everything and seek out some of Pops's no-nonsense, use-the-good-sense-God-gave-you advice. Now, he was afraid Pops would be talking as much about his own personal life as advising him on his. He didn't think he was up to peeking at that particular insight. "I'm fine." He cleared his throat. "By the way, this…person you stayed with last night. Anybody I know?"

Silence greeted his question. He turned back to see Pops grinning. "Uh-huh."

"Care to share who?"

"Uh-uh."

Mitch stood in the middle of the kitchen, watching in amazement as his father left the room, whistling as he went.

Mitch left the coffee on, snatched up his truck keys, then headed for the door. He needed to get out of the house. All this…whistling was making him feel lousier.

AH, THIS WAS more like it. Good, familiar company, a hot cup of coffee, and peace in which to drink it.

One of the many advantages of having traded his P.I. cap in for his new one as a horse breeder was his ability to structure his day however he liked. During the week it was easier to drop in at Bo and Ruth's Paradise Diner for breakfast and lunch before and between chores than to cook something up for himself. And on those occasions when he traveled into D.C. to work on the few cases he'd held on to or to check in with Mike and Renee, he did so in the afternoon. He glanced at the date on his watch, reminding himself that he'd planned to head into the city tomorrow.

He'd completely forgotten.

Stiffening, he told himself that he was *not* going to think of the person behind his recent distracted state.

Mitch leaned his elbows against the counter and took a deep breath of his first cup of joe. Even on his good days he couldn't come close to imitating Ruth's unique blend. And today was definitely *not* one of his good days.

But it was getting better.

Farther down the counter he listened with half an ear as the ever-present Darton brothers argued about whose turn it was to buy breakfast, and behind him he heard Ezra, owner of the town's only gas station, order his usual pizza, despite that it was nine o'clock in the morning. But it was Sharon's, the waitress's, tight little uniform that got his attention as she reached for a plate of bacon and eggs on the other side of the counter. What a great pair of legs.

She's too young for you, his conscience taunted.

She's legal, his libido argued back.

The cash register free of customers, Ruth stepped up to fill a glass of water for him. Mitch dragged his gaze from Sharon's legs and smiled his greeting.

"Didn't expect to see you in this morning," Ruth said. "You and Sean normally eat breakfast at the house on Sundays, don't you?"

Mitch's grin waned. "Pops had, um, other things on his agenda today."

"I see."

He slowly sipped at his coffee. No doubt Ruth saw a whole lot more than the rest of them did. Born and raised in Manchester, she took great pride in letting everyone know she was never interested in living anywhere else. A good twenty years Mitch's senior, she had an uncanny ability to figure out what was going on before anyone else did—including those involved in the goings-on.

"By the way, pass on to your brother that Bo and I had a grand ol' time at the reception last night. It's been so long since anyone from these parts has gotten married, I'd forgotten what a wedding looked like."

Mitch put down his cup. "I'll tell Marc when he and Mel get back. I get the impression calling home isn't going to be at the top of their list right now." He waved at Bo through the open kitchen window. Bo raised a meaty hand in response, looking more like a bouncer than a cook. "For a couple that likes to close down the joint, you guys left a little early, didn't you?"

Ruth busied herself clearing the spot next to him. "Bo was a little tired, that's all. Things were pretty hectic around here yesterday, and what with the drive into Maryland and all…well, I guess it all caught up with him last night."

Mitch frowned as he watched Bo flip a few pancakes then drag the back of his hand across his forehead. Bo never got tired.

Ruth sighed. "Nice girl, that Mel. And pretty, too. Who'd have thought Marc would hook someone like her?"

Sharon angled her way back behind the counter to pick up an order. Mitch watched her absently. "Yeah, who'd have thought."

"Enjoying the view?" Ruth asked as she dragged a rag across the counter in front of him.

Mitch grinned at her. "Yeah."

Sharon shot him a coy little smile as she squeezed out from behind the counter to take Ezra his breakfast pizza. Ruth put her rag away and leaned closer to him.

He told himself he didn't care what she was about to say. He lifted the cup to his lips. Nothing was going to stop him from enjoying his first cup of coffee.

Ruth said, "You'll probably enjoy the view a whole lot more tomorrow morning when Liz comes back to work."

Mitch spewed the coffee out all over the counter. What precious little peace he'd managed to find scattered to the four winds, and his frustration level surged past the danger point.

Ruth smiled, tossed him the rag to clean up the mess, then walked pleased as could be toward the kitchen.

ADMIT IT, McCoy, you're thinking with the wrong body part.

Mitch pulled his pickup over a low rise and slowed to a stop on the weed-choked gravel road. He stared at the hulking Victorian some fifty yards away. Not just any hulking Victorian, but Liz's hulking Victorian. Just knowing she was in it—alone—did interesting things to his body.

He dragged in a deep breath and let loose a line of unmatched curses. Who in the hell had decided to boot him out of his familiar life and into a twisted version of Oz?

Mitch scrubbed his hand over his face. In this particular instance, he could count the bricks that led to the unfamiliar territory in which he now wandered around stupidly. First, Liz had slunk back into town in that shiny new car. Next, Pops had rambled in, looking like he'd come fresh from licking some woman's neck, his off-tune whistling chasing Mitch straight from the house, bursting with the urge to do some of his own neck-licking. Then Ruth had spilled the beans about Liz's returning to work at the diner. Soon thereafter he found out word was already all around about her impulsive return. Everyone at the diner was abuzz with the news. Even Josiah—who did little more than rock in his chair on the general store porch—had said something about her still being the tallest drink of water this side of the Appalachians. This when the old guy had barely said anything to anyone for years.

That had been the last straw. Who else but Liz could invade every corner of his life in less than twelve hours without even trying? So he'd abandoned his plans to have breakfast then return to the house to start laying pipe from the house to the new barn, and headed out to the old Braden place.

Mitch took his foot off the brake and steered his truck over the remainder of the potholed, deeply rutted drive. Goliath barked beside him. He looked at the little traitor. How, after living in D.C. with him for several years, could the damn dog remember this ramshackle house and the fact that Liz lived here?

Correction. Had occasionally lived here. She might be visiting, but Mitch had no illusions that Liz was staying, despite her having taken on her old job. She was merely a visitor in a place she, herself, had once described as never really having been home.

He ground the truck to a halt next to a weeping willow and shut off the engine. While Old Man Peabody had managed to keep time from touching the house itself much, the surrounding greenery had been left to run wild. Trees that had been little more than saplings now towered over the truck. The lilac bush was so overgrown, it would take a chainsaw to cut it back. The grass was nearly up to the middle of his shins....

The sight of the grass sent him reeling back to a time when he was seventeen and had decided to make a good impression on Liz's grandmother by offering to mow the yard. A grand gesture that had turned into a disaster when he found out exactly how *much* grass he would have to mow. Using Minerva Braden's old push mower, it had taken him all afternoon.

Ah, but it had been worth it. He smiled. The sun had been setting, the lights inside the house just switching on, and he'd caught a glimpse of Liz—who would have been all of a tender fourteen then and well on her way to being built like Marilyn Monroe—through her bedroom window, exploring her blossoming curves in a full-length mirror. He'd watched her skim her hands lightly over her breasts, pinching her pink nipples. Then she slid her fingers down over her still-boyish hips, then back up over her inner thighs, pausing where her soft curls sprang against the white cotton of her panties....

Sweat caused by a whole different source had soaked him, his own shallow breathing sounded foreign to his ears...much as it sounded now.

Mitch closed his eyes to banish the vivid image and to

ease his acute physical reaction to it. It was only natural that
being near Liz again would open a door to the past. He only
wished that door would reveal as much of the bad as the
good.

He couldn't help wondering if he'd be in the sorry state
he was if he and Liz had ever…well, if they had ever had sex.
If they hadn't waited for the wedding night that had never
come, and if he had had what he'd been only dreaming about.

He reached for the ignition, then dropped his hand again.
For the fifth time that morning, he told himself he'd be better off to lie low and wait for her inevitable departure to happen. But he couldn't. Not when he knew the only reason
she'd have returned to Manchester would be because she had
to be in some sort of trouble.

And not when his testosterone level had reached an all-time
high, leaving him little more than a quivering sack of lust.

He climbed out of the truck and waited for the aging Goliath to leap down. His stout body appeared to shudder as his
paws met the hard earth, then he lumbered in the direction
of a stand of trees on the north side of the property. Shaking
his head, Mitch shut the door and stepped around the side of
the house, noting the weeds pushing through the thin gravel
of the drive. Near the one-car garage some twenty feet behind the house, he spotted the Lexus. A large green tarp he
suspected was a tent was draped over the roof and hood. Little was visible except for half the Massachusetts license plate.

Interesting….

He might have believed she'd covered the vehicle to protect it from the elements, if it weren't for the bloodstained
wedding dress she'd been wearing when she drove the car
into town. And her elusive answers to his questions.

"Hello?" he called through the screen door. He made out

the tinny sound of a radio and stared through the screen at wet wading boots in the mudroom…right next to the pair of strappy red shoes she'd been wearing last night.

He called out again—no response. He grasped the tarnished handle and tugged the door open, cringing at the bone-chilling screech of the rusty hinges.

"I'm in the kitchen!"

Mitch stepped over the boots, knowing it had to be Liz who invited him in. Who else would welcome Lord only knew who into the house? He froze in the open doorway to the roomy, sun-filled kitchen.

"Oh, it's you. Tell me why I'm not surprised," she said casually. She stood in front of the sink, yards of white fabric pooled around her feet. She yanked on the material, stuffing a good portion of it under running water.

Mitch tried to come up with a finely honed comeback, but doubted the words would make it past his closed throat anyway. His gaze moved of its own leisurely accord. Up from her slender bare feet and purple-painted toe nails, over the shapely length of her long, tanned legs to where a pair of cut-off jeans barely covered her firmly rounded bottom. He shifted until his gaze rested on the jaggedly cut edge of the Georgetown University T-shirt, an indecent scrap of cotton that came dangerously close to hiking up over her breasts. Breasts he guessed were bare given the way they swayed as she shoved the white material into the sink.

Seven years ago the outfit had been tomboyish on her almost too-slender body. Now it was downright sinful given her fuller, lusher curves.

He pushed a swallow past his dry throat and stared at her golden hair.

"You're blond," he said, staring at the way the sunlight

made the shoulder-length straight tresses glow. The impact of her looking so much like she had before was like a blow to the stomach.

"Life as a brunette wasn't as lucky as I thought it would be," she said, motioning toward an empty box of hair coloring on the cluttered counter. He caught her gaze. There must have been something on his face that gave him away because she bit her bottom lip and touched a hand to her head. "What's the matter? Did I miss a spot or something?" When she plopped her hand back in the sink, water splashed onto the threadbare front of the T-shirt. Mitch caught sight of the tightening of her nipples beneath the soft cotton, then forcibly wrenched his gaze away.

"No, it's fine. It's great. Couldn't you find anything else to wear?" He plucked a travel brochure from the table and held it strategically in front of himself where his jeans had grown snug. He hadn't gotten a hard-on so easily since... He cursed. Since he'd last seen Liz in the same outfit.

He stared at the other items on the table. More brochures, maps and travel guides littered the top, some dog-eared, others apparently untouched. He frowned and slid a map of Dallas aside, finding another pamphlet on Miami underneath.

"I don't know if you noticed, but I didn't exactly have a suitcase with me when I rolled into town." Liz drew his attention back to her. She turned off the water and rubbed the shining wet material together.

Oh, no you don't, he warned himself, as his gaze yearned to watch how her breasts responded to the vigorous movement of her arms.

"It was the only thing in the house I could find that still fit," she said between determined attacks on the dress.

Fit. She was certainly stretching the definition of that

word. Then again, his own jeans had fit just fine until he came into the house.

Agitated, he rustled the brochure he held and focused his gaze on her slender hands. It suddenly struck him what she was doing.

She's washing the bloodstain from the wedding dress.

Or at least she was trying to. Judging from the puddles of water on the countertop and around her bare feet—were her toenails really painted fluorescent purple?—she had been trying for some time with little luck.

If anything could have cooled him down, her intentions did. He put the brochure back onto the table. "What are you doing, Liz?"

She shrugged off his question as she wiped her damp forehead on her shirtsleeve. "Thought I'd do a little laundry this morning."

He was frustrated, not only by her evasion of his question, but by the way his libido was so acutely focused on her tight little behind and the delectable curves of her flesh. He stuffed his hands into his jeans pockets, wincing as the coarse denim pulled tighter across certain strategic areas.

"Uh-huh."

She looked at him then, her hazel eyes filled with amusement while her hands kept up their rapid motion. "You wouldn't happen to know how to get rid of bloodstains, would you?"

Mitch pinched the bridge of his nose. "Try sponging on some peroxide."

Her luscious mouth curved into a smile.

"I was raised with four brothers, remember?"

She turned back to the sink, giving him full rein to do what he would with the view. "How could I forget? Your brothers hardly left us alone for a minute."

"That's because they were all in lust with you." *And so was I.*

Her throaty laugh made him want to groan. "I can't imagine Jake being in lust with anyone."

"Yeah, well, you never saw the shrine he built for you in his room." Mitch quickly reached his patience level, which was odd, because he hadn't known he had one. He stepped forward and grabbed her arms, forcing her to face him.

"Liz, what in the hell are you doing back here? And just what…what in the hell is going on?"

The surprised shadow on her face made him want to groan all over again. Now that she had returned to her natural hair color, the electric shade of her eyes was enhanced, making it nearly impossible to look anywhere else.

Nothing about this woman was constant, smooth. Not her personality, not her actions, and certainly not her physical traits. Her nose sloped, her chin was an angular work of art with a tiny little dimple in the middle. But it was her too-wide, lavish mouth that had always done him in.

"Mitch?" she practically purred, and, if anyone could purr, Liz certainly could.

"Hmmm?" he hummed distractedly, falling into the hazel depths of her eyes.

"I hope you realize you're going to be the one to mop up the mess you're making."

Mess? He hadn't made a mess yet, but give him a couple more seconds, and—

He blinked, watching as her hands dripped water on the floor.

"I just spent the morning mopping up the basement after a pipe burst. I don't much want to clean up the kitchen floor, too."

He released her so fast, she nearly toppled to the floor. He remembered the wet hip boots in the mudroom.

"I hope you turned off the electricity before you went trudging through that water," he grumbled, trying to get a handle on himself. He was supposed to be trying to convince her to get into her car and head for the road, not entertaining thoughts of getting her between the sheets.

"What electricity? Old Man Peabody kept the water on, but it's going to take some money to get the electricity switched back on."

Mitch glanced at a one-eyed propane burner on top of the obsolete stove, and a lantern near a cot in the corner. "So that's why you took your old job back at the diner."

She tilted her head and slid her gaze over him suggestively. "Are you going to tell me what you're doing here, or am I going to have to guess?" She tugged on the bottom of her T-shirt, pulling it tight against her breasts in a provocative way, though she was likely preventing the scrap of material from revealing more than was decent. "Or did you just come out to hassle me?"

"It depends on your definition of hassle," he said, not trusting the spark of mischief that compelled him to grin. "If you categorize wanting to know what you're doing as hassling you, then we have a problem."

"The only problem I'm having now is getting the stain out of that dress."

Mitch stared at the sopping wet material puddled on the chipped tile floor. "That's just it. Why would you want to get the stain out?" He eyed her. "Unless, of course, you intend to use the dress again."

He didn't miss her amused expression. She turned from him and hoisted the dress up onto the counter.

He stepped closer until he was nearly flush with her backside. The subtle scent of wild cherries drifted over him, inciting another uncomfortable response in the lower half of his body.

"Tell me, Liz, why is it there's a car parked out back that costs more than some houses and you can't afford to have your electricity turned on?"

His breath stirred her honey-blond hair. He felt satisfied at her soft sigh.

He reached around her and touched the satiny material of the wedding dress, purposely skimming his arm against hers. "And why are you trying so hard to wash that stain out?"

She turned in his arms, staring up at him as if she just now realized how close he was. The tips of her breasts grazed his chest and this time *he* sighed—or choked, more accurately. A reaction she didn't miss if the teasing smile on her lips was anything to go by.

"What's the matter, Mitch? Are you thinking that this time I didn't just run out on my groom? That maybe this time I did away with him?"

He narrowed his eyes. Despite the way she trembled, she was acting too casual, too self-composed. "Well, that would certainly answer a lot of questions." He caught a lock of her blond hair and twirled the silky strands around his finger. "The first being why you came back to Manchester."

A SHIVER swept down Liz's neck despite the late June sunshine that drenched the kitchen through the window above the sink. The combination of hot sunshine on her back and one hundred percent Mitch McCoy at her front was a lethal one. She pressed her rear against the sharp edge of the counter.

"I already told you why I came back."

"No, Liz," Mitch shook his head. "You didn't tell me why. You said what it would take for you to leave. More specifically, that things had to settle down in Boston before you could move on." His gaze shifted to her mouth and she had to fight not to lick her suddenly dry lips. "What I want to know is what things need to settle down and why."

Liz felt incredibly, wickedly, exposed standing like that in front of him. Hardly a thing in her old bedroom upstairs fit. And despite her affected nonchalance when he'd commented on her apparel, the first thing she'd wanted to do when she'd spotted him in the doorway was cover herself from his searing gaze. The problem was the only other things that fit were her wedding dress and—thankfully—her old waitressing uniform.

She rode out a shiver that began at the tips of her toes and flitted all the way up to her scalp. Who would have thought that after seven years Mitch would still make her want to strip naked and run through the cornfields with him?

"Don't worry, Mitch. I'm no longer the damsel in distress you once had to rescue at every turn. I'm perfectly capable of taking care of myself now."

His green eyes darkened. "This isn't a matter of stealing a candy bar from Obernauer's, Liz. Or your filling Peabody's firing-range cans with cement. Answer my question."

Her smile was decidedly playful. "Is that why you came all the way out here? Because you think I'm in some sort of trouble?"

His expression grew teasing as his gaze raked her humming body. "I'm just trying to protect the residents of Manchester, Liz."

"From little ol' me?"

"Yes, from you. From you and whoever is following on your heels."

Following on my heels. So he hadn't forgotten what she'd said on the dark road last night. Her smile widened.

"Don't worry. I'd never put anybody in Manchester in danger."

"Why don't you let me be the judge of that? For once, why don't you tell me exactly what's going on?"

She wriggled to free herself without touching him. An impossible task with him so near. She shifted to her right and he compensated for the move, leaning in closer. Her highly sensitive nipples brushed against the hard width of his chest a second time and she gasped, arousal heating her insides and a thrill of awareness tingling across every inch of her skin, exposed or otherwise. His hands caressed her arms and she shivered.

"I...I wouldn't do that if I were you," she whispered, overly interested in the nearness of his mouth.

"Do what?"

"Kiss me."

A maddening grin played on his all-too-tempting lips. "Then stop me."

He made the inches separating them disappear, pressing the solid muscles of his thighs against her legs, the scrape of rough denim against her tender skin excitingly erotic. His mouth stopped a hairbreadth away from hers, his minty breath fanning her heated cheeks, his eyes inviting her to finish what he had begun. She swallowed hard, incapable of stopping him...incapable of stopping herself. She groaned.

Oh, how she'd missed the feel of him against her.

Thrusting her fingers into his thick brown hair, she drew

him the rest of the way, crushing his lips against hers, challenging him to a duel of tongues, an exchange of pleasure she'd never felt as powerfully with anyone else. He responded with consummate flair, pulling her bottom lip into his mouth and gently biting down on it, then claiming her in a way she remembered all too well. Liz's entire body caught fire. She restlessly, instinctively sought closer contact. A low whimper caught in her throat as the ridge of his arousal pressed provocatively against the cradle of her thighs.

Her hands were suddenly all over him. In his hair, tugging his T-shirt from his jeans, sculpting his firm backside. She couldn't seem to touch him nearly enough. From rough denim to velvety hot skin to the thick strands of his hair, her hands sought something she couldn't hope to define…not until his fingers found the skin over her rib cage.

She caught her breath, her mouth stilling beneath his, her eyes locking with his half-lidded ones. *Touch me,* she silently pleaded. Her nipples strained painfully against the thin cotton of her shirt. Her chest rose and fell as she regained her breath and dragged in precious air. Irrationally, she thought she'd die if he didn't touch her.

His fingers slid up, gently cupping the underside of her breasts. Heat, sure and swift, swept over her in dizzying waves. Liz nearly collapsed to the floor in a puddle of shimmering need. One callused thumb moved over her right nipple. She moaned.

"Ooh," she whispered, tugging her mouth from his, trying to catch her breath, calm the thick pulsing of her heart.

Mitch suddenly jerked back, taking his warmth with him. Liz propped her hands against her knees, filled with the sudden urge to laugh.

The picture really was quite ludicrous. Yesterday she had

been about to marry another man. Now she was practically devouring Mitch.

This didn't make any sense at all.

"Why don't we continue this conversation another time?" she asked, dragging the back of her knuckles across her swollen lips. "I have a lot of things I need to do today, and your kissing me isn't going to help get them done."

His grin was decidedly devilish, despite the questioning glint in his eyes. "I didn't kiss you, Liz. You kissed me. Remember?"

Oh, yeah, she remembered all right. And if he didn't leave *now,* she was going to pin him to the table.

"Answer my question and I'll be happy to let you get on with your list of chores."

Liz straightened. "Well, then, I think you oughta just strip and let's get on with it."

He stumbled backward as if she had physically pushed him. The edge of the table stopped his progress. "What?"

"That's the real reason you came here, isn't it, Mitch?" There was something wonderfully delicious about the expression on his face. "You came to get what you couldn't have seven years ago."

CHAPTER THREE

YOU CAME to get what you couldn't have seven years ago.

Mitch clenched his coffee cup, mulling over what Liz had said the day before. He shifted uncomfortably on the diner stool. He cursed, remembering how he'd beat a hasty retreat out of her house like a panicked roadrunner.

It was past noon on Monday. The diner was packed. His coffee was getting cold. And he should be on the road to D.C., where he'd planned to catch up on some office work and check in with a couple of clients…as well as do some more checking on the ghost of weddings past and present. Instead, he was in the diner, gaping at the broken pieces of his sorry life, and staring at the bomb in a waitress uniform that had broken it.

Leaving Liz's house yesterday after relearning the taste of her mouth, feeling her hot, slick flesh against his, had been one of the hardest things he'd ever done. How much he'd have liked to have slid his fingers up under the frayed hem of her jean shorts and explored the hot, pliant flesh there. How much he had yearned to claim—as she had so slyly suggested—what had been denied him so many years ago.

But the instant she'd offered up what had once been forbidden fruit, he'd hightailed it out of there.

He'd spent the bulk of this morning alternately taking cold showers—it was a hot day, damn it—and checking with the Virginia and Massachusetts state law officials. Several calls yielded no outstanding warrants. There was absolutely nothing on her listed at the FBI's National Crime Information Center, including info on whether or not the Lexus was stolen. Not stopping there, he contacted the Massachusetts Department of Motor Vehicles; the plates on the Lexus were hers, as was the Lexus itself, though he found it interesting that the Boston address in the DMV's files was no longer valid.

What bothered him was that he couldn't verify one way or another whether or not she had skipped town *before* or *after* her wedding ceremony. An irritating clerk he had talked to at the licensing bureau refused to tell him anything that wasn't already a part of public record and said she wasn't his gofer. If he wanted the information, he'd have to go fish it out himself…when it was publicly posted in a week or two.

At least his next call had gone better. He'd found Liz listed as owner of Braden Consulting in the State Board of Corporations' books.

He stared at the address and phone number to that business now and sucked in a deep breath, puffing his cheeks out as he released it.

He stuffed the number back into his pocket, telling himself he should be more concerned with all the work that had gone undone around the McCoy place, and just when, exactly, he planned to head out for D.C. He'd wished Pops had been around, but the old man had been gone when he returned from Liz's yesterday, and Mitch had the sneaking suspicion he hadn't made it home again last night.

Mitch sipped his cold coffee, masking the uneasiness twisting inside him like a twenty-foot length of knotted razor wire.

Down the counter from him, he tuned in Moses Darton

complaining about the puny size of his Heavenly Pineapple Ribs for the third time and asking Liz if she couldn't scare up a bigger slab. She sighed in exasperation and slid the refused plate onto the counter to go back into the kitchen.

"Your halo's slipping, angel," he said to her in a voice almost too low to make out in the packed diner. Hell, figuratively speaking, her halo had fallen off a long time ago.

"After yesterday, I think you passed on the chance to call me angel, Mitch." She tugged on the hem of her white skirt to hide the thighs he'd already taken an eyeful of.

"Hmm." He tilted his head, taking in his fill. He openly followed the line down the front of her uniform, then stared at her legs. "Maybe."

He watched that simmering, wicked smile light her eyes before she tugged up the edge of the *Manchester Journal* he held.

"Read your paper, McCoy. I wouldn't want you to miss an important news flash."

"Funny, I was just checking for any possible news on you."

He peered over the paper to find her running that pink tongue of hers over her lips. His gut-deep reaction almost made him groan.

What was it about this one woman? Just when he thought he had finally shaken off the baggage he'd been hauling around since she'd left and was eager to re-start his life, she popped back in and piled the overpacked trunks back up on his shoulders again. Reminded him that he had never completely cleansed her from his system.

Perhaps it was time he did.

The thought snagged in his mind and held.

He grinned. He'd been uncomfortable ever since scurrying from her grandmother's house yesterday. Now he knew why. He should have stayed. Should have peeled those skimpy shorts down her long, long legs and taken what she'd offered. Maybe if he had, he wouldn't be sitting there wondering what would have happened if he had. Maybe he wouldn't be sitting there wanting her more with every breath he took.

He grimaced. And maybe he'd be even worse off.

During training at Quantico, he'd learned to look at problems from all angles, and that particular angle bothered him. Having sex with Liz Braden might very well be just what he needed to rid her from his life forever. It might also be the catalyst to finding himself in the same damn boat he'd been in seven years ago.

He lifted the paper this time, hiding himself from her curious gaze.

What other alternative did he have but to finish what had been started so long ago?

And just consider the fringe benefits….

He rustled his paper. "Angel? You mind giving me a warm-up over here?"

WARM-UP?

Liz glanced at Mitch McCoy. She didn't miss the suggestion threaded through his innocuous words, or the all-too-familiar emotions that emerged whenever she looked his way.

Taking the coffeepot from the warmer, she poured some of the hot liquid into his almost-full cup. It was all too…weird being here again, in the same role she'd played so long ago, as soon as she was old enough to apply for the waitressing job. In a town the size of Manchester, where "downtown" consisted of little more than a city block, the only choice she'd had job-wise was at the diner, since the general store was well-manned by Charles Obernauer and his wife, Hannah.

Then there was Mitch....

It wasn't what Mitch said that got to her. It was the way he said it. Whenever he talked to her, a wicked proposition hummed through his words, sending tiny little shivers scooting everywhere.

Mitch took a long sip, then grinned. "Oh, and I could do with a piece of Paradise Pie, too."

"Oh, you could, could you?"

"Uh-huh."

She removed the apple pie from the counter display and turned out a healthy piece, smothering it with vanilla ice cream and sticking a candy cherub on top. She pushed the plate in front of him as his gaze slid over her tight white uniform and lingered on the hem. Tiny tingles followed his path and Liz drew in an uneven breath.

"Am I getting under your skin, Liz?" he asked. "You used to like it when I teased you."

Her gaze flicked from his eyes to his mouth as he took a hefty bite of pie, then quickly to his eyes again. She quietly cleared her throat, finding him far more appealing than was safe. A little closer and she'd give him a repeat performance of what had passed between them yesterday.

Yes, he was getting under her skin, by making her want to feel him all over it.

He lifted his eyes to hers, that damnable teasing glint giving him a wholly devilish appearance. "Are you going to answer me?"

"Answer you?" She cleared her throat, trying to recall the question. Oh, yes, her skin and his getting under it. "It's been a long time since...then." So long she had a hard time recognizing the woman who once thought she could make a man like Mitch happy.

Her gaze riveted to a dab of vanilla ice cream at the side of his mouth. She longed to be able to lean over and lap it off.

"And the next thing would be?" he prompted.

"Next thing?"

He nodded and swallowed another bite.

I want to know why you never came after me, her heart answered.

Her breath caught and she raised her gaze to his eyes. Flames seemed to backlight the green depths as he apparently tried to gauge what she was thinking.

"Don't you dare look at me that way," she said.

"Look at you what way?"

Her voice was little more than a throaty rasp. "You know what way. That look that, um, says you'd rather be watching me melt instead of the ice cream in front of you."

The right side of his well-defined mouth budged up a fraction of an inch as he licked off the ice cream. "It is what I'd rather be doing, so why shouldn't my expression say that?"

Liz smoothed the collar of her uniform. "Because I don't want to be your ice cream, that's why." *Liar.* She eyed his left hand slowly inching across the counter. His fingertips lightly grazed her arm in a maddening path he followed back and forth.

"What…what are you doing?"

"I'm thinking."

She moved his hand back across the counter and planted it in his half-eaten pie. "Since when does it take fingers to think?"

"Since your explanation of why you don't like my attention has nothing to do with your lack of attraction to me."

He watched her while he cleaned the ice cream from his hand with a napkin, then he dipped his fingers in his water glass and shook them once in her direction.

She wiped the droplets of water from her cheek, surprised they hadn't sizzled against the heat of her skin. "Lack of attraction? Are you trying to say what I think you are?"

"What?" He picked up his fork and stabbed another piece of pie. "That you're wildly attracted to me and don't know what to do about it?"

"Wildly attracted?"

"Uh-huh." His eyes challenged her.

"I, um, at one time I might have been very attracted to you, Mitch McCoy—" her voice softened "—but now I wouldn't even consider…"

"Sleeping with me?"

Her muscles liquefied, but somehow she managed to push out, "You already missed your opportunity there. From here on out, something like that will only happen in your dreams."

He nodded. "Yep, there, too." He finished the last of his pie and shook his head. "Only I know for sure I'm not dreaming now. Because if I were, you wouldn't be on the other side of the counter, and you wouldn't be wearing that uniform, no matter how cute you look in it."

"Oh? And where, um, would I be?"

His pupils widened, threatening to take over the green of his eyes. "For starters, you'd be stretched across this counter with those long legs of yours…"

Liz quickly took a step back, her pulse leaping. "That's enough. I think I get the picture."

"But darlin', you didn't even let me get to the part about what *I* was doing."

A bolt of awareness sliced through Liz's abdomen. No, he

hadn't told her what he'd been doing in his dream, but she could very well imagine. And the images were more than distracting, they were downright provocative—especially when combined with the confusing heat that still lingered from the day before. She cleared her throat and turned away. She'd never look at the long, narrow slip of counter the same way again.

"Look," Ezra called out from a corner booth. "Lizzie is quiet. Looks like Mitch has struck a chord."

"I don't have any chords to strike," Liz lied. "I was just thinking that Mitch's vivid imagination is exactly why everyone calls him a dreamer." Still, she tried to ignore the sensation similar to a quivering harp string twanging straight through her.

"Hey, Mitch," Ezra said, "are we all included in your little…dream?"

Liz stared at him as he slowly shook his head. "Nope. Sorry, Ez, it's just me and Lizzie in this scenario. That's what makes it a dream."

His gaze said a whole hell of a lot more than his words. Was he threatening her? Was he saying in a cryptic way that the next time they were alone she might not get off so easy?

This flirtatious attitude was the last thing she'd expected from him. Where were the questions? Evidence of the huge ding to his pride? After all, seven years ago she had left him standing at the altar. She wiped the counter, then stuffed the rag back into her apron pocket. He showed neither. Instead, he slanted her a few unexpected zingers that short-circuited her own emotional wiring, leaving her inexplicably responsive to his teasing.

He picked up the paper folded at his elbow, his grin telling her he knew he'd hit his mark.

She looked around the diner and found nothing out of the ordinary. Which was laughable because anyone else might find *everything* out of the ordinary. From the padded pink vinyl booths, the corny cherubs on the tabletops that swayed back and forth when the customers moved, to the townsfolk who were as peculiar as the decor, Liz had forgotten how…eccentric the town was. How familiar and reassuringly unchanged. All too easily she recalled how Gran brought her here for lunch every Sunday after church service. How the McCoy bunch had teased her when she was fourteen and had finally grown breasts. How she had screwed up every order on her first day at work, and how everyone had covertly played musical plates when they thought she wasn't looking and had generously tipped her anyway.

She turned the pages of her order pad and tallied up the total for table one.

She was just being sentimental. Yes, that's what it was. That's the reason she'd succumbed to the desire to kiss Mitch in Gran's kitchen, why his nearness and flirting had such a hot effect on her now. Certainly nothing that would get in the way of her plans to move on with her life, go somewhere where she could set up her business all over again. Plans that had nothing to do with Mitch or Manchester or the nineteen hundred and ninety-nine residents that inhabited the north-central Virginia town, no matter how reassuringly familiar they all were. Plans she fully intended to see succeed before her thirtieth birthday less than two weeks from now.

Thirty years old. She nearly groaned and wondered if she should order her headstone now.

Mid-tally, Liz halted her pencil and flipped to another page in her order book. Tearing it off, she slid the white slip under the wall of the *Manchester Journal*.

Mitch dropped the newspaper a few inches, gazing at her with those teasing green eyes of his.

"Not in a hurry to get rid of me, are you, angel?"

"Now, Mitch, why would you say that?" She leaned her hips against the counter and offered up a smile. "How many times do I have to ask before you stop calling me angel?"

He shook his paper as if to straighten it, though his gaze remained riveted to her face. "Ask as often as you like. I'm not going to stop. Not as long as you're in front of me wearing that white uniform." The grin that threatened grew into blood-heating reality.

Every inch of her roused to glorious life. "Is that your way of saying you want *me* to leave?"

"That's not my way of saying anything except what I said." He rustled the paper again.

She twisted her lips and allowed her gaze to flick slowly over his face. *This is his way of getting back at me,* she realized. No angry demands to know why she'd left. No attempts to get her alone for a quiet talk. Not even any mention of the time they'd been together or the scorching kiss they'd shared yesterday. No, Mitch McCoy intended to make her time here as miserable as possible. And if he could speed up the process of her leaving, it was all for the better.

The maddening thing of it was that, despite everything, she wanted to have him hosed down and brought to her tent...*pronto*.

"Isn't there someplace you should be getting back to? Doesn't the world need saving or something?" she said, reaching for his paper again. He moved the *Journal* out of reach.

"I didn't know you paid that close attention to my comings and goings."

She crossed her arms over her chest. "The diner's pretty full. We could use the spot you're taking for someone interested in eating." She smiled. "Anyway, I'm more interested in your goings than your comings, Mitch."

"Funny, I'd say you're more interested in *your* goings than your comings." He stretched lazily, offering every solid part of his T-shirt-covered abdomen for inspection. Liz covertly admired the enticing wall of muscle, then turned away, a slow burn beginning in the pit of her stomach. She was wrong. More had changed about him than his unpredictability. No longer was he the corded teenager, then young man for whom she had once hungered. A few pounds of added muscle made his physique more intriguing, more enticing, and much more irresistible than it had ever been.

She pushed open the kitchen door, aware of his keen attention.

"Hey, Bo, how are the burgers frying?" She flashed a smile at the harried cook and half-owner of the diner.

"They're...frying," he said gruffly.

"Mind if I use the phone for a minute?"

"Naw." He waved toward the extension on the wall near the door. "Go on ahead."

"Thanks."

She plucked the receiver from the old rotary phone, dialed the area code for Boston, then the number to her office. She'd called her personal assistant, Sheila, from the general store yesterday. She only hoped she'd like the answers she was going to get today.

"Hello?"

Liz wound the tangled cord around her finger. "Not even Braden Consulting anymore, huh?"

Sheila sighed heavily into the receiver. "Nope. My boss

told me the business is defunct as of yesterday." Despite her words, Liz imaged the young woman smiling. She'd promised her a severance that would equal six months pay, enough for Sheila to follow her dream of opening her own dance school. "Hi, Liz. Funny you should call this second. I just hung up with your mother."

"Sunny?" Liz repeated, surprised. Why would her mother be calling her?

"Yeah. She seemed rushed and didn't talk long, but said she's been trying to contact you since the day of the wedding that never was."

She cringed at the description. "What did you tell her?"

Sheila hesitated. "In all honesty, I wasn't sure what to tell her. So I told her nothing."

That meant her assistant had stuck to the story she'd given her, which was to basically claim she hadn't talked to her and didn't know where she was. Liz bit her bottom lip. "Did she leave a number I can call?"

"No. She said she's unreachable now, but that she'd try back."

Good ol' consistent Mom. She was likely in between moves and didn't have a phone. The cell phone Liz had given her for Christmas had been lost, never to be found again. She suspected Sunny had tossed it out the same day she got it. Too restrictive, is how she'd viewed the modern piece of technology.

"So, what do you have for me?"

Sheila paused, then said, "You want the bad news, the bad news…or the bad news?"

"Why don't we start with the bad news?"

She heard the closing of a filing cabinet and guessed Sheila was already closing up shop. "You were right.

Beschloss froze all your accounts, business and personal. And he filed assault charges against you. The cops were by this morning."

Liz rubbed her forehead. "And the bad news?"

"You broke his nose." There was a short burst of laughter. "He's got this…contraption on his face that makes him look like an alien from *The Next Generation.*"

Liz groaned.

"Serves him right, really. I always thought he was a reptile."

"I only wish I had listened to you."

Another whoosh of a cabinet drawer. "Hmm…I seem to recall you couldn't hear me over the ticking of that biological clock of yours. Something about turning thirty—"

"Call me in six years and tell me how you feel then, smartie pants." She really was going to miss Sheila. She'd been like a little sister to her for the year she was in Boston.

"Liz? You want me to call those cops back and report Beschloss? I could probably have access to your accounts by this time tomorrow. And it might get that charge of assault dropped." She paused. "Either that, or you could come back and straighten everything out yourself."

"Can't do that," Liz said quietly. That was Rule One in Liz's Moving On Handbook. She never returned to a place she'd left behind. Well, except for Manchester, but that didn't count because she had a house here. In fact, yesterday she'd made arrangements to have Sheila pack up her stuff and put it all into storage, including her personal belongings when Rich finally came to his senses. Then once she was settled, Sheila was to forward it all to her new address.

Besides, going back to Boston meant speaking to her ex-fiancé, something she really didn't want to do right now—

especially since it wouldn't change anything, and it might very well find her spending a little time in a jail cell.

No, she would wait this one out.

She sucked in her bottom lip, then sighed. "No. He's bound to cool down in a few days, which will take care of both problems." As much as the prospect of having Richard arrested appealed to her, he'd suffered enough. It couldn't have been easy for him to have to explain the situation to his snooty parents and the who's who of Boston society.

She spotted Mitch watching her through the open window that looked out over the dining area and waggled her fingers at him. "You go ahead and take what's in the petty cash drawer and we'll work everything out later, when things are back to normal, okay? Look, I've got to get back to…I've got to go."

"Wait. You didn't let me get to the last piece of bad news," Sheila reminded her.

Liz sighed. "You mean there's more?"

"Yeah. This guy called up this morning asking all sorts of questions about you and the business. I told him, sorry, I couldn't tell him anything because I didn't know a Liz Braden, and that we were closed for business, but he kept on. In fact, he got pretty agitated with me after asking the same questions twice."

Liz perked up. "Did he give you his name?"

"Yeah. Yeah, he did. Hold on a sec…."

Liz gazed back at the man sitting at the counter.

"Here it is. It's Mitch. Mitch McCoy."

She laughed so loud even Bo looked up from the grill. She cleared her throat and turned toward the wall. "I see."

"I take it you know this guy?" Sheila asked.

"You, um, could say that." She scratched at the body of

the phone with her thumbnail. "Did he leave a number where he could be reached?"

"Yes, he did. Asked that I call him if I decided I wanted to spill."

She smiled. Sounded just like Mitch.

A few moments later, Liz hung up the receiver, then straightened the skirt of her uniform.

"Everything all right, Lizzie?" Bo asked.

"Hmm?" She looked at the man who could mirror Mel of the sitcom *Alice* right down to the white cap rolled up on his balding head. He stood behind her now. She turned to smile at him. "Shh, the guy on the other side of the window might hear you. The last thing I need now is the FBI breathing down my neck."

Bo chuckled. "Who? Mitch? Hell, Lizzie, he quit the bureau going on something like three years ago now. I thought you knew."

She mentally chewed on the tidbit. "No…I didn't."

"Not that it matters any, mind you. He started his own P.I. company along with a couple of partners in D.C."

"P.I.?" Liz scanned the features that had aged more than the years she'd been away. "What's he doing in Manchester then? Vacation?"

Bo shrugged. "Can't say as I know. Awful long time for a vacation. He came back home about eight months ago, hangs out here a bit, but doesn't talk a whole lot except for the usual conversational stuff. His brother Marc got married, did you know?"

"Yeah. I heard. Shocking, huh?" she said absently.

"Yeah. All of us around here figured out of that McCoy bunch, Mitch was the most likely to marry first."

And we both know what happened there, she added silently.

Bo headed back to the grill and she for the door. The instant it closed behind her, her gaze slammed into Mitch's.

Mitch? A P.I.?

This bit of news managed to dampen her amusement at finding out he'd been checking up on her. He'd been a tried-and-true FBI agent when she'd left. Even the one time she'd attempted to broach the subject of a career change, he'd stiffened and rattled off the reasons why his job was important to him. "Every McCoy for the last four generations has been in law enforcement, Liz. I won't be the one to break that tradition."

Now, she stared at him curiously. Something had to have happened to make him break free from that familial obligation. He was back in Manchester, wearing faded denim jeans and T-shirts that clung too perfectly to his body, reminding her of the teen he'd been before he'd taken on the responsibility that came with being born into a family where men were men and women were... Well, where women were nonexistent.

"Tell me, Liz," he broke into her thoughts. "Did a ring come with that wedding dress you were wearing the other night?"

"Ring?" she repeated, pretending not to know what he was referring to. She ripped off the tally for table one. "Why don't you tell me?" She smiled at the narrowing of his eyes.

"Call me old-fashioned, but usually when someone's wearing a wedding dress, it means they just got married," he baited. "Then again, I'm beginning to think a wedding dress is everyday apparel for you."

"Oh, low blow, McCoy." Liz picked up the plate Bo slid onto the window ledge. She rounded the corner, ignoring the way her skin warmed beneath Mitch's gaze.

"Here you go, Ezra, your Garden of Eden Pizza with lots

of snakes, just the way you like it," she said, plopping down the anchovy- and cherry-tomato-covered pie onto table five.

"Thanks, Lizzie. I've got just enough time to give in to temptation before I've got to get back to the gas station," he said, wiping his hands on his purple and gold cotton shirt with *Ezra* sewn above the pocket. Liz piled up the empty plates left by his tablemates.

"By the way, you never did answer the question I asked earlier," Ezra said, stuffing an anchovy halfway into his mouth then sucking the rest of it in.

"What question is that?" Liz hoisted up the empty plates. "Wait, don't tell me. You're talking about that ridiculous bet again, right?"

Myra overheard her from the next table and leaned toward Liz as she passed. "You only think it's ridiculous because you're afraid of losing."

Liz eyed the wiry-haired waitress, half expecting to spot antennae hidden in the dark mass to explain the way her old friend heard everything said.

"Sorry, Ez, but I'm not much of a gambling woman."

Ezra grinned at her. "Hell, Lizzie, you used to be the first one to put your money down."

She started, realizing he was right. Then again, she used to be a lot of things she wasn't anymore. "Sorry, maybe next go-'round."

She followed Myra back behind the counter, trying to forget that Mitch sat a mere ten feet away—which was just about as easy as forgetting water was wet.

"I don't even know what this bet is about. How can I lose something I'm not even involved in?" she asked her long-ago summertime friend, pushing the dirty dishes onto the window ledge.

"You're about the only one who isn't involved." Myra's brown eyes sparkled as she plucked a leftover French fry from a plate. "Practically the whole population of Manchester has money riding on it."

Liz confiscated the fry from Myra's hand before she could eat the secondhand food. "I don't know why anyone would be interested in me."

Myra laughed and reached around her to pick at another plate. Bo pulled it into the kitchen. "Girl, your roots are buried in this town just the same as mine, even if you only nourished them during the summer. Of course everyone's interested in and concerned about you. They're also interested in the cat-and-mouse game you and Mitch have been playing since he came in this morning."

"Trust me, nothing is going on between me and Mitch."

"Come on, Liz, you can't pull the wool over this one's eyes. Anyway, it's never taken much for Ezra to start a betting pool. This particular one has to do with whether you two are going to repeat history."

Repeat history? She went still, feeling as if every drop of blood had drained from her head. In her mind's eye, she vividly remembered their wedding day....

"Oh, no," Myra said quickly. "Not *that* history. Lord forbid you should do that again. People are still talking about that."

"What history, then?"

"Well, it has something to do with the night you two were caught in here, you know, after hours, the lights on for all to see—"

Liz smiled, the sensual memory one that still haunted her dreams. "I get the picture, Myra. And I don't believe for a second that's what this bet is about."

Myra chuckled wickedly. "You're right. The only thing they're betting on is how long before you and Mitch hook up with each other again."

Liz's stomach gave a funny little lilt. "Yeah? What do the odds say?"

Bo slid an order onto the counter and Myra dropped her voice an octave. "That Mitch doesn't stand a chance in hell of staying single."

Myra's laugh followed her as she collected the meals from the window and squeezed out from behind the counter to deliver them.

Liz's attention slid back to the other victim involved in the bet. She wondered just who, exactly, was supposed to be the cat and who the mouse.

She grabbed the water carafe and stepped down to refill Mitch's glass.

"Hey, Lizzie," Ezra called out. "Thought you'd like to know I got another five dollars down on the bet."

Liz looked at Mitch. "Are you responsible for this?"

"Responsible for what?"

"This bet Ezra's got going."

Mitch grinned. She felt like slugging him.

She put the water pitcher back where it belonged and rubbed her rag against the counter. "Okay, McCoy, let's get this over with right now. Ask me out, I'll tell you no and we can go on from here as if this silly bet never happened."

His grin widened. "Nope." He slowly shook his head, the overhead lights catching the golden strands otherwise lost in his thick mane of chestnut-brown hair. "I don't go out of my way to invite rejection. Not anymore."

What an odd thing to say—

"How 'bout it, angel?" he asked in that voice that rubbed

her in all the right…no, *wrong* ways. "You ready to put your money where your mouth is?"

Liz dug in her pockets for her morning's tips. "How much you got down?"

"Uh-uh."

"Fine. Don't tell me then." She crumpled what she knew was no more than ten or so dollars' worth of tips. She crossed the room and put the pile of crumpled bills on the table in front of Ezra. "I don't need to know anything more than I already know. Nothing is going to happen between Mitch and me."

"Lizzie, rules are nothing over five dollars," the mechanic said quietly.

She smiled. "Is that what you're really worried about, Ez? Or are you afraid of losing your own money now that I've joined in?"

"I'll cover it."

Liz didn't turn. Didn't need to. She'd recognize the voice and the teasing tone anywhere. Mitch moved to stand behind her, carefully placing the matching funds on the table before her.

"You know, Mitch, you're really starting to ruffle my feathers," she said.

"That's my whole intention, angel."

She turned around to face him. She was unprepared to find him so…near. Before she could react, he captured a stray lock of her hair and twirled it around his thick finger, the near-white strands contrasting against his tanned, callused skin. The cocky, confident way he stood pulled his jeans tight against his muscular thighs. Her eyes followed the denim down to where his brown cowboy boots were dusty and scuffed. She swallowed.

"You don't stand a chance in hell, Mitch," she told him, mimicking Myra's words.

He tucked her hair behind her ear. "Good, 'cause that's not the place I'm counting on to help me out on this one."

THE DINER mostly emptied out after lunch. Midway through bussing table one, Liz slid into the glossy pink booth near the window, her back to Mitch, the man she feared would make her time there a study in tolerance. Oh, sure, he might have turned tail and run yesterday, but she had the sneaking suspicion he wouldn't be running anywhere else anytime soon. And after her experience with her last relationship, another man in her life was very low on her list. Especially Mitch. She'd screwed up with him before. She wasn't about to do it again. No matter how deliciously provocative his counter fantasy. Just thinking about being stretched across that counter at his complete and utter mercy made her hot all over.

She stared at the red candied cherub swaying back and forth on the table, then snatched the cheerful object from its metal spring. What had she been thinking?

"Things haven't settled down in Boston yet, huh?" Myra glided onto the seat across from her, having exchanged her uniform for a black cotton shirt and bedraggled jeans. Liz watched her tug the shirt down slightly over one smooth shoulder, her black bra strap plainly visible.

"No. In fact, they're a little worse than I expected they'd be right now." Liz accidentally snapped off one of the cherub's wings.

Mitch's rich chuckle filled the diner. Liz guessed he was still talking to Charles Obernauer, the owner of the general store. She rubbed the back of her neck to ease the tingle there.

"I know you don't know what's going on, Myra, but I do

appreciate you not pushing the issue." She strained to hear the words of Mitch's conversation, then broke off the cherub's head. She tossed it onto a plate. "You were always a good friend."

"So were you."

Liz looked at her. Aside from a postcard here and there, and a few sporadic holiday cards that revealed nothing, she'd lost touch with Myra over the years. But her ex-maid-of-honor treated her as graciously as if they'd spoken daily.

Myra rummaged through her fringed, black purse and offered her a piece of fruit-flavored candy. *A Lifesavers moment.* Liz laughed and accepted the offering.

"Come on, Liz, I know if you could tell me, you would. Anyway, it really doesn't matter why you came back. What does is that you did." She wrinkled her nose. "Did that make any sense?"

"More sense than you know." A burst of gratitude warmed Liz's heart. Myra had taken her in hand the minute her mother had plopped her on her grandmother's doorstep. The outgoing woman before her had also been a friendly girl and she'd made Liz participate in kiddy, then teenage, social life, such as it was in Manchester County. If not for her, Liz would have set up shop at Gran's until summer vacation was over. Just like she shut herself in her new bedrooms whenever her mother dragged her from town to town, apartment to apartment. Sunny Braden could never much figure out her daughter. The way she saw it, her frequent moves opened up a whole new world of opportunity for the girl. Instead, Liz had always felt shut out. And so very, very alone.

She cleared her throat. "If it makes any difference, you are the best friend I ever had."

"Same here."

For a long, quiet moment, neither said anything. Then a grin enlivened Myra's attractive, uneven features and she leaned back in the booth. "Besides, now that you're back, I can take this trip Harvey has planned for us without worrying about leaving Bo and Ruth shorthanded."

"I knew there was an ulterior motive," Liz said wryly. It wasn't likely that Richard would come to his senses before the weekend. And the banks would be closed for the coming holiday anyway....

Myra must have taken her prolonged silence as reluctance. She said quickly, "Well, you said you wanted to keep busy. With me gone, you'll be that and more, especially with the July fourth festivities. You are going to help with Ruth's booth, right?"

Ruth's booth. With the busyness of the morning, Liz had nearly forgotten about the food booth Ruth and Bo always manned at any holiday or county event. She twisted her lips.

"Have you known anybody to say no to Ruth and have it stick?" she asked. "Enough of that. I want to know where you and Harvey are going. Have you decided?"

During mini-breaks throughout the day, Liz had had Myra fill her in on the past seven years. The chitchat let her find out about what her friend had been doing, and it also saved her from having to talk about the comical mess that was her own life.

Myra had told her she'd opened her own flower shop a few years ago only to watch it slide into debt under the weight of Manchester's weak economy. The only businesses that unfailingly survived in the small town were the general store, a nearby bar, Ezra's gas station and the diner. Even the dead went to an outside mortuary for final arrangements.

Liz had learned Harvey was her on-again, off-again boyfriend of the past year or so. He was from the neighboring county, and from what Liz could surmise, he was a bit of a rebel with his Harley and unplanned trips arranged to escape small-town life for a short stretch.

"Don't know where we're going this time," Myra finally said. "He should be here in a few minutes. We'll probably just jump onto that Harley of his and ride."

"Harvey and his Harley. Ingredients of every girl's dream."

"Maybe not yours," Myra said easily. "But definitely mine."

"So why don't you marry him?" Liz eyed her.

She shrugged. "He hasn't asked."

Liz choked on her response. Myra handed her a previous customer's half-empty glass of water.

"I'm joking," Myra said with a laugh. "You know, you don't fool me with those saucy smiles and zinging remarks of yours, Liz. You're as uptight as ever. While I'm gone you should really have a little fun. You look like you could use some." She gestured over her shoulder. "Why don't you take advantage of what life has to offer? Especially that prize customer of yours."

Liz's throat tightened. "Mitch doesn't tip well enough to be a prize customer."

"He always leaves me good ones." Myra's silver bracelets jangled as she pushed all five of them up her forearm.

"You're probably saying I should have some fun with Mitch because of this stupid bet."

"Don't put that one on me. You got yourself into that jumble all by your lonesome."

Liz looked up. "Speaking of which, who did *you* put your money on, Myra? Me or…him?"

"Hmm?" Liz watched Myra pretend an interest in putting back together the dismembered cherub scattered across the table.

Liz kept an eyebrow raised, noticing that the subject of their conversation had gone quiet as well.

"Okay. Let's put it this way, Elizabeth Braden. I still have hopes for you."

Myra had bet against her. "I can't believe you!"

"Yeah, well, believe it. While you and Mitch may have had a run at it before and failed, there's not a single reason why you can't have a little fun with him now. The type of fun that involves sheets, preferably of the silk variety. You know, at least until things settle down in Boston and you can get on with your plans."

If only her plans extended beyond waiting for Richard to calm down, maybe she'd feel better. Truth was, her plans' well was currently empty. And she didn't need help imagining that fun with Mitch would involve silk sheets. She cleared her throat. "This from a woman who dates a man named Harvey with a Harley."

"At least I have a man I want to run away with, not from."

Through the tall glass windows that looked out over manicured Main Street, Liz watched someone who could only be Harvey pull up on a chopper. His black hair was a tangled mass around his stern features, the tattoo of a skull vividly displayed on the fist-size muscle of his right arm. His dark attire matched Myra's, the exceptions being a red bandanna tied loosely around his tanned neck and the absence of a bra strap.

She gasped. "My God, Myra! If there was ever anyone to run from."

Myra quickly hugged her. "The tattoo washes off with soap and water and Harvey's an accountant in his day job."

"Call if you need anything, okay? Like if Harvey leaves you stranded out in the middle of nowhere with a hefty bar bill."

Myra laughed. "I will."

Liz stood and dragged the pile of plates to the edge of the table. "Oh, and about that bet, Myra." She smiled. "You're going to lose every stinking penny."

CHAPTER FOUR

THAT FRIDAY at the Fourth of July county fair, Liz leaned against the food booth she was helping to man and drew in a deep, satisfying breath. There was nothing quite like the smells of sunshine, popcorn and cotton candy. Not to mention the aromas that wafted up from the table before her. She reached over and drew her fingertip across the bottom of the barbecue rib pan, ignoring the wobble of the table as she stuck her finger into her mouth.

She briefly closed her eyes, only to throw them open again when an enticing vision of Mitch emerged front and center. She dragged her finger from between her lips. She was beginning to suspect an image of him was forever etched into the backs of her eyelids. Even last night, when she'd tried to write an apologetic letter to Richard, thoughts of Mitch had distracted her. "Dear Richard, I know you don't know where I am, but rest assured I'm in good hands...." Then for the next ten minutes she'd thought about Mitch's hands and the many things she wanted him to do with them.

She'd plodded on. "I'm sorry for popping you in the nose. I'm not usually a physical person, but since I've gotten into town, all I can think about is getting even more physical...with Mitch...."

She'd crumpled at least eight such drafts before giving up on the endeavor entirely.

She shifted uneasily, and the table lurched.

"Oh no," Liz said under her breath, fastening a death grip on the corner as the back leg gave out.

She'd seen it coming since she'd set up for the three-day event hours earlier. Watched the wobbles when people bumped the front of the booth. The teeters when she and Ruth busily served ribs, potato salad, pork and beans and French fries to the harried lunch crowd. But the table hadn't given out then. Oh, no. It had to wait until Bo and Ruth had taken advantage of the present lull in customers to check out what else was going on around the fairgrounds. Until she was alone. Until, once again, thoughts of Mitch had completely distracted her.

The afternoon sun beat down on Liz's head, overheating her skin and dappling the leftover food spread across the tabletop. She leaned back, trying to get a look at the damage under the table.

"Need some help?"

Speak of the devil.

Mitch stood a few feet away, arms folded across his chest, his cowboy boots solidly planted on the hard dirt of the pathway. Liz nearly lost her grip—literally and figuratively. Damn, but the man had a way of chasing every thought, every intention from her mind.

She glanced up at him. "Depends on what it's going to cost me."

He grinned that maddening grin. "At this point, I think I can afford to throw you a freebie."

The corner she held dipped an inch and the food platters clattered ominously. "Are you going to help me get this leg back under the table now, or are you waiting to surprise me on my birthday?"

He uncrossed his arms. "It's my mission in life to help you with your legs, angel." He lazily dropped his gaze to where her khaki shorts ended and her tanned skin began. She'd bought a few things the day before with her first check, not that it mattered. The heat in his gaze made her feel completely naked, or at least made her yearn to be.

"Mitch McCoy, in two seconds everything Ruth and I spent two days making is going to end up on the ground. Now are you going to help me or not?"

He narrowed the distance between them, then knelt down and propped the table leg up. His forearm brushed against her bare calf. A delicious shiver shimmied up the back of her leg.

"Sorry," he murmured.

Scooting what few inches she could away from him, she tested the repair work, then released her grip. "You can get up now, Mitch."

"Hmm…I like the view better from down here."

"I bet you do." Liz admired the way the sun reflected off his brown hair, livening the fair highlights, the wind teasing the thick, soft strands. She wanted to tunnel her fingers through it and tug that grinning mouth of his to hers. "But if you don't get up now, you're the one who's going to need help fixing one of your legs."

With a quiet chuckle, he rose to his feet. Liz swallowed hard, trying to determine whether or not he'd grown taller since the last time she saw him.

"Are you threatening bodily harm, Lizzie?"

"Uh-huh."

His brows lifted skeptically. "Not a particularly wise thing to do considering the trouble you're already in."

For the first time since she'd seen him standing backlit by the sun, she felt like smiling. And did.

"Okay, this time I'll bite. The circumstances surrounding my return are eating you alive, aren't they?"

It was satisfying to watch him cross his arms defensively. "I don't particularly like the imagery associated with what you just said, but, yeah, I'll admit I'm a little curious."

"A little?"

"A little." He stood his ground.

"Good." She bent over and repositioned the ribs that had slid slightly when the table gave out.

"Is that it?" Mitch asked, coming to stand close. Too close.

She shrugged, though the last thing she felt was unaffected by his nearness. He was so…big. "Given your former occupations, I've no doubt you've already checked with the Virginia and Massachusetts authorities. And since you haven't said anything, I trust both checks came back clean."

"Should they have?"

"I'll let you be the one to figure that out." Kneeling down, she opened the portable refrigerator and took out a bowl of potato salad. "Want some?"

"No, thanks."

Picking up a plastic fork, she took a healthy bite of the blessedly cold food, though she suspected a freezer full of ice cubes wouldn't be enough to cool her off. And her condition had nothing to do with the summer sun. "Are you sure? Ruth really outdid herself this time."

He fairly growled. "I don't want any damn potato salad, Liz."

Sucking on the end of the fork, she watched him. She was really getting to him, wasn't she? Which was good. Because he got to her in a way she couldn't begin to fathom.

"Hey, Mitch."

Liz watched Mitch's brother, Jake McCoy, step up to the booth. Seeing as she'd been back for almost a week, she'd expected to run into more McCoys by now. She knew Marc was off on his honeymoon, but where were Connor and David? Around five years older than Mitch, Jake had always been the quietest of the brothers. Darker, more intense, he reminded her somewhat of the actor Jeff Goldblum.

"How are you, Elizabeth?"

She smiled at his formality. She couldn't remember one time when he'd called her Liz. "Fine. And you, Jake? I have to say, you're looking as good as ever."

She watched the tips of his ears redden, but little else betrayed what he was feeling. "Fine. I'm fine." He turned his attention toward Mitch, who looked anything but fine. "Where's Pops?"

Mitch grimaced. "He's not at the house?"

"No."

"Then, I don't know where he is. I haven't seen a whole lot of him myself lately."

Jake raised a brow. "Okay. Guess I'll catch up with him later."

Jake nodded at Liz, started to walk away, then hesitated. "I like how the place is coming along, Mitch."

Mitch jammed his fingers through his hair. "Thanks."

"Let me know if you need any more help."

"Sure."

Liz's gaze trailed to Mitch after Jake had disappeared down the fairway. "Everything all right with your father?"

"What? Yeah, sure, Pops is fine. But he isn't the one on my mind right now."

"Oh, now I know what you're worried about," she said jokingly. "It's the bet, isn't it?"

Again, he stepped closer. Liz backed up, her body on alert.

"No, angel, I'm talking about something entirely different."

Her throat grew dry. "Mind telling me what?"

"Well…" He scraped a rough fingertip along the cotton strap over her right shoulder. "Actually, it has to do with you telling me something I've been waiting seven years to hear."

The ground shifted beneath Liz's feet. She didn't have to ask him what that something was. She knew.

"Why did you leave me, Liz?"

In direct contrast to his chilly tone, his finger slid from the cotton to her bare shoulder, searing her flesh. A slight shift and his hand would rest over her breast. Oh, how she wanted to feel him there, cupping her, testing the weight in his palm.

She quickly moistened her lips and searched his eyes. The teasing there surprised her. She would have thought he'd be a little more serious when he broached the subject. As it was, he acted as if their conversation concerned nothing more than the color of her tank top.

"You know why," she whispered.

His gaze raked her face. "I do?"

"Yes…no…you know what I mean."

He slowly shook his head. "No, Liz, I can't say as I do." He suddenly shoved his hands into his jeans pockets and shifted his weight from one boot to the other. "Tell me, is the reason you left Boston the same reason you left me?" He held her gaze with a potency that had her mesmerized.

Liz searched his face, learning the new shadows of hurt and disappointment that lurked there. She wanted to reach out to smooth away the wrinkle of his dark brow and coax back the humor that made his eyes twinkle. But she didn't. The silence that clanked down around them wouldn't allow it. There was no room for soothing, for jokes. Their conversation had moved to more serious ground and now she would just have to stand on it. She fought to keep her gaze locked with his.

"No. The choice I made now," she said carefully, quietly, trying to respond in a way that made sense, "is nothing like the choice I made seven years ago."

The pain that shadowed his face turned into a grimace. "You know, Liz, you've always been about as clear as a muddy river." He cursed under his breath. "What did you expect from me when you came back? That I would have forgiven you for something I can't begin to understand?"

"I don't expect anything from you, Mitch. You asked me if the choices I made were similar, and I gave you an answer." She clasped her fingers around her opposite arm. "Now if you want to talk about choices, then let's talk about the ones you gave me when I asked to postpone our ceremony."

"A request you made on the day of our wedding."

"Yes, on the day of our wedding." She caught herself rubbing her arm and dropped her hand. "What choices did you give me then, Mitch?"

He was silent, so she provided the answer for him. *"Either you marry me now, Liz, or you leave me and Manchester forever."*

She didn't need to remind him that she'd never been good with ultimatums. She'd spent her entire childhood waiting for that moment in time when she'd have control over her life. When she was no longer at the mercy of her mother's constant restlessness. When she was the one calling the shots. And his response…well, it had threatened that control. Sure, she'd known he'd said the words out of anger. But the moment they were out, they were out, hanging between them in large, bold, capital letters. It didn't matter that he didn't mean them, or that she'd loved him more than anything. The whole dynamic of their relationship had changed in that one moment. And that was something Liz couldn't live with. If she had stayed…well, she hadn't, had she?

Long minutes passed, then Mitch finally cleared his throat.

"That doesn't explain why you asked for the postponement," he said.

"You didn't seem too interested in knowing why then," she said. She'd asked for the postponement because she was petrified. Terrified that she might not be the right woman for Mitch. Paralyzed with dread that she didn't belong.

She shook off her uneasiness, surprised to find those emotions remained even now.

Which was dumb, because they had both done what they had to.

"That was a long time ago, Mitch. Been there, done that, bought the T-shirt. No amount of talking about it now is going to change things, so why even bother?" She tucked her hair behind her ear, steadily holding his gaze. "You see the world one way. I see it another. We're just not suited for each other. Not for a kiss, not for a date, not for forever. Don't ask for any further explanation than that, because I don't think I can be any clearer than that without cussing."

Kids that had been hanging back neared the front of the booth, prodding at the food Liz had been putting away. They were laughing, but she couldn't concentrate on what they were saying.

"You've really thought about this, haven't you?" he asked, the sides of his mouth beginning to turn up.

She lifted a finger. "Now don't go making more of this—"

"Admit it, Liz, you've stayed awake nights fortifying your reasons not only for running out on me, but for not being with me now."

She felt as if he had stripped away her blanket on a cold winter's night. Or peeled back her clothes on a hot summer's day, just like this one. The contrast left a tantalizing tingle in her belly that refused to go away.

"Still, I want to remind you none of your reasons has anything to do with attraction."

Oh, he had her there. As far as the attraction angle went, she didn't think she could burn for a man more without self-combusting. Still, she said, "It takes more than attraction, Mitch."

"For marriage, yes, it does. For one date, how much more do you want? I'm not asking you to marry me again, angel."

"Date?" Of course, date. They were back to the cursed bet again. "Nice try, but you're going to have to do a whole helluva lot better than that if you hold out any hope of winning this bet."

He grasped her upper arms and hauled her closer. So much for not self-combusting. Flames seemed to lick over her skin from forehead to feet. "Forget the bet, Liz. I just think it fair for me to warn you: I want you. And, damn it, I'm not going to stop until I have you."

CHAPTER FIVE

TWO DAYS LATER Liz sat at a pink booth, the squeak of her bare legs against plastic echoing through the empty diner. She absently tugged the hem of her silk shorts down farther to cover her skin. After three days manning the food booth at the fair, she, Bo and Ruth had finally closed up shop earlier tonight in preparation for the Fourth of July fireworks. Since everyone was at the fairgrounds anyway, the diner was closed, and Liz was left with nothing to do but think.

Not that there was much to think about. She propped her chin in her palm. Okay, so her plans for her future were basically a blank slate, but she couldn't do anything about that until Richard unfroze her assets. Something he had yet to do, as Sheila had told her the day before. Still, she couldn't seem to concentrate on anything other than what Mitch had said about wanting her, and about his obvious absence since making the declaration. Both things that had kept her up late into the night, yearning for an unnameable something that she was beginning to think no one but Mitch could give her.

She stared through the window next to her at the darkening sky. About a half mile down the road at the fairgrounds, the bright tail of a skyrocket heralded what would soon be the beginning of the fireworks display. Liz hadn't known she'd sighed until she heard the wistful sound break the silence of the empty diner.

Everyone would be at the fairgrounds now, stretching blankets out on the dewy grass, reaching into coolers for colas and beer, lighting sparklers for the kids, having fun that wouldn't end with the fireworks. She shifted, wincing when her skin peeled from the plastic again. *Fun.* She hadn't had much of that in recent years. If she were honest, aside from the brief snatches of promise the first few days in a new city brought, she hadn't had near the adventure she had sworn she'd have when she'd left Manchester.

First she'd gone to Cleveland, where she'd lived with her bohemian mother and taken some night school courses at a local college, earning her bachelor's in business. Then the harsh lake-effect winters had chased her from the bustling city to Chicago, which was laughable, because the winters had been even worse there, and the busy metropolis had certainly earned the title Windy City during the year she had stayed.

Next had come St. Louis and Philadelphia.

In the meantime, as a consultant she'd steadily moved up from helping small business and restaurant owners turn a healthy profit to signing large contracts with major industrial firms and service agencies.

Then there was Boston and her biggest contract yet with a centuries-old bank. Only, that contract had a handsome, charming male attached in the shape of a vice president named Richard Beschloss.

Liz absently gathered the brochures littering the table in front of her into a pile, feeling much as if she was gathering scattered playing cards. Only she had yet to find an ace in this deck. For days, she'd been toting around the pamphlets she'd picked up on her way to Manchester trying to figure out where she wanted to head next. Dallas, L.A., Seattle, Miami? She had solid contacts in each of the cities, contacts she could use to re-establish herself. And she could get letters of recommendation from nearly everyone she'd worked with. Except for Richard, of course. But none of the places had jumped out at her. Wherever she decided to head, she had enough capital to get herself up and running again—if she could ever regain access to her personal and business accounts in Boston, that is.

She'd never thought Richard Beschloss would be so vengeful.

She bent the corner of the brochure on Atlanta back and forth. Just before she had become engaged, a professional headhunter had approached her with a job opportunity in the southern city. The position would mean working for somebody else instead of herself, but the company was good, and job security was guaranteed.

A clang of metal drew her attention back to the well-lit street. Liz slid over the booth, closer to the window, immediately recognizing the red truck parked in front of the general store across the street. Mitch climbed out, leaving the door open only long enough for Goliath to jump out after him.

"Mitch McCoy, where in the hell have you been?" Liz murmured in the quiet of the diner.

It wasn't like him to drop a bombshell such as the one he had the other day, then disappear. Then again, did she really even know *what* he was like anymore? She was beginning to think she didn't.

Why wasn't he at the fairgrounds? And why in the world was he re-stocking the two vending machines that stood sentinel at either side of the entrance to the general store?

He lowered the tailgate of the truck, the dog barking and nipping at his heels.

"Down, Goliath," Mitch ordered, his voice drifting through the open diner door. He freed his right hand and scratched the dog behind one of his ears.

Goliath knocked him off balance. A few foil bags of chips slid from the box and scattered across the sidewalk. Mitch didn't even frown as he put the box down, gathered up the items, then used his keys to open the large, glass-fronted door of the first machine.

My, but he has a great pair of buns.

When she saw him like this—with several yards separating them and no curious onlookers around—Liz admitted she'd always liked looking at him. No, *like* wasn't the word. *Relished* was better. He had the type of body that commanded attention. Long, slender and solid. More than that, Mitch exuded a strength she wondered at. It was more than the tight fit of his T-shirts, the just-right shade of his faded jeans and his broken-in cowboy boots. It was the man himself. A man who never seemed flustered by anything. In fact he gave the impression he was quite pleased with himself and his life, even in moments when nobody was around to watch him.

Still, none of that explained why Mitch was stocking vending machines when he should be at the fairgrounds, settling in with the rest of the town for the fireworks display. She plucked at the brochure. He should be with a pretty, single woman, mapping out plans for starting a family. Living the life they had once planned to live.

An anxious sense of loneliness sank into Liz. She'd never much liked the "what if" game, but lately she'd found herself coming back to this one. What if she had stayed? What if she had never asked for the postponement, thus provoking his ultimatum? Compelling her to leave?

Goliath abruptly turned toward her and started barking. Liz was suddenly aware that she sat spotlighted in the empty diner, though it wouldn't surprise her one bit if Mitch had known she was there all along, ogling him. He shifted his head, noting her Lexus parked on the street, then stared right at her through the window. He offered up his devilish grin and her heart thudded. Liz tugged her gaze away from his and jerked the cover on the brochure on Atlanta open in front of her.

"What is it about you, Mitch, that won't let me chase you from my heart?" she muttered.

Goliath's nails clicked against the tiled floor and the sound of footsteps followed. Liz shivered, despite the sultry heat of the night.

She pulled her notepad closer and wrote down words that made absolutely no sense. Something cold and wet touched her calf and she jumped. She laughed at her own high sensitivity and bent to pet Goliath. "Come here, you big slobber puss. How did you get in here?" She cleared her throat and looked at Mitch where he stood near the door. "Oh. I didn't hear you come in."

Liar. Even if she hadn't heard or seen him, she'd have known he was nearby just by taking a deep breath of his warm, outdoorsy scent.

His eyes momentarily darkened, but his grin didn't waver.

Goliath's tail thumped against the side of the booth and Liz petted him again.

"Coffee sounds good right about now," Mitch said.

She poked a thumb toward the half pot she'd made a little earlier, still on the hot plate behind the counter. "I'm off duty." She gave the dog a final pat and turned back to her brochures. "Anyway, the diner's closed. Didn't you see the sign?"

He ignored her and walked toward the counter. He blew into a clean cup, filled it, then turned back. He took the seat across from her.

She glanced up from where she pretended to scour the brochures. "There are at least twenty other tables to sit at in this diner, Mitch."

"Yeah, but none of them have an angel sitting at them."

She plucked an ever-present cherub from its spring stand and tossed it his way. "That's going to have to do, because I'm a little busy right now."

He picked up the cherub from his lap and tossed it back onto the table. "I can see that." He fingered a brochure, then drew it in his direction. He raised a dark brow. "Miami?"

She snatched back the brochure with a picture of a pink flamingo on the cover and stuffed it under the others. "Why aren't you at the fairgrounds with everybody else?"

His grin widened. "I have to say, Liz, your interest in my activities never ceases to amaze me."

At least she hadn't asked him where he'd been—which was just as well, because she had the sneaking suspicion he wouldn't tell her.

She scribbled on the notepad, overly aware of the way his gaze slid over her hair, face and neck like a caress. "Don't tell me. Your new career stocking vending machines is what's keeping you busy."

"Vending ma—" He apparently realized what she was talking about and chuckled. "I'm just looking after those for Klammer. He's on his yearly pilgrimage to Key West to see his old friend Ernest. Should be back sometime next week."

Liz straightened the strap of her silk tank that had slipped down over her shoulder. Her skin was hot to the touch and she wondered if she was as flushed as she felt. "Somebody ought to tell him Hemingway died over thirty years ago."

"I thought you did once."

She met his gaze and smiled. "Yeah, I guess I did. Not that it did any good if he's still going down there."

A loud boom reverberated through the night air. She turned toward the window to find the first of the fireworks shooting across the sky.

"I answered your question. How about you answer one of mine?" Mitch said.

"Depends on what it is."

"How come you're not at the fairgrounds?"

She peered under the table at Goliath, who had taken up residence on one of her feet. Her heart felt impossibly light— the sight, the circumstances, the company all too familiar. Of course, seven years ago Goliath had been little more than a few years old. She'd adopted him as a puppy from one of her neighbor's litters only to find out her grandmother had a violent allergic reaction to him every time he got within smelling distance. She looked at the grown dog now, grateful that Mitch had kept his promise to look after him.

She heated under his probing gaze, realizing he was waiting for an answer to his question. "I figured now was as good a time as any to get my plans together."

He ran his callused thumb over the rim of his cup. "Does that mean whoever you're running from has found you?"

She laughed. Trust him to remember something she'd said to bait him.

"No, it doesn't mean that," she murmured. "Besides, I didn't say I was running away from anybody. I said I needed to get away from someone. Big difference." She twirled the pencil in her fingers, cursing softly when it slipped from her grip and dropped to the floor. She bent to pick it up and bumped against Mitch's hand as he did the same thing from the other side of the table. A flush of awareness hastened up her arm and she slowly pulled her hand back, sitting up to take the pencil from him.

Mitch grinned at her mischievously. "So I take it you haven't noticed the strange guy in town then."

CHAPTER SIX

MITCH WATCHED LIZ closely for her response. Not so much as a batting eyelash gave away her thoughts.

When he'd spotted the fiftyish stranger in the late-model Chevy hanging around the fairgrounds two days ago, then on Main Street yesterday, he'd asked David to run a check on the plates through DCPD's central computers. It had come back as a rental out of Dulles airport. The youngest McCoy had asked if he wanted him to check further, to get the name and address on the rental contract, but Mitch had declined, deciding to use the information he had to get answers from Liz first.

Her hazel eyes seemed to challenge him. He wasn't going to get any more than he'd already gotten from her, which was precious little.

"What strange guy?" she asked. "I think everybody in this town is a bit strange."

She glanced through the window at her Lexus, and he followed her gaze. It was the first time he'd seen her drive it. Since she'd arrived, the car had sat under that damn tarp in her backyard and she'd been catching rides with Ruth into town. Why had she used it now? And why was she looking like it had been a mistake?

"What's the matter, Liz? You seem a bit jumpy tonight."

"Maybe it's because I've had one too many cups of coffee," she answered and rose from the booth. "But, what the heck, one more won't hurt."

He held up his half-empty cup and she ignored him. He put the cup back down and looked under the table to where Goliath shifted to sit on his foot instead of Liz's. Briefly, he wanted to nudge the little Judas away, but allowed him to settle. After all, the dog wasn't the only one who wanted to touch Liz. Only Mitch had much more than just her foot in mind.

His gaze strayed to her walking away from him. Her hips were lush and inviting under the thin silk of her peach-colored shorts. He told himself he should be glad she was wearing something other than those cut-offs and that Georgetown T-shirt, but he honestly could say that the curve-clinging silk was worse. It clung to her rounded bottom like a second skin when she walked, and seemed a lighted billboard advertising just how soft the flesh was that the material covered.

He didn't try to hide his interest in her figure as she walked back to the table with the coffeepot, surprising him by topping off his cup before filling her own. She put the pot on the table. He curved his fingers around her wrist, holding her in place.

"Tell me, is it really the coffee, Liz, or is it the company making you so nervous?" he murmured, his gaze sweeping her upturned face.

Her skin was cool and velvety under his callused fingertips. So cool he thought he might scorch her. A slow burn began deep in his groin.

She laughed a little too lightly, still standing next to the booth. "I've never been nervous in my life, Mitch McCoy. You know that."

"Maybe that was true of the old Elizabeth Braden," he said quietly, scraping his thumb against her wrist and down to the sensitive area of her palm. The movement of his rough skin over her lotion-soft hand felt incredibly provocative. She shuddered and something answered inside him. He halted the movement of his thumb and formed his masking grin. "But this Liz—this new Liz—seems plenty nervous to me."

She tried to tug her wrist away, only serving to tighten his grip. Her breath came in shallow gasps, and he could feel her thundering pulse under his thumb.

"What? You don't really think you're the one making me nervous, do you, Mitch?"

He stared at a shiny, saffron lock of her hair swept against her tanned shoulder. Impulsively, he wanted to rake it back from her enchanting face.

"The thought had crossed my mind," he drawled.

"Well, you better let that thought just keep on going, because you don't have a thing to do with my being anxious. And I'm not saying I am anxious, by the way."

"Of course not," he readily agreed. "Anyway, if you were nervous, it could have as much to do with that stranger in town as it does with me, right?"

She narrowed her hazel eyes. "Is there really a stranger in town, or are you pulling my leg?"

"Oh, if I were pulling your leg, you'd know it, angel. Trust me."

She tried to tug her arm away again, catching him unawares. He tightened his grip and the movement had a reactive effect that hurled her directly into his lap. He stared at her startled expression. She wriggled against him. While the predicament wasn't one he had planned, one particular part of his body readily welcomed her lush bottom pressed against him—a physical response Liz didn't miss if her soft intake of breath was anything to go by. And he was betting it was.

"Well, nice of you to drop in so unexpectedly," he murmured, the sweet smell of wild cherries filling his senses.

She wriggled to free herself from his grasp, serving only to elicit a groan from his suddenly raw throat.

He encircled her waist with his arms, bumping the table in the process, nearly spilling his coffee. "Would you stop struggling a minute before you end up doing some serious damage?"

"I'm not going to stop until you let me go."

Realizing this wasn't fun and games anymore, he released his grip. While her being planted in his lap had been an accident, he could see where she might view it differently given his manipulative behavior lately. Awareness surged through him like an express steam-engine with one destination, but he would never physically press himself on her. No, she was going to be the one coming to him. Willingly. Hungrily.

She stopped struggling, her hazel eyes all sexy and warm.

"What is it?" he murmured. "You're free to go. So go."

She stayed right where she was.

His gaze flicked over her flushed face. The damn woman confused him more than she ever had. Who else but Liz would fight like a spitfire to free herself, then stay as if to spite him? Didn't she realize what she was doing to him? He swallowed, his gaze skimming her pink lips. Or maybe she knew exactly what she was doing and he had just opened a wide passage for her to exact her own brand of revenge.

"Funny, but, um…I don't want to go anymore," she murmured.

An emotion stronger than any he'd ever experienced quaked through him. "I'm warning you, Liz. If you don't get up right now, I won't be held responsible for my actions."

Her teasing little smile made his mouth water. "Aren't

those usually my words?" She lifted a hand and ran her fingertip along the ridge of his jaw. "Looks like the tables have turned, haven't they?"

"Speaking of tables, you realize you're two seconds away from ending up flat against the top of this one, don't you?"

"Yes, well, maybe it's about time we ended up horizontal together somewhere, isn't it?"

Heat blasted through his veins. For the second time, Liz was kissing him. But where the first one in her house had been tauntingly carnal, her exploration now was haltingly sweet, reminding him of stolen kisses when they were teenagers. A groan clogged his throat and he moved his hands from where they rested at his sides so he could tunnel his fingers in her golden hair. He molded her mouth against his, drawing from her all the promises that had gone unfulfilled, glimpsing all they could have had if only he hadn't chased her away.

That glaring truth caused a second groan to follow the first. Even as he parted her lips and gained access to the rich depths of her mouth, he knew that's what he'd done: he had chased the only woman he'd ever cared for from his life.

Pushing the coffee cups out of the way, he lifted her so her bottom sat on the table. With a shaking hand, he nudged her thighs apart and slid his fingers up the leg of her shorts. His knuckles brushed against the damp front of her panties. She whimpered, kissing him harder as she moved her hips closer. He placed a stilling hand against her stomach, then began working the hem of her silk tank top up until her matching silk bra was exposed.

He caught his breath. No one could quite fill a bra the way Liz could. Not too big, not too small, the supple flesh curved just so over the top of the cups, tempting his mouth. He ran his tongue slowly across one slope, dipped it into the shallow valley, then trailed it across the other, before fastening his lips over her right nipple.

Her shuddering response edged up his own need. The silk of her bra was soft, the nipple beneath hard and round. He pulled at it through the material. She restlessly moved her hands through his hair, holding him there, aiding him when he moved to lavish attention on the other breast, leaving a round wet spot in his wake.

She tasted so good…so damn right.

He skimmed his fingers down her sides, over her thighs, then slipped them again under the hem of her shorts. She went completely still, her heartbeat a rapid staccato against his ear. He closed his eyes, savoring the amplified quiet of the moment. Enjoying the sweet anticipation. Then he gently probed her engorged flesh and dipped the tip of his fingers in her dripping heat.

Her moan, deep and soft, wove its way around him.

"Oh, how I want you," he ground out, his erection pressing painfully against his jeans.

Her eyes, half-lidded and drugged, stared at him. "Then take me, McCoy."

He bolted from the booth toward the row of lights near the kitchen door while she yanked closed the caf-style curtains at the windows. Within seconds, the diner was dark, the door closed, and he had her sprawled across the top of the table. She ripped at his T-shirt and the buttons on his jeans. He tugged off his boots, then her tank top, shorts and panties.

She was the most beautiful thing he'd ever seen.

In the golden light shining in from the top of the windows, her skin shimmered richer than the silk he'd taken off her. Her breasts were two peaks that rose and fell as her breath quickened, topped with pale, engorged nipples. He slid his hands up from her waist and cupped the firm globes, running his thumbs over the puckered nipples, wondering at their hardness. He hungrily lowered his mouth to capture first one, then the other, afraid he'd never be able to kiss them enough to make up for the past seven years. Afraid that if he didn't take her now, he'd never have the chance again.

Liz alternated between shoving his jeans down his hips, then bracing herself against the table, the restless sounds she made driving him onward. Finally, his jeans fell to the floor and he stepped out of them, stopping only long enough to get the condom from his wallet before again positioning himself between her thighs.

The sight of him poised just so against the pale tangle of curls between her legs made him pause. His breathing stopped. His heart beat loudly in his ears. How many times had they made it this far before only to pull back? One or the other of them regaining control of their actions and stopping before things went too far?

His gaze swept up to her face. The need, raw and undiluted, that shone in her eyes told him there would be no turning back now. There was no wedding night to wait for. No preconceived ideas on just how, exactly, their first time should play out. Not a champagne glass, a heart-shaped bed, or red satin sheets in sight. Only her, him and their pure, physical need for each other.

He hadn't realized he'd closed his eyes until he felt her fingers slide the condom over his pulsating shaft, then settle the tip between her soft folds of flesh. She leaned her hands far back on the table, then thrust forward, surrounding him with her slick, tight flesh, hungrily drawing him in. A groan gathered in the back of his throat as he grasped her hips, holding her still, holding her near. He stayed like that for a long moment, ignoring her quiet pleas. He'd waited too damn long for this. He intended to make it last.

Slowly, he counted backward. Ten…nine…eight…

Her sleek muscles flexed around him. The groan ripped from him and he thrust deeply into her, feeling her expand to accommodate him, feeling himself hardening all the more.

He'd never wanted a woman more than he wanted Liz Braden right now.

She wriggled free from his grasp and wound her legs around his waist. He nearly died right then and there when she lifted her hips with the sheer strength of those same legs and ground against him needfully. His ears were filled with her soulful moans, his body surrounded by her sweet, sweet flesh.

He thrust into her once. Then again. And again and again. Each and every move only making him want to move more. Over and over. Harder. Deeper.

Grabbing him by the shoulders, Liz lifted herself from the table until only his thighs rested against the side, the shift allowing him to go deeper still. He wrapped his arms around her silken body, flattening her breasts against his hair-peppered chest, squeezing her luscious rear with his hands. Then he slid his fingers between her legs from behind until he felt her slippery wetness, felt where they were joined.

His climax seemed to spiral up and up from the soles of his feet, gaining speed, gaining potency, until he exploded into her with his own unique brand of fireworks. Her own orgasm followed and she gripped his shoulders for dear life.

He stood like that for what seemed like forever—buried in her sleek flesh, his legs locked, his fingers clutching her soft bottom, her body quivering against his. She lifted her head from where she'd thrown it back. He kissed her, passionately, then dragged his mouth across her temple to push the damp wisps of hair back there.

Their eyes met.

In the dim light from the streetlamps outside the window, he read in her eyes everything he felt. Wonder. Amazement. Hunger. A seemingly insatiable hunger that even now had him hardening inside her again.

He claimed her swollen mouth with his own, moving his hands to rest on either side of her satiny neck as she clutched his shoulders. He gave himself over to the squall of agitated emotions swirling in his chest, punctuated by the boom of distant firecrackers in the warm night.

Liz slowed their kiss, then nipped at his bottom lip, catching it between her slightly crooked white teeth, her hazel eyes holding him transfixed. The affectionate gesture reminded him too much of the past. Of torturous moments looking at her and fearing he could never have her. Of feeling she wasn't a woman of flesh and bone, a person he could hold on to, but a wild exotic butterfly constantly soaring just beyond his reach. A butterfly whose ceaselessly flapping wings did the most amazing things to his insides. A butterfly that fled when he tried to catch her with his net.

Liz broke off the kiss, her breath coming in quick gasps. She smiled and rested her forehead against his.

"You're…I'm…that was…incredible," she whispered, her tongue dipping out to moisten her just-kissed lips.

"Yes, I'd say that was worth seven years of absent foreplay," he managed to push from his raw throat.

She flexed her leg muscles around his waist, causing the tightening of other muscles as well. He groaned. She laughed, a low, raspy sound that affected him as much as her nearness.

"Mitch, tell me, why didn't you ever...well, why hadn't..."

He tilted his head back to get a better look at her. Now that they'd finally made love she was even more enchanting...and just as elusive. And he felt himself being reintroduced to the ripping, consuming, adolescent love he'd always felt for her.

Aw, hell.

"What?" he asked. Telling himself he should put her down, push her away. But unable to do either.

"Never mind," she said quietly, to his relief.

The shrill ring of the phone sliced through the needy cloud accumulating around them again. But instead of moving to free herself, Liz burrowed further into his chest.

Goliath scratched the door from the kitchen where Mitch had shut him in.

"Um, don't you think you should get that?" he asked, suddenly urgent to escape the vacuum-like suck of the past. Because, even as her familiar scent tempted his nose, inviting him to breathe her in, he suspected that what had just happened between them had little or nothing to do with the present. He was afraid their lovemaking had come as a result of completing something they'd never had.

She stiffened in his arms, and he reluctantly lowered her to the floor, wondering if she was thinking the same as he was. The damnable thing about the whole situation was that he really didn't want to let her go. Not to move away from him. Not to get the phone. Not to leave Manchester.

He grimaced as he reached for his jeans. So much for casual sex.

EVERY INCH of Liz's skin tingled, every nerve ending sang as she quickly threw her clothes on, then made her unsteady legs carry her to the cash register and the phone. Leaning against the glass-topped case, she pushed her tousled hair back from her face and groped for the receiver. She noticed a dark spot on her tank top and pulled it away from her torso to follow the stain onto her shorts. A glance at the table told her it must be coffee. The new shorts set was ruined, but she couldn't seem to make herself care.

"Hello?" she croaked, then cleared her throat, looking to where Mitch had gotten dressed and turned on the lights. He stepped behind the counter and scooped ice into a glass and filled it with water.

Static crackled over the telephone line. "Hello?" she said again, more clearly. "Bo and Ruth's Paradise Diner."

"Liz, is that you? Thank God you're there. When I didn't see you at the fairgrounds, I hoped you might be at the diner…."

The connection was bad, but Liz thought she made out Ruth's voice. "Ruth? What's the matter?"

"The matter? Well, let's see, aside from the fact that this call is being transmitted through the state police over a radio because I'm in the back of an ambulance heading for D.C., everything's just peachy."

Liz's knees went weak for a second time. "Ambulance? My God, what's happened?"

There was a brief moment of silence. Liz guessed Ruth was trying to pull herself together, an image that was hard to form because Ruth was the most together person she knew. Something was very wrong.

"Bo had a mild heart attack, Liz. The paramedics say it's

not serious. He must have just tired himself out this past weekend, what with the festivities and all…."

Liz felt Mitch's hands on her arms and she automatically leaned into him. He tightened his grip.

"What is it?" he asked quietly.

Liz covered the mouthpiece with her hand. "It's Bo…he's had a heart attack."

His expression held all the concern she felt.

Ruth's voice continued in her ear, sounding more like herself than she did a moment ago. "I told the big oaf he needed to start watching his diet, more vegetables and less of that artery-clogging stuff. But did he listen? No. He wears that belly of his like it's some kind of trophy he's won."

Liz smiled shakily, hearing the sound of a man's voice in the background.

"Would you just shush a minute and let the man do his job," Ruth said. Relief flushed through Liz's frazzled mind. "That's Bo." Ruth confirmed her suspicion. "He's giving the paramedic a hard time. Big surprise. Look, I can't talk long, but I wanted to let you know they're probably going to keep Bo at the hospital in the city for a couple of days, you know, for observation. And I—"

"—want to stay with him," Liz finished for her. "Of course you do. Don't worry. I'll look after the diner." She briefly bit her lip, surprised to find herself near tears. "Is there anything else you need?"

Ruth told her no, that she was having somebody else look into getting them a change of clothes, then Liz quickly told her to give Bo their love. She didn't catch her mistake until Ruth paused.

"Who's *our*?" the older woman asked.

"Our?"

"You said, 'Give Bo *our* love,'" she pressed. "Is there somebody there with you? It's Mitch, isn't it?"

She glanced at the man next to her.

"Mitch? Of course he's not here. I said 'our' in terms of the whole town. As in, give Bo Manchester's love." Liz cringed, afraid she was sounding as crazy as the town's other occupants. Mitch's chuckle didn't help matters much, either. She elbowed him in the ribs.

"Uh-huh," Ruth said, unconvinced. "You're a terrible liar, Liz. Anyway, tell your company that I fully expect him to help you out while Bo and I are gone."

"I'll tell him whenever I see him next. Goodbye, Ruth," Liz said firmly. "Call me from the hospital once Bo's settled in."

She quickly hung up the phone and turned around—and put herself squarely back in the cradle of Mitch's arms.

"He's going to be okay, I take it?" he asked, his gaze scraping her heated cheeks.

"Um…he was arguing with the paramedics, so I think that's a pretty good sign."

Mitch chuckled. "Bo will probably argue with St. Peter."

Liz cleared her throat, unsure how she felt after everything that had happened tonight. She glanced over his shoulder to where Goliath again slept under the table. "Looks like you're going to have to carry him out of here."

The night was silent and Liz realized the fireworks display must have ended. Everybody would be heading home soon, a good number of them passing through town with a clear view inside the diner. She suddenly realized that anyone passing too close to the windows might have seen them….

"So, what time should I be here to help you open up in the morning?" he asked, his gaze fastened to her mouth.

"Time?"

He grinned. "I take it from your side of the conversation that Ruth had something she wanted you to pass on to me. I'm assuming it was to help you out with the diner."

Liz forced her attention away from him and his sexy green eyes. "Yes, in fact she did. But you don't have to help. You already have enough to do, what with your private investigating…the vending machines…and…" She stared at him. Lord help her, but she wanted to push him back to that table and continue acquainting herself with his body.

"Is six okay?" he asked, ignoring her protests.

"Six?" she echoed, realizing she was repeating his words a lot.

"Five?"

"No, no. Six is fine."

He hesitated. "Then I guess I'll see you at six."

"Yeah, six. You want me to swing by to pick you up?"

His brow budged upward.

"You know, since it's on my way and everything. No sense both of us driving in separately."

"Sure. Why don't you pick me up."

She eyed his mouth, fervently wishing he would kiss her again. And scared to death that he wouldn't. Instead, he let loose a low whistle and Goliath slowly scrambled to his feet, stopping for a goodnight pet from Liz before sauntering out the open diner door with Mitch.

MITCH SAT in the McCoy kitchen alone, realizing after a half hour he hadn't turned on the lights. If anything was capable of putting his libido in check, the news about Bo should have been it. But not even his concern for a man who had pretty much been a constant fixture in his life could stop him from thinking about what had passed between him and Liz at the diner. His pulse still throbbed a steady rhythm, and he swore he could still taste her sweet flavor on his tongue. In the back of his mind ever since she'd driven back into town was his fear that things would be as good between them now as they were back then. Trouble was, he'd discovered that things were even better.

Better? Hell, he'd had a hard time not peeling those silk shorts from her hips and taking her all over again.

The sound of truck tires on the gravel drive snapped his attention toward the door. Pops. He'd probably been at the fairgrounds for the fireworks display and was just now coming home. Mitch quickly switched on the lights, then sat back down at the table just as the door opened.

"Hey there," Connor said as he walked in, followed by what appeared to be the entire McCoy clan, minus Marc, still honeymooning with his new bride. Lucky Marc.

Mitch stifled a groan, warily eyeing his brothers and father. "Hey, yourself."

David walked to the refrigerator and pulled out beers one by one. Jake took the seat across from Mitch and accepted his along with a glass. He poured the golden liquid inside. "I didn't see you at the fairgrounds tonight, Mitch," he said almost accusingly.

Mitch refused the bottle David offered as the rest of them took their regular seats around the table. "Maybe that's because I wasn't there." Which had probably been a mistake. In a town as small as Manchester, often a person's absence was more worthy of comment than his appearance.

Pops popped the tab on a soda. "Then you probably didn't hear what happened to Bo."

"Actually," Mitch said slowly, "I did hear. I'm, um, going

to be taking over his responsibilities at the diner. You know, until he's well enough to come back."

The kitchen went silent—which was saying a lot, because when there were this many McCoys in the house, the place was never silent.

Mitch leaned back in his chair and absently patted Goliath. For the past week, he'd been dying for someone, anyone, to talk to about Liz, and what was going on. Now that he had the chance, he wanted to be alone.

Didn't make a lick of sense. Then again, sense seemed to have flown out of town the instant that Liz drove in.

Jake leaned his forearms on the table. Wearing a crisply pressed oxford shirt and khakis, he was the best dressed of them. He always was. "Where'd you get the news? Somebody call you here?"

Mitch's hand stilled on Goliath's head. Even if the house was full of men in law enforcement, it didn't take a badge to figure out that something was going on here. "Nope. I happened to be at the diner when Ruth called."

David took a long pull from his bottle. "Hey, what's this, the third degree? Who cares who heard what when?"

Pops agreed, "I second that."

Mitch snapped his head up. In his father's eyes he saw recognition and understanding, which only confirmed his suspicion that there was more going on here than casual conversation.

Jake was like a bulldog with a rabbit caught in his teeth though. "Was Liz there with you?"

There it was. The reason for this midnight showdown in the McCoy kitchen.

Momentarily, Mitch empathized with every illegal alien in the country. If this was the way Jake, the INS agent, questioned his own brother, he shuddered to think what he did with total strangers who had actually broken a law.

Then again, maybe *he* had broken a law. One right out of the Jake McCoy Rules of Conduct Handbook. *Thou shalt not fraternize with those who have left you standing at the altar.* He grimaced. That sucker was probably as thick as the D.C. public phone book.

Connor nearly choked on his beer. "Liz? Did you just say Liz?" David shrugged, obviously as in the dark as he was. No one else answered him. "We're not talking little Lizzie Braden here, are we? She left eons ago, didn't she? The day—" His words abruptly cut off.

Connor merely swore succinctly.

Pops leaned back in his chair, the wooden creak serving to heighten the tension. "How's she doing, Mitch?"

He jammed his fingers through his hair and let loose a gusty sigh. "Fine. She's doing fine, Pops."

Jake muttered, "She ought to be tarred and feathered for what she did to you."

Tarred and feathered? Mitch nearly laughed at the absurdity of the situation. He figured it was good Jake hadn't been the one to cross paths with Liz the night she rolled into town. He had a feeling she'd still be in the local lockup.

"Self-imposed exile not enough for you, eh, Jake?" Pops said, his blue eyes throwing mischievous sparks.

Jake sat back in his chair and cracked his own smile. "It's a start."

The tightness in Mitch's neck eased a bit. Perhaps it was his own frustration brought on by the night's earlier events that had him raring for a confrontation, purposely misreading his brother's intentions. Oddly enough, he didn't want his pound of flesh from Liz for walking out on him. He wanted all her delectable flesh to do with as he pleased.

His remaining tension shifted to other parts of his anatomy.

"So Liz is back, huh?" David said, shaking his head in wonder. "She still as much of a looker as she was back then?"

Connor chuckled. "If life was fair, she'd weigh five hundred pounds and look like Attila the Hun."

Mitch laughed. Not because of what Connor had said so much as the realization that he'd likely still want Liz no matter what she weighed or looked like.

"Well, we all know life is not fair," Jake said with a long-suffering sigh. "The damn girl is as gorgeous as ever."

Mitch hiked a brow. "I didn't know you noticed things like that, Jake."

"Hey, I notice a whole lot more than you guys give me credit for." He sat a little straighter.

David slapped him heartily on the back. "I can vouch for that. He's a pain in the ass when we go out together in D.C. Can't keep a conversation going for more than a minute without his attention wandering to the latest girl walking by." He shook his head. "The pisser is there seems to be something about that tall, dark and brooding bit that women go for, because they're all over him."

Connor set his bottle onto the table with a thud. "I think it's more of the hard-to-get thing, myself. Women always want what they can't have."

Mitch watched Jake closely. Was it him, or were his brother's ears growing a little red at the tips?

But it was Connor's comment that rang through his mind. *Women always want what they can't have.* Could the same be said for men? He didn't like the looks of that dark mental road and reined in his thoughts.

Pops coughed. "You guys are as bad as a bunch of old women at a bridge game. Talking about each other's sex lives like that."

Mitch's gaze homed in on him. "Speaking of sex lives, yours seems to have picked up momentum recently."

His brothers' heads nearly snapped off as they turned toward their father. "Pops? Sex?" David fairly croaked.

Connor elbowed him hard, nearly forcing him off his chair. "Yeah, you know, that thing he did way back when to conceive your sorry butt."

"Who? What? Where? When?" Jake said without pause, glancing at Mitch when their father didn't answer.

Mitch shrugged. "Haven't been able to figure it out yet, and he's not giving up the info. Can't be anyone local, though, or else I'd have heard about it."

Pops waved the interest away, but his wide grin told Mitch that things must still be going well with his mysterious lady friend. "I'm not about to justify this line of questioning with a response. Did I say you were as bad as old women? I stand corrected. You're far worse."

David grinned. "Speaking of sex, has anybody heard from Marc and Mel? I'll bet they're having a lot of, um, *fun* on that cruise ship."

"I wouldn't be too sure," Mitch said, telling them Melanie had called the house the day before. "I guess there's been an incident or two involving motion sickness."

Pops sighed. "I told that boy it wasn't a good idea to take a pregnant woman on a boat, no matter how big."

"Marc's the one who's sick."

Everyone at the table erupted with laughter.

Pops started to get up from the table. "I think this is the point where I call it a night."

Mitch grinned. "'Night, Pops."

Jake stared at him. "You're not just going to let him leave without giving us some answers, are you?"

"What would you have us do, Jake? Tie him to his chair until he 'fesses up?"

"Not a bad idea."

Mitch grinned. "Yeah, right up there with the tarring and feathering suggestion."

"So I'm a little protective when it comes to family. Shoot me."

David got up and put his bottle away. "Don't tempt him. It may have been a while since Mitch has carried a gun, but I bet he can still beat the hell out of all of us at target practice."

Connor got up, too. "Yeah, well, maybe you should concentrate on your own sex life there, Jake, and keep your crooked nose out of everyone else's."

Absently, Jake reached up and ran his thumb and index finger down the length of his nose.

Connor stepped to Mitch and grasped his shoulder. "You do what you need to with Lizzie, ya hear? And if this guy gives you any trouble, just let me know. I'll set him straight."

David angled around Connor to look at Mitch. "Ditto for me."

"I'm heading back into the city. You coming, Jake?" Connor asked.

"Yeah, I'll be out in a minute."

Connor left the house, the slap of the screen door marking his departure. Mitch couldn't help thinking that Jake still had something to say, given the way his gaze rarely left Mitch's face. They both looked at David, who leaned against the counter.

"What? I'm crashing here for the night. I sucked back one more than I should have. Either of you have a problem with that?"

Neither Mitch nor Jake said anything.

Finally, David pushed from the counter. "Okay, okay, I can take a hint." He loped from the kitchen and up the stairs, leaving the two of them alone.

Mitch leaned back. "I, um, take it you have something more to say on the Liz front?"

Jake nodded soberly. "Yeah, that I do."

Goliath stretched and yawned at his feet, reminding Mitch that he hadn't gotten much sleep in the past week himself. "So…?"

"So, I'm worried about you, that's all." Jake shifted awkwardly. "Look, I always liked Liz, Mitch. And despite what I said earlier… Well, I can't help thinking she had her reasons for, you know, doing what she did." He cleared his throat. "It might be a good idea for you to find out those reasons."

Mitch stared at his brother. He'd really never had a heart-to-heart with Jake, not even when Jake had agreed to be Mitch's best man seven years ago. Now he realized that it was because Jake didn't quite know how to put thoughts with an emotional twist into words.

"Aw, hell, you know what I mean."

Connor lay on the horn outside. A moment later, Pops yelled at him from an upstairs window to keep the racket down.

Jake pushed from the table. "The more things change, the more they stay the same, huh?"

Mitch wondered if he was referring to the exchange outside, or Liz. Either way, he would be right. "Yeah. I guess they do."

Something landed squarely in the middle of the table. Mitch stared at it, then at his brother, incredulous.

Jake rubbed the back of his neck looking as uncomfortable as hell. "'Night."

Mitch was shocked beyond speech as his gaze flicked from his brother's retreating back to the item he'd left behind.

As the truck tires outside crunched the gravel drive, he slowly reached out, turning the package over and then over again. A box of condoms. And not just any condoms, either. Latex, he'd suspected. But ribbed? Multi-colored? Flavored?

He burst out laughing, wondering what his brother would think if he knew the gift had come a couple of hours too late.

CHAPTER SEVEN

LIZ TOSSED her new handbag into the front seat of her Lexus then climbed behind the wheel. She was way too early. The sun was little more than a promising smear across the eastern sky. But she hadn't gotten much sleep last night, and if she sat around the house one minute longer, she'd go nuts. She'd rather wait at the McCoy place than here if Mitch wasn't ready yet.

Mitch...

She floored the gas pedal and tore out of the drive, nearly forcing an old pickup off the road. She waved her apologies to the driver and continued on through the cloud of dust her tires had kicked up.

What was it Mitch had said last night after...well, afterward? That their finally coming together had been worth waiting seven years for? Or something along those lines anyway. She tucked her hair behind her ear, then straightened the collar of her uniform. The words had haunted her all night. Despite his running from her that day at Gran's house, she suspected he'd planned on getting her between the sheets since the moment she arrived back into town. Well, okay, there hadn't exactly been any sheets.

Anyway, she couldn't quite shake the feeling that for him their...experience...had meant little more than to satisfy his curiosity. And that didn't sit well with her, which in turn caused her to be all the more upset with herself. After all, she wasn't exactly a despoiled virgin who now expected unwavering devotion from the man on whom she had bestowed her gift of chastity. She was a single female who'd had her share of consensual, intimate relationships with the opposite sex. Okay, she'd had all of two sexual relationships. Still, she had never felt this burning need to know exactly how the man felt about her after they'd…been together.

"I can't even *think* the words. Had sex. Made love. Did the nasty." She cringed at the last description, then forced herself to slow the speed of the car. At this rate, she'd end up passing the McCoy place.

Her agitation with herself and the world at large continued for the entire five-mile ride to his family's house. She tried to concentrate on the rolling landscape on either side of the road, to memorize the vivid green of the rows of corn and tobacco rushing toward maturity, to drink in the sweet smell of fresh earth and things growing, but all she could focus on was the further mess a single hour with Mitch had made of her life.

Finally the sprawling colonial farmhouse that Mitch had been raised in came into view. She immediately recognized some changes it had undergone since she'd last seen it. Where the exterior had been painted an austere white with black shutters before, it was now a heather gray, and the ornate cornices and remarkable lattice work shone a cardinal red. Her gaze swept up from the newly constructed front porch to the roof where the original smooth, tin sheeting shone. She squinted from where the just rising sun reflected off new curved windows with sunburst designs above each. Off to the right of the house a new red barn sat away from the old barn, which was little more than a haunted, gray monster.

She pulled into the drive, counting two cars and a truck

in the drive. The truck was Mitch's. One of the cars likely belonged to his father. The other? Jake's?

She looked back up at the house, just then noticing that on the stretch of tin roofing over the porch sat Mitch in a pair of jeans and T-shirt. He was looking off toward the sunrise, seemingly unaware of her arrival. She moved her hand from the horn and instead got quietly out of the car.

She'd forgotten about his habit of climbing out of his bedroom window to sit on the roof. She slowly neared the porch, studying the serious lines of his face. He'd once told her he'd spend the entire night on the roof if he had a particularly tough problem to work out. Of course, back then his problems had come in the form of final exams and runaway pets.

She wondered what he worried about now. Was he, too, thinking about what had happened last night? Did he want to do it all over again? Her body hummed to life at the mere thought of being flesh-to-flesh with Mitch again. Or…

She caught her bottom lip between her teeth.

Or did he regret it?

Oh, this is ridiculous, she firmly told herself. Didn't she have enough to worry about? Did she really need to heap second-guessing his worries on top of all that?

"Liz? Lizzie Braden, is that you?"

David McCoy was stepping out onto the porch from the front door. At the sound of his brother's greeting, Mitch spotted her as well, his eyes smiling as he caught her gaze. She felt suddenly warm all over, then quickly stomped the reaction down.

"I heard you were back in town." David's gaze skimmed her figure in the waitress uniform. "I'd also heard you were as gorgeous as ever."

"Oh?" Mitch was talking about her. That was a good sign. Wasn't it?

David grinned. "Yeah, Jake filled us all in last night."

"Jake?" she said, unable to squelch her disappointment. "I didn't think he noticed things like that."

Within moments, Mitch had used a nearby tree and porch railing to lower himself to the ground, then came to stand next to her. "Me neither. Go figure, huh?"

Liz felt herself blush. She never blushed. Yet this was the second time she'd reacted in such a way since returning to Manchester. She fastened her gaze on David's face. He was her own age, and they'd shared a few summer catechism classes in younger years—that is when David could pull himself away from the girls and bothered to show up for them.

She smiled to herself. "So what have you been up to, David? Still hanging around the house, I see."

"Actually, I just stayed here for the night. I have a place in the city."

"Oh? Are you still in the army?"

"Nope. With DCPD now." He leaned against the porch column and crossed his legs at the ankles. The fairest one of the five brothers, he'd always had a way with girls, then women. In fact, Liz was probably the only one in the tri-county area who hadn't gone out with him.

He didn't miss her perusal and flashed one of his to-die-for grins. "Hey, I was thinking about coming back next weekend. If I do, you wanna catch a cup of coffee or something?"

Liz heard Mitch make a growling sound, then he stepped up to put his arm around her shoulders. The gesture made her feel...wanted...angry...confused. She shrugged his arm off and heard him say, "Sorry, little bro, but all Liz's cups of coffee are reserved for me."

"What is it with men and the issue of ownership?" She stepped from touching distance. "If I'm still around, I'd love to, David. We can do tea."

Mitch waved to his brother in mock dismissal. "Why don't you and your hormones go back inside? Liz and I have to be getting to the diner anyway."

"You be sure to let me know if you guys need any help, you hear?"

Liz smiled at him. "We'll do that, David."

Mitch crossed his arms and stared at her through narrowed lids. Liz's uncertainties returned tenfold.

She knew that the male posturing that had just gone on meant little. The McCoys were legendary for their public skirmishes. If there wasn't an honest-to-God conflict to engage them in combat, they'd been known to make one up. In fact, she'd once watched Connor chase David up a tree just for looking at him wrong.

"So…" she said slowly. Why wasn't he saying anything? She didn't care what. He could at least make some inane comment on the weather. Something, anything, to stop her mind from reeling both from the nearness of him, and her fear that he regretted the night before.

"So," Mitch repeated.

Oh, that was just grand. Her gaze snagged on his mouth. That skillful, enticing mouth that had said and done so much yesterday, but was now quiet and unmoving. She cleared her throat. "Well, I guess we'd better get going. You know, to the diner."

"Yes, I guess we'd better."

She led the way, acutely aware that she walked in front of him and that he was probably watching her. A glance verified that his gaze was glued to her backside. She quickly got into the car and he did the same on the passenger's side.

They were halfway to the diner before either of them said anything.

"I wanted to talk to you about last night," she said.

"The consulting business must be good to afford this baby," Mitch said.

They stopped, looked at each other, then laughed.

"Go ahead," Mitch said.

"No, you first. I…I really didn't have anything to say, anyway." *Liar.* What was it with her? Lord knew she was the first to voice her opinion on anything. If she had a question, she asked it. And boy, was this question a doozy. Then why was she doing the mental equivalent of tucking her tail between her legs and making a run for it?

Mitch's wide grin told her he wasn't completely oblivious to her dilemma. And, damn him, he didn't appear ready to help her out of it either. She watched him stretch, then drape his arm across the back of her seat. "I was just saying that the consulting business must be good. You know. Your car and all."

She glanced around the rich interior without registering a thing. "Oh. Yeah. It's been very good." She relaxed slightly. Okay, maybe they were getting somewhere. "Ah, you've finally decided to share that you've been checking up on me, have you?"

He shrugged, the muscles beneath his T-shirt bunching then relaxing. She slowly drew the tip of her tongue across her parched lips.

He watched the movement, then turned to stare out the passenger window. "I figured it couldn't hurt, seeing as I'm getting nowhere fast in my investigation."

"I rate an entire investigation, do I?" She was acutely aware of his arm resting on the back of her seat. She tussled with the desire to lean her head back to entice contact.

"Uh-huh. Only problem is, I haven't been able to get answers to some very important questions."

"Such as?"

"Such as, Did you marry the damn guy or not, Liz?"

DAMN, but he wanted to touch her again. Anywhere. Everywhere. He'd been aware that finally having sex with her might offer up as many problems as solutions. What he hadn't counted on was wanting her even more now than he had before. Now that he knew exactly what making love to Liz was like, he had a helluva time thinking about anything else, including this damn investigation.

And her provocative, closed mouth wasn't helping matters any either.

"So?" he prompted.

"So what?"

He pulled his arm back from her seat, away from temptation. "Come on, Liz, did you run out on the guy before or after the 'I do's' were exchanged?"

He didn't trust the way she kept her gaze trained on the road, or the way her lips tilted up slightly at the corners. "Explain to me why it matters, and maybe I'll tell you."

He felt the sudden urge to punch her expensive dashboard. "Call me old-fashioned, but I don't make a habit of sleeping with somebody else's wife."

She finally glanced his way, but she'd lost the look of wariness she'd worn when she'd pulled up in front of his house. In its place was playful amusement. "Well, then, you should have thought about that before, don't you think?"

Mitch ground his back teeth together. Forget hitting the dash. He'd rather wrap his fingers around Liz's pretty little neck until something that resembled the truth came out of that wicked mouth of hers.

"We're here," she announced lightly, pulling behind the diner and parking between a Dumpster and the building.

He looked around the deserted alleyway, then grasped her wrist before she could get out of the car.

"Why didn't you park out front, Liz?"

She blinked several times in what could have passed for innocent confusion. Only he knew she was a long way from innocent and she was never confused. "You don't have to make a federal case out of it, ex-Agent McCoy. I just thought I'd leave the spaces out front for the customers."

She laughed and he released her. Spaces for the customers, his ass. Why did he have the sneaking suspicion he was being led on a wild-goose chase?

And why did he feel like wanting to do a little leading of his own?

CHAPTER EIGHT

TWO DAYS LATER, Liz hoisted the money tray out of the cash register, probing for the roll of quarters she was sure she'd seen somewhere in the drawer that morning. She smiled at the short line of people waiting to pay their lunch bills, then grabbed an extra roll of dimes instead, filling her palm with change before handing it to Charles Obernauer, the general store owner.

"Sorry, Charlie, I'm all out of quarters."

He jangled the small pile of dimes in his hand. "I'll have one of my boys run you over a couple of rolls when I get back to the store."

"Thanks. You really do have a heart, despite what everybody says about you."

He chuckled and ambled toward the door. Liz quickly took care of the other two patrons before grabbing the broom to sweep up the potato chips someone had dumped on the floor earlier and everyone else had tracked throughout the diner.

"Order up!" Mitch called.

Liz stared at him through the window that opened into the kitchen. He winked at her, then turned back to the grill, which was about the extent of their interaction since temporarily taking over the running of the diner two days earlier.

How was it that she felt so drained and he looked like he had just awakened from twelve straight hours of restful sleep in a big, soft, decadent bed? Especially since he'd been there since six that morning, the same as she had. And aside from burning a couple of pancakes early on, he'd slid into his old occasional role as short-order cook like a pro.

She remembered their last conversation, or at least what passed for a conversation, and wondered if not telling him she was as single as the day she was born had been a good idea. She knew it was only a matter of time before he found out that she and Rich had never even made it to the justice of the peace on the Beschloss lawn, much less gotten anywhere near saying the words *I do*. Ever since, Mitch had flirted and teased but kept his distance. He refused her offers to give him a lift into town. He gave her a casual wave at day's end. Nowhere was there any mention of the…incident…on that very table over there three days ago, much less any sign that they would be repeating the experience anytime soon.

She'd realized she'd left out an important option when she'd considered his possible reactions to their coming together: his ignoring the experience completely.

Liz bumped into Sharon, who had grudgingly agreed to come in on her day off to help. The young woman juggled the two plates she held.

"Sorry," Liz murmured.

"No problem," Sharon muttered back.

Liz made short work of the sweeping, then put the broom up and reached for the order Mitch was placing on the ledge. He opened his mouth.

"Don't you dare say it," she warned.

He leaned a tanned forearm against the window ledge, his ever-present T-shirt revealing a healthy length of toned biceps. "Say what?"

She snatched her gaze away from his tempting flesh. "You

know what. Bo never yells 'order up.' He never has to, because we can see when someone's food is ready." She put the plate back on the ledge, forcing his arm off. "You forgot the cherub."

He stabbed the top of the Heavenly Hamburger bun with a chubby candy cherub and eyed, a little too openly, the way she straightened the skirt of her uniform. "Now, angel, you're never going to make enough tips to get out of this town if you don't adjust that attitude of yours."

"Good thing I don't need the tips then, huh?" she flung back, satisfied by the narrowing of his eyes.

"My, my, we got up on the wrong side of the bed this morning, didn't we?"

Liz tucked a stray strand of hair back up into her ponytail. The image of Mitch together with her bed made her hot all over. "And just what would you know about my bed, McCoy?"

Liz's feet ached, she was sure she would never regain full movement of her stiff neck, and she was positive she never wanted to see another rack of Paradise Pineapple Ribs, another Garden of Eden Pizza or Heavenly Hamburger again. She knew her ill humor wasn't just about Myra being gone until Lord knew when, or about every person in Manchester stopping in to check on Bo's status and having a meal while they were at it. Both of those things she could handle, for Bo's sake. It was Mitch and his constant flirting, his enjoying himself at her expense, that frayed her nerves and made her remember at the most inopportune times how intoxicating his kiss was…how intimately he had touched her…how wonderful he had felt between her thighs…and how much she secretly yearned for a repeat performance.

She put the plate of pizza down in front of the owner of the gas station.

"Ezra, do you order the same thing every day?" she asked the amazingly clean man with the sloppy eating habits.

"Yep. Look—" he fingered a slice of pepperoni with the tip of his finger "—it covers all the food groups. Everything a growing boy needs."

She tallied up his order and put the white slip of paper next to his untouched napkin. "I hate to be the one to tell you this, Ezra, but I think you stopped growing twenty years ago." She smiled at the five-foot-six man with his graying hair and unusually proportioned face.

"Aw, Lizzie, and here I was about to update you on where things stand with the bet."

Liz's hands paused as she stuffed her order pad into her uniform pocket. In the busyness of the past few days, she'd completely forgotten that stupid wager she'd gotten herself into. She glanced at the man who had started it all and found him stacking two more plates on the ledge and calling 'order up!' with much relish.

"What do you mean, update me?" she said, stepping to the neighboring table and collecting empty plates. "I should think things are pretty much the same, aren't they?" She hiked a stack of dishes onto her hip. "Unless, of course, I stand to make more money than I did."

Ezra took a monstrous bite of pizza and grinned. "I'd like to tell you that was the case, Lizzie, I really would."

"But?"

"But…the odds have evened out. At this point, from what my figuring tells me, you and Mitch are running neck and neck."

Liz nearly dropped the plates to the floor. Neck and neck? Whatever happened to the favorable odds she had enjoyed only a few days earlier? The only odds that made any sense because no matter how preoccupied she was with the physical side of her relationship with Mitch, that's where she intended to keep things with him: physical. And very secret. That is, if she ever found herself alone with him again.

Why would she want a man to complicate things? Her life was an out-and-out mess already. The career she'd worked so hard to build for herself didn't exist. Besides, she'd just left one man. She'd be nuts to switch her sights to another. Given her own allergic reaction to anything resembling an altar, she was coming to see that the whole marriage thing just wasn't in the cards for her.

"What?" she said.

"That's right." To her surprise, Ezra used the napkin instead of his purple-and-gold work shirt to wipe his hands. "Rumor has it you two were in the diner together alone the other night setting off fireworks of your own. Can't tell you how many people put their money on Mitch after that." His upper lip curled into what passed for a smile. "Good thing for me, too, 'cause I was coming out on the losing end of this bet if I had to cover all the wagers on you the first day."

Liz stood stock-still. Someone had spotted her and Mitch in the diner? Just exactly how much was seen? Her cheeks blazed.

"Guess that blush of yours says the rumor's true," Ezra crooned. "Want to join me for some of this pizza and tell me about it?"

Liz eyed the stringy anchovies snaking over the top of the pie and her stomach turned. She quickly squashed the temptation to pump the gas station owner for more information on what exactly the rumor going around town was. She recalled a similar such situation seven years before. An innocent food fight with Mitch over who would get the last bite of a shared bowl of ice cream had been made out to be something very carnal indeed by the time that rumor had made its way back to her. Liz rubbed her forehead with her free hand. Of course, not even that incident could equal what had happened there the other night.

"Sorry, Ez, but Eden pizza doesn't particularly appeal to me right now." She grabbed the empty cups on the table she was clearing and moved toward the kitchen. In fact, the only thing that appealed to her at that moment was exacting revenge against the man responsible for this whole mess.

She swung the door inward and crossed the kitchen to the sink where she unloaded the contents in her arms.

"You didn't collect your orders," Mitch said from behind her.

She turned toward him. "Mitch McCoy, what do you have to do with this rumor floating around town?"

"Rumor?" He quirked a brow and flipped a burger.

She picked up a rag from the counter and wrung it in her hands. "Don't play cute with me. You know perfectly well what rumor."

"I hate to disappoint you, but I've been stuck in this kitchen for the past two days." His grin did funny things to her stomach and she twisted the rag tighter. "I haven't exactly had time to indulge in any gossip."

He glanced to the rope she'd made out of the rag. She forced herself to stop wringing it. "Yeah, well, maybe you haven't had time to indulge in any, but you sure as heck could have started it."

"Oh, I see. I think I understand what this is about. Someone saw us in here the other night, didn't they?" His gaze slammed into hers. "How much did they see?" He skimmed her warm cheeks. "Never mind. We both know how little it takes to get rumors rolling in this town."

Liz cleaned off the cutting board he had used to slice onions, her eyes tearing in response to the pungent vegetable. She swiped at them with the back of her hand. "*Rolling* is about the word for it, considering that's probably exactly what the gossips have been saying we've been doing with each other."

His amused chuckle drew her gaze to him. She scanned his solid torso and the way his faded jeans hugged his delectable rear end. A twanging yearning vibrated through her. Good thing he was busy slapping the cooked burgers into altogether different buns or else he'd have made her pay for her lingering attention.

She cleared her throat. "You know, Mitch, there's something I'm having a difficult time understanding." She spotted Sharon picking up an order on the other side of the window and quickly asked her to look after the two customers she had left. The attractive young woman sighed. "Okay, but I get half the tip."

Liz motioned her off and turned back to Mitch.

"Why aren't you upset by all this attention the two of us are getting?" She examined him thoroughly.

"Upset?" He scraped the greasy cooktop with a metal spatula. "Why would I be upset?"

"Well…." She stepped a little closer to him so they wouldn't be overheard by the lunch customers who preferred the counter. "I would think that after…when I left… Well, the rumor mill probably worked overtime for months."

She regarded the tightening of his fingers on the wooden spatula handle. But when he looked at her there was nothing but that damnable gleam in his green eyes. "So?"

"So…." she said slowly. "Why would you purposely court more gossip about yourself now, especially since you know I'm going to be leaving again soon?" And especially since the other night was seeming more and more an aberration.

As far as she was concerned, there wasn't nearly enough rolling around being done to warrant any gossip.

His devilish grin sent shivers shooting everywhere. "We're not anywhere near an altar now, Liz."

She crossed her arms. "So this is all just your idea of having a little fun then, is it?"

"Hmm, you could say that."

She took the net from her hair and shook the restrained tresses loose. She didn't miss the slight darkening of his eyes. Mitch McCoy wasn't nearly as unaffected by her as he pretended. His cool, teasing behavior might be a puzzle to her, but one thing remained plainly clear: he still wanted her. She only had to figure out what to do so she could give herself to him. Again. And again after that.

She eyed his mouth. She didn't think even Myra's definition of fun included what had happened between her and Mitch—and what she hoped would happen again. At least once before she left, she quickly added.

In fact, she had hoped last night would prove just the opportunity. She had just turned off the house's lights when she heard a vehicle come up the gravel drive. She was pretty sure it was Mitch. But by the time she went downstairs and unlocked the back door, his truck was long gone. Needless to say, she'd gotten far too little sleep after that. She still trembled whenever she thought of the sizzling manner in which he had responded to her, the restraint he had used in the beginning, and the shaken way she had felt when they'd broken away from each other.

"You know, Mitch, if I didn't know better, I'd think you were purposely avoiding being alone with me."

He eyed her. "We're alone now."

"Sure, with half of Manchester just on the other side of that window."

She popped a blueberry left over from breakfast into her mouth. "I'd never have pegged you as the type to make late-night visits then back out at the last minute."

She turned toward the sink, nearly losing her balance when he grasped her arm.

"Late-night visits?"

She stared at him, heat stealing up from the touch of his fingers against her cool skin.

"Yeah, late-night visits." She felt her breasts tighten, warmth pool in her belly. She was in a sorry state if such a simple touch almost did her in. "Don't even try to tell me you weren't the one who drove up my driveway, then chickened out last night. Because I'm not going to buy it."

His passionate curse surprised her. "As much as I'd like to repeat what happened the other night, Liz, I didn't go anywhere near your place last night. Until I get some answers, I don't intend to go within a mile of your place."

She searched his face. She'd never gotten a look at the vehicle in her driveway. She had automatically assumed it was Mitch. Obviously she had been mistaken.

She shrugged. "Guess I was wrong then. Maybe someone used the drive to turn around." She took off her apron and folded it once. "Anyway, I've got a few errands to run."

Mitch's movements slowed. "Errands?"

"Uh-huh."

"First you tell me some stranger's watching your house—"

"I said I thought I heard a car pull up."

"—and now you're just going to take off without explanation?"

She loved to see him all worked up like this. "Yep." Liz glanced at her watch. "The lunch rush is over, and there are only a few people left. You and Sharon should be able to take care of things until I get back. I want to run over and ready Ruth and Bo's house for their return from D.C. tomorrow. And…well, I have a couple other things I want to see to."

"What things?"

She planted her hands on the metal island separating them and leaned closer to him. "Nothing that would help your investigation, I assure you."

He followed her lead, their mouths mere inches apart above the counter. "Frankly, at this point, everything you do would help my investigation."

She smiled, enjoying the surge of power that came with her present position. "Still having a hard time, Mitch?"

"You're damn right I am." His gaze raked her face. "Why don't you wait until tomorrow to see to these other things so I can help you out with them?"

Oh, but that was plum. Mitch was actually showing a little emotion, proving he wasn't as unaffected by her as he seemed. But it was not exactly the type of emotion she was aiming for. "Help me out? Why would I need you to help me out?"

"Come on, Liz, let me in on this, will you? All I know so far is that you drove into town in the middle of the night wearing a bloodstained wedding dress, you're running from someone—"

"—I needed to get away from someone," she corrected again.

"Same difference," he shrugged, clearly aggravated. "It doesn't matter that I haven't been able to dig up anything more than that you've left a perfectly profitable business behind, and you no longer have a residence in Boston. As circumstantial as it all is, it adds up to you being in trouble."

She smiled. "But I'm not *in* trouble, Mitch. Why won't you trust me on this?"

He eyed her. "It's not you I don't trust, it's your judgment. What are the odds that you could be underestimating your situation and you could be in some sort of danger?"

"About zero to nil," she said, liking this conversation and her control of it a little too much. She stared at the unbending line of his lips, tempted to kiss the tightness from them and make him grin that irresistible grin again. "Anyway, if you want to talk odds, Ezra told me we're running neck and neck in this bet you got me into."

Mitch scowled. "Forget the bet. Our conversation doesn't have anything to do with that."

She glanced down at her uniform, wishing she had time to change out of it. But she was going to have to hurry as it was if she hoped to get back to the diner in time for the dinner crowd. "Oh, but you're wrong. Everything between us has to do with that bet, Mitch. That's the way you made it."

She started to turn away, then changed her mind. This opportunity was just too good to pass up.

Leaning farther over the counter, she tasted his lips with a quick flick of her tongue. She'd fully intended to stop there. Give him a little something to keep him guessing. But at the hungry look in his eyes, she couldn't resist meeting his lips full on.

It had been a long two days. He tasted of iced tea and mint. And his mouth was hot, so hot. She hated that the food counter separated them. Hated still that just beyond the window all conversation had stopped.

Yet all she could concentrate on was the quickening of the blood through her veins. Mitch's hand where he had thrust it through her hair to pull her closer. The tightening of her breasts beneath the fabric of her uniform. And the sensual sliding of Mitch's tongue against hers.

When she finally did pull away, she found herself as much a victim of her little tease as Mitch. Lord help her, but she wanted to vault over the counter and prove to herself that the other night hadn't been a figment of her imagination.

"Um," she barely managed, quickly licking her lips, loving the taste of him there. "I'd better get going."

"Yeah. I think that's a good idea."

She turned on her heels, the heat swelling in her belly chasing her exhaustion away.

CURSING UNDER his breath, Mitch checked on the meat items he had estimated he would need for that evening's orders, then stepped to the window overlooking the area of the diner for the fifth time in as many minutes. No one was visible except for old Josiah on his chair in front of the general store. Where in the hell was Liz? She'd been gone more than two hours. But it was more than her prolonged absence and the reason behind it that bothered him: the stranger he had spotted in town a few days ago was sitting at the same booth he and Liz had taken advantage of on the Fourth of July.

Given the relative emptiness of the diner—it was four o'-clock and the only ones in there aside from the stranger were the Darton brothers, talking over coffee—the stranger stuck out like the red pair of shoes Liz had had on with her wedding dress when she'd driven back into town.

The guy had come in a half hour after Liz left, and, immediately upon spotting him, Mitch had adjusted his guess of the man's age as nearer to sixty than the fifty he'd thought before. He had graying blond hair, slightly aristocratic features, and was dressed in a lightweight summer suit, the white shirt he wore underneath looking as if it had come right out of the package. Those observations combined with the knowledge that the car the man drove was a rental told him that the stranger was convinced that what he sought was in Manchester or he wouldn't keep popping up there. It also told him that the stranger was very likely Liz's late-night visitor.

He watched Sharon serve him what had to be his third piece of cherry pie, the stranger obviously trying to involve her in conversation. The young waitress turned away from the table and Mitch called, "order up." Sharon stared at him, puzzled, but came to the window anyway.

"I don't have any orders," she said, ignoring his gesture to keep her voice down.

The stranger appeared not to hear her, his attention instead on the street outside, leaving the fresh pie untouched.

"Do you recognize that man?" Mitch asked.

"Which man? Oh, you're talking about my last customer. No. Never seen him before."

Mitch grimaced, realizing he wasn't talking to one of Manchester's most observant people. "What did he say to you?"

Sharon shrugged, evidently beat by the long hours she'd been putting in along with him and Liz. "Not much. Just asked if I knew somebody named Betsy something-or-other."

The stranger looked their way and Mitch handed Sharon a whole pie for appearances' sake. "Do you? Know anybody by the name of Betsy, I mean?" Mitch asked.

"Nope." Sharon sighed and reluctantly took the pie.

"Do you remember the last name?"

The waitress frowned. "I'm not very good with names. When he said Betsy, I already knew that I didn't know anybody with that first name, so I didn't pay much attention to the last. Why?"

Mitch watched the stranger reach into his pocket and deposit a couple of bills on top of his check and rise from the table. Trust Sharon to get curious now.

"Never mind. I just noticed he's new to the area and wondered if he needed any help."

Sharon sighed. "You want me to ask him?"

Mitch shook his head. He didn't want Sharon to strain herself. "No. Anyway, he just left."

The young woman looked relieved that she had one fewer customer to worry about and turned a beseeching look on him. "Can I leave now? I've already missed my favorite soap, my feet are so swollen there's not a chance they'll fit into the shoes I want to wear on my date tonight, never mind that I won't be able to put those new decals I bought for my fingernails on in time—"

Mitch stopped her with a wave of a hand. He glanced at the clock on the wall, then back at the tired Sharon. "Sure, go ahead. But would you mind coming in again tomorrow morning?"

"Do I have to? What with Ruth coming back and all…"

"I'd really appreciate it if you could," he said.

"Okay," she said grudgingly, pulling her purse out from inside a closed cabinet. "I'll see you then."

Mitch turned from the window and headed for the kitchen door. By the time he left the kitchen, Sharon was long gone, and the two Darton brothers were in need of refills. Trading gibes with them, he saw to their needs, then crossed to the table where the stranger had been sitting. He picked up the order and the money, then slid into the booth, watching the late-model Chevy pull from the curb across the street. The man had left a five-dollar tip.

Reminding himself to pass it on to Sharon in the morning, he stuffed the bill into his pocket and kept the remainder for the cash register.

Just sitting at the table again after what had happened on the Fourth did strange things to him. He ran his hand over the smooth, clean surface, practically seeing Liz stretched across it in all her naked glory. He instantly grew hard. A brief look told him the thick folds of his full-front apron hid the proof of just how much he still wanted Liz.

Staying away from her for the past two days had been a virtual hell for him. Watching her move around in that tight little uniform. Catching the longing in her own eyes when she looked at him. Listening to the sassy little remarks he was sure were designed to get a rise out of him—and oh boy, did they—every time she came into the kitchen. All combined to leave him a shaking pile of lust when he finally got home. And he'd learned the hard way that cold showers were powerless against his growing need of her.

He tunneled his hands through his hair. But until he got some answers, the last thing he needed to do was sleep with Liz again. What if she *was* married to another man? What if the blood on her dress belonged to that man, and even now his decaying body was floating to the surface of the Boston Harbor? What if the guy just in here was a police detective come to question Liz about her husband's disappearance?

He let loose a series of mismatched curses. And what if he was the biggest fool alive because of his inability to read her? Problem was, he'd once thought he knew her better than anybody else. Then she had run out, telling him he had never really known her at all.

The flash of afternoon sunlight reflected off an approaching vehicle. He turned to stare at an old, battered…was that a Pacer? He hadn't seen one of those since the mid-eighties.

The large, rounded car parked at the curb, and he noticed the temporary tag in the back window, right above where the bumper hung from two wires.

Liz got out of the driver's side.

Mitch rose from the booth so quickly, he nearly knocked the table from its anchor.

"What in the hell?" he muttered, hurrying to the door. Only Liz didn't head for the diner. Instead, she took that cursed wedding dress from the back of the car and crossed the street, walking in the direction of Peter's combination dry cleaners/men's wear/custom-tailoring shop. Glancing to where the Darton brothers stared at him from the counter, he offered up a half-assed grin, then turned to scowl out the front door. Changing his mind, he stepped to the counter and pulled the Dartons' freshly filled cups away from them.

"Sorry, guys, but the diner's closing for a half hour so I can get ready for the dinner rush," he said, keeping an eye on the cleaners across the street.

Moses Darton balked and reached for his cup. "Ruth never closes the diner."

"Yeah, well, Ruth's not here right now, is she? She's in D.C. looking after Bo." He grinned and stashed the cups under the counter. "Right now, I'm in charge, so blame me if you must, but I need you out. Now."

He budged the two from their stools and ushered them toward the door, not in a placating mood as he spotted Liz leaving the cleaners and heading in the diner's direction.

"Hey, there's Lizzie," Moses pointed out. "Bet she'll let us stay."

"Bet she won't, because neither one of you are going to ask her." Mitch patted them heartily on the back. "That is if you want me to let you run up your tab until your next pay-check from the mill."

Moses stopped short. "You're not saying you're going to cut us off, are you, McCoy?"

"This may come as a surprise, Moses, my man, but in a word, *yes*." He opened the door for them.

Moses looked at his brother. "Did that sound like a threat to you?"

His brother led the way down the sidewalk, dragging his feet. "Yep, sure did sound like a threat to me...."

He watched them hesitate as Liz passed, but neither of them said anything more than hello to her. Mitch held open the door so she could enter, then hung the closed sign and turned the lock.

Liz blinked at him. "Why did you do that?" She glanced around the empty diner. "And where is everybody?"

Mitch advanced on her. "I told Sharon she could go home because she was dead on her feet. The others...well, I kicked them out."

A flicker of amusement colored her hazel eyes. "Why did you do that? The Dartons always stick around until din—"

"Enough of me answering your questions," he cut her off, glancing to her hand holding the key to what he guessed was the Pacer. "I think it's time you started answering mine."

The sides of her provocative mouth turned up into a sexy little grin. "Such as?"

He scowled at the way she eyed him suggestively, then grasped her arm, finding her skin sun-warm and much too silky. "Uh-uh, not here. Let's go into the kitchen. I don't want to be accused of setting you up again."

He lightly kicked open the swinging door and dragged her inside. He turned to find her smiling.

"It really doesn't matter much where we talk, Mitch. That closed sign you just hung will be enough for everybody. In fact, it's probably even better, given what the town already thinks."

Mitch fumed at her breezy attitude. "To hell with what the town thinks. I want to know what you're doing driving that clunker parked on the street."

She hiked a feathery brow. "Clunker? That's my new car."

"New ca…" He let loose a string of curses and restrained himself from giving her a good shake. "What did you do with the Lexus?"

She smiled coyly. "I got rid of it."

"You…got…rid of it," he repeatedly slowly, thinking her words made no more sense than she did. The expression on her face was that of innocent amusement. Too innocent. "Why would you do that?"

She shrugged. "It was more trouble than it was worth." She tucked a glossy strand of hair behind a tiny ear. "Besides, I always wanted a Pacer. They're so unique."

He narrowed his eyes. "You wanted a Pacer over a Lexus," he deliberated aloud.

An insistent knock sounded at the front door. Liz stepped to the window.

"It's Myra," she said. "She must be back from vacation. I'd better go let her in."

Mitch curved his fingers around her arm a second time, infuriated by the way she was stringing him along—and wondering just how long that string was. "I don't think that's such a great idea."

She stared up at him in raw need.

Every last thought threatened to fly straight from his head as he eyed the way she ran that sweet tongue of hers across her lips.

Then it struck him that she knew exactly what she was doing. Just as she had turned the tables on him emotionally two days ago, she had found another way to torture him and was doing a class-A job of it as well. He admired her lush little mouth, and wished he didn't want to reclaim it.

Liz glanced back through the window. "Mitch?"

"What?"

"I thought you might like to know that the Darton brothers are not going to leave now that Myra's back. They're all sitting on the edge of the planter outside waiting."

"Then let them wait," he ground out. He blamed his lack of diplomacy on the long day, on her tempting, frequent forays into the kitchen in her tight uniform, and on the growing list of unexplained, suspicious things she had done. What could possibly be next? A smoking gun?

He tightened his grip on her arm. "Now tell me...who's Betsy? And don't even think about telling me you don't know, because I know your pretty little behind is in trouble."

All trace of teasing drained from her face.

CHAPTER NINE

MITCH RELEASED HER, confident he had earned her full attention. Confident, too, that if he kept touching her, he wouldn't be able to stop.

"Betsy?" she repeated dully.

"Uh-huh. Betsy." He crossed his arms. "You want to explain who she is? Or could it be that I'm looking at her right now?"

Another knock sounded at the front door, but Liz didn't budge. In fact, she appeared not to have heard it at all. Mitch rounded her and spotted the Darton brothers flanking Myra, all three standing with their hands cupped over their eyes against the glass, trying to see inside the diner. Mitch turned back to Liz.

"Remember that stranger I told you about? The one I saw in town the other day, and at the fairgrounds?"

He wished he knew what was spinning through that beautiful head of hers.

"Well, he stopped by the diner right after you left earlier. Ordered three pieces of cherry pie, but only ate two. He seemed to be looking for someone."

"Did you talk to him?"

"No. I was stuck back here in the kitchen. But he did ask Sharon a few questions. One of them was if she knew a woman in town named Betsy. Now, normally that wouldn't get my attention. After all, I don't know any Betsy." He tilted his head. "Or do I?"

She gave him a small smile then picked up a tray of re-filled sugar containers. "I can't say as I know what you're talking about."

"Can't?" he murmured, gently forcing her to face him again. "Or won't?"

She stared at his chest and he found her sudden interest in his anatomy frustrating...and all too provocative.

"Come on, Liz. We both know Betsy and Liz are nick-names for Elizabeth. I'm not going to let you wriggle out of an explanation for this one."

She caught her plump bottom lip between her teeth. He repressed the urge to suck the pink stretch of flesh into his own mouth, then run his tongue along the smooth line of her teeth.

"What did he look like, this guy?" she asked, her gaze still riveted to his chest.

"What does it matter?"

She finally lifted her gaze to his. If he didn't know better, he would have sworn he felt her shiver. But whether it was because of the stranger they were talking about, or the need she must have glimpsed on his face, he couldn't be sure. "Just tell me, Mitch, what did he look like?"

"Put it this way, he didn't look like your type." Then again, what did he know about her type? He had fooled himself into believing *he* was her type long ago. "He was somewhere in his mid- to late-fifties, graying blond hair, nice suit."

He might have been way off about her shivering, but he was sure her muscles relaxed under his fingers. The sensation was backed up with a dazzling smile from her that nearly made him stumble backward.

"Like I said, I don't have a clue what you're talking about," she said, suddenly all sass and light. She glanced pointedly at his hands, then dragged her gaze up his arms, over his chest, then up to his eyes, making *him* shiver. Mitch could have sworn she had touched him, but her hands were calmly at her sides. If only he didn't want her to touch him. All over. Now.

His jaw tensed. "Liz—"

A series of knocks sounded again at the door, this time unceasingly impatient. He thought of all the questions he needed answered, all the little mysteries that followed in Elizabeth Braden's wake, and was filled with the desire to tie her up until she answered and solved every one. Let every person in Manchester knock at the door and wonder what was going on inside, he didn't care. They couldn't do much about it, short of dragging Ruth back from D.C. early. He stretched a kink out of his tense neck. The image of the curvy, luscious woman before him with her wrists and feet bound with lengths of rope and at his complete and utter mercy elicited a response in him that was downright dangerous.

He silently cursed and slid his hands from her warm arms.

"We're nowhere near done with this conversation, Liz," he said, unable to resist smoothing her collar, feeling the heat of her flesh just below the surface of the stiff material. "Like I said before, you may look one hundred percent angel, but both of us know there's more devil in you than is good for either of us."

WHAT SHE WOULDN'T GIVE for her cell phone right about now.

In the middle of her grandmother's living room, Liz sat back on her heels, admiring her handiwork. She'd never cleaned so much so often in her life. She tilted her head to the side and frowned. A smudge was still apparent on the surface of the wooden side table. She pumped another spray of furniture polish on it and rubbed it from sight. Sexual frustration sure made for a spotless house.

There was only one man who could alleviate her problem, and since two nights had passed without a trace of him, she might as well put the polishing supplies away and plot out the next item she wanted to clean, scrub or strip.

If only she could keep her mind off stripping a certain someone instead of something, she'd be fine.

She felt like a sex fiend. Never had she been so fixated on something, completely incapable of thinking of anything else. She got up and headed for the kitchen. She hadn't realized how obsessed she was until she caught herself tracing highly suggestive shapes in the dust on the buffet table. She pushed her hair from her forehead with the back of her hand and flicked on the kitchen light, smiling when the room filled with warm, glorious light. She'd never realized how important electricity was until she didn't have it. Kind of like sex. Well, at least after you've had the right kind. And, oh boy, had Mitch ever showed her what *that* was like.

She put the can of furniture polish away, dropped the rag into the garbage, then leaned against the counter. The mere pressure against her hips made her shiver. Maybe she should give some thought to investing in some…pleasuring tools. She laughed aloud. They were sex toys, pure and simple. And she wished she had one or two about now. If only she was anywhere near convinced they would do the trick.

After washing her hands, she lethargically thrust the back window open a little farther, hoping for a breeze to cool the thick night air. No such luck. Air didn't come any hotter or more humid. She glanced at the clock she'd reset on the wall—11:00 p.m. Was that all? At this rate she was going to end up jogging to Mitch's in her T-shirt and white socks, his father and visiting brothers be damned.

If she did have her cell phone, who would she call? Ruth in D.C.? Sheila? She filled a glass with cold water and sighed. Ruth was probably already tucked in at her hotel room. And Sheila? She realized she didn't have a clue what her ex-assistant would be doing right now. Sleeping? No. She'd told her once that she was very much a night owl.

At any rate, both of them were doing something more than she was at this moment.

The sound of tires crunching against the gravel drive caught her attention.

Mitch?

Her heart skipped a beat. She'd be damned if she didn't get all wet just thinking about him coming here now.

Then she recalled the night before and how she had mistaken that late-night visitor for him.

Stepping to the wall, she killed the lights. She listened as the vehicle moved farther up the driveway. Was it the stranger Mitch had told her about? If so, who was he? A P.I. Rich had put on her tail? A lawyer? Or had Rich hired his own police officer to come all the way down here and have her arrested for assault?

She crossed her arms tightly, then rubbed her fingers along her neck. Then again, it could be Rich himself.

No.

He'd never show up himself in the flesh. He'd send one of his cronies to bring her back.

Not that she'd go, mind you—

The slamming of a car door told her she was going to find out who the person was soon enough.

Out of a sense of self-preservation, she stepped silently back into the shadows, watching the open window. A figure walked by. It was too dark to make out who it was. But as he walked by the window, she noted the guy—and she was sure it was a guy—had to top six feet.

She bit her bottom lip. She should have turned on the outside lights.

Oh, this is ridiculous, she thought. Mitch and all his ravings about her being in trouble. For a minute there, she'd actually thought herself in trouble.

Still, when she heard the turning of a key in the lock, she grabbed the broomstick before flipping on the lights.

The man stepped into the kitchen.

"Jesus, Mitch, you scared the hell out of me."

Standing with his booted feet planted firmly on the tile, he considered her standing practically one with the wall, the blunt end of the broomstick pointed at his midsection. "If I had been an intruder, do you really think that would have done any good?"

She looked at the broom, then him. "Hey, don't knock it. You've never seen what I can do with one of these."

His grin made her feel alive all over. "Yeah, I hear a splinter in the backside can be quite deadly." He crossed his arms. "Tell me, Liz, what are you so afraid of?"

She propped the broom against the wall. "Nothing." *Now,* she added silently.

"Wrong wording. What *were* you afraid of?"

She shrugged. "You tell me. It's eleven o'clock at night. I'm a woman alone in a big ol' house. And there's a stranger in my driveway." She gave him a coy little smile. "Wouldn't that be enough to scare anyone?" She tucked her hair behind her ear, realizing what a mess she was. Unbrushed, sans makeup, cleaning products smeared across the front of her T-shirt, her old white socks bagging around her ankles, she probably looked a sight.

Why was it then that Mitch was looking at her as if she was the sexiest thing he'd ever laid eyes on? And why did she suddenly feel that way?

She cleared her throat. "What are you doing out here this late, anyway? Make a habit of dropping in on women in the middle of the night and using their spare key to get in?"

"Only one woman in particular. And I'm here for the same reason you felt compelled to arm yourself with a broom. I was concerned for your safety."

She shivered under the weight of his suggestive look. "So you're here to protect me," she said, her voice sounding foreign to her own ears—rusty and far too suggestive.

She wanted to tease him. Continue the game of cat and mouse they indulged in at the diner. But her body had something else entirely in mind. Her nipples hardened to aching peaks. Her belly filled with a heat so intense she thought for sure he must feel it across the room.

Oh, how she wanted him. She wanted to feel him in her arms. Between her thighs. In her. Above her. Around her. She longed to feel him in every way there was for a human being to feel another.

And judging by the dark expression on his face, he wanted the same.

Mitch had struggled since earlier that evening with his decision to come over here. But the later it got, the more agitated he became. Yes, he told himself, part of the reason he was there was due to his concern for her well-being. Until he found out who the stranger was, and what exactly he wanted, he didn't like the thought of Liz being alone.

But his body reminded him of what his more compelling motivation was.

He wanted Liz.

As if reading his mind, she crossed the room and threaded her fingers through his hair, her pupils so large they nearly eclipsed the color of her irises. "So protect me then, McCoy," she murmured.

He claimed her saucy mouth with savage intensity. Damn it, he didn't care if she *was* married. If she *had* done away with her husband and stashed him in a Dumpster somewhere. Neither of which he'd been able to prove or disprove. He'd give everything he was to be connected to her again. Everything. To lose himself in the feel of her sleek flesh surrounding him….

He hauled her against him, feeling the sway of her breasts beneath her T-shirt. Reveling in the hunger so clearly evident in her kiss. Loving the feel of her hands running wildly over his body.

He moved his hands up the backs of her thighs, then slipped them up under her skirt. His thumbs found the thin elastic of her panties and he slid them underneath. God, she felt so good. So damn right. He swallowed her low moan and plunged his thumbs into the narrow valley between her cheeks. Her breath caught. He thrust his tongue deep into her mouth even as he gently parted her, finding her sopping wet.

Groaning, he moved his arm to the backs of her knees and swept her up against his chest.

"That way," she said on a raspy sigh, pointing toward the hall door.

He didn't need directions. He'd traveled this route at least a thousand times in his mind. He just wished it wasn't so damn far. It seemed forever passed before he laid her down on the canopy bed in her room upstairs. His breath came in ragged gasps. His body felt about to explode.

He quickly stripped himself, then her, then lay down next to her, reaching for the condom in his back jeans pocket.

Before he knew what hit him, she was taking the foil packet from his fingers, tearing it open with her teeth, and quickly sheathing him. He nearly lost it right then and there.

He'd wanted this, their second time, to be better than the first. He'd wanted to go slow. To taste the sweet pleasures that lay between her thighs. Show her he could please her without pleasing himself. But she wasn't having any of that. Already she was straddling him, her palms against his abdomen, her breasts swaying tantalizingly just beyond his reach.

Then he was exactly where he wanted to be. Deep inside her.

She rocked her hips forward once. Then again. He grabbed the sheet under him in his fists. It took every ounce of self-control he had to just lie there, let her find her rhythm.

Finally she did.

And Mitch moved with her.

Never, ever had he seen a more beautiful sight than Liz, sitting astride him. Her mouth shaped in a perfect oval as she fought to hold off her climax. He thrust deeply up into her, watched the bounce of her breasts, the glistening of sweat beginning to accumulate on the velvety skin between them.

It was then he knew that he couldn't bear for her to leave. He'd realized after their first time together at the diner that sex with Liz was not merely the satisfaction of a long-burning lust. When he joined his body with hers, he was, pure and simple, making love.

He swallowed hard, now fighting off his climax. He let

go of the sheets and cupped her breasts in his palms, plucking at her distended nipples, his gaze drawn to where their bodies were joined together.

He clamped his jaws tightly together. *No, no. Not yet.*

He needed a plan. He needed to find a way to convince Liz to stay. To show her they could have more together than just mind-blowing sex.

But how—

Liz's movements quickened, then ceased altogether as she needfully ground herself against him.

Mitch slid his arms under her knees, then lifted her. He ignored her soft protests and held her there for a long, torturous moment. Then with an almost violent thrust of his hips, he plunged deeply inside her. Once. Twice. Again.

His entire body quaked as she cried out above him.

His climax seemed to go on and on. Spasm upon spasm gripping him from deep within as her sleek muscles convulsed around him.

Long moments later, she lay on top of him, spent and breathless. He reached to push her hair from her face, distantly surprised to find his hand shaking.

"Liz?"

She softly hummed her response.

"When Bo and Ruth return—when we have time to ourselves—I want you to spend the day with me at my place. I have...I have some things to show you."

She didn't say anything right away. He listened as her breathing slowly returned to normal. Then she said quietly, "okay."

He closed his eyes and pressed his mouth against her temple. God help him, but he didn't know what he was going to do if he couldn't convince her to stay.

CHAPTER TEN

FINALLY, the chaos of the past couple of days held all of the promise of a return to normalcy when Ruth swept into the diner the following afternoon. Liz looked up from cleaning the last of the tables from breakfast, as did Myra, who was restocking the pies in the counter displays. Mitch belted out a hearty hello from where he cleaned up the kitchen. The only two customers, the Darton brothers, turned on their stools, holding up their coffee cups in salute.

Liz stuffed her rag into her pocket and rushed to hug her. "You don't know how good it is to see you," she said, leaning back to take a look into Ruth's strained eyes. "Is Bo with you?"

"No, after the trip from D.C., I made him go home and lie down. After all those tests, and the fear the doctor put into him, he was pretty beat."

Liz touched Ruth's arm. "You said you and Bo weren't going to be back until later tonight."

Ruth glanced around the clean, nearly empty diner. "That's because I wasn't up to a welcoming committee with a truckload of questions. I'm going to have to deal with them soon enough."

Ruth hugged her again so tightly, she crowded the breath from her lungs. Tears pricked Liz's eyes. What had brought this on?

"I can't thank you enough for looking after the place while we were away," Ruth murmured and Liz caught a whiff of the lilac powder she always wore.

"Hey, don't I get some of that?" Mitch chided, emerging from the kitchen, his white apron securely in place.

"Of course you do, you big lug." Ruth hugged him as well. Her eyes twinkled mischievously as she eyed him. "Though I have to wonder if you'd have been so generous with your time if our Lizzie wasn't back."

Our Lizzie. Shifting from foot to foot, Liz tried to avoid meeting Mitch's gaze, but couldn't.

"Any other time I would give you guff for that remark," Mitch said. "But just because you and Bo are back safe and sound and healthy, I'll go easy on you."

Ruth grimaced. "Safe and sound we are, but healthy is a little ways down the road. Speaking of which," she began, pushing her hands against his chest and angling him back toward the kitchen, "I think we three ladies are going to review the diner's menu right now. I know you don't mind looking after the cooking a little while longer until we're done."

"Review the menu?" Mitch repeated with a droll grin. "That wouldn't happen to be synonymous with gossiping, would it?"

"That's none of your business. Now go. And I don't want to catch you listening in, either, you hear?"

Mitch feigned a grimace.

Liz crossed her arms and indulged in one of her favorite pastimes: watching Mitch walk away. Myra stepped up beside her.

"He looks as good going as he does coming, doesn't he?" her friend murmured, crossing her arms.

Liz elbowed her, and glanced at Mitch just in time to find

him looking back at her. She didn't miss the devilish tilt to his lips, nor the wink that told her that that wasn't the last she was going to see of either his front or back side. She shivered in anticipation.

Ruth glanced toward the two men at the counter. "Moses and David, you're going to have to see after yourselves for a while, but we're right over here if you need anything."

"Yes, ma'am," they said in unison without turning around.

Liz slid into the nearest booth when Ruth gestured for her to do so. Myra slipped in next to her.

"What's this really about?" Liz asked as Ruth collected a plate of cookies from the counter and sat across from them.

The diner owner plucked one of the plastic menus from its perch next to the sugar container and opened it in front of her, pushing the plate of chocolate chip cookies in Liz's direction. "What I said it was. We're going to revamp the meals we serve here."

Liz shared a glance with Myra, then took her notepad out of her uniform pocket. She pushed the cookies toward Myra, who grimaced.

"First of all, anything that moos goes," Ruth muttered, tapping her index finger against the long list of meat dishes the diner offered.

Myra's gaze shifted from the cookies to Ruth. "Are you serious?"

"As a heart attack."

Liz carefully reached out and closed the menu. "Ruth, are you sure you want to do this? I mean, while adding healthier selections is a good idea, you don't want to eliminate the plates that draw the people in."

"You mean the artery-choking killers?"

Liz experienced a burst of sympathy. Ruth was serious about altering the menu. And she guessed the decision was strictly an emotional one, a way to vent her fear about what had happened to Bo without letting on that it had bothered her. Only Liz could see it bothered her too much.

"Ruth? You can't turn the diner into a health food place." She carefully worded her argument. "This is not some trendy district in New York here. Manchester is full of meat-and-potatoes people. They may order your pineapple ribs, and they may like them, but you have to remember it's the ribs that pack them in, not the pineapple."

Myra leaned back to stare at her. "You really are a business consultant, aren't you?"

Liz ignored her, transfixed by Ruth's pinched expression and obvious dilemma. "I've got a suggestion, if you want to hear me out."

Ruth pulled a napkin out of the nearby holder and made a show of dabbing at her makeup, though Liz knew exactly what she was doing—drying the tears that had seeped from her eyes. "I don't know. Depends on what it's going to cost me."

Liz smiled softly and caught Mitch peeking around the kitchen window. Her cheeks heated and she lowered her voice. "It's not going to cost you a cent. Even though in my last contract I got…" She quoted a figure.

Both Ruth and Myra stared at her in thinly veiled shock.

She laughed. "No joke. But, hey, I made the mistake of getting involved with the boss. That same boss froze my accounts when I broke our contract."

Myra gave in to temptation and broke off a piece of a cookie. "Froze your accounts? How could he do that?"

Liz noticed that the shine of curiosity had returned to

Ruth's eyes and she relaxed slightly, deciding sharing a little of herself to help Ruth concentrate on something other than her own ordeal was worth it.

Still, it was a bit difficult to push the words past her throat. Especially since Mitch—despite Ruth's stern warning—was trying his level best to hear what was being said at the table across the room.

She stumbled back on subject. "How could he do that? Simple. He, um, my boss was the vice president of the bank where I had my personal and business accounts."

Ruth leaned her forearms on top of the closed menu. "This the guy you were going to marry?"

Liz nodded, relieved she had put it that way. After what had happened between her and Mitch seven years ago, Ruth could easily have said, "This the *other* guy you were going to marry?" But what had occurred between her and Richard Beschloss in no way, shape or form came close to what she had once felt for Mitch. What she still felt for him.

She swallowed and waited as Myra rose from the table and brought back three cups and a full pot of coffee.

The Darton brothers groaned about the loss of their coffee and Myra told them to put a sock in it.

The quirky brunette sat down again and sighed. "So that explains why you took your old job back here. You really do need the money."

Liz folded the top sheet of her notepad, purposely not mentioning the hefty money order she had mailed to Sheila that morning to cover her severance pay. She'd gotten more than she expected for her Lexus in the neighboring county and had sent half of it. Even with the mere pittance the Pacer had cost deducted from it, she had more than enough with which to move on. Funny thing was, she didn't feel in a hurry to go. "Guess I like to learn things the hard way."

Myra sat back in the booth. "Learn what? That all men are dogs?"

This time it was Liz's turn to stare. "Dogs?"

"We wouldn't happen to be talking about Harvey now, would we?" Ruth asked.

Liz glanced out the window, seeing old Josiah across the way rocking in his chair. "I didn't hear the infamous Harley when you came in yesterday."

Myra twisted her lips. "Yes, I'm talking about Harvey, and no, you didn't hear the Harley because I rolled it into a ditch night before last somewhere outside Moody, Alabama."

A laugh exploded from Liz, earning a glare from her friend. "Sorry," she said, and tried to make herself look as if she was. "But I was just imagining Harvey's face when you did that."

Myra shrugged her slender shoulders. "Wish I could tell you. Truth is, I did it after he fell asleep at a motel, and left before he had a chance to find out what I'd done."

The three of them exchanged glances, then burst out laughing.

"What did the dog do?" Ruth asked. Liz eyed her, comforted to find little trace of her earlier worry visible.

Myra leaned closer. Liz noticed that Mitch very obviously stood in the kitchen window drying a large pot, and the Darton brothers had grown awfully quiet at the counter.

"*Dog* isn't exactly the word I'd use to describe him, Ruth. That wolf…coyote…dingo…well, as soon as we got down to Mobile—that's where my mother's family is from—he made this big production of having something to give me.

Something, he said, that I'd been wanting for a long time." She paused and closed her eyes. "I swore he meant to ask me to marry him. I went out and bought a new dress, got all dolled up. Then over dinner at a crab place—" her eyes flicked open, revealing flames licking in the brown depths "—he gave me this...this box. You know what was in it? A dog collar."

Liz blinked at her. "Did a dog come along with it?"

"Yeah. Harvey." Myra rolled her eyes. "Of course a dog didn't come with it. It was a collar for humans. You know, a thick piece of black leather with silver spikes that you wear around your neck?" She half circled her own neck with her index finger and thumb. "This one had a tag attached. It said Harvey's Biker Chick."

Liz cringed and looked at Ruth, neither of them finding the information particularly shocking. Myra had a long history of choosing thoughtless guys. This was the first time, however, that Myra had dumped one of them, instead of waiting around and being dumbfounded when they deserted her.

"You're better off without him," Ruth said, giving her forearm a squeeze.

"That's what I thought." Myra sniffed.

Liz handed her a napkin, and Myra took a swipe at her arm. "Knock it off, Braden. Your luck with men isn't any better than mine."

Ruth raised a penciled brow. "She's got you there, Lizzie." She shot a reprimanding gaze at Mitch and the Dartons, who were openly watching them now. "If you guys don't want to lose your stool privileges, you'd best be about your business."

Mitch disappeared from sight and the brothers promptly

turned back toward the counter and grabbed their empty coffee cups.

Liz laughed, loving that Mitch was curious as hell about
what they were discussing.

"Speaking of Mitch…" Ruth trailed off, looking at her.

"Oh, were we? I didn't hear his name come up," Liz said,
swearing sometimes the woman could read her mind like an
open menu.

Ruth smiled knowingly. "I want to know what you two
were doing in here alone together when I called on the
Fourth."

Myra pretended to be about ready to fall out of the booth.
"What?"

"Oh, quit it, you two. His stopping by was completely innocent." Well, at least that much was true. They didn't have
to know what happened after that. Or what had happened
again last night….

"Uh-huh." Myra finished the cookie she was working on,
and part of another, then pushed the dish toward Liz.

Ruth took one herself. "That's not what I heard. In fact,
word is the odds on that bet is tipping over into Mitch's
favor."

Liz stared at her.

"You guys *are* repeating history," Myra mumbled, clearly
dismayed.

Ruth waved her hand dismissively. "Never mind her,"
she said to Liz. "She'd gone out with every available guy
in the tri-county area by the time Mitch came back. The
instant he rolled into town, she thought her prospects had
improved."

Myra poured cream into her coffee. "Until Liz came
back, too."

Liz stared at her friend. Why was she the last one to hear this? "You're interested in Mitch?"

Myra shrugged and stirred her coffee. "Not interested really. I guess *curious* is more the word. I always wondered what you two used to do together to look so…blastedly happy."

Ruth munched on a cookie and studied Liz's face. "They couldn't have been too happy or Liz would never have left."

Feeling as if she had revealed too much about herself already, Liz plucked a cookie from the small stack remaining. She began to put it back, then instead took a hearty bite. "Can we get back on topic, please?"

Ruth wiped crumbs from her hands and stared at the menu in front of her again. "Do you really have some ideas about changing the menu?" she asked.

Liz nodded, relief suffusing her tense muscles. Why was it whenever Mitch was brought into the conversation, she immediately found herself on the defensive? She stole a glance toward the kitchen, but he was nowhere in sight.

Myra slipped from the booth. "Don't look now, but the flocks descend."

Liz stared through the window overlooking the street. Charles Obernauer, along with a couple of his cronies, approached from one side, while Ezra headed another group closing in from the other. Liz popped the remainder of her cookie into her mouth, regretful she didn't have time to chase it down with some coffee.

Myra gathered the pot and the cups, but Ruth refused to give up the menu.

She glanced at Liz. "Guess we're going to have to wait until these guys' rumbling stomachs are filled before we can finish this conversation."

MITCH COOKED his way through the dinner rush. Ruth had attempted to take over, but he had chased her out of the kitchen to her usual job of tending the cash register and catching up on the books Liz had looked after the past couple of days.

He flipped four burgers, then peeked around to catch a glimpse of Liz waiting tables. The early-afternoon sun slanted in through the windows, setting her glorious blond hair aglow and bringing her lush figure into relief under her white uniform. He lowered his gaze to her nicely curved legs and the gentle sway of her hips. The woman could put a real angel to shame. What was amazing was that the beauty she radiated on the outside came from a very deep source within. Somehow, over the course of the past week and in the shadow of their private midnight meetings, he had forgotten that.

But while she had sat with Ruth and Myra discussing whatever it was that women talk about, his gaze had been drawn to her time and again, catching the warmth and compassion in her gestures, her smiles, the way she gave whoever she talked to her complete attention. What he would have given to be able to hear what they were talking about.

He caught a whiff of something burning. Biting back a curse, he rushed back to the grill. One of the burgers was a little darker than it should be, but, irritated, he slapped it on a bun anyway.

Now that Ruth was back, it was time to put his own plan into motion. One that would, he hoped, throw a permanent monkey wrench into her plans.

He slid the four ready plates onto the ledge. "Order up!" he bellowed.

Liz jerked to stare at him and he couldn't help grinning,

until he got a gander at Ruth's questioning gaze. Clearing his throat, he turned back to his duties, keeping an eye out for Liz.

"Ruth's going to have a piece of your rear end for that one," she quipped, taking two of the four plates while Myra gathered the others. "And it's a shame really, seeing as it's nice just the way it is."

Mitch moved toward her, relieved six inches of wall and two counters separated them, because he wouldn't have been able to resist tasting her sassy lips otherwise. "Why is it, Liz, that you're all mouth when others are around, but you clam up when we're alone?"

The Darton brothers and Charles Obernauer chuckled from the counter. She glared at him, as if daring him to say something more. Like how she wasn't so quiet when they were alone after all, and, in fact, could get quite loud. But he kept the words, arming himself for the next time he could corner her.

Myra rolled her eyes and turned from them. "You two make me sick."

Liz squeezed out from behind the counter to deliver the orders.

Mitch didn't miss the amused expressions on the other men's faces as he made a point of watching her walk away. She wasn't the only one who could enjoy a great departure. The sexy sway of her hips, and the slight upward tilt to her chin, made her all the more attractive.

"Whew, things sure are getting hot in here," Moses Darton said, fanning himself with his paper napkin. "Ruth! You want to turn the air up a bit?"

Laughter rumbled through the diner and Liz nearly dropped the plates she'd cleared from an empty table. Mitch wiped his hands on a towel and had begun to turn away when the flash of the sun reflecting off the opening door stopped him. From the beige-and-white checked suit jacket up to the new arrival's graying blond hair, Mitch scanned the unwanted visitor.

Mitch crushed the towel in his fingers, his muscles tensed to the point of snapping as he stared at the man. He had no doubt that Liz's late-night visitor from two days ago was now seating himself at the booth she had just cleared.

Myra's head popped into the window. "You got Ezra's pizza ready yet?"

Mitch stared at her; her frizzy dark hair blocked his view of the stranger.

"It'll be out of the oven in a couple of minutes," he answered automatically, trying to look past her to where Liz poured the stranger a glass of water and appeared to take his order. The guy looked at her a little longer than necessary, but nothing in his demeanor spoke of surprise or curiosity.

That means he already knows who she is.

Mitch's stomach tightened and Myra drummed her midnight-blue fingernails on the ledge then turned away with a sigh.

But if he already knew who she was, then why didn't she recognize him?

The questions lined up one after another as Liz moved to the pie display and served—what else?—a piece of cherry pie.

He threw the towel to the preparation counter in front of him and started for the kitchen door to find out exactly who this man was and what he wanted with Liz. Halfway there, the oven timer buzzed, halting him in his tracks.

Not bothering to hide his irritation, he let loose a string

of curses that would curdle the cream in the customers' coffee. He was forced to abandon his hasty plan…for now. But he would confront the guy the moment the lunch crowd let up.

Nearly burning his hands as he removed Ezra's pizza from the oven, he slid the food onto a serving plate and hurried back to the window, staring at the way Liz moved around the place as if not a thing was wrong.

Didn't she remember the stranger he'd told her about? Didn't she see the guy was staring at her right now? Judging by all her normal reactions he guessed no. Then again, he reasoned, she had been gone seven years. And even back then she hadn't come near knowing all the residents the way he had. He frowned. As she herself had said, everybody in Manchester was strange to her.

Urgently, he put the pizza on the ledge. Near the cash register, he spotted Liz taking off her apron, the stranger's gaze focused outside the window, then trailing to her.

"You didn't say 'order up,'" Myra complained, popping up in the window again.

"So sue me," he challenged without looking at her.

Liz was saying something to Ruth, then she laid her apron on the counter and strode toward the door. Myra picked up the plate, and Mitch grabbed her arm.

"Where's she going?" he asked.

"Who?" Myra stared at his hand. "Liz? She said she had something she wanted to pick up at the cleaners before they close for the afternoon."

Realizing he still had a grip on Myra, he quickly released her, his gaze plastered to the stranger watching Liz cross the street outside the diner. Adrenaline pumped through his veins.

If the guy was a cop, then Liz was going to hand him his first and most damning piece of evidence against her.

He began to untie his apron, then abandoned it, telling himself he didn't have enough time. As busy as it was at the diner, Liz didn't dare stay longer than a couple of minutes at the cleaners.

He pushed open the kitchen door and stalked directly to the stranger's table.

"You looking for somebody?" he grumbled.

Dragging his attention from the street and Liz, the stranger blinked up at him.

"Pardon me?"

Mitch met the man's stare. "I asked if you were looking for somebody."

"No." He gestured to his untouched food. "I just stopped in for a piece of Bo's famous cherry pie."

Mitch seethed. How good could the guy be if he didn't even do his research? "It's Ruth's," he pointed out.

"Okay," the stranger said slowly. "Then Ruth's famous pie. With two names on the diner, I had at least a fifty-fifty chance of getting it right, eh?"

Mitch reined in the desire to take the pie and make the guy swallow it in one bite so he could kick him out. But he couldn't, not without knowing if he was some sort of police detective from another city. Say, Boston?

Ruth hurried up to him. "Mitch, are you hassling my customers?"

He said nothing.

"No, ma'am, Mitch…isn't it? Mitch and I were just having a harmless conversation," the man said and flashed a cool smile.

Ruth hovered uncertainly, looking about ready to grab Mitch by the arm and yank him away from the booth.

"Actually, we were just about to take our conversation back to the kitchen, weren't we…Dick?" he added the name for good measure, drawing a surprised expression from the neatly dressed man seated in front of him.

Ruth sighed in exasperation. "Well, then, go on and do it. You're disrupting people's lunches out here."

Mitch swept his arms in the direction of the kitchen door. "After you."

Reluctantly, the man rose from his seat and started in the direction he indicated. Mitch flicked an uneasy gaze toward where Liz was just entering the dry cleaners.

"Have we met somewhere before?" the man asked.

The kitchen door swept closed behind them and Mitch grasped his nicely tailored lapels and carried him to the wall where he flattened him against it.

"I want to know who you are and what you're doing in Manchester," he ground out, hardly recognizing the dark tone of his voice. "Are you a cop?"

Beads of sweat broke out on the older man's forehead. "A cop? No, no. I thought you knew who I was when you called me Dick out there. I'm…I am a private dick…detective from Massachusetts. If you'll just let me go for a minute, I'll show you my card."

Mitch stared him down. All at once, everything came together, and what the man was saying made perfect sense. He should have known from the first. He'd always been so capable in his jobs as FBI agent and as P.I. But add Liz to the picture, and he missed even the most obvious of clues.

Reluctantly, he released his grip and smoothed down the wrinkled lapels. His hands shaking, the stranger rifled through the inside pockets of his jacket, finally pulling out a bi-fold identification that listed him as Don Secord, P.I.

Mitch eyed it long and hard. "You're not in Massachusetts anymore, Secord."

The stranger blinked at him. "No, I—"

"Who are you working for?" Mitch interrupted.

A peculiar clicking noise sounded as Secord swallowed. "I can't tell you that. That's privileged information."

"Well, I'm making it unprivileged." Mitch stepped ominously closer to him.

"I'm telling you I can't give you that data. But—but I can tell you who I'm after."

Mitch waited.

Secord rifled through his pockets again, this time coming out with a three-by-five photograph. Mitch snatched it from his fingers and turned it around. His throat tightened as he stared down at the dark-haired woman. *Liz.*

"Her name's Betsy Braden. Someone at the store across the street told me she worked here. I didn't recognize her at first, but I'm positive she's the blonde that just left the diner."

Mitch cringed. *Betsy Braden?* Whatever possessed Liz to take on such a pretentious name? He eyed the man before him, noting his expensive clothes and his smooth demeanor. Given his own experience in the field, this guy was no B-movie private dick. He was a professional. And professionals cost big money.

He stuffed the photo into his back jeans pocket, and, in the same move, slid out his own identification. "Well, Don Secord, P.I., I'm Mitch McCoy, ex-FBI, now fellow P.I.," he said, laying on a heavy southern drawl. "And I don't much like northerners down this way bothering the residents of my town."

"FBI?" The man eyed his apron and the kitchen they stood in.

"Yeah, ex-FBI." Mitch grabbed his lapels again and swung him toward the door. "I'm going to give you two minutes to reach the county line. If you're not out of here by then, I'm going to have a few of my old buddies introduce you to a little cell up D.C. way."

The man reddened. "You can't hold me."

"Try me," Mitch challenged, wondering if Connor or David could help him out if push came to shove.

"On what charge?" Secord sputtered.

"Harassment for starters. Trespassing on private property if you make things difficult, and a whole host of other charges, including stalking, that will find you in the area longer than you planned, if you want to press the issue."

The dick shrugged and nodded. "I'm gone as soon as you let me go. In fact, I'll be out of here so fast you'll have to wonder if I was ever here."

Mitch tightened his fingers, wondering if Liz was still at the cleaners. To be on the safe side, he jostled the P.I. toward the back door.

"Go out the back way."

"What about my bill?"

Mitch scowled. "I'll get it."

He released the man, and, true to his word, he scrambled toward the door in two seconds flat, nothing left of him except the lingering smell of his expensive cologne.

Stuffing his ID back into his pocket, Mitch entered the main area of the diner just in time to see Liz coming through the front door, hanging the clean wedding dress up on the coatrack just as a flash of beige scrambled past the window. Moments later, the blue rental car squealed away in a streak of color.

He let out a long breath and hung his chin to his chest.

Thank God. Didn't Liz realize that no bloodstain could ever be completely cleaned from any material? That the chemical Luminol could illuminate the tiniest of traces? He dragged his fingers through his hair and glanced up to find everyone in the place staring at him.

Ruth faced him.

"Cough up your apron, McCoy. As of this moment, I'm officially retiring you."

Liz strode up to stand behind her.

He reluctantly reached to unfasten the ties behind his back. "Were the reports on my cooking that bad?"

Ruth looked ready to boil him fully clothed. "On the contrary. Your cooking gets raves. It's your manner with the customers that leaves something to be desired." She took the apron he offered. "First I hear you chased two of my best customers out of here yesterday afternoon then closed the joint. Now you're just plain chasing customers out. What's gotten into you?"

He nearly told her it wasn't *what* had gotten into him, but *who* had gotten into him. Namely Elizabeth, alias Betsy, a.k.a. Liz, Braden.

He watched Liz reach over to a nearby table and halt a bobbing cherub, trying to keep a straight face but failing miserably.

"Boy, the thanks I get," Mitch mumbled as he slanted a gaze toward the Darton brothers still seated at the counter. Moses Darton cleared his throat.

Mitch looked at Liz. "So are we on for tomorrow? Shall I pick you up at, say, eleven o'clock?"

"Tomorrow?" she repeated.

He nodded in Ruth's direction, hoping Liz hadn't forgotten last night when she'd said she'd spend the day with him as soon as they had a day to themselves. He had but one shot to convince her to stay. And, damn it, he was going to take it.

Liz's face flushed with color. "Oh. Yes. Yes, um, eleven's fine."

Mitch reached into his pocket and handed Ruth a five-dollar bill. "To cover the pie."

"Gee, thanks. Now go on. Get out of here."

He grinned at the quick way she took the offered money. "Do I still get to come back as a customer?"

Ruth smiled back. "The place wouldn't be the same without you."

CHAPTER ELEVEN

THE FOLLOWING MORNING, Mitch lay on the horn, unsurprised by the lack of movement in Liz's house. Goliath, sprawled across the bench seat, whined. It was ten after eleven. If he had known Liz had no intention of making it on time, he could have checked a couple more items off the list of things to be done around the one-hundred-and-sixty-four-acre McCoy spread.

Where was she?

Switching off the engine, Mitch climbed from the truck, hesitating only slightly to allow a reanimated Goliath to jump out before closing the door. He strode toward the back of Liz's grandmother's house. Finding the key over the back window again, he then opened the screen door, and settled his hand over the tarnished door handle. It turned easily without the key.

"Damn it, Liz, you should know better."

He stepped into the mudroom and was nearly knocked over when Goliath barreled inside, sniffed around his feet, grabbed something then ran back outside. Banging his knee on a low-lying table, Mitch groaned and clutched his leg until the throbbing pain passed. He groped around, plucking a shoe from the floor. He stared at it. It was not just a shoe, but one of those maddening red shoes she'd been wearing the night she rode into town.

Holding the shoe, he carefully made his way into the

kitchen. The room was dim, in spite of the hot sun outside. He blinked, adjusting his eyesight, then settled his gaze on the window. He stepped over to it and opened the curtains that blocked even the dimmest ray.

He turned to find a cot set up in the far corner. He was almost sure it hadn't been there the night before last. Liz's slumbering outline was plainly visible under the tangled, thin cotton sheet, both it and a pillow pulled over her head. A bare foot and part of a shapely calf stuck out the end. He resisted the urge to run a finger over the delectable arch.

There would be time enough for that later.

"Liz?" he said, searching for signs of life.

Still holding the shoe, he reached over and closed his fingers over a corner of the sheet—a corner well away from her foot.

"Oh, Elizabeth?" he tried again, this time a little louder.

Not even a twitch to indicate she had heard him. Staring at the sheet he clutched in his fingers, he debated yanking it back. He shifted his gaze to the form underneath, trying to discern if she wore anything. The woman didn't lock her door, wasn't even alert to the fact that there was someone in her temporary bedroom/kitchen. It wouldn't surprise him in the least if she was sleeping in the buff.

He jerked his hand back empty. Oh no. He knew his limits. And a naked, sleepy Liz was a sight even he wouldn't be able to handle, plans or no.

"Betsy!" he yelled, crossing his arms.

She sprang up so quickly she startled *him.* He stepped back, well out of attack range, watching her toss the pillow to the floor. Her hazel eyes were wide and unfocused, her blond hair a captivating tangle around her sleep-creased face.

"Wh-wh-what?" she whispered, her gaze darting around the kitchen, then back to him.

She moaned and flopped back to the mattress. "Oh, it's you. For a minute there I thought you were…"

It would have been the perfect opportunity to pump her for information on exactly who that was. But the truth was, he couldn't have pushed anything past his tight throat if he tried.

Liz wasn't naked. But she *was* the next best thing.

He eyed the sheet bunched around her knees, his searing gaze dragging upward to where a triangular scrap of lace and satin barely covered the lush wedge of hair beneath. A brush-fire swept through his groin. He forced his attention away from the naughty string bikini and up her toned, perfectly molded torso to where the cropped T-shirt barely stretched over the satiny swell of her breasts, the undersides clearly visible. He watched the movements of her chest as she lazily reached for the sheet.

"Mitch McCoy, have you no shame?"

"What?" he asked, quirking a brow and enjoying the rosy flush that crept up her lovely neck and across her cheeks. "I was just noticing that you've been doing some shopping." He swallowed hard. "Anyway, you don't have anything I haven't seen before."

Which was the truth. He had seen it all. He'd sampled the luscious wares, too. And he'd be damned if he didn't want to do it all over again. He shifted from foot to foot, trying to find a comfortable position where his jeans didn't hurt so much. If he didn't cool it, he'd end up between those toned thighs before she could blink her sleepy eyes. The arousing image made his jeans even tighter. He eyed the rickety cot, wondering if it would support both their weights….

"What are you doing sleeping in a cot in the kitchen, anyway?"

"It got a little too hot upstairs last night," Liz said, dangling her tanned legs over the side of the bed. "What are you doing holding my shoe?"

He stared at the red, strappy object in his hand. It took a moment to remember how it got there. He tossed it onto the bed next to her, resisting the temptation to ask her to put it and its partner on, just so he could see how she would look in her present attire...and the red shoes.

Briefly closing his eyes against the rage of emotion threatening to erupt, he dragged in a deep breath and counted backward from ten. By the time he opened his eyes again, she was standing, the sheet draped haphazardly around her waist.

"The thing nearly killed me when I came in the door," he said, watching her navel wink at him as she tucked in the sheet. "A door, by the way, that you left unlocked all night."

She pushed her jumble of shiny hair back from her face. "I did not. I woke up this morning for a potty break and I unlocked it then." She smiled up at him. "I figured I probably wouldn't hear your knocks because I'm a pretty heavy sleeper."

"I'll say."

He battled to keep his gaze above neck level, but didn't find the view there any less attractive than the rest of her. Liz had the type of face that inspired men to sculpt. He gazed into her wide eyes and altered the thought to paint. But it would take years of experimenting with different shades of blues, browns and greens to duplicate the remarkable color of her eyes.

He made a point of looking at the watch on his wrist.

"Well if you have any more potty breaks you'd like to take, I'd recommend taking them now." He'd known it would be a mistake to come in here this morning. That's why he'd sat for fifteen minutes in the truck, blowing the horn. "And put something on."

Her tempting little lips bowed into a smile. "Do you really want me to do it?"

"Yes. Now get a move on. Time's a-wasting." She started to walk toward the bathroom. "And you can wear anything but that shirt and those skimpy cut-offs. The whole point of this adventure is to spend some time together outside of bed, if that's all right with you."

She halted in the doorway, smiling at him. What was she up to now? He found out when she dropped the sheet to the floor and provocatively stepped from the puddle of material and away from him. He noticed then that the panties didn't have a back. The heat in his groin gushed through his limbs as he stared at the red satiny ribbon that came dangerously close to disappearing into the shallow crevice between her firmly rounded cheeks.

He closed his eyes, trying to remember what they called the downright indecent undergarment. But for the life of him, he couldn't concentrate on anything other than the image of her tight, lush rear end, her narrow waist, and the provocative way she had teased him.

The bathroom door slammed and he relaxed, if only a bit. He quickly strode one way in the cramped kitchen, then the other. The woman was bad enough when she *wasn't* trying to provoke a reaction.

The toe of his boot caught something. He stared down at what looked like a blue dart on the warped linoleum. He picked up the fine-pointed game piece and weighed it in his hand. What was Liz doing with a dart? Possibly throwing it at a picture of him? Slowly turning toward the opposite wall, he discovered the answer.

Far from the picture of himself he half expected, the wall was covered with the various brochures he'd seen her with over the past week. Brochures on cities as far away as Seattle, and as near as Richmond. Puzzled, he counted twenty of them, all brightly colored, flashy displays of the best the places had to offer. Peppering the wall between them were darts sticking out at all sorts of wild angles, as if she'd thrown them from various positions in the room.

Smack dab in the middle of the display one of the darts had hit. He stepped closer and tugged the projectile out, eyeing where it had pierced the second *a* in Atlanta. But where the other darts had entered the wall at an angle, this one appeared to have been deliberately put there, the pin deeply embedded.

He turned toward the sink where a box of unopened hair dye waited. Vibrant Auburn, the top read.

"I'm ready," Liz said from behind him.

Out of her line of vision, he tugged the Atlanta brochure from the wall and stuffed it into his jeans pocket. Then he briefly closed his eyes, almost afraid to find out what new way she had discovered to torture him. Clutching the darts in his hands, he slowly turned, letting out an audible breath when he found her dressed in a pair of baggy khaki shorts and a beige tank top, a crisp white blouse worn loosely over it.

Thong. The word popped into his head as he recalled exactly what Liz Braden had on under all those respectable clothes.

She grabbed her purse then faltered, catching sight of the darts he held. "What are you doing with those?"

He frowned. "I think the question here is what are *you* doing with these?"

"I'm not doing anything," she said, taking them away from him. "At least not anymore."

The high color in her cheeks told him all he needed to know: she had used the darts to choose her next point of destination.

He jostled her toward the door, made her lock up, then ushered her into the truck cab.

He tightly gripped the steering wheel to prevent the truck from bouncing out of one of the potholes directly into the thick brush on either side of the narrow drive.

"You know, you really should get somebody other than Old Man Peabody to look after this place for you," he said, trying to find a safe subject. She wasn't gone yet. And he'd be damned if he didn't try every trick in the book to get her to stay. He glanced over to find her tempting Goliath into her lap. The dog only too willingly agreed and blissfully tilted his head back to allow her to scratch his chin.

"Better yet, you should sell it," he said.

Out of the corner of his eye, he watched her cease movement. Goliath whined, upset by the cessation of attention.

Bull's-eye.

"Sell it?" she fairly croaked.

He nodded slowly. He'd long suspected that Liz hung on to the house as a safety net. Hell, even he'd clung to her ownership, hoping she'd someday come back. The mere prospect of her selling her grandmother's old place, cutting off all ties to Manchester, might be just the splash of cold water she needed to help her realize she didn't want to leave at all.

The stunned, hurt expression on her face nearly made him regret the suggestion, despite his intentions. Nearly, but not quite.

"If you're honest about your need to move on, to leave Manchester, then why are you hanging on to this old, decaying piece of the past?" He looked at her meaningfully. "Unless, of course, you do plan to stay."

Absently, she drew her fingers down Goliath's back, her gaze fixed on Mitch's face.

"You want me to sell the house?" she asked again.

He closely guarded his expression to keep his amusement from showing through. Looked like Liz wasn't the only one good at manipulation. "If you're leaving, then yes," he said finally. "Yes, Liz, I think you should sell the house."

He made a conscious effort to ease back his foot from the gas pedal. A dull pang of fear assaulted his stomach as he considered the possibility of her taking him up on his suggestion. The mere thought of the pile of lumber behind them not belonging to Liz anymore… Well, he only hoped he hadn't taken this thing too far.

HE WANTS ME to sell the house.

She really didn't know why his words bothered her so. But they did. Up until that point, she'd never really thought about Gran's place much. It was enough that she always knew it was there. Sell it? She'd never even considered the option. She absently scrubbed under Goliath's ears. She supposed circumstances might be different if she needed the money. But she didn't. Well, at least she wouldn't as soon as she had access to her accounts, which shouldn't be too much longer now.

Before she knew it, the McCoy place came into view. She scanned it, again noting the changes, yet cherishing the things that had stayed the same. She'd never thought of herself as particularly sentimental. Of course, there had been little opportunity for such emotion given her chosen lifestyle.

Now? Well, now she found herself sweetly bombarded with all things familiar.

What was it Gran had once said? You always had more fun remembering the events of your life than living them? Was that what was happening now? Was that why she was upset by the prospect of letting her grandmother's house go?

She glanced at Mitch and felt the expected jolt of fiery electricity dance along her nerve endings. Oh, she seemed to be enjoying the present just fine, thank you very much. She could just imagine what she would feel when she looked back on this brief time with Mitch again.

She wasn't sure what made this time different, somehow better, than when they'd been together before. Maybe it was because they'd finally slept together. Or perhaps they'd both grown up during their time apart. Yes, she'd loved Mitch then. But there had been so much uncertainty. So much about herself she didn't know and needed to find out.

Now….

Her throat tightened. Now, she suspected that love had never truly gone away. It had stayed locked up in a secret place in her heart, waiting until this moment to spring out and surprise her with its potency. The only problem was that in order to keep the woman she'd become intact, she had to move on. So much of her depended on her work. And Manchester just wasn't big enough to support her career.

"Your father's done a lot of work on this place, hasn't he?" she said, clearing her throat.

"Pops?" Mitch pulled onto the freshly raked, white-gravel drive that led to the house some hundred yards back from the road. "Pops wouldn't care if the ground opened up and swallowed the place whole. I bought my mother's family's part, the Connor division of the spread, from him a month ago, which includes the house. He still lives here, though. And all my brothers come back a lot. As you've already seen." He smiled wryly. "It was the only way my four brothers would tolerate the house changing hands, even though they had no interest in the money pit, as they call it."

She blinked. "This place is yours?"

"Yep. All one hundred and sixty-four acres of it."

Her hand halted on Goliath's soft fur. "I don't remembering it being that big."

"That's because it wasn't. Connor objected to my purchasing the McCoy part, which granddad used to farm, so I bought a large annex from the neighbors on the other side."

"Connor didn't want you to buy the old McCoy stretch? Is that house really still there? It was practically falling down when we were kids." She vaguely recalled it was miles on the other side of the property. It had taken her and Mitch nearly all morning to hike there once. Then neither one of them had had the guts to go inside. With its sun-bleached exterior and broken windows, she'd been convinced it was haunted. Needless to say, they'd never gone back.

"Yeah, it's still standing—barely—and, yeah, Connor objected. We're all still trying to figure that one out."

He pulled up to the side door of the impressive, two-story structure that was part of the old Connor spread and shut off the engine. Liz stared up at the house. What would Mitch want with such a huge place? From what she could piece together from memory, there were at least six bedrooms upstairs, a den, a full-sized family room, a sitting room she'd never entered, along with a formal dining room and an eat-in kitchen downstairs....

She turned back to find him watching her, the expression on his face curious.

"What?" she asked.

His grin made her go soft inside. "Nothing. Come on."

Liz followed him from the cab of the truck, holding the door so Goliath could jump out after her. She reached down and patted the dog, then he ran off toward the opposite side of the parking area. She watched him go, spotting a large fenced-in area where a mismatched menagerie of animals stood at attention, some wagging tails big and small, others chomping at the metal links penning them in.

She counted two goats, a mule, a pig, a St. Bernard and a cow, while just outside the fence lay three overfed cats, sunning themselves.

Mitch stepped over to the fence and fed the mule something from a bucket hanging on a nearby post. She could practically see his broad shoulders relax.

"I'm beginning to think I should start calling this place The Final Pasture," he murmured, drawing his fingers along the sleek nose of the mule. "I don't have any of these animals by choice. One of the goats I took off the neighbor's hands about a month ago when he said he couldn't handle him anymore. The mule came from Old Man Klammer. After that, it seemed everybody in town had an unwanted animal they needed to unload." He gestured toward the cats. "The black one I found in a box near the curb a couple of days ago, along with her six kittens." He scanned the freshly mown grass. "The little devils should be around here someplace. Sheba never leaves them too far behind."

"Sheba?"

"Yeah. You only have to watch her for a while to figure that one out." His grin rivaled the brightness of the sun shining over his shoulder. "If you're good, maybe I'll tell you the rest of their names."

Liz shaded her eyes with her hand, an agreeable tranquillity flowing through her. "So, time's a-tickin'. What did you want to show me?"

His grin widened. "Follow me."

CHAPTER TWELVE

HE HAD HIS WORK cut out for him, that was for sure.

Still, everything was going better than he'd planned so far.

Mitch leaned against the side of the new barn, crossing his legs at the ankles. He took a fresh look around him, drinking in his surroundings through another's eyes, namely, Liz's. And he liked what he saw.

What was not to like? In early July, central Virginia was at her most beautiful. Everything was green and lush. The air was full of the pungent smells of wildflowers and all things growing. The sky bluer than any he'd ever seen, with fluffy white clouds skidding across it. The rolling hills heading off to the west and the magical Blue Ridge Mountains.

He glanced back inside the barn where he'd left Liz patting the old pig he'd agreed to take from Old Man Peabody. He'd given her a tour of the house and quietly, careful not to appear too eager, shared all the plans he had to renovate the interior. He'd taken her out back to where he'd planted a half-assed vegetable garden and watched her pull a couple of weeds from between the crooked rows, her fingers looking at home in the rich earth. Then he'd led her through the barn, ready with the answers to her questions.

She hadn't begun asking those questions yet. But she would. He was sure of it.

When he'd sat down at the kitchen table last night to map out his plan, he'd called it the Seduction of Liz. But far from the physical connotations the title suggested, he was out to seduce her heart. He wanted her to remember that she'd once loved Manchester as much as he did. That she'd once loved him. Still did, if he was any judge of character. But he wasn't about to trust his judgment that far. It was enough to see her responding to his tour in the eat-everything-up way that she responded to everything else. In his estimation, it would only be a matter of time before she realized that this was where she belonged. Here. With him.

And that was his major enemy, wasn't it? Time. He restlessly pushed from the barn. With Ruth back at the diner, Bo soon to follow, Myra returned from her vacation and life pretty much back to normal in town, it was only a matter of time before Liz straightened out whatever mess she'd gotten herself into in Boston and moved on.

He couldn't let that happen.

LIZ LANGUIDLY WALKED down the long aisle of the newly constructed barn in the direction Mitch had gone. She peeked at the stall doors she passed, noticing they weren't mere chains blocking entrance or exit, but solid wood with places for brass nameplates. She slowed her stride and looked inside one, finding a fresh bed of hay blanketing the floor, and what looked like a feed bucket hanging just inside the gate.

A feed bucket? She tucked her hair behind her ear and continued toward the door. Probably where the mule slept.

As she neared the pool of sunlight streaming in from the towering, open doors of the barn, she stopped, her breath catching. The sight of dust motes floating in the shaft of warm light caused a surge of memories to burst forth in her heart rather than her mind. Memories of long, lazy summer days when she and Mitch would walk hand-in-hand in the cornfields, loll about in the grass, feed each other a light lunch Ruth would sometimes put together for them. How long ago that time seemed. Before she had earned her degree. Back before Gran had died. Before Mitch had proposed to her on the front steps of the general store because she'd found the ring in his pocket.

Someone sighed wistfully. She realized it was her. How simple life had been then.

She stepped into the light, then beyond, picking Mitch out instantly, crouched down near the bed of his truck. In one of his large hands were two-black-and-white puffs of fur. He was trying to coax a third out from under the truck with a length of rope.

Liz's stomach did an odd sort of somersault.

As she slowly made her way across the gravel toward him, she wondered exactly what Mitch's agenda was. First he'd suggested she sell Gran's house. Then he was showing her around his. Goliath bounded up to her. She petted him, her gaze fastened on the man across the drive.

Mitch pulled the rope out from under the truck, a brown-and-tan kitten clutched onto the thick cord in a mixture of fear and playfulness.

"There you are, Spike." He picked the tiny thing up with his other hand and brought it eye-to-eye. The kitty batted at his nose. "How many times have I told you and your siblings here that the truck is off limits, hmm? The last thing I want is kitty pancakes." The kitten burrowed into the side of Mitch's face, appearing to hug him close, rather than bat at him. It purred so loudly, Liz could hear it from ten feet away.

Oh, how good Mitch was at making her purr.

She cleared her throat.

Mitch looked over his shoulder at her, his grin widening. She noticed the warmth in his green, green eyes. And for the first time she wished she had a camera, to capture this unguarded moment.

He walked over to the fenced-in area and gently dropped the kittens inside, watching until they scampered toward their mother, who had eyed the entire rescue operation while bathing herself.

Liz tore her gaze away from his all-too-handsome face, feeling suddenly restless. She admitted to herself that one of the reasons she'd come out here today was to prove to herself that she still didn't belong. That the fears that had racked her seven years ago applied even today. She'd needed to prove to herself she'd done the right thing when she walked out on Mitch McCoy.

But she found comparing today's circumstances to yesterday's impossible. Mitch was no longer an FBI agent prone to long absences due to assignments. And she no longer thought herself a woman with no worth—she'd proven herself very capable of forging a good career and a life for herself…outside Manchester.

She briefly closed her eyes, then opened them again, focusing on the lush grass that seemed to stretch to forever behind the house. She tried to superimpose the image of her office in Boston. An office she would reconstruct in Atlanta. But her mind and heart weren't having any of it.

"Looks like a summer storm is brewing," Mitch said next to her.

Liz checked the southwestern horizon to find dark gray clouds resting on top of a sloping hill. She leaned next to him against the truck. Out of the corner of her eye, she caught him crossing his arms over his green-cotton-covered chest.

There were a few things that didn't completely jibe. Why would Mitch want to put fences up along his property line? Certainly he wasn't afraid of his crops running off. She absently rubbed her arms. Then again, she hadn't noticed any crops. When he'd said he'd bought his father's property, she had assumed he would take up farming. But she'd spotted no neat rows of corn dotting the horizon, or small, leafy bean plants covering the brown earth like nature's blanket. In fact, if she wasn't mistaken, the only thing planted was grass. Grass that appeared to have been mowed. She could imagine the size of *that* lawn mower.

"You're up to something, McCoy. I haven't figured out what yet. But I will."

"I don't know what you mean."

She smiled. "Sure you don't." She crossed her arms loosely under her breasts. He watched the movement a little too closely. "Tell me this, Mitch. You're a P.I. now, right? What, are you on vacation? Between jobs or something?"

He chuckled. "I'm more than between jobs, Liz. I'm retired. I still hold interest in a partnership in D.C. and I held on to a couple clients, but otherwise I'm…free."

She eyed him standing in the direct sunlight. Damn the man, but he looked better than any man had a right to. The breeze brought his soapy scent to her nose, his skin smelling as good as it had when he'd picked her up that morning.

It was then she put her finger directly on what was bothering her: her lack of knowledge of him. Not knowing what made him tick now. She'd been so wrapped up in stringing him along, struggling with her physical needs for him, she hadn't taken a closer look at him and what he'd become, beyond the obvious. But this uninterrupted time was giving her plenty of room to get to know this new Mitch. And she found herself more drawn to him than ever.

He gestured toward the truck. "Ready?"

She glanced at the red vehicle. "What? Day over already?"

"Oh, no. It's just getting started, angel."

She felt a peculiar little flutter in her belly as he put Goliath in the pen with the rest of the animals, then helped her into the cab. She flipped the sun-visor down and clicked open the vanity mirror. She noticed a smudge across the bridge of her nose. Now how had that gotten there?

Mitch climbed in next to her. The engine hummed to life.

He sat for a long moment, staring at her, then reached out a hand and thumbed her nose. She automatically tried to tug her head away from him, but he caught her chin.

"Would you hold on a minute?" he said, his voice rough and low. "I'm trying to get something off."

Liz held her head still, watching him dampen his thumb with his tongue, then rub at the spot on her nose. She fastened her gaze on his inviting mouth and wondered at the heavy staccato beat of her heart.

"Are you done yet? For God's sake, it can't be that big," she croaked. Another moment of him touching her, no matter how innocent the purpose, and she was afraid she'd straddle him right where he sat.

He drew his hand away and chuckled. "Guess I'm as done as I'm going to get, huh?"

Mitch backed out of the spot near the house. But instead of heading for the driveway and the road beyond, he pointed the nose of the truck in the direction of the fields behind the house. Liz gasped and grabbed the dash as the wheels left the gravel and bounced along the uneven grassland.

Surprised laughter burst from her throat. "Mitch! What are you doing?"

"You'll see soon enough. Why don't you just sit back and enjoy the ride?"

She flattened one of her hands on the ceiling of the cab to prevent her head from hitting the roof. How many acres had he said he had? One hundred and sixty or thereabouts? Why did she have the feeling he was going to ride over every single foot of that acreage?

And why in the hell was she liking it so much?

MITCH PATTED a spot next to him on the red-and-white checked blanket he'd spread beneath the overhang of trees. Liz caught her lip between her teeth, looking at him as if torn between wanting to make a sassy remark and needing to run.

"Don't tell me, McCoy. You have this picnic fantasy you want to play out."

He breathed a sigh of relief when the sassy remark won out. "Yep. And I've cast you in the starring role."

Her laugh was low and raspy as she sat down next to him. "I haven't been on a picnic since…"

Mitch opened the wicker basket Ruth had helped him put together that morning. He'd been banking on her not having been on a picnic for as long as he had—which would make it the week before their wedding seven years ago. He remembered that afternoon all too clearly. Not because of what was to come, but because they'd come very close to breaking their vow to wait until their wedding night.

He willed his growing erection away and reached into the basket.

"It's been a while for me, too," he said.

All her favorites. He'd gone all out to make sure he had

every last one of them. Lasagna in a warmer. Greens with olive oil and lemon. Fruity red wine. Crusty baguettes and soft white cheese. Tapioca. Everything a growing girl needed. He swept his gaze over her body where she rested back on her elbows, her ankles crossed over the edge of the blanket.

For long minutes neither of them said anything. Merely passed the dishes to each other and slowly devoured the food he'd brought along. Afterward, Liz helped him clean up, then lay against the blanket, staring up through the swaying tree branches.

He lay back with her.

"Now I'm really suspicious," she said quietly.

Mitch drank in her profile, wondering at the serious shadow in her hazel eyes. "Oh?"

She turned her head toward him. "One of the first pieces of advice I give to my clients is know your market. Be sure you know what you're selling, then package your product accordingly. Then target that market head-on."

He grinned. "I'm not selling anything, Liz."

She was silent as her gaze slowly scanned his features. "Oh, but you are, Mitch."

He folded his hands behind his head. "Maybe it's the wine, but I don't think I'm following you. What product? And what market am I targeting?"

In direct contrast to her serious tone, she got up on all fours, then straddled him. The feel of her soft feminine parts pressing against his hard—and growing harder all the time—male parts made him groan. She smiled and squeezed her thighs together.

"I find I can explain myself better if I have the audience's undivided attention."

Oh, she had his attention all right. But he didn't think it

was where she wanted it. He fought to keep his hands behind his head. Then again, maybe this tactic was purely diversionary in nature. If so, he was in deep trouble. Because with her moving her hips in that rhythmic way, he wasn't sure how long he'd be able to decipher her words.

A crack of thunder sounded off in the distance.

"Go on," he croaked rather than said.

"You see, I knew you were up to something, but I wasn't exactly sure what. At least not until you brought me here and opened that damn picnic basket."

She ran her hand down his T-shirt-covered abdomen, then slid it between them. Through the thick denim of his jeans, she found his erection, then positioned it so it ran the length of his zipper. She resettled herself, his hard shaft lining up neatly with the juncture between her legs. He watched her moisten her lips with the tip of her tongue and groaned.

"You've lost me again," he said, commanding himself to concentrate on what she was saying rather than what she was doing.

"All my favorites were in that basket, McCoy." She ground against him. Her shudder nearly shattered his best intentions.

"Your favorites...."

"Uh-huh." She braced her hands against his shoulders, her hair tumbling around her face. "You see, in that one moment, everything came together." His gaze flicked to where her breasts pressed against the thin cotton of her tank top. "I figured out that I'm the target audience." His control was dwindling fast. "And you're the product."

Liz's head felt light from the wine, her body on fire from being provocatively pressed against Mitch, but neither state completely stopped her thought processes. And she'd concluded that Mitch was playing her as adeptly as she'd been playing him this past week.

Thing about it was, his actions excited her all the more.

She leaned down and ran the tip of her tongue along his lower lip. When he tried to kiss her, she pulled away.

"Product?" he repeated.

"Uh-huh." She leaned down again, pressing her lips against first one temple, then the other. Mercy, he tasted good. "Only thing is—" she pulled back, directly meeting his gaze "—you don't have to sell yourself to me, McCoy. I already have my money out and ready."

Before she could blink, he had rolled her over onto her back. If there was such a thing as two people fitting perfectly together, then they were it. His hips fit just so between her thighs. His height was just right to allow him to kiss her while he also saw to other things.

He hungrily claimed her mouth, then pulled back. "Problem is, Liz, I'm not exactly sure what you're buying."

She tightened her legs around his waist. "This." She reveled in the sound of his deep groan.

He cupped her breast through her tank top. She caught her breath as she stared into the intoxicating depths of his eyes and heard him whisper, "That's not all I'm selling."

She kept her eyes open and watchful as he again dipped his head toward hers. She was still as he licked one side of her mouth, then the other. But when he fastened his lips over hers, she completely lost herself in his kiss, instantly forgetting why she had felt that momentary pang of panic.

Moments later, rain channeled through the sieve of the tree branches above them. For long moments, neither of them noticed—until a deafening crack of thunder sounded directly overhead. Reluctantly pulling apart, they gathered everything together and dashed for the truck.

CHAPTER THIRTEEN

MITCH GROUND the truck to a halt near the side door, shut it off and together they made a run for the small overhang protecting the steps from the elements. Liz felt the drop in temperature as she followed him through the mudroom into the kitchen of the large old house. Central air. She trembled. Not because it was too cold, but because her skin was damp. On the wall, she barely registered an old aerial picture of the house, likely shot from a crop duster.

"I plan to get an after shot taken once I get everything in order," Mitch murmured.

Liz shivered, finding his words didn't have to go too far to drift into her ear. He stood mere inches, if that, away from her backside, his breath teasing her neck.

"Order?"

"Uh-huh."

His nearness blocked out everything but the sensual heat that radiated from his tall, rock-solid frame behind her. He reached around her to open a drawer. The movement brought him flush against her, his erection pressing insistently against her bottom. Liz caught her breath, nearly groaning when he took two tea towels from the drawer then turned her around. Her gaze was riveted to the droplets of water clinging to his lashes while he languidly drew the soft terry along the side of her neck. The searing hunger in his eyes multiplied her state of arousal tenfold. Her knees weakened and she leaned back against the counter for support.

"Mitch?" she whispered, staring at his tempting mouth, longing clenching her stomach.

"What?"

He drew nearer and she swallowed hard, her heart pounding an uneven rhythm in her chest. "Do you have a thing for counters?"

His advance halted and his gaze flicked up to her eyes. "I'm thinking I must."

She parted her lips in anticipation of his kiss, a shudder running through her as a loud roar of thunder shook the floor beneath her feet.

"Me, too—"

His mouth descended on hers, trapping whatever other words she might have uttered under the welcome weight of his kiss.

A moan surged up Liz's raw throat. He tasted of red wine and smelled of soap, but the feel of his powerful body crowded against hers was one hundred percent pure Mitch McCoy.

A welcome shiver skittered across her skin as she wound her arms around his waist and dug her fingers into the flesh of his back through his T-shirt. Swiftly, his kiss grew more exacting, more dominating, seeking a response she was only too willing to give. Arching into him, she wanted more than the limited embrace allowed. Dragging her fingers down the length of his back to his sculpted rear, she pulled briefly away from the kiss, drawing a ragged breath.

Holding her gaze, Mitch nudged her knees apart with one of his, sliding his leg between hers. She whimpered deep in her throat, a slow burn starting at the contact of his leg against her pelvis. He tangled his hands in her hair, hauling her mouth back to his, his tongue delving deeper, challenging hers to a duel of passions.

She jerked her hands to his abdomen and restlessly tugged his wet shirt from the waist of his jeans, stopping only when her fingers rested against the hard, hot surface of his chest. The coarse hair felt marvelously tantalizing as she inched her fingertips toward his nipples, feeling them harden beneath her attention. Pulling her mouth from his, she fastened her lips around a tiny nub, generously laving one, then the other, reveling in the soft groan of pleasure she coaxed from him.

"Get up here," he demanded, grasping her shoulders and forcing her to eye level.

Her chest rapidly rose and fell as she drank in the devilish gleam in his intoxicating green eyes. She curved her fingers halfway around his thick, pulsing erection, frustrated by the heavy denim preventing her from making closer contact.

She heard the tearing of fabric, and jerked to find Mitch drawing the sleeve of her shirt down her arms, and ripping her tank top loose, gazing hungrily at the flesh he revealed inch by inch. He halted when the material skimmed over and past her right breast, exposing her frilly white bra, her pale pink aureola clearly visible through the lacy fabric. She pulled in a ragged breath, watching as he hesitantly brought his hand within millimeters of cupping her, then drew away.

When he fastened his mouth over her breast through the fabric, she gasped.

Unbearable heat gushed through her limbs, coalescing in

a monstrous pool in her lower abdomen. She moaned and pressed herself more powerfully against his leg, relishing the delicious emotion taking possession of her.

Another tear and her back-fastening bra popped open in the front. Through lowered lids, she watched him stare at her, grinning mischievously. "I always end up ruining your clothes, don't I, angel?" he murmured, running his hot tongue from one of her hardened nipples to the other, devouring both in one ravenous sweep.

An answering reply was on the tip of her tongue, but never made it past her lips as he thrust his leg more fully against her. She nearly shattered, gripping his shoulders to steady herself as he boldly plucked at her aching nipples.

The raw yearning that transformed his face as he gazed at her sent a new sensation skating down her spine—the powerful sensation of knowing she could imbue so much longing in him with merely a look. He slid his hands up from her waist, probing her rib cage, curving his fingers under each of her breasts and lifting them, marveling at the gentle slope of her tender flesh. Bringing his lips down, he covered her right nipple, tugging it into the depths of his mouth where his tongue stroked it.

The heat puddled in Liz's stomach changed into a terrible ache as the fingers of his free hand trailed a path down to her shorts. He lessened the pressure of his leg so he could outline the triangle of her engorged womanhood with his fingers. Liz bit down on her bottom lip, trying to slow down her climax, needing to wait until he could join her to give herself over to the delicious paroxysm.

When he cupped her in his palm and squeezed, her restraint vanished.

Liz exploded, liquid heat flooding her body. She gasped

in shock, writhing restlessly against him, thrusting her hands into his hair, pulling him closer, needing him closer still.

Her quivers subsided and she lessened the grip on his hair. He lifted to gaze at her, his eyes full of devilment.

"Nice to know some things never change," he murmured, flicking his tongue out and across her upper lip. "I could always make you come apart with one touch."

She nipped at him but he drew his tongue back into his mouth and grinned.

"Oh, but Mitch," she murmured, "I'm hoping you're going to do a whole lot more than touch me now."

His grin expanded and he hastily kissed her, then kissed her again.

"You have no idea," he whispered, wrapping his arms around her and thrusting the ridge of his arousal fully against her.

She shuddered and ripped at his shirt, yanking it halfway up only to restlessly abandon it to grope for the metal button of his jeans. Within moments, she had it undone.

His deep chuckle tickled her ear and he caught her hands. She stared at him, puzzled, until he broke away and started to lead her from the room.

Liz saw little on their rushed trip up the stairs to his old bedroom. She had a quick glimpse of an iron bedstead covered in a stitched, white coverlet, and four large windows that overlooked the front of the property, before he virtually flung her to the bed, then lunged on top of her.

The old bedsprings groaned beneath their combined weight, and Mitch grinned.

"You don't know how long I've fantasized about this," he murmured, catching her right earlobe between his teeth. "About having you stretched beneath me, just like this, on this bed." He slid the tip of his tongue inside her ear, causing her to wriggle fitfully against him. "Wondering what the springs would sound like when we made love."

Made love….

The words warmly invaded Liz's clouded mind. She savored the feel of him on top of her, forcing the air from her lungs, bracketing her body with his arms.

"Of course," he began, drawing back from her, "in my fantasies you're naked."

A low laugh vibrated her stomach. "That's easily fixed, you know."

He grinned.

She's incredible, Mitch thought, reluctantly rolling off her to lie on his side. He propped his head on his hand. Everything about Liz was incredible. From her magnificent blond hair, down to her purple toenails, she was one remarkable piece of work.

Teasingly reaching out, he peeled away what little remained of her top and her bra, then undid her belt. Flicking a gaze up to where she watched him with a sort of detached wonder, he slowly, with some help from her, dragged her shorts down past her slender hips, and over her legs, his gaze following his movements. He tossed the khaki material to the floor, then trailed his gaze back up to the naughty underwear she'd given him a flash of that morning. A streak of lightning brightened the dim bedroom, illuminating every precious millimeter of her. The resulting rumble of thunder mirrored the need coiling within him.

She squeezed her thighs together and shuddered, but he refused to let her stay that way for long, no matter how much he liked watching her. He spanned his fingers over her right knee, then slid them inward and upward, over the velvet of her inner thigh, and gently forced her legs apart. She hesitated, and he feared she might close them again, but then she relaxed, opening more than her body to him.

His hardened shaft twitched against his stomach as he stared at the scrap of lace and satin barely covering the dusky wedge of her womanhood before disappearing into the enticing crevice between her cheeks. *Oh, my, these things should be illegal.* Restraining himself, he hooked his index finger under the flimsy side string and tugged, fascinated, as she arched her back to make his task easier.

The moment the thong bikini hung from his finger well away from her lush, slick body, she curled against him, forcing him onto his back where she straddled him.

"I think you've stolen my reputation as a tease," she rasped, her hazel eyes wide and enchanting as she fumbled for his zipper.

She recklessly jerked his T-shirt, jeans and briefs off, her hot gaze taking in every inch of his exposed body from where she still hovered above him.

She began to straddle him again and he quickly grasped her wrists.

"Uh-uh, angel. This time I want to start things the old-fashioned way."

The fierce expression on her bewitching face told him he was in for an argument. He quickly flipped her over and covered the length of her. To circumvent the debate, he slid his fingers down the satiny skin of her belly, simultaneously claiming her mouth with his, swallowing her gasp as he probed her soft curls. Catching the velvety bud between his thumb and forefinger, he gently squeezed. She bucked from the mattress so wildly, he thought he'd caused her to climax again. But she was reaching for him, thrashing against him, drawing him nearer.

"Please…no more teasing," she whispered urgently. "I…can't take any more."

Slipping his fingers into her sleek aperture, his own body shuddered as he found her more than ready for him.

The shudder melted into a quake as she wrapped her fingers around his erection, grazing her thumb against the length before guiding him to press against her.

Reaching for and finding the box Jake had left for him, he quickly sheathed himself with a purple condom. Then he coaxed her open, clenching his teeth as her moist satin heat closed around the tip of his shaft. Exquisite sensation swelled through his body, and he grasped her hips, holding her still even as she strained upward against him. She was so exceptionally tight, so remarkably sleek.

He increased his grip on her hips and she whimpered, begging him to enter her more deeply, to satisfy the hunger raging through them both. In one smooth move, he granted her wish and plunged nearly all the way in, until he reminded himself that she needed time to grow accustomed to him.

She grasped his buttocks, pressing him down, her legs tangling with his, trying to force a deeper union. He gazed into her passion-glazed eyes and the jumble of hair around her face, thinking she truly was an angel. Shaping her wet mouth with his, he slid even deeper into her velvety depths, trapping her moans with his mouth, basking in the overpowering feeling of her surrounding him. Her sweet smell, her roving hands, her inviting body….

He released her hips and groaned when she thrust up against him with such urgency he almost lost it. It took every bit of his self-control not to give in to the glorious emotions roaring inside him as powerfully as the thunderstorm raged outside. But this slow stuff was not getting them anywhere. He withdrew halfway, then thrust into her with such abandon a sob ripped from her throat. Instantly, he feared he had hurt her. Then she gazed up at him and smiled, straining to meet him halfway when he withdrew again.

Together, they set a wild pace to their lovemaking, his ears filled with her passionate cries, his fingers stroking the soft flesh of her breasts, his mouth hungrily pulling at hers, his back enduring the sometimes violent grate of her nails. As the storm outside grew in intensity, so did his thrusts, a ball of fire amassing, burning a savage hole in his stomach, the pressure in his groin building to aching potency. No longer able to restrain the rush of climax, he grasped her hips and tilted them upward, allowing him to plunge deeper, farther. Her answering cry crowded all coherent thought from his mind and his muscles went rigid, held in awe of the feel of her convulsing profoundly around him, compelling him to fill her, demanding he follow her into the incandescent light that eclipsed all semblance of sanity.

As the shuddering of their bodies slowly subsided, and their gasps for air became manageable, Mitch lifted to stare into her face, smoothing her golden hair back. Her red lips looked well-kissed, her hazel eyes glowed in the aftermath of their lovemaking. She smiled, running her fingers over his sweat-dampened chest, down to where they were still joined.

"You know, sex like that is almost enough to keep me here," she whispered, lifting to press her lips gently against his.

He earnestly studied her in the dim light. "And if I told you I loved you?"

Outside the thunderstorm had passed, and the only sounds in the room were the lazy rubbing of her leg against his, and the ticking of his wind-up alarm clock.

He held his breath. Waited for her answer. This was it. This was the moment when he'd learn if she was his completely.

"Well," she said slowly, "I don't know, Mitch. Why don't you tell me and find out?"

She flexed her inner muscles around him and he groaned, feeling his erection grow within her.

She smiled wickedly, curving her fingers over his buttocks.

I just did tell you, his mind said even as his body took over. But he couldn't be sure if he'd said the words or not.

She pushed a fresh condom into his hands, then rolled over and got up onto all fours, straining her lush bottom against him. It was all he could do to shakily change the condom before thrusting into her with wild abandon.

This time there was no waiting, no hesitant attempt to take it slowly. He plunged deeply, reveling in the feel of her straining against him, taking every bit of him into her. He slid his hands to her shoulders, guiding her in a provocative rhythm. Through half-closed lids, he observed himself delving into her velvety heat, then retreating. He dragged his fingers down the column of her spine, watching as she automatically arched her back, her silken hair creating a fringed, golden curtain over her flawless skin. Clutching her hips fiercely, he gave himself over to the sensations pulsing through him, thrusting into her again and again until the world exploded in a bolt of wondrous, white light.

LIZ SLUGGISHLY DRAGGED herself out of the haze of slumber, the mattress beneath her unfamiliarly soft, the play of light on the opposite wall foreign. Next to her lay something warm and furry. At her start, Goliath whimpered, then licked her face. She sat up and the crisp sheet fell to her waist. A waist free of clothes, her bare breasts shimmering in the dim light wafting in through the windows.

"Mitch?" she whispered, finding the other side of the bed empty.

She hesitantly lay back down, not wanting to disturb the languid tranquillity saturating her tired muscles. Draping an arm across Goliath's back, she smiled, luxuriously reviewing the past few hours she and Mitch had shared...and back farther, to when she first returned to Manchester.

When she'd arrived, she remembered wondering if fate had somehow intervened in her life by tugging Mitch back into it.

She laughed quietly and closed her eyes, recalling the array of animals that called the new barn their home, the fence he was erecting around his property, the horse-breeding operation she suspected he planned to start. So different from the cold one she had forged for herself, his was a wonderful, seductive life full of peace and peppered with the excitement provided by the town's distinctive population.

It was a life she was growing to love more than she ever had before.

She went still, expecting the anxiety that had plagued her her entire life to claim her, the dubious voice in her head to tell her she didn't fit in, didn't belong here. Didn't belong anywhere.

The apprehension never came as she stared at the ceiling, transfixed. Is this where she belonged? Could this be the place she had always been destined to settle? The same place she had run away from so many years before?

After fighting the idea for so long, she found the concept incredible, astonishing.

Suddenly restless, she swung her feet to the floor and rummaged around for her panties. She came across Mitch's T-shirt and tugged that on as well, then padded toward one of the windows, open, letting in a muggy, after-storm breeze.

Shivering, she pushed aside the sheer, jumping when she spotted Mitch sitting on a stretch of tin roofing on top of the front porch overhang.

"Mitch?" she whispered. "What are you doing out here?"

He didn't answer. Instead, he scooted to the side, indicating she was welcome to join him.

Glancing down at his T-shirt skimming her thighs, then out to him wearing only his jeans, she carefully climbed through the window. The roof didn't slope much, just enough to let the rain run off, and the tin sheeting was cool and dry under her bare feet. She crouched down, tugging the cotton shirt to protect her bottom before sitting.

Resting her back against the house, she felt a rush of recklessness, of doing something outside the norm and having it appeal to her. Nearby, male crickets chirped, and the sweet, heavy scent of honeysuckle filled her senses. She smiled and shifted her head to stare at him.

She wanted to reach for his hand, but saw that he had both of them locked between his bent knees.

The crescent of moon winked out from behind a wisp of cloud, bathing the horizon in its silvery glow. Liz wondered at the furtive quality of the light, the way it outlined the trees and kissed the rolling hills like a fleeting lover. She sighed.

"This is nice." A sated yawn seized her and she quietly laughed. "How long was I asleep?"

He shrugged. "An hour or two."

She stared at him. "Have you been out here that long?"

"Nearly." He dragged in a breath and released it.

She looked back at the horizon, for the first time truly opening her heart to the stretch of land, much as she had opened herself to the man next to her. The sensation proved remarkably liberating, imbuing her with the strength of belonging.

She sensed his gaze on her and she turned to look at him. "What?" she asked, her cheeks heating as she fluffed her sleep-rumpled hair. "I look awful, don't I?"

He said nothing for a long moment, his eyes black in the silvery light. Finally, he shook his head. "No, Liz, you don't look awful. You look beautiful."

Which was part of the problem, wasn't it? Mitch thought. Liz had always been, and always would be, beautiful to him.

"What, exactly, do you have planned for the land?" She rubbed her palm against the edge of his T-shirt. "I mean, I didn't see any farm equipment in the new barn, and it's obvious you didn't plant this year." She looked at him. "Then there's the fence...."

He raked his gaze over her flushed face, but said nothing.

He'd thought she'd remember, if given the chance. Maybe he'd been wrong. They'd only talked once about his dreams while meandering through the neighbor's cornfields at harvest time. He might recall the conversation word for word, but there was no reason for her to remember it at all. After all this time and everything that had happened, perhaps it had been unreasonable to expect her to know what he had in mind.

"You're going to breed horses, aren't you?" she said, breaking the silence.

He relaxed against the house and grinned. "Yes."

She smiled back at him.

His grin slowly ebbed. Over the past eight months, all he'd planned, he'd planned to do alone. He hadn't counted on Liz rolling back into town. And he hadn't planned on loving her again. And with that love came the instant insertion of her into every aspect of his life. While touring the house, he'd readily discarded his ideas for decorating and instead wondered which color scheme and designs she would choose. He'd found himself thinking how his mother's old sewing room with the window facing the east would make a great nursery. When they'd toured the barn, he noticed how the back room would make a wonderful office for her to run the business end of things.

He tunneled his fingers through his hair restlessly. When he'd told her he loved her, she hadn't directly responded. Rather, she'd turned the tables back on him, then made sure he couldn't pursue the matter by distracting him with sex.

What she *had* said continued to demand examination: "Sex like that is almost enough to make me stay."

Almost.

Maybe it was long past time to admit that nothing could keep her here. That the ace he thought he'd held by opening up his life and dreams to her had turned out to be a powerless joker. And as soon as he figured out how to clear up the trouble she was in, she would drive out of town as easily as she had driven back in.

He couldn't believe he'd been so stupid. Again.

"Mitch? Is something wrong?"

"Wrong?" he repeated. "Yes. I suppose you could say that." *Talk about understatements.* He looked her full in the face. "Don't you think it's time you stopped stringing me along? Tell me, Liz, what in the hell are you running from in Boston?"

Her sexy smile threatened to chase all thought from his head. He battled the urge to haul her back inside and forget about why she was here. Forget about Boston and when she was going to leave. But he couldn't. Not anymore.

"I can't believe you're still worrying about that."

"Yes, well, I am. And I think it's time for you to give me reason to stop."

Twin beams of light cut through the darkness. He looked toward the road to find a car pulling up into the driveway, illuminating them where they sat on the roof. Liz tugged at the hem of her T-shirt and he cursed. Hell of a time for Pops to decide to come home.

The car stopped.

"That you, Liz?" his father called as if he'd just run into her on the street. "I'd heard you were in Manchester. Welcome home."

"Thanks, Mr. McCoy," she said.

The old man put his sedan into gear, continued up the drive and parked.

"I think we've just been busted," Liz whispered, leaning into him.

Mitch didn't respond. Couldn't respond.

"Is something wrong?" she asked quietly.

Everything's wrong, Mitch wanted to say. Instead, he stood up and offered her his hand. "Come on. Let's get you home."

MITCH WASN'T SURPRISED to find Pops waiting up for him when he returned from dropping Liz off. He stepped into the kitchen, acknowledged him with a nod, then poured himself a cup of the coffee that was always on the warmer when his father was home.

"Seems like old times, eh?" Sean McCoy said, taking a long sip from his own cup.

"Excuse me if I don't feel like talking right now, Pops. All I want to do is go to sleep."

With a move of his foot under the table, Sean pushed a chair toward him. "From what I can gather, you've been getting as much sleep as I have lately—which ain't much. Sit down."

Mitch looked at him over the rim of his cup, then sighed and took the chair. Saying goodnight to Liz without revealing what was going through his mind had to be one of the hardest things he'd ever done, especially since she was an expert at noticing change in demeanor. And, boy, had his demeanor taken a notable nosedive.

"So what's up?" Pops asked.

Mitch scrubbed his face with his hand. "Let's just say things are resembling old times a little too much."

"Ah." Sean sat back, looking at nothing in particular.

Mitch sat back as well, quietly examining his father. He'd been wanting to turn to him for counsel ever since Liz's return. This wasn't exactly what he'd had in mind. "Ah? Is that all you have to say?"

Sean shrugged. "Don't know that there's much more to say."

The house was quiet, nothing but the sound of the light summer breeze occasionally billowing the kitchen curtains, now that he'd turned off the air-conditioning and opened all the windows.

Maybe Pops was right. Maybe there wasn't much more to say. He'd known going into this that Liz's leaving was a probability more than a possibility. And when he'd made the decision to convince her to stay, he'd done so knowing his chances of success were marginal.

Still, it had been so easy for him to dupe himself into believing he'd made a difference. That her passionate responses to him were a sign that she was coming around. That this time they could make it work.

His chair legs screeched against the tile as he shifted uneasily.

He looked at his father. He needed something, anything, to get his mind off his own problems. "So what's been up with you?" he asked, figuring turnabout was fair play. Besides, Pops looked about as good as he felt.

Sean shrugged. "Not much."

Mitch grasped his coffee cup. "Could have fooled me. As much as you've been around here lately, I'd say a lot was up."

"*Was* being the key word."

He hiked a brow. It was then he realized Pops had made it home the past few nights. A little late, and he'd been gone even before Mitch got up in the morning. But he'd been home.

He took a long sip of coffee. Was it him, or was this conversation strange? Him and his father both down in the dumps because of women?

Mitch cleared his throat. No matter how uncomfortable it made him, he at least owed Pops a show of sympathy. "I'm sorry things didn't work out. You know. Between you and your…um, lady friend."

The sparkle of amusement returned to Sean's blue eyes. "Who said they didn't work out?" He ran a callused thumb over the rim of his cup. "Sorry to disappoint you, boy, but things with me and my 'um, lady friend,' are working out just fine, thanks for asking." His voice lowered. "Too fine, if you ask me."

Mitch grimaced. It was bad enough his father *had* a love life to talk about. That his should be succeeding where his own was not...

He silently cursed. Now what had caused that stupid thought to skid through his mind? "Ah," he said in much the same manner as Sean had.

Pops squinted at him, emphasizing the lines that fanned out from the corners of his eyes. "Now what's that supposed to mean?"

Mitch shrugged. "Oh, nothing. I'm just guessing that your lady friend must be pushing the commitment issue."

"Actually she's not. It's just gotten to that stage, you know, where you either decide to take things further, or you just drop everything altogether. You know?"

Yes, Mitch did know. All too well. "You mean, like letting your families meet each other. Little details like that."

Sean sat back and sighed. "Yeah. Something like that."

Mitch wondered if his father had been taking lessons from Liz on the art of ambiguity. "I don't know what the big deal is. I mean, sure, your seeing someone on the sly was a little surprising to all of us." He cleared his throat. "But if you're serious about this woman, then why don't you just bring her around for dinner one night?"

"It should be so simple." Sean got up and topped off his cup. Mitch waved him away when he moved to do the same to his. He had enough trouble sleeping. "I am assuming that either you or Liz must be pushing the commitment issue at this point." He retook his chair, the squeak of the old wood punctuating his sentence. "My guess is it's you."

"Kind of."

Sean frowned. "Well, either you are or you aren't. Which is it?"

Mitch's fingers tightened around his cup. Distantly he wondered if he could shatter the thick porcelain if he tried hard enough. And whether or not it would make him feel any better. "I've been thinking about, you know, the issue. But I haven't exactly said anything to the other party. At least not in so many words."

Sean merely stared at him. "I won't pretend to know everything that's going on here, Mitch. Because I don't. None of us knows what really happened between you two seven years ago. All I've got to say is that you should stop putt-putting around and use the good sense God gave you."

"Gee, thanks, Pops."

He waved off his remark. "What I mean is, you've got to decide whether or not to tell the woman how you really feel. Or…"

"Or?" Mitch prompted.

"Or live with the consequences."

If only he didn't believe the outcome would be the same either way.

The way he saw it, Liz had already made it plain as day that she was leaving again. He wasn't about to make an even bigger fool out of himself than he had before. Better he should let her think he didn't care one way or another about her leaving. Adios. See ya. It's been nice knowing you again. That kind of thing.

The funny thing was, coming to the decision didn't make

him feel any better. But at least he now knew what the future held. And for better or worse, it didn't include Liz.

He got up from the chair. "Thanks, Pops."

Sean blinked at him, clearly confused. "Sure."

CHAPTER FOURTEEN

THE FOLLOWING EVENING, Mitch sat at the counter at Bo and Ruth's Paradise Diner, his jaw clenched so tightly he thought he might grind his teeth to dust. The coffee before him was cold and bitter. And not even Ezra's jubilant disposition as he entertained the people crowding the eatery could lighten the leaden weight crushing his shoulders.

Ruth's dark head appeared in the kitchen window.

"Liz has got to come," she said as Bo stepped up beside her. "She has to or all my planning will be for naught."

"Wouldn't be the first time." Bo grimaced and scratched at a spot near his chest. Ruth swatted him, likely for the comment and for scratching the area that received the majority of the attention following his minor heart attack.

Mitch automatically lifted his coffee cup to his lips, ignoring Ruth's frown as she looked at him. For the past hour, the diner owner had been driving herself crazy with worry over whether or not Liz would swing by as she'd promised. It was all he could do not to remind her that Liz was infamous for not keeping her word.

According to Pops, she had called the house for him twice that day. And had swung by once. He'd been away at the vet's at the time, having taken the six kittens in for their first shots and their mother in to be spayed. Pops had just stared at him expectantly when he'd passed on the news. Mitch hadn't responded, though a part of him had wanted to ask for the details. How had she sounded? Did she leave a specific message?

He grimaced. What was it with him? Psychology had been part of his training at Quantico. He judged himself a hairbreadth away from being classified as some sort of masochist who was co-dependent on Liz's heartbreaking ways. An enabler who allowed Liz back in even knowing she was going to rip out his heart again.

The bell above the door clanged. He turned, half expecting to see Liz breezing in. Instead, he narrowed his gaze on a tall, blond guy who stood just inside the door, looking around the diner. Mitch judged him to be about his own age and height, but that's where the similarities ended. Where he was more comfortable in jeans and T-shirts, this one looked right at home in his dark Brooks Brothers tailored suit. He stiffened, then glanced through the window and caught a glimpse of someone familiar.

Outside stood that damn private investigator from Boston.

The P.I. met his gaze, then ducked off out of the line of vision. A moment later, Liz's old Pacer sputtered and coughed up to the curb.

Mitch absently scratched his head, wondering what the hell was going on. And whether or not he should do anything to stop it.

"Here she comes," Ezra called out.

The instant she entered, the packed diner erupted in a lusty, out-of-tune rendition of "Happy Birthday."

Everyone sang, Mitch noticed, except himself and the newcomer, who stood off to the side, a grin on his face, his arms crossed neatly over his chest.

Who was this guy? And why did he have the feeling he wasn't going to like him?

Liz appeared surprised and touched as Ruth and Bo carried out a gigantic cake in the shape of an angel, halo and all, from the kitchen. Mitch eyed the way the hand she lifted to her mouth trembled as the cake was held out in front of her, and he tensed against the sound of her sexy, throaty laugh.

The singing ended, and after a few robust shouts that she make a wish, silence took over.

And Liz stood completely still. Mitch realized it wasn't because she didn't know what to say, but because she'd noticed the guy standing off to the side.

Mitch shifted on his stool as her gaze sought and then found his. He told himself to turn away. Told himself to keep it light, keep his feelings to himself until after the celebration. But he couldn't. He met her questioning gaze with his stony one. Then he watched her pale.

"Blow out the candles, Liz," Ruth urged.

"Yeah, all thirty of them!" Moses Darton called out.

"You would have to remind me of the number, wouldn't you, Ez?" Liz's gaze flicked around the room, gratitude mingling with confusion in the hazel depths of her eyes. Mitch cleared his throat and stared at his boots, not looking up again until he heard the sound of her blowing out the candles moments later.

Clapping and roars of approval filled the diner and Bo and Ruth shifted to put the cake on a table. Ezra stepped up to Liz, draping an arm over her shoulders.

"I'd like to say one of your birthday gifts is the return on your wager," he said. "But truth is, you lost this time around."

Her gaze snapped to his so quickly, Mitch didn't have time to avoid it. He grimaced and shook his head, trying to dispel the challenge in her eyes by indicating he hadn't said anything. He hadn't had to. Pops hadn't been the only one on the road last night. From what he could gather, the Darton brothers had gotten an eyeful of him kissing Liz goodnight when he'd dropped her off. And they'd told everyone who'd listen.

"Gifts! Gifts!" Myra shouted, giving her friend a bear hug, then thrusting a small package into Liz's hands.

The stranger stepped into the center of the room, next to the cake. "Please. I'd like my gift to be first."

The diner lapsed into a silence so complete, Mitch could swear he heard Liz's heart beating.

She looked down at her feet. Everyone was expecting her to say something. And Mitch didn't think 'thanks for the cake' was going to cut it.

"Um, everyone, I'd like you to meet Richard Beschloss. My, um, former fiancé from Boston."

Former fiancé? Mitch eyed the man again, finding he was right. He didn't like the guy. Not one bit.

At the same time, though, two other realizations materialized. Number one, the guy was alive. Number two, Liz hadn't married him.

Both made him feel as if a fifty-pound weight had been eased from his chest. They also made him feel like the biggest sucker this side of the Blue Ridge Mountains.

The rich guy cleared his throat. "Sorry to crash your party, Betsy." Mitch tensed to the point of shattering at the use of the name. "But when I found out where you were, I felt compelled to come and give you this." He held out something. It looked suspiciously like a purse.

Liz took it. "I don't know what good this is going to do me if my accounts are still frozen."

"They're not. Not as of half an hour ago." He shrugged his expensively clad shoulders. "Sorry I didn't do it sooner. I wanted an opportunity to apologize to you for my behavior in person. The only way I could do that was by limiting your resources."

"You're apologizing to me?"

Beschloss toyed with his tie. "Yes, I am. I know I was a real jerk when you said you couldn't marry me. Instead of threatening you with a lawsuit for breach of contract and assault, and freezing your accounts, I should have thanked you. You were right. We'd have only made each other miserable."

Miserable. Now that was a word. Mitch grimaced then thrust his fingers through his hair. *Miserable* about summed up what he was feeling right now.

He couldn't believe he'd gotten so worked up over something so simple. Liz had refused to marry Mr. Rich. He'd threatened her with a lawsuit. She'd decked him. Mr. Rich had frozen her accounts.

He was such a fool.

Liz silently went through her purse, then slung the strap over her shoulder. "Does this mean you dropped the assault charges?"

Mitch watched Beschloss raise his hand to his nose. "They were never officially made. Sure, I contacted the police, and they did some asking around. But Father was afraid that if I signed anything, it would be all over the tabloids the next day."

Liz bit her bottom lip in the way that drove Mitch crazy. "I guess I'm now the one who should be apologizing. I'm not usually a violent person. You must have had a hell of a time explaining that broken nose."

Down the counter from Mitch, Moses Darton elbowed his brother and snickered.

Surprisingly Beschloss chuckled. "Actually, you ended up doing me a favor. I'd broken the damn thing winter before last on the slopes of Vermont. The doctor said it never healed quite right. Your punch…well, it kind of knocked it back into place."

Liz's laugh tinkled through the diner. "Well, if you need any help knocking anything else back into place, you let me know, huh?"

The look in Beschloss's eyes was a little too warm. A little too damn intimate. Then he bent down and kissed Liz. He lingered a little too long for Mitch's liking. He started to get up from the stool, but Bo held him back.

"It's on the cheek," Bo told him. "Just cool your heels, McCoy."

Mitch forced himself to turn back to his coffee, unable to watch.

A moment later, he heard the cowbell clang again. A glance verified that Beschloss was climbing into a late-model sedan driven by the Boston P.I.

The drama over, Myra stepped forward again and shook her dark head. "Geez, woman, if that guy and Mitch are your throwaways, you're doomed to be alone forever." She thrust her gift into Liz's hands. "I don't know if this can compare to what just happened, but take it anyway."

Mitch's gaze slammed into Liz's. She blinked several times, as if trying to see his thoughts. Then Ruth patted him on the back and set a healthy helping of the chocolate cake and vanilla ice cream in front of him. His grimace deepened. They'd given him the damn halo.

"And this one's from Mitch," added Myra.

FOR THE FIRST TIME in her life, Liz didn't know what to do.

She stared at the wrapped box in front of her, then at the man whom it was from.

Ever since last night on the roof, she'd sensed a distance between herself and Mitch. A distance that had grown even more pronounced when he'd dropped her off at Gran's house. Oh, yes, he'd kissed her until her toes curled. That hadn't been the problem. That he had looked at her so seriously, almost grimly, had. And when he'd said goodbye…well, she couldn't help thinking it had been one of those forever kind of goodbyes.

Then she got the very distinct impression that he'd been avoiding her all day.

And now this.

After all his probing and prying into her life over the past ten days, she would have expected him to leap from the stool and grill Richard like a murder suspect. Instead, he just sat there looking on, as if he didn't care one way or another about the truth the unexpected encounter had revealed.

Liz sought his gaze, but found him sitting stiffly at the counter, his back to her. His odd behavior made her dread even more opening the box in front of her.

"Well, go ahead now, open it," Ruth encouraged.

Surprised to find her fingers shaking, she carefully opened the ends of the red-and-gold wrapping, no longer able to put off finding out what lay inside the box.

Her heart thudded painfully against her rib cage. What she discovered was that the item wasn't in a box at all. The box was the gift. More specifically, the sturdy, leather suitcase was. She looked up to find that Mitch had finally turned her way.

"Open it," he said quietly, the stony expression on his face warning her against following his directive.

Ezra stepped up from where he was taking bets on Lord knew what. "Yeah, open it."

Hesitantly, she unzipped the piece of luggage, holding her breath as she stared at the plain white envelope lying inside. She opened it. Inside was a fresh array of bills.

Ezra peered over her shoulder, puzzled. "It's the money he won on the bet."

Crumpling the envelope in her hands, Liz stood rooted to the spot. Unable to blink. Incapable of drawing a breath.

The reason she had thought Mitch's goodbye last night was so final was because it had been.

THE FOLLOWING MORNING Liz sat numbly on the floor of Gran's kitchen, her hands clasped tightly between her raised knees.

Gran's kitchen.

She took in the yellowing walls, the outdated appliances, the chipped linoleum floor. That's exactly what this place was, and would always be: Gran's house. A place where she had spent her summers. A collection of rooms chock-full of memories. While it had been the only constant during her otherwise unsettled life, the neglected old house had never been home.

Liz forced herself up from the floor and crossed to where all her belongings were neatly stacked on the narrow counter. Belongings that included the precious few things she'd collected when she was younger but had never taken away because she had always thought the place would be there.

She fingered a faded blue ribbon she'd won in a spelling bee at the Manchester County Fair when she was twelve.

Her heart expanded and tears flooded her eyes. Mitch was right. She needed to sell the house. To finally close the door on a past that was better off forgotten. Especially now that she knew Manchester no longer held anything for her.

Scanning the barren room, she picked up the suitcase Mitch had given her and began piling the few clothes she'd bought inside.

She didn't know what, exactly, had happened with Mitch. One minute everything was perfect, then the next...

The next he acted as though none of it mattered.

Could it be as she suspected after their first time together at the diner? That his intention all along had been to get what he couldn't have seven years ago? She tightly closed her eyes, thinking about how willing a participant she'd been. She honestly didn't think the words *casual sex* were part of his vocabulary. After all, he'd waited how long before their wedding night?

A night that had never come.

She bit down hard on her bottom lip. She supposed that maybe this was exactly what she deserved for having done what she had so long ago.

She slowly pushed her hair back from her face, and swiped at an errant tear. At a couple of weak points during the day, she had hoped Mitch would come ambling through the back door, that endearing mischievous grin on his face. Give her a cocky "Well, how did that feel, Liz?" Then she would whack him and forgive all. It was the only reason she had stayed through the morning rather than waiting at Dulles airport for the first flight out to Atlanta. But his crushing absence from her doorstep told her it wasn't going to happen. He had meant what he said, and the only thing left for her to do was leave.

She laughed caustically and folded the top of the bag.

Who was it who had said Manchester was but a pit stop on her way to another city? Was that her? Not that she noticed that person anymore. She now knew that the instant she'd run into Mitch on that deserted road, she had reached her final destination.

Taking one last look around the kitchen to make certain everything was in order for the Realtor she planned to contact, she grabbed the bag and stepped toward the mudroom. The setting sun slanted through the open door, shining a spotlight on one of the red shoes she had worn into town.

She reached over and plucked it up off the floor, unable to locate the other. It occurred to her that the shoes were her running shoes. No sneakers for her. When she left some place behind, she did it in style. She should have known the instant she traded her white satin pumps for her red shoes the morning she was supposed to marry Richard that she wasn't going to exchange wedding or any other vows that day. She stared down at her beige macramé sandals that matched her tan skirt and blouse and frowned. She was ruining her image. At any rate, she was tired of moving around. Come what may, the instant her plane touched down in Atlanta, her feet would never leave the ground again. Emotionally as well as physically.

Tugging the door closed and stashing the key on the nearby window ledge, she headed toward her Pacer, tossing the lone shoe into an empty trash can as she passed.

CHAPTER FIFTEEN

COULD THINGS get any worse?

Liz stood in front of the baggage-claim conveyor belt, then looked at her watch. There was no way in the world a puddle-jumping flight from D.C. to Atlanta should have taken so long. But, as the pilot had informed them when they started to make their descent into the southern capital, due to a violent line of thunderstorms, their plane had been rerouted...through Detroit. *Detroit,* for crying out loud. A destination two hours in the other direction. Tack onto that the one-hour take-off pattern after they had landed, and another two to make it back to Atlanta, and she was suffering from a major case of airplane sickness. Not the kind that required a small paper bag, but that necessitated getting far, and fast, from any and all airports.

Heaving a hefty sigh, Liz watched the same luggage make the rounds again, hers nowhere to be found. When she'd left Virginia, the sun had been shining....

For the tenth time in as many minutes, she found herself wondering what Mitch was doing. And for the tenth time she ordered herself to stop it. She didn't care if he was at the diner chatting it up with Bo and Ruth. Or home with his father and whichever brother or brothers had decided to drop in. She didn't want to think of him feeding his mismatched menagerie of animals, or throwing fresh straw in the stalls in preparation for the thoroughbreds he'd soon be breeding there. Or how much she would like to breed with him. In fact, she didn't want to think about him at all.

Liar.

All she yearned to do was think about Mitch. She wanted to check into a hotel room, put the Do Not Disturb sign on the door, order up everything room service had to offer, raid the mini bar and pretend clocks didn't exist until the acute ache in her heart began to ease. Only she thought that the ache might never ease. She didn't have enough resources for never. But she could swing a good month if she had to.

She finally spotted what she thought was her suitcase being spit out by the luggage monster. As the bag slowly made its way toward her, she hoped the limo service had been able to arrange for someone to meet her. "Can't promise anything," they'd told her. "Seems everyone and their brother wants a limo today, what with the concert and all." She hadn't bothered to ask what concert.

She eyed her new suitcase. It was so battered, she questioned ownership, and almost didn't reach out in time to grab it. A man helped her, mumbling something about stupid females in response to her thank you. She ignored him and hurried for the door.

Through the crush of people, she searched for the white sign with her name on it. Please let them have sent someone. She really didn't feel up to waiting for a taxi in the rain. Then again, if it got any wetter, she could just float to her hotel.

Someone bumped into her from behind, forcing her into the person ahead of her. Her breath rushed from her in a sharp whoosh and her suitcase slid from her grasp. She watched in paralyzed horror as it skidded across the marble tile, thunked down onto its side then sprang open.

At the same time, she spotted the sign with her name on it. Good, someone had made…

She froze. Slowly she read the sign a second time. Elizabeth/Betsy/Liz Braden was written across it crookedly in black marker.

Her heart skipped a beat. Then another. But she couldn't seem to take her gaze from that sign, even when the person holding it lowered it to hip level.

She moaned aloud. She'd recognize those jeans-clad hips anywhere.

Mitch.

Mitch shifted his weight from one boot to the other. *Come on, Liz, look at me, damn it. I have to know my coming here isn't another in a long line of major mistakes.*

She had yet to lift her gaze to his face.

He squared his shoulders and stood a little straighter. Mistake or no, he wasn't going anywhere. He'd camp out on her doorstep if he had to, he didn't care. Because sometime between last night and this afternoon, he'd realized he hadn't been a fool for loving her. He'd been a fool for never letting her know how much he loved her. How much he needed her in his life.

Of course, the realization had come after Pops had practically shouted, "You did *what?*" at him when he told the old man what had happened. Then Sean had let him in on exactly how he'd misread his advice two nights before. When he'd said he should be prepared to live with the consequences, he'd meant *after* he'd told Liz exactly how he felt. And didn't it just beat all that he was sitting back like a dumb fool as the love of his life left town…again.

Of course, he'd only felt lousier after the talking down. And it had taken him a whole hour of pounding fence posts into the ground a mile away from the house before he figured everything out.

Liz hadn't had to come back to Manchester…she'd *chosen* to.

Even though Liz's accounts had been frozen until yesterday, she'd had the resources to leave town after selling her Lexus…but *hadn't*.

Liz hadn't said she didn't love him, he had *assumed* she didn't…even though every gut instinct he'd ever had told him differently.

And when Liz had said "sex like that is almost enough to keep me here," that hadn't meant she was leaving. It had meant she was waiting for him to offer her another reason to stay.

And, like an idiot, he'd instead given her every reason to leave.

He bit back a curse. Damn him and his stupid pride. He'd been so afraid of history repeating itself that he'd basically guaranteed that it would.

Finally, Liz's gaze moved up his torso, lingered on his neck, then shifted to his face. She looked like she'd been through hell and back. And she'd never looked so damn beautiful.

He gave her the biggest grin ever, dropped the sign and held out his arms. She catapulted toward him so fast, she got her shoe caught in her open suitcase and he had to catch her before she hit the hard tile headfirst.

She stood back to look in his face. "How did you know where I was? How did you get here before me?" She waved her hand in the air. "Forget the second question. You probably could have driven here faster. Just answer the first."

He slid the brochure he'd taken from her wall from his pocket and put it in her hand. "Remember this?"

She sighed and flung herself into his arms again.

He held her so tightly he was afraid he'd snap her in two. "Lord, woman, do you have any idea how much I love you?"

Liz kissed him. On the mouth. On the chin. On the brow. "Not half as much as I love you, McCoy." She drew back and slugged him in the arm. "Now what in the hell took you so long?"

He chuckled. She hit him again. He grasped her wrists and hauled her until she was flush against him. "Know of any good hotels in this town?"

Her eyes narrowed even as she ran that naughty little tongue of hers across her lips.

"A hotel with a grade-A jeweler in the lobby?" he added.

She didn't say anything for the longest time. Then a smile slowly spread across her face. "Ask me, Mitch."

He cleared his throat. "Should I get down on one knee?"

She struggled against his hold, presumably to hit him again.

"All right, all right." He planted his boots solidly on the floor. Gave his head a toss to loosen the kinks in his neck. Then he gazed deep into her eyes. Eyes he hoped he'd be looking into for the rest of his life. "Will you marry me, Elizabeth/Betsy/Liz Braden?"

She kissed him so hard, so thoroughly, he wanted to tug her into the nearest men's room and have his way with her in one of the stalls.

"Yes, Mitch McCoy, I'll marry you."

He gathered her close and took a deep breath of her sweet-smelling hair. It was then another realization dawned. The excitement he'd been seeking in his life could never be found in any job. That's why he'd quit the FBI, retired from private investigating. And he knew now he wouldn't have found it in horse-breeding, either. Liz was the only one who could provide the kind of excitement he was looking for. The only one capable of keeping him guessing, keeping him running, keeping him attuned to what life and love were truly all about.

"Does this mean we can go home now?" she asked.

He swept a damp tendril of hair back from her face. "Yes, angel, it does."

EPILOGUE

WHAT A DIFFERENCE three weeks makes.

Mitch stood at the end of the aisle, tugging at his bow tie. Jake stood next to him, once again playing the role of best man. Every chapel pew was filled to capacity, the occupants, decked out in their Sunday best, waving fans or songbooks to combat the heat. He was somewhat relieved that he wasn't the only one who felt like he was on a hot plate. But the sweat dotting the back of his neck had very little to do with the fact that the small chapel wasn't air-conditioned.

Could it be that he'd suddenly developed a case of stage fright? He realized his uneasiness had very little to do with standing up in front of a crowd, really. What made him feel like rushing for the door and hurling behind the nearest bush was being in front of *this* crowd, prepared to marry the *same* woman…and being scared to death that the same damn thing would happen all over again.

He nearly groaned.

Pops motioned to him from the front pew, indicating his tie was crooked. Mitch toyed with the stiff material until Sean nodded.

God, everything about this day eerily mirrored that life-altering day seven years ago. Even the townsfolk seemed to be sitting in the exact same spots they had been back then.

Liz's mother Sunny sat up front and center on the bride's side, looking more like Liz's sister than her mother in her crinkled skirt and tank top. The Darton brothers fidgeted in what had to be the same brown suits near the back of the chapel. Ruth sat smiling at him from the bride's side. Ezra poked someone in front of him, likely hammering out the details of his latest betting pool. Even Josiah stood quietly in the back, having relinquished his rocking chair in front of the general store for the day.

Then there was his family, the McCoys.

Aside from Jake, who stood next to him, they sat in the front right pew. He caught Pops's gaze and swallowed so hard the old man must have heard it, because his grin widened. He still hadn't found out exactly who Sean McCoy was dating, none of his brothers had, but they weren't going to stop until they came up with a name.

Connor sat to Pops's right, his attention more on his watch than the events around him. Mitch glanced at his own watch, the heat factor vaulting higher as he realized they were already running ten minutes late.

Despite his initial attempt to laugh it off at the house, Connor was the one who took the news of Pops's secretive, apparently serious, dating the hardest and let Pops and everyone know it. Before the ceremony, he'd heartily slapped Mitch on the back and offered his condolences. Despite his anxiety, Mitch cracked a smile. Leave it to Connor to equate marriage with death. Out of the five of them, Connor seemed to be the one who took seriously their childhood vow never to marry.

His gaze slid to Jake, and he amended his assessment. Jake took everything way too seriously. Tall and sober, he was the only one who looked comfortable in the monkey suit he wore. Not surprising. If it was confining and required rules to work, wear or eat it, then Jake was right at home. At one point, dyed-in-the-wool Trekkie Marc had nicknamed him Spock. But it hadn't stuck. Could have had something to do with the chokehold Jake had put on him. It wasn't so much the physical act that had nipped the name-calling in the bud. It was the calm way Jake had done it: one minute he'd been passing Marc in the hall, the next Marc had virtually been part of the wall.

Next came David, who elbowed Connor in the ribs and whispered something. Connor gave him a threatening look and David laughed. Mitch guessed being the youngest gave David much of his cocky confidence. They all took more guff from him than they'd ever taken from one another. As he looked at the great-looking blond kid—kid? Sheesh, he had to be pushing thirty—he sometimes wondered if they'd all been raised in the same household. It was more than the physical characteristics that made them different. Where he and the others had always been cautious in their relations with women, David had pretty much compensated by dating so many women they had stopped trying to keep track of their names long ago. Then again, his youngest brother's approach might be different, but it ultimately found him in the same spot as Connor and Jake—unmarried.

His gaze fell on Marc. Some of the tension melted from his shoulders. Where everything else was essentially the same as seven years ago, here was a palpable difference. Go figure. Marc was not only married, he was due to be a daddy in a few short months. And while his and Melanie's honeymoon had been a disaster, all one had to do was watch them watching each other to know that those two had the stuff it took to make it.

The first opening strains of organ music snapped his attention away from his family and back to the unbearably long aisle in the small chapel. He slipped a finger under his bow tie and tugged, then felt it to make sure it was still straight. Myra's wiry form filled the doorway, festooned in purple satin from head to toe. Mitch didn't know if it was just him, but Myra seemed determined to take an inordinate amount of time stepping down the flower-strewn aisle. *Baby steps,* he thought. She was taking baby steps. If he didn't know better, he'd think she was deliberately trying to delay things….

Behind her, Bo came into view. Mitch nearly slumped in relief at the appearance of the short, beefy cook. With no male family members of her own, Liz had again asked the gregarious Bo to give her away. A role Bo readily agreed to play.

Finally, Myra stood across from him and the organist began pounding out the "Wedding March."

Mitch's heart skipped one beat, two, then beat so loudly, he could hear nothing but its throbbing tattoo. Bo looked behind him, then quickly to his left. When he turned to face the chapel again, a panicked expression creased his aging face. Mitch's stomach bottomed out.

Oh, God, she's going to do it again.

Sensing that something was amiss, a low murmur began among the guests. A hum that mimicked the ringing in Mitch's head. Out of the corner of his eye, he saw Connor begin to get up, then Pops slap a hand on his arm. Bo disappeared from the door and the din in the chapel grew to a noisy roar. Even the organist stopped playing.

A sudden, suffocating silence settled over the room as, one by one, the guests turned their solemn eyes to him.

The past was playing itself out all over again. His feet

seemed cemented to the spot up to his knees. His body eerily frozen. He could do nothing but stare at the spot where his bride should have appeared ten minutes ago. Nothing….

Then came the unmistakable rustle of fabric.

"Aw, Lizzie, you're going to rip the damn thing." Bo's voice wafted down the aisle.

Everyone snapped their attention back to the still-empty doorway. Mitch's gaze had never moved.

"To hell with the dress, Bo, I've got a groom to marry."

Then, suddenly, all that was Liz filled the doorway. Yards upon yards of puffy white fabric swirled around her figure, hugging her in all the right places. Mitch blinked once, twice, certain he was seeing things. Then Liz nearly fell to the side before Bo steadied her. It was then that Mitch noticed she was tugging on her skirt. A loud ripping rent the air, finally freeing the material from where it was caught on the heel of her right shoe. Ah, but they just weren't any old shoes. Mitch felt a grin begin to edge across his face when he spotted the purple skyscrapers that came into view as she grabbed her skirt in both hands and lifted the material free.

His gaze slammed into hers. She was flushed, but the sparkle in her hazel eyes nearly knocked him over. Before the organist could even resume playing, she started toward him, her step quickening the closer she got, until she was at nearly a full run by the time she crashed into him.

Mitch caught her shoulders to steady her, his fingers digging into her soft flesh beneath the ruined dress.

"Sorry I'm late. I ran into, um, some problems." Her voice was breathless and emotion-filled. Mitch's heart again skipped a beat. But this time it was for all the right reasons.

"I was afraid…I mean, I thought…"

She laid a white-gloved finger against his lips. "Shh."

The pastor cleared his throat. "Ladies and gentlemen, we are gathered here today—"

When Mitch hauled Liz against his chest, a collective gasp filled the chapel, along with a few awkward chuckles. "What say we get this over with, angel? Say 'I will.'"

Liz blinked at him several times. Then realization dawned on her sweet face. She smiled. "I will."

"Me, too." Together they pushed and tugged and pulled until her veil was lifted and lay askew on her head. Then he did what he hadn't been able to wait to do: he kissed her. Truly, madly, deeply kissed her. His intention was to make those toes of hers curl inside those purple things she called shoes.

EZRA'S TRIUMPHANT SHOUT filled the otherwise silent chapel, followed by low groans. Liz reluctantly allowed Mitch to tug his mouth away from hers, welcoming his quick nip after he pulled away.

"All right everybody, pay up," Ezra said, racing around the chapel and snatching the bills nearly everyone pulled from their pockets.

Liz blinked. "What's going on?"

Mitch tightened his arms around her, his nearness warming her. "I don't know, but somehow I think our bet wasn't the only one going on around here."

Ezra hooted and counted out some of his winnings, handing a portion to Ruth. "Mitch, my dear boy, you're darn right there was another bet going. It started the moment you ran into Liz on that dark road." He grinned and hugged Ruth to his side. "This fine lady here and I started the wager that you two—" he shook a finger at them "—would end up married yet."

Mitch chuckled and buried his face in Liz's neck.

"Liz?" he murmured.

She entangled her fingers in his soft hair. "What?"

"I need you to do me a favor." He glanced up at her, his gaze serious. "I need you to get rid of that damn suitcase I gave you. 'Cause angel, you won't be needing it anymore."

Her laugh mingled with the boisterous conversation swirling around them.

Oh, yes, this was definitely different from what had happened seven years ago, Mitch thought. And he liked this much, much better.

There was no escaping it. He was, and always would be, the spy, P.I.... Oh, hell, just the plain old guy who loved her.

FOR HER EYES ONLY

CHAPTER ONE

"JAKE, DO I EVER HAVE THE woman for you...."

Jake McCoy tucked his chin toward his chest and squinted against the September morning sunlight. If any words could put the fear of God into him, those were it. Melanie, his younger brother Marc's new wife, had said them at the McCoy place last night—right after his other brother Mitch's new wife, Liz, took a perfectly good chicken and mutilated it beyond recognition for Sunday dinner.

His measured footsteps echoed off the asphalt of the parking lot across the street from the Immigration and Naturalization Service field office building in Arlington, Virginia. He hadn't responded to Mel's frightening proposition. Marc had answered for him, reminding his pregnant wife that Jake wasn't interested in a woman. That none of the McCoy men were. They had to be bitten in the ass before any of them would even consider the idea of marriage.

Jake had been embarrassed by the resulting laughter.

Then again, how was Marc to know how very close he'd come to getting married? Long before his younger, brash brother had even had his first sexual experience.

He tightened his grip on the files he held in his left hand, then absently moved his other hand to pat the breast of his jacket. Perhaps *close* wasn't exactly the word for his only brush with the M word. *He'd* been close. The woman he'd been dating, Janice Tollerby, was shocked when he'd pulled out the simple gold ring and proposed on their fourth date.

He still couldn't figure that one out. He'd known on their first date that he and conservative Janice could form a workable union. It was unimportant that he was new to the dating scene and that they hadn't known each other long.

For the first time he'd cut loose, taken a chance. And for the second time, he'd lost an important woman in his life.

He'd never taken a risk like that again.

He was a simple man, with simple tastes. He respected and appreciated routine, stability, discipline. He got up every morning at five-thirty, no matter what time he made it to bed. His need for simplicity was what led him to work for the INS. Those who didn't belong within the country's borders, or were no longer welcome, he sent home. Couldn't get neater than that. In fact, if not for his brothers, he'd probably never use any of his vacation time. It was difficult for him to justify leaving important cases in limbo even for a day. In an unpredictable world, he liked predictability. It comforted him to find the same selections in his refrigerator. When he replaced his furniture, he bought like pieces. And he had six identical dark brown suits in his closet. One for each workday, and an extra just in case.

His older brother Connor especially took great joy in teasing him about what he referred to as his anal tendencies. It didn't bother him. Well, most of the time, anyway.

It was a mystery still how David had managed to talk him into five days of hiking—hiking, for cripe's sake—through the Blue Ridge Mountains. With everything they needed strapped to their backs. Jake grimaced.

He patted the left breast of his suit jacket again. The familiar billfold holding his INS agent ID wasn't there. It hadn't been lying on his bedroom bureau that morning when he got up. And a thorough search of his apartment and car hadn't turned it up, either. He supposed it was possible he'd left it at the McCoy place last night, though not probable. There was no reason for him to have taken his ID out of the back pocket of his Dockers.

Then again, he wouldn't put it past one of his brothers to lift the sucker so he'd have to take his vacation, which officially started today.

Vacation. What David had planned sounded more like hell on earth.

He crossed the street, then looked at where his identification usually filled out the front of his jacket—and rushed headfirst into someone barreling in the other direction.

Jake didn't know how he'd overlooked the female who was pushing away from him. She had curly black hair and round brown eyes. Perhaps it was her height, which couldn't be more than five foot four to his six two. Or maybe it was her build, which was somewhere between skinny and petite.

"Excuse me," he said, running his fingers down the length of his tie.

She looked a million miles away even as she stared at him. In the bright sunlight her skin was a shade lighter than freshly milled paper, her lips colored a rich burgundy. She wasn't the type of woman he'd normally find attractive. Aside from the obvious contrasts in their sizes, she was too…tousled, as if she did little more than finger comb her dark curls. Curls that a light breeze tousled even further. And her mouth… His gaze fastened on it. Her mouth was too…distracting. Provocative.

Her gaze finally seemed to focus on him. She murmured something under her breath, then brushed past him in the direction of the parking lot.

Jake stood stock-still. He felt as if he'd just been sucker punched in a way he'd never experienced, and Lord knew he'd weathered his share of punches. He couldn't seem to draw air into his lungs; his knees felt ready to give out.

Slowly, he continued toward the building, wishing the sensations away. He'd have to make a point to watch where he was going from here on out. He held open the door for a small group exiting the building. First item on his agenda: unload the documentation he promised to bring over from the investigations unit. Second: locate his identification.

Keys jangled. He glanced over his shoulder. In the lot across the street, the woman was unlocking the driver's side door of a battered old Ford. A once-over told him the tires were bald and he suspected she hadn't had the oil changed in the past ten thousand miles. His inspection also told him that she had incredibly shapely calves. And that she was probably much shorter than five foot four when she took off the impractical, thick platform heels she had on.

He caught a glimpse of a man walking in her general direction at a brisk pace, likely on his way to his own car.

Jake turned toward the door he held. No one else was exiting. A statute ought to be enacted disallowing women to have legs that looked as good as hers did. He caught the ridiculous thought. Well, at least they shouldn't be able to wear skirts that complemented those legs as nicely as hers did. It was downright distracting.

He absently patted his empty jacket pocket again, then slid another gaze at the woman's legs.

The man moving in her direction quickened his pace. Jake dragged his attention away from her long enough to figure out that the guy wasn't hurrying to get to his car, but was rushing for her.

He let go of the door, watching as the man knocked her over and grabbed her purse. Jake broke into a run, too far away to stop it from happening but close enough to catch up to the figure. The guy slowed to pull something out of the handbag, then dropped it. Jake swept up the purse, then lunged for the envelope the guy had taken, snatching it away. Their gazes locked. Just as Jake reached to grab him, the guy turned tail and ran. He disappeared into the depths of the city, the clap of his shoes quickly blending into the sound of car engines, blowing horns and a nearby siren.

MERDE.

The concrete pavement was cold and hard under Michelle Lambert's behind. She stared at a scratch on the driver's door of her car, her legs spread-eagle in front of her, her hair hanging in her face. After everything she'd gone through today, there didn't seem to be much point in moving lest she stumble into yet another nightmare. Yes. Better she should sit there. Breathe. Pretend what was happening wasn't. Wait until someone woke her from what had to be some sort of twisted sequence of events from an artsy, senseless independent film, the type that won awards in Cannes, not far from the town she'd grown up in in France.

Someone had snatched away everything that verified her existence: her passport, her plane ticket home, her money.

She forced herself to blink. Was it really just that morning that she'd discovered the manager of the crummy motel she was staying at had forgotten to give her her phone messages? By the time she'd called that swindling private detective she'd hired, he was gone for the day. His gum-smacking secretary had told her he'd need at least five hundred more American dollars to continue on the case. Dollars she hadn't had before her purse was stolen by some greedy, bloodsucking American.

She clamped her eyes shut. But the simple move wouldn't let her escape. She groaned, remembering her appointment with the INS mere minutes ago. The immigration officer's voice had been so clear, she could practically still hear it. *"Sorry, Miss Lambert, but we can't honor your request for an extension on your B2 tourist visa. You'll have to go back home to France tomorrow."*

Home.

France.

Without Lili.

She'd jump out of the plane window before she let that happen.

She opened her eyes, a foolish, tiny thread of hope winding through her. If she didn't have her passport, they'd have to let her stay, wouldn't they? At least until she could get replacement papers—

"Ma'am?"

Her gaze snagged on a shiny pair of men's shoes, then slowly drifted upward to a man's chest—a tantalizingly wide chest belonging to someone who towered over her like some sort of silent, handsome sentinel.

She looked into his face. "It's you." It was the man she'd bumped into earlier. The man who had large, slender hands and even larger calm gray eyes.

He held out her purse.

Michelle nearly burst into tears on the spot. *"Merci."* She choked the word out in French, forgetting for a moment to speak in English. She rifled through the contents of her bag. Her passport. Her return plane ticket. Her compact, hairbrush, a snapshot of Lili she lingered over for a moment, multicolored receipts she'd accumulated over the past six weeks. Where was her money?

Her movements growing jerky and quick, she started looking through the contents again.

"Here." The man held her slender bill holder toward her. She noticed the way his gaze slid over her compromised po-

sition, his pupils huge, his throat working around a swallow.
A bolt of unexpected awareness spiked through her as she accepted the money from him.

"That's all he tried to take," he said. His voice seemed to
come from somewhere very deep within him and vibrated
right through her. "Are you...okay?"

Michelle pushed her hair from her face, looked where she
clutched her purse in her lap, then stared at the run in her nylons. Her last pair of clean nylons. She felt like crying all over
again. "No. I think you should just take me out back and
shoot me."

His quiet chuckle drew her attention from herself and
zoomed it in on him. He reached down. Michelle stared at his
long, tapered fingers. Nice hands. Strong. Sexy. She placed
her right hand in his, his strong grip lifting her to her feet.

"You hear about the crime, tell yourself you're being safe,
you know, looking over your shoulder to make sure no one's
following you. Checking the back seat of your car in case
someone is hiding there. Double wrapping the strap of your
purse to make it a difficult target. Then—bam! Some degen-
erate pig gets you anyway."

She sank her teeth into her lower lip. The more she bab-
bled, the closer she moved to the tears she tried so hard to hold
at bay. That's all she needed on top of everything else that had
happened that day. To collapse into an unflattering pile of hys-
terical female in front of this very virile man.

She shivered at the undiluted heat that traveled from his
hand to hers, only then realizing his fingers were still neatly
wrapped around hers.

He cleared his throat, then withdrew his hand and patted the
front of his jacket as if looking for something that wasn't there.

"You are an ex-smoker, yes?"

"Excuse me?"

She gestured toward where he patted his jacket. "I know many ex-smokers who keep the habit of reaching for a cigarette long after they've quit. My father is one." She slid the money envelope into her purse, then slung the strap over her shoulder.

"No…no, I don't smoke." He glanced away, as if caught looking at something he shouldn't be. Michelle glanced down. Aside from the run in her nylons and some dust on the back of her skirt, she supposed she looked all right. He cleared his throat again. "Shall I call the police? Or do you want to go to the hospital first?"

"Police?" Michelle's mind caught and held on the word. No, she definitely didn't want to waste any of the precious time she had talking to police. Every moment that ticked by was one more she wasn't using to find her daughter. "No, no." She lifted her purse for his inspection. "See, he didn't steal anything, yes?"

The corners of his sexy, generous mouth curved upward. "No."

"So no police."

"No police."

"Good." Michelle couldn't seem to tug her gaze away from his mouth. In every other way, this man appeared disciplined and ordered. But his mouth…. She ran her tongue along her teeth. His mouth looked downright delicious.

"Coffee then?"

"Coffee?" she repeated, blinking at him.

"Or tea." He seemed to grow inches taller as he straightened. "You, um, look like you could use a cup. You know, to settle down before you get back on the road again."

He nodded toward her hands. They shook slightly. No doubt the day's events were beginning to take their toll, but she didn't know how coffee or tea or anything with caffeine could remedy the situation.

He nodded to the right. "There's, um, a café a couple of blocks away."

His gaze was direct. His eyes clear. And just being near him made her feel safe in a way she hadn't felt in a long time. In at least eight weeks. Before Lili was taken.

"Okay," she said quietly.

The man seemed surprised by her response, which didn't make much sense. Why should he invite her out if he expected to be turned down?

She followed him across the street where he picked up a manila file folder he must have dropped when he tore after the purse snatcher. He straightened the papers in it, looked at the INS building, then at her. "I guess I should introduce myself, shouldn't I? I'm Jake. Jake McCoy."

"Michelle Lambert." She thoroughly looked him over, thinking herself certifiable for agreeing to have coffee with this beautiful stranger, much less pondering all the other possibilities his nearness presented. But those same possibilities made her feel gloriously alive in a way she hadn't for a long, long time.

THREE QUESTIONS puzzled Jake. Who was this woman? What was he doing here with her? And why couldn't he shake images of her naked and moving restlessly beneath him from his head?

He sat across the bistro-style table from her, slightly turned to the side because he was too tall to sit as designed. Michelle Lambert took a generous pull from a latte, or at least that's what he thought she'd called it. She sat back with a satisfied sigh, licking the white foam from her upper lip in a provocative way that made him want to groan before he looked around to see who was watching. "It is not like mine, but it will do," she said.

Jake found himself running his tongue along his top lip,

wondering not only how the foamy concoction would taste, but how it would taste on her.

He looked away. Everything about this woman seemed to throw him for a loop. Her sweet, spicy scent was light, almost nonexistent, making him want to lean closer and breathe it in. Her accent, decidedly French, was heavy… sexy, which was a way he'd never viewed a foreign accent before.

He didn't know why he'd suggested coffee with her. He also didn't know why he was in the trendy coffee shop he must have passed a hundred times but had never entered. He glanced around the busy place. It seemed they served everything *but* coffee—at least as he knew it. He supposed part of the reason he'd extended the invitation was he couldn't see her getting into that car in the shape she was in. Besides, for a brief, telling moment, she had looked like she'd…needed someone. And he'd felt an inexplicable urge to respond to that need.

That he battled against a completely different need of his own was another matter entirely.

"Thank you," she said quietly, her small fingers curled around a cup that could have doubled as a soup bowl. "I…I really needed this. I haven't had a cup in six weeks."

He raised a brow. Six weeks? His mind clicked. He assumed that she hadn't had a cup of whatever it was she was drinking because she'd been in the country for that long. If that was the case, and if she was in the country on a B2 tourist visa, then it should be about to expire, if it hadn't already.

He didn't like his train of thought. Especially since it didn't seem to change his almost unbearable attraction to her one iota.

"My pleasure," he said in delayed response to her thank you.

She smiled. The action sent his stomach down somewhere in the vicinity of his knees. "You don't speak much, do you?"

"I've been told it's not one of my stronger suits."

"That's okay. I'm of the personal opinion that people, as a

rule, talk too much anyway. You know, when your friends tell you, 'I'd really like to go back to university,' or 'I keep meaning to lose that last five pounds,' my response is always that they shouldn't talk about it, they should just do it. Sometimes it seems the moment they say it, the importance attached to the statement loses all impact, you know what I mean? Anyway, how exactly do they expect you to respond? I think it's their way of asking you to share all those things you've been meaning to do but haven't, as a type of shared misery." She waved her hand. "I don't go in much for that."

He stared at her. He hadn't known a woman could say so much without taking a breath.

She smiled. "Then tell me what is."

"Excuse me?"

"You said talking isn't one of your stronger suits. What is?"

He noticed that her eyes were a light, light brown, matching the color of her designer coffee. He found himself returning her smile. "Well, I'd have to talk to tell you that, wouldn't I?" Her laugh was as smoky as he thought it would be. "Um, my job." Oh, but that was lame.

"Your job?"

"Yes." He didn't offer more. It was suddenly important to him that she not know he was with the INS. He was drawn to her openness. Her teasing smile. And he suspected that if she knew what he did for a living, she'd close all that off to him. He didn't want that to happen. Not yet, anyway.

He was relieved when she turned her attention toward the sugar decanter. She straightened it, then the napkin holder behind it, her gaze scanning the café's interior. "I once wanted to open a café."

His brow rose again, but for a completely different reason.

"Oh, not here. In Paris. Until Papa pointed out that the last thing Paris needed was another coffee shop." That smile again.

She tucked her mass of unruly hair behind her right ear. Jake was inordinately fascinated with the move and found himself wondering if her hair was as soft as it looked. And pondered how it would feel trailing a path across the sensitive skin of his abdomen. "So I switched my plans to a restaurant."

Her laugh caught him unawares. What was funny about that?

"You know. If Paris doesn't need another café, it needs another restaurant even less?"

"Oh." He cleared his throat again, then blurted, "You seemed distracted."

She squinted at him slightly, as if not understanding.

"When we bumped into each other earlier."

The light in her eyes diminished. "Yes. I was distracted."

She took another pull from her cup, and he looked at his own. He wasn't sure what it held. Was afraid to find out. "Any particular reason?"

He noticed then that she bit her nails. They were too short, barely crescents on her fingers. Unpainted. "Yes. There is a reason. Tomorrow, I'm told, I must leave your country full of swindling private detectives and bloodsucking purse snatchers. Go back home."

He held his gaze steady on her. Just as he suspected.

She gestured with her hands. "They, those people don't care that I need to stay here. That I need to find my daughter. They tell me they can't help me. They can't grant me an…"

"Extension." He finished her sentence.

She squinted at him again, making him wonder if she normally wore glasses. He scanned her features, imagining her with all that unruly hair pulled into a smooth twist—

"Yes, an extension."

"So you can find your daughter."

Her hands stilled on her cup. "Yes. Her father, or the man

who calls himself her father when he didn't want any involvement in her life before now, came to Paris two months ago and…took her. Brought her here."

"Your husband?"

She shook her head. "No. He and I, we had a brief—how do you say it?—relationship. No, no, an affair. You use the same word, yes? Five years ago. He was an American living in Paris. I was a waitress. Lili was the result."

Jake stared at her. Not so much shocked by what she'd said, but shocked that she was saying what she was as easily as she was. And that he found it impossible to tug his gaze away from her animated face. She was a single mother who'd had her child out of wedlock. And she was *foreign*. Not that he had anything against foreigners. At one time or another, all Anglo-Americans had been *foreigners* to this land. But in his job as agent for the Immigration and Naturalization Service, the word foreigner took on a whole new meaning.

Not knowing what to say in the situation, he asked, "So your daughter's four?"

She briefly closed her eyes, her long, dark lashes casting shadows against her pale skin. She murmured several sentences in French. The thick, nasal sound wound around him in a way he wasn't sure he liked. It made him feel…lustful. He found himself wishing he knew the language so he could understand what she'd said, though he was sure it had nothing to do with his increasingly uncomfortable state. "Yes. She will be four this Saturday…five days from today." She stared at the tabletop, but he doubted she saw it. "I should have never given Gerald a copy of her birth certificate when she was born. I'd wanted to include him, yes? Instead, he used it to get her an American passport and take her away from me."

She looked so helpless at that moment. Much as she had

in the parking lot when he'd returned her purse. He was filled with an inexplicable, urgent need to pull her into his arms. To smooth her curly hair. Tell her everything would be all right.

On the heels of that sensation followed a physical pull that left him feeling as if he'd downed a pitcher of beer in a single sitting.

The reaction was so completely alien to him, he wasn't sure how to respond. No one had ever stirred such a complete physical response in him. He had stopped paying attention to the countless hard-luck stories he heard on a daily basis about six years ago. Stopped counting the number of illegals he'd taken to the airport and put on the next plane out. Why Michelle Lambert's sketchy situation should affect him so baffled him.

"Have you visited the States before?" he asked quietly.

Normally he might not have noticed the slight coloring of her skin, but he'd been staring at her so much, any variation was noticeable. He wished he knew exactly what it meant. "Yes…I visited the west coast years ago. Vacation."

He grimaced. "So you're going home tomorrow?"

A waitress approached their table. "Can I get you two something else? A warm-up, maybe? The elephant ears are fresh."

Michelle waved her away. "No, thank you. I don't wish for anything more." She looked at him. "You've been far too generous already."

"Please," he said.

"No. No, thank you." She gathered her purse and got up. "I really must be going now."

Jake rose so quickly, he nearly knocked the table over. All he knew was a sudden, overwhelming urge to stop her from leaving. He curved his fingers around her arm. The heat that swept through him and pooled in his groin was instantaneous.

She gazed into his face, clearly puzzled. Then her expression changed. Her pupils widened, nearly taking over the tawny brown of her irises. The open sensuality he saw in the coloring of her cheeks, the softening of her mouth, made looking anywhere else impossible.

She slowly leaned forward, tilted her head and pressed her mouth firmly against his. Jake couldn't have acted more surprised had someone zapped him with a live wire, but he'd be damned if he could pull away. She tasted of chocolate and coffee. Smelled of fresh air and open interest. He wasn't sure, but he could have sworn he felt the quick flick of her tongue over his bottom lip before she pulled away.

He stood dumbfounded. Had that really happened? Had she just kissed him? His almost painful erection told him she had. And that he wanted her to do it again.

"Why...what did you do that for?" He barely recognized the low, gravelly voice as belonging to him.

She glanced quickly away, then gave a slight shrug. "Just curious."

"About what?"

Her gaze slid to his face, and she smiled. "Curious as to whether your lips felt as good as they looked."

She began to move away again, and he let her. Near the door, she turned toward him. "By the way, they do."

She stepped through the door.

Jake stood for a long moment watching her, an ache the size of Virginia in the pit of his stomach.

CHAPTER TWO

HE DECIDED to blame it on all the time he had on his hands. Jake stood waiting for the elevator to reach the second floor, only belatedly thinking he should have taken the stairs. And thinking of the prospect of having time on his hands. He'd passed his most pressing cases to fellow agent Edgar Mollens. His desk was clean even of dust. The only thing that stretched before him was five days trekking through the Blue Ridge Mountains with David.

He cringed. He'd be the first to admit that spending the night in a tent wasn't exactly his idea of a good time. In his mind, roughing it was being stuck in a hotel room without CNN. But even his reluctance to snap on his new backpack and tie his new boots wasn't to blame for his unusual interest in a certain provocative Michelle Lambert.

Then there was her kiss.

He forced the thought from his mind even though his body immediately responded.

At any rate, it was better that his chances of seeing her again were zip to nil. She'd never answered his question, but he was certain she'd be heading to France tomorrow. The elevator doors opened, and he stepped out. What he couldn't help wondering was when she was due to fly out.

Bypassing the administrative offices where he usually left any papers, he walked through the jam-packed waiting area in Room 200, vaguely aware of a number being called and an elderly woman likely of European descent using her cane to rise from her chair. He strode down the long hall leading to his office. His interest in Michelle should have been equivalent to his interest in the European woman. Less, even, because Michelle violated at least ten of his appearance rules.

Yet his mind kept venturing to her. The way she ran the small pad of her thumb across the rim of her cup while she spoke. Sat slightly leaning to the right, her legs crossed. Looked as if she could see inside him, appearing candidly interested in what was there.

Jake stopped outside an immigration information officer's cubicle and waited for the officer to finish with a young man presumably of South American descent. The kid finally left holding a sheaf of papers that likely reflected the details of his life thus far.

Pauline turned toward her computer, putting her back to him. "Good thing you're so tall, Jake, or else nobody would know you were there."

Jake entered the office. "What do you got on a Lambert, Michelle?"

Pauline entered the name in her computer. "French. Point of entry, Dulles. Extension denied." She swiveled slowly toward him. "Why?"

"Who handled the case?"

"Brad. You didn't answer my question."

"Thanks." Jake stepped out of the cubicle and headed to one down the hall.

"Jake McCoy, one of these days I'm going to cut off your special privileges. Then where will you be?" Pauline called after him.

He grinned.

Brad Worthy was between cases. Jake repeated his request

for information on Michelle. Information that either hadn't yet been or wouldn't be entered into the computer.

Brad leaned back in his chair and tossed his pen to the desktop. "The Frenchwoman? Quite a looker, that one, eh?"

"I hadn't noticed."

"Yeah. You wouldn't." He shuffled through the files on his desk. "Extension denied."

"What else you got?"

Brad stared at him from under lowered brows. "What's the interest?"

Jake suddenly felt uneasy. He had a hard time explaining that one to himself. Maybe if he knew she was heading out, leaving for France, he'd be able to get her out of his head. "Indulge me."

"Okay." He opened the file and scanned the contents. "Lambert, Michelle. Twenty-eight years of age. Chef. Came in on a B2 tourist visa, though it's noted she tried to get a special travel visa. Claims her three-year-old daughter, Elizabeth aka Lili, was kidnapped by her biological father and brought to the States two months ago."

Jake digested the information. Chef. A transient profession. If she chose to violate the terms of her visa and stay in the country, she could find a way to stay indefinitely. "Why was her request for an extension denied?"

Brad sat back again. "She lied on her initial application about her criminal past. Information we didn't have when she came in but we since got."

Jake frowned as he recalled her vulnerability when her purse had been stolen. "Kid stuff?"

"Not this one." Brad shook his head. "Her visa's up at midnight tonight. But I can already tell you she's going to defy."

"How do you know that?"

Brad grinned. "Because she told me so. Let's see, how did

she put it? That if I wouldn't give her the time she needed to find her daughter, she'd take it. Yeah, that's it. If she wasn't such a looker, I'd have had her detained on the spot." His grin widened. "Anyway, I'm planning to pass her file on to Edgar in the morning."

"Edgar?" Jake repeated. What could she have possibly done to warrant high-profile attention? He and Edgar Mollens took on the high-risk cases. Suspected terrorists. Drug runners. Russian Mafia. Sweatshop owners. What could Lambert, Michelle, possibly have done to earn the same regard?

And would her file have been passed to him if he wasn't officially on vacation?

He was about to ask for specifics on the conviction when Brad's phone rang. "Hang on a minute." He swiveled his chair away to speak to the caller. "Brad Worthy." Jake inconspicuously turned Michelle's file in his direction. The Four Pines Motel. He noted the address.

Jake's cell phone vibrated in his jacket pocket. He slipped it out and stepped closer to the door. "McCoy."

"How about that? There's a McCoy here, too."

Jake grimaced at the sound of his youngest brother's voice. "What is it?"

David chuckled. "You know, one of these days you're going to have to work on those phone manners, Jake. Then again, your entire demeanor could use a little work. Something I'm hoping to start on first thing in the morning."

"Are you at the house?"

"Yep. Thought I'd hang around until you got here."

"Listen, I can't find my INS ID. Have you seen it around there?"

"Can't say as I have. Boy, you must be feeling awfully naked. Anyway, I don't think you're going to need it where we're going, unless there are some illegal aliens hiding out in a cave or two."

"Right." Jake watched Worthy hang up the phone. "I'll call you back."

"Jake, don't you dare—"

Jake pressed the disconnect button and slid the phone into his pocket. Brad had closed Michelle's file and was motioning a new applicant to enter. That was it. Just like that, Brad had drawn their conversation to a halt. No more information. To press the matter would not only put him at a disadvantage, it would make his unusual interest in the sexy Frenchwoman even more obvious than it already was.

With a reluctant wave, Jake left.

"Hey, you're welcome, McCoy."

MICHELLE HAD NO IDEA why her extension request had been denied. If she had, maybe she could have done something to fight it. But the best she could come up with was that stupid situation she'd gotten herself into in San Francisco so long ago. Though why that brief period in her life meant anything to the American government, she couldn't begin to fathom.

She plucked her nylons and panties from the shower curtain rod, then stuffed them into her back pack on the double bed. She was blind to the crummy state of the room. The cigarette-burned carpet. The torn bedspread. The stained bathtub. Not because she'd been there long, but because in the course of the past six weeks she'd seen virtually identical rooms across the country. Truth be told, she'd lived in her share of such tacky places in Paris when she'd first struck out on her own. In Kansas, at least the rooms had smelled better, but North Carolina had to be the worst simply because of the bug population and the strong metallic smell of the well water.

The low-rent rooms were all she could fit into her budget. Actually, she'd have found they tested her budget if she'd sat down to think about it. The money she'd been saving to open her own place in Paris's Left Bank couldn't have run out faster had someone stuck a vacuum hose in her handbag and flipped the switch. And gone also was the additional money her father had wired to her two weeks ago. Of course, she hadn't expected her search to be so long, America so very large.

The mattress sagged pitifully as she sat on the side and tugged on her shoes. At least she'd finally gotten a decent latte, thanks to tasty Jake McCoy. In fact, she was thankful to him for much. If not for his quick reaction, she'd be sitting here with even less than she was now.

She absently rubbed her palm along her bare leg. And why had he reacted the way he had? In Paris, she'd had her purse snatched no less than two times, a third thwarted because she'd been determined, the thief careless. She'd been surrounded by people both times, but no one had lifted a finger to help. But Jake...

She sighed gustily, remembering her impulsive kiss and the masculine taste of him on her lips.

She wasn't certain which interested her more: the fact that she was thinking of someone other than Lili for the first time in so long, or that the someone on her mind was a man.

She pushed from the bed and smoothed the creases she'd made. Her mother had once told her, a year or so before she died, when Michelle was ten, that men were the one thing women could never live without. Michelle hadn't believed her. She'd forgotten the advice when she'd met Gerald Evans at the Jardin des Tuileries one rainy morning. He'd offered her his umbrella. She'd given him her heart, then, nine months later, a daughter.

She smiled wryly. Awfully high price to pay to keep a little rain off one's head. But she'd never looked back. Gerald had left Paris shortly after Lili was born. And Michelle and her daughter had forged a life of their own. A wildly variable life she loved. A laughter-filled life—shattered when Gerald had popped up two months ago.

She intended to get that life back.

A leisurely walk in the park with his daughter, he'd told Michelle. That's all he wanted. He was only in town overnight. Could she please allow him a brief time alone with Lili?

She had. And had regretted the decision ever since.

She rifled through her purse, extracting a sheet of paper. After leaving Jake McCoy at the café, she'd paid a visit to the private detective's office. Contrary to the information his secretary had given her that morning, John Bollatin had been in. And ten minutes later she'd left shaking with anger and clutching the address in her hand.

Canton, Ohio.

In a dusty corner of her mind, she remembered Gerald saying something about growing up in the Midwest. She had assumed it was Kansas. Going by the map, it should have been. And Bollatin had told her the same. But the address she held was in the northeastern corner of Ohio. An address for Gerald's parents.

She took out the billfold holding her money from her purse. She sighed at the pitiful amount, then slid it back in. She supposed she could call her father again, plead with him to send her more. But by now Jacqueline had learned about his sending her the other money and would have convinced him that sending more would be irresponsible. After all, they had three additional children to think about. It was an argument that had worked especially well on her father throughout Michelle's teenage years. And she had no doubt it was even more effective now, seeing as two of their children were still attending university.

No, she wouldn't put her father in that position. She was the only one who understood how devastated he'd been after her mother's death from breast cancer. It was as though a part, a very important part of him had died with her. Michelle took an odd sort of comfort in knowing that only she was aware of this. She didn't want to cause him any more pain.

Besides, living with Jacqueline and her three brats was enough for any man to have to bear.

No, she would have to find her way on her own.

And it was time she started. Now.

THE CAR'S TIRES spit up the spotty gravel as Jake pulled into the motel's parking lot. He put the gear in Park, then shut off the engine. The sound of traffic zooming by on I-295 was deafening, making him wonder how anyone could sleep with all the racket. His apartment was located in Woodley Park, in the older section of D.C. Quiet, tree-lined. A bit of Norman Rockwell and old America in the middle óf bustling downtown.

He stared at the closed door to Room Three. He couldn't begin to explain to anyone what he was doing there, much less come up with a rational explanation for himself. He'd tried already. It hadn't worked.

So what if Edgar was out of town until tomorrow, wrapping up a case in Georgia? Edgar was just as efficient as Jake was. And he had more years on the job. It didn't matter if he got the case today, tomorrow or the next day. Edgar would find Michelle quicker than she could blink those latte-colored eyes.

He shifted uneasily on the leather seat. The feeling was foreign to him. Very little made him uncomfortable. But not knowing what deeds lurked in the shadows of Michelle Lambert's past did.

At least that's what he told himself.

He shifted again, recognizing the statement for the lie it was. He was drawn to this woman. It was as simple…as complicated as that. She ignited something within him impossible to ignore and equally foolish to pursue. But pursuing it he was.

He scrubbed his face with his hands. He realized part of the reason he was intrigued by her was that her reason for being in the country had nothing to do with finding a better job than she could back home. Or because she was in search of the American dream. She wasn't interested in any of that, as many foreign nationals were. She hadn't applied for a green card. She'd merely wanted an extension on her visa. So she could find her daughter.

There. There it was again. That bottomless feeling in the pit of his stomach.

And the image of Michelle sitting in a rocking chair with a dark-haired child in her arms. Her thickly lashed eyes sparkling with warmth. Smiling.

He left out of that thought the possibility that he wouldn't see her again. Despite that her beat-up Ford was parked a few yards away from him, she could have already skipped town. And knowing what she'd told Brad, he was convinced she would live up to her threat. There was a strength about her. A determination he couldn't help but be fascinated with.

His hand automatically patted his empty jacket pocket. He sighed, then slipped his cell phone out of his other pocket. Within moments, his father answered his call.

"Yeah, Pops, David around?"

There was the sound of clinking silverware. Jake envisioned the kitchen of the house he'd grown up in, finding some comfort in the familiar. Of course, so many things had changed since Mitch's wife, Liz, had moved in, but he chose to concentrate on those that had stayed the same.

"Hey, yourself, Jake," Sean said with that ever-present smile that had been in his voice lately. "He is. But are you sure you want to talk to him? He's mad as hell that you're not here yet. Not that I can blame him." There was a heartbeat of a pause, then his father's voice lowered. "It's not like you to be late for anything. Everything all right?"

"Just running a little behind." Jake grimaced. There were some drawbacks to having a family who knew him so well. He didn't doubt that if he were face-to-face with Sean, he wouldn't have gotten away with such a vague statement. "Any luck finding my identification?"

"Nope. Turned the place upside down earlier. Not even a fiber. Wait. Here comes David now."

Movement outside the car caught Jake's attention. Michelle was coming out of her room, a backpack slung over her shoulder.

"This better be good." David's voice filtered over the line.

Jake pressed the disconnect button then opened the car door.

MICHELLE SLUNG her pack onto the passenger's seat. This was it. All she had left was an address. Nothing more. And there were no guarantees that this address would be any better than the ones the detective had gotten before. She took one last look at the closed door to Room Three. But what choice did she have? She would not, could not go home without Lili.

"Going somewhere?"

Michelle turned at the sound of the familiar voice. Given how little he'd said to her earlier at the café, she didn't know why it should be familiar. It was more her body's reaction to the deep timbre than anything that told her Jake McCoy had followed her to her motel.

The funny thing was, she wasn't surprised by his appearance—maybe because she couldn't seem to get him out of her mind since bumping into him in the parking lot of the INS building.

She gripped the top of the door with her left hand. "Yes. I suppose I am."

He came to a stop before her. His back straight. His hair impeccably neat. His suit clean and pressed. She felt the sudden inexplicable desire to muss him all up.

"You wouldn't happen to be going to the airport now, would you?" he asked.

Her fingers tightened on the hard metal of the door. "Airport?"

"Yes. You know, for your flight home." He patted the breast of his jacket the same way he had at the café, then grimaced, as if not finding something that was usually there.

"No. No, I'm not going to the airport." She tucked her hair behind her ear. "What are you doing here?"

It occurred to her that he couldn't have followed her to the motel, because she hadn't gone directly there after they left the café. She'd stopped at the detective's office.

That meant he was either a stalker or else he'd known where to find her.

"Don't tell me. You work for the INS, don't you?"

He stood a little straighter, if that was at all possible, stretching that lean torso, drawing her gaze to his slim hips and legs that appeared muscular even through the light material of his slacks. "Yes, I do." He held out a business card. She took it, running her thumb over the raised lettering. Jake McCoy, Immigration Agent.

She closed her eyes and swore in French. "This day keeps getting better and better. Only I could meet a guy I'm attracted to for the first time in what seems like forever, kiss him, then find out his mission in life is to make mine miserable." She stared at him. "Does this mean *you're* taking me to the airport?"

He seemed to hesitate. "Do you want me to?"

She tucked the card into the waist of her skirt. "Do I have a choice?"

He glanced at a plain silver watch on his wrist. "Until midnight, you do."

She slid her hand from the door. "You have to be kidding." She regarded his clear, direct gaze and realized he wasn't.

"Have you eaten yet?" he asked.

"Eaten?"

"Yes. Supper."

She thought of the granola bar she had stashed in her backpack. With the meager amount of money she had left, she didn't have enough to splurge on little extras like food.

"Do you want to, you know, go catch a bite?"

"A bite?"

"Yes."

She crossed her arms under her breasts. On another woman, the move might have been provocative. Not with her. Like everything else about her, her breasts were small. Nonetheless, she watched his gaze skim the front of her shirt, the darkening of his eyes telling. Her nipples hardened beneath the thin, soft cotton, and a slow, arousing shiver tickled her spine. "Let me, um, get this straight. Isn't that how they say it? You're telling me you're with the INS. But you're not taking me to the airport. You can't. At least not until midnight. But you want to take me out to dinner. Is that right?"

He cleared his throat. "Yes."

She glanced at her digital watch. "It's only seven. Where were you planning on taking me?"

A glimpse of a grin played around his full lips. "I know this nice place that serves great French food."

She raised a brow.

"In Baltimore."

Her burst of laughter surprised even her.

There was no playing with this guy. He was as straight as they came. If she asked him how many times a week he took his suits to the cleaners, he'd probably not only answer her, but answer her accurately, down to the time of day he took them in.

She wondered if those same painstaking characteristics would make him thorough in his lovemaking, as well. He'd take his time. Explore every crevice and hollow. Make sure he was giving more pleasure than he was taking.

She caught her bottom lip between her teeth. "Sorry, but I've already eaten." She grasped the door again. "Thank you, though."

She climbed into the car, half expecting him to stop her. He didn't.

She rolled down the window.

He leaned over, his hands tucked into his pants pockets. "Mind if I ask where you're going?"

"No, I don't mind. But even you'd have to agree I'd be stupid to tell you."

He nodded. Her gaze was riveted on his mouth. While everything else about him bespoke discipline and order, his lips hinted at a passion she didn't think even he knew the depths of. She remembered the firm, silky feel of them against hers. His initial hesitation. Then his soft groan, and the confident pressure of his mouth as he returned her instinctual kiss. She could almost still taste him there, on her tongue.

She started the car's engine. "You're not going to follow me, are you?" The thought both excited and scared her, but not for the reasons she would have thought. While Jake McCoy posed a threat to her freedom to find Lili, she got the distinct impression it was an altogether different autonomy he threatened.

Then again, one night with this man who looked at her in a mixture of wonder and desire might not be such a bad idea.

"Probably," he answered.

She settled on excited.

"Okay. Guess I'll be seeing you on the road, then."

"Yeah. On the road."

CHAPTER THREE

THE NERVE-GRATING CHIRP of the cell phone filled the otherwise quiet interior of the car. Jake fumbled in his jacket pocket then pulled it out. McCoy Place, the display read. He reached over and chucked the phone into his glove box. Until he saw what was going to happen over the next few hours, there was no point in talking to David. Michelle Lambert and her intentions took priority over a hiking trip. He glanced into the back seat, where all his new gear was tucked neatly into an oversize blue nylon backpack. The manager of the sports equipment store had told him everything he'd bought was top of the line. A sleeping bag no thicker than his linen bedsheets was guaranteed to keep him warm when the temperatures dipped below freezing, and dry when it rained for days on end. He leaned forward and stared at the sky. It definitely looked like rain.

He put both hands on the steering wheel and zoomed in again on the rusted Ford two car lengths ahead of him in the right lane. He was sure there was a law against the amount of exhaust the tailpipe was spewing out. And the wire holding her back bumper in place looked ready to snap. His gaze trailed to the open driver's window. Every now and again, tendrils of Michelle's curly hair trailed out and whipped in the wind. Like now. He watched her run her fingers through the unruly mass, casually gathering it on the other side of her head.

Jake adjusted the car's interior temperature. It was the first time he'd ever turned it past the sixty-seven-degree point. But that didn't bother him. What did was the irrepressible urge he had to turn the damn air conditioner off and roll his windows down. To feel the early evening air skim through his short-cropped hair like a woman's fingers.

He smoothed the front of his jacket and focused on the overhead sign coming up. Welcome To Pennsylvania. He'd driven this route before many times. Up through Maryland to Penn State, then either west to Pittsburgh or Cleveland or east to New York or Boston. When possible, he preferred driving to flying, and oftentimes he got there faster on these shorter routes. They had yet to make a business-class airplane seat with enough leg room to keep him happy.

He relaxed a bit. The Pennsylvania turnpike was the only direct route through the mountainous state this far south. Not even he would attempt navigating off the four-lane thruway.

Off to the west, the sun was sinking toward the horizon, thin summer clouds throwing off shades of pink and purple. The vibrant colors made him think of the woman in the car ahead of him. Of her provocative nature. Of her small, round breasts. Her great legs. Her chattiness. His mind wandered, and he let it. As his doctor told him last week, there was no safer sex than mental sex. No one ever got pregnant or contracted an STD by indulging in fantasy. And sex with Michelle Lambert was—and would stay—nothing more than a harmless fantasy.

Images of rumpled bedsheets, an empty wine bottle and a Do Not Disturb sign on the door conjured a scene that made him squirm in his seat. She would be a talker in bed, that one. Pleading with him to touch her just so. Knowing instinctively just where to touch him. She would be insatiable....

Whoa.

Jake made a quick steering correction, then stared at his lap. The last time he'd gotten a woody just *thinking* about a woman was when he was a teen. And he'd never indulged in fantasies about an overtly sexy, attainable female. While Farrah Fawcett had been his brother Marc's angel of choice, Kate Jackson always had been his favorite. Trim, neat, ordinary. Watching her in her high collars and conservative slacks had really flicked his switch.

Why, then, was he lusting after a woman who was a puzzling combination of Sophia Loren, Audrey Hepburn and va-va-voom Raquel Welch? One that went in for plunging necklines and short, short skirts? Didn't make any sense at all.

The wind caught Michelle's dark curls again, jerking Jake's mind to those bedsheets. They would be white and crisp, a contrast against all that inky black....

Tearing his gaze from the car in front of him, he pushed the button to turn off the air, then rolled the windows down.

JUST KNOWING Jake McCoy was behind her made Michelle feel erotically appealing. She'd never had a man literally pursue her before. Okay, his reasons weren't exactly what she'd like, but she'd bet his job wasn't the only thing on his mind.

She turned down the radio station cranking out rock and roll oldies, then gazed into her rearview mirror. She spotted Jake and his dark Caprice immediately. He never let more than two cars separate them and stayed for the most part in the left-hand lane, except to let others pass. How charitable of him. She caught herself smiling, then cleared her throat. She should be thinking of what lay ahead of her in Akron, Ohio, south of Cleveland. Instead she watched Jake. Noticing the way he held his hands on the steering wheel in the traditional three o'clock position. His correct, upright posture explained part of the reason his suit appeared barely wrinkled.

One hand on her own wheel, she reached down and plucked off her shoes, then slid them under her seat. Her speed let up a bit, and she instantly compensated. Jake did the same behind her.

The radio announcer told her it was eleven. Would Jake do as he'd said and take her into custody at midnight? He appeared to be a man of his word. Then again, if he'd thought her a real threat, he'd have stopped her from leaving D.C.

She focused more prudently on the road. It was completely dark. The only lights were her headbeams, which illuminated the monotonous, seemingly endless white lines that separated her lane from the next.

If Lili were with her right now, she'd be giddily trying to count those lines.

Michelle bit into the flesh of her bottom lip. It often seemed that everywhere she looked, everything she did, she imagined what her nearly four-year-old daughter would see or do in the same situation. Her absence was like a colossal hole, always present, forever threatening to swallow her up, bogging her down in the details.

What was Lili doing right now? Had she had her bath? Had she eaten? Did Gerald know that a certain name brand of baby care products irritated her sensitive skin? Or that he had to comb her hair just so to get out the tangles? Was she scared?

Michelle dragged in a deep breath. While she was fluent in English, Lili only knew a few basic words, and then only when used in conjunction with French. Would constantly being surrounded by the foreign tongue confuse her?

Oh, how she missed her daughter. Missed tasting her skin when she kissed her temple. Tickling her round, hard belly. Smiling at her rambunctious laugh. Missed playing hide-and-seek with her and Julianne, her frazzled stuffed pet elephant and constant companion.

She reached out and took Julianne from her backpack, running her thumb along her nubbed belly, then lifting the toy to her nose. After nearly eight weeks of sleeping with the animal, it smelled more like her than Lili. But every now and again she swore she could make out her daughter's sweet, little-girl scent.

The sign ahead was blurry. She blinked, realizing that fog wasn't to blame for the haziness, but tears.

Stuffing Julianne in her temporary home, Michelle pressed her foot down on the pedal, watching as Jake dropped farther and farther back. Indulging in a bit of escapist flirtation was one thing. Allowing it to derail her plans was another entirely.

OKAY, SHE WAS finally making her move.

Jake flicked off the cruise control and eased his foot onto the gas pedal. He was mildly surprised she hadn't tried to shake him before. Then again, she might think being so far away from D.C. put them at the same disadvantage. Smart woman.

He easily caught up with her Ford, pulling parallel with her in the left lane. She flashed him a wide smile, making that peculiar weightless sensation more acute. He saluted her. But before he could put his hand back on the wheel, she slammed on the brakes then turned off the exit ramp to her right.

Letting rip a string of hardly used curses, Jake pulled to the shoulder of the road just on the other side of the on ramp, then flicked on his hazards. With his gaze glued to the rearview mirror, he slid the top button of his shirt open, leaving his tie to cover it.

Before Michelle had made her move, he'd kept a close eye on the road signs. This particular exit had no rest facilities, and the next exit was twenty-two miles down the highway. Michelle would soon realize she had no choice but to get back onto the turnpike.

At least he hoped she'd realize that.

After five long minutes with no sign of the battered Ford, he jerked the car into reverse. Traffic was sparse, and he ignored the honking of horns from what little there was. He finally backed up far enough to exit, then raced toward the tollgate. The guard remembered Michelle—probably no other cars had exited since hers—and said he thought she'd gone east. Jake paid the toll then headed in that direction as well, scouring the dark farmland surrounding him. Nothing. No lights. Nobody driving. Nothing but a long, lonely stretch of two-lane road.

He drove for exactly three miles then stopped. He'd been had. It was as simple as that. He suspected that the instant she saw him turn off, she'd doubled back and was already well down the turnpike by now.

Then again, what she could be looking for could be here somewhere.

Trusting his first instinct, he turned around. He could only hope he was right.

On the turnpike fifteen minutes later, he saw that he was.

He pulled onto the shoulder then cruised to a stop behind Michelle's disabled Ford. The back left tire was flat. He climbed from the car and buttoned his jacket, careful of passing traffic as he made his way toward the driver's side.

No Michelle.

He leaned inside the open window. She'd left the keys inside. He used them to unlock the trunk. Why wasn't he surprised that there was no spare? A tractor and semitrailer roared on by, the resulting gust of air plastering his suit to his body. He stared down the road after the truck. Just then, it began to rain.

MICHELLE CLIMBED DOWN from the monster-size truck cab then slammed the door. There was a loud grinding of gears, then the trucker rolled slowly away from her, leaving her standing at the side of the road in the rain.

She shivered. It wasn't that she was unaccustomed to male attention. But the way the trucker had come on to her made her want to scratch something—that is, if she'd had any nails left with which to scratch. In France, men—no matter how old or attractive—at least hinted at the promise of or openly boasted of an ability to satisfy a woman. This guy had been moderately handsome, but he'd made it sound as if she'd owed him one. As though even if she wouldn't enjoy a sexual liaison with him, he didn't care one way or another, just so long as he could cop a feel.

Completely unlike Jake, who would probably never come on to a woman unless he were sure his attention was welcome.

She turned toward the lights on the other side of the toll-booth not too far away.

At least this exit included life of some sort. The one she'd pulled off in the hopes of losing Jake had been completely dead. She spared a glance behind her, half expecting to see the dark Caprice bearing down on her. Hiking her backpack a little higher on her shoulders, she headed in the direction of the tollbooth. She hoped they could direct her to a bus station or even a nearby train station, any place where she could curl up on a chair out of the elements, then continue on in her trip toward Ohio.

She hadn't counted on that flat tire. Then again, she hadn't counted on much of what had happened to her during her trip. She'd known when she'd bought the car that it didn't have a spare. It's how she'd gotten the dealer to go down thirty dollars on the price. She'd figured she'd gotten the better part of the deal, since the spare had been as bad as the rest of the tires. But even that would have been better than what she had now, which was nothing.

Headbeams illuminated her from behind. She stepped farther onto the shoulder as she walked. The way her luck was running, someone would hit her from behind, and she'd be stuck in an American hospital for the next month or so. Or, worse yet, in a cast up to her neck on the next plane to Paris.

She stepped up to the tollbooth. A woman in her forties eyed her critically. "Pedestrians aren't allowed on the turnpike."

"My car, it broke down—"

The attendant leaned forward and frowned. "I can't understand your accent, miss. Pass that by me again."

Michelle grimaced. "Is there a bus or a train station nearby?"

The woman apparently understood her. She leaned back and crossed her arms. "Nope. The nearest bus station is about twenty-two miles east, at the last exit."

Merde. She'd have to be careful, or the next thing she knew, she'd be arrested for loitering outside the tollbooth. "I don't suppose there's a cab service here?"

"Excuse me?"

Michelle shook her head. "Nothing. Thanks for your help."

JAKE FLASHED his high beams, then passed another eighteen-wheeler. He glanced at the truck cab. Michelle could have been in any one of the dozen or so such vehicles he'd seen in the past five minutes. Or in one of the cars, which easily doubled that number.

"What are you doing, McCoy?" he muttered to himself.

He gripped then released the steering wheel. His reasons for following her in the first place were shaky at best. And now that she had lost him...well, there was very little point in continuing without more information or an official reason for doing so. And since he had neither, he'd be better off turning tail and starting on the long road for home.

What had he been thinking? Or, more accurately, which body part had he let do the thinking for him? He grimaced. He'd never done anything so irresponsible in his life. When he was younger, he'd opted out of stealing candy bars from Obernauer's general store while Marc was busy stuffing his pockets full. Not because he was afraid he'd get caught, but because it was just plain wrong. Later, when Connor had surprised him with a stripper on his twentieth birthday, he'd handed her money rather than slip it in her G-string, and had kept his gaze carefully focused on a point just past her toned, undulating waist.

Why, of all times, he'd chosen now to let his hormones get the better of him, he didn't know. Especially since Michelle was nowhere near the type of woman he was usually interested in.

It stood to reason that that's exactly the reason he did find her so intriguing. But that didn't help him any now.

He slowed down to exit the turnpike so he could head in the other direction when the muffled chirping of his cell phone caught his attention. He reached over and fished it from a box of Kleenex in his glove compartment. He didn't recognize the number spotlighted in the display. Pulling onto the shoulder of the exit ramp, he clicked it on.

"Jake? It's Michelle."

He didn't need to be told that. Just her saying his name made his pants a little tighter. He closed his eyes and exhaled silently. It was weird, this physical reaction to her call. More acute than the first time he'd given his number out and the girl had called him.

Michelle told him where she was, then paused before saying, "Can you come get me?"

He knew how very much it must have taken her to call him. He also knew he shouldn't be feeling half the relief he was, either.

He glanced through the windshield at the tollbooth just ahead. He made out Michelle's silhouette instantly. She was leaning against the side of the booth, the toe of one platform shoe on top of the other as she plugged her opposite ear.

"I'll be right there," he said, then flicked off the phone.

Within moments, he was pushing open the passenger's door and paying the toll.

"That was quick," the guard said, openly interested.

He didn't answer her. He was more interested in Michelle as she climbed into the car and quietly closed the door. He pulled from the booth.

An air of defeat seemed to cling to her damp shoulders. Her sensual mouth was stoically unmoving, offering no babbling commentary on what the past half hour had held for her. She looked like a woman who had faced one too many disasters for one day and was ready to pack it in. He remembered who she was, who he was, and realized that the moment she'd called him, she'd done just that. She'd given in.

He fought a fierce urge to reach out and touch her. Pull her closer to his side.

"You about ready for that bite?" he asked instead.

She slowly turned to look at him. "Bite?" she repeated. "Oh, yes, food."

"I don't know about you, but I could eat a horse."

Michelle smiled. "Gerald used to say that all the time. Used to drive me nuts. Especially in the beginning, when I didn't know he didn't mean it literally. But why would anyone want to even joke about eating a horse? I mean, yes, I get the whole size thing…." She let the words drift off, her gaze traveling the length of him, then back again. The color in her cheeks made her eyes seem to sparkle.

He smiled at the reemergence of her chattiness, then wondered why the mention of size had caused her to look him over so thoroughly. "Gerald, your...ex-boyfriend?" He caught himself before he said ex-husband.

"Lover," she said, avoiding his gaze and crossing her arms. "And sorry, I don't frequent restaurants that serve equine animals."

"I'm afraid it's not an invitation."

Michelle closed her eyes, then looked at him. "Is it past midnight already?"

He nodded once.

"Then I'm suddenly very hungry. Ravenous, even. But I think I'll leave any horse they might be serving for you."

CHAPTER FOUR

MICHELLE WELCOMED the vibrating hum of the hair dryer as she fluffed her freshly washed hair with her fingers. Her limbs felt rubbery. Her shoulders unbearably heavy. The long, hot shower had helped. So had dinner beforehand. At least what little she'd been able to make herself eat of the traditional American fare of meat loaf and mashed potatoes, the only selections available this late to her and Jake at the greasy spoon next to the motel. Even the tall, quiet INS agent who sat outside the bathroom door had appeared to lose his appetite as they sat across from each other. A pregnant silence had filled the air between them like so many unsaid, useless words. Unsaid and useless because Michelle knew that no matter what happened, Jake would be taking her to D.C. in the morning and putting her on the first flight to Paris.

She switched off the dryer and stared at the warm plastic in her hands. The steady drone of rain outside the slatted windows made it sound as though someone were taking a shower in the bathtub behind her.

She would be returning to France. Without Lili.

The thought that she might never see her daughter again caused a tightness in her chest that made it nearly impossible to breathe. What was she going to do without Lili crawling into her bed on rainy nights like this one, complaining about her inability to sleep, though she usually dropped right off once she'd curled her warm little body against Michelle's? She supposed her life would come to resemble what the past eight weeks had held for her. Emptiness.

She caught a glimpse of her haunted eyes in the mirror, then reached out to wipe a small circle of steam from the surface.

A sound from the bedroom caught her attention. She realized Jake McCoy must have switched off the television. The tinny sound of voices was gone.

Jake McCoy.

Instantly, the tension in her chest unwound and snaked lower. She wasn't sure what it was about this man that affected her so. It could be his awkward way around her. His solicitous grin. The way he blushed—actually blushed!—when he found out they would have to share the one room left at the motel and when she caught him looking at her breasts. Or when she curiously eyed certain parts of him. Whatever it was, the attraction she felt for him was strong enough to, if not fill the hole left by Lili's absence, at least distract her from it a bit.

She cursed at herself in French. Six weeks in America and she was already beginning to overanalyze like an American. What was it with these people that made them question every feeling, every action, as if seeking a deeper meaning that wasn't there? She was used to going with her feelings. If it felt good, she did it. And the prospect of making love with Jake McCoy felt very good indeed. It held all the promise of complete and total escape, at least for a few brief, precious hours—enough to get her through the night and on into the morning, when her situation might not look so dim.

It would also satisfy the flash of desire she felt whenever he was near. Give her an outlet for the emotional turmoil dogging her. Allow her a physical release she'd forbidden herself for far too long.

She caught her tiny smile in the mirror, envisioning Jake's

reaction when she made her intentions known. Would he run for the door? Or would he surprise her with an equally interested response? Either way, she viewed it as a win-win situation.

She took body lotion from her handbag and began smoothing it over her skin. Her neck. Her breasts. The balls of her feet. No, she would not by any means be mistaken for a seductress. Her black camisole was pure cotton, and her panties were plain. But she didn't think even straight-shooting Jake McCoy could miss her message when she walked into the bedroom.

Fastening her attention on her hair, she smoothed it first this way, then that, frowning as strands sprang free like thick, unruly corkscrews. With the help of a little water and one of Lili's rubber bands she found in her purse, she managed to pull it back in what resembled a twist, every wild strand smoothed, tucked and pinned in place.

Her fingers encircled the doorknob and she hesitated—likely the first time she'd ever hesitated in her life. Why, she couldn't be sure. But in that one moment she knew a fear of rejection she was unfamiliar with.

Aside from their kiss at the D.C. café, there was no solid proof Jake was attracted to her. Yes, his gaze ignited the most delicious of desires within her. But her reaction could be based on nothing more than her need to escape the gravity of her situation.

She released a gusty sigh. There she went again. Analyzing everything too much.

She turned the knob then pulled the door open, standing in the passageway with only one thought in mind....

JAKE TURNED his cell phone over in his palm again and again. He really should call David, or someone at D.C. headquarters. But he couldn't seem to make himself do anything more than listen to the sounds on the other side of the closed bathroom door.

He'd never been in such close quarters with a woman before. Well, yes, he'd been with a few women, and took some amount of pride in the fact that they numbered more than the fingers of one hand, but he'd never listened to one take a shower before. The images that slipped through his mind were just this side of pornographic and long past carnal. He could practically see the warm water sluicing over Michelle's compact little body. Dampening her hair. Rolling over those soft, soft lips, tempting her tongue out to catch a drop or two. Splashing over her pointed breasts, causing them to swell and the tips to harden. He turned the phone over faster and faster as he inserted an image of himself standing in that shower with her. Bending down to claim her hot, wet mouth—

The bathroom door opened. Jake lunged for his cell phone, which had jumped from his hand.

Dear God, help me.

His gaze slid over her well-shaped frame. From the high-cut panties that gave her legs the appearance of being extremely long. To the camisole that clung to her torso and her breasts in a way his fingers itched to, to the way her hair was slicked back from her face, emphasizing the width and depth of her dark eyes, the fullness of her mouth, the long curve of her neck.

She couldn't have provoked a more complete physical reaction from him had she walked out in nothing at all.

He forced himself to stare at the phone in his hands. "I put your pie on the nightstand next to the bed," he forced himself to say.

She didn't move.

He didn't, either.

"Thank you."

He shrugged off her thanks and reached for the remote control. But the blasted thing refused to work. After a couple of moments spent futilely punching at the buttons, he tossed it onto the round, scarred table.

"I thought you could sleep in the bed closer to the bathroom," he said.

"So you could be closer to the door."

He looked up to catch her smile and felt the irresistible desire to smile back. "Yes."

She slowly crossed the room to the bed in question and began folding back the hideous bedspread. "I had another thought in mind."

Stick to her face, McCoy. Stick to her face.

She propped up the pillows on both sides of the bed. "I thought we might share one bed."

Jake nearly crushed his cell phone altogether.

She sat down and pulled her knees close to her chest. Far from the femme fatale her words implied, she acted as though she'd just suggested they engage in a long chat about the change in the weather. "Our being so...close would allow you to keep even a better eye on me."

Jake cleared his throat. "Um, yes, that it would."

"You object?"

He shook his head, then nodded. With a strangled sigh, he slipped his phone into his jacket pocket then pulled the jacket closed. "I find you very...attractive, Michelle. There's no denying that. But it would be..." *Unprofessional? Crazy? Decadent?* "It would be, um, imprudent for me to entertain ideas of you and I...well, making love."

He realized he hadn't even considered that this might be some sort of ploy on Michelle's behalf to gain her freedom. In his usually highly suspicious mind, he was notably unwary of her motives. Perhaps it was because of the way she looked at him, as though she was as interested in exploring the sparks that flew between them as he was. Or maybe it was the casual, unaffected way she invited him into bed with her. Either way, he knew, just knew on a deeper level he was hesitant to explore, that her desire to sleep with him was a result of just that—desire.

"Imprudent?" she questioned, the word rolling like melted sugar off her foreign tongue.

"Wrong," he said.

"Oh." She wriggled her toes until they were tucked under the white sheets. Her skin was as pale as the crisp linen, and appeared softer. "Because of your…job."

"Yes, of course, because of my job." Suddenly agitated, Jake stood. What he wouldn't give for a little of her chattiness right about now.

"I see."

"Good." He stepped to the curtains and pulled them back to stare outside. Rain came down in drenching sheets, making the night dark and intimate.

He watched her reflection in the glass as she got up and went into the bathroom again, then came out with her monster-size purse. Within moments, she was on the bed, propping something up on the nightstand next to the generous helping of cherry pie from the all-night diner next door. He slowly turned, finding her running a fingertip along the surface of a picture. Then she sat against the pillows and closed her eyes.

"Your daughter?"

She blinked and looked at him. "Yes."

He sat on the other bed and folded his hands tightly between his knees. The little girl looked nothing like he'd imagined she might. Rather than the dark hair and eyes he'd given her, she had straight blond hair that shone nearly white, and large green eyes.

Nearly four years old and she'd gone without seeing her mother for eight weeks. Jake ran his hand over his face then rubbed the back of his neck. He'd been seven years old when his mother had died. And the days afterward, recovering from the shock, had seemed like months. Years.

Michelle propped her chin onto her bended knees and gazed at him. "Explain to me why your job makes it—what is the word that you used?"

"Imprudent."

She pressed her mouth against her skin. "Yes. Imprudent. Imprudent for us to have sex."

Jake shifted on the mattress, which reminded him that he was sitting on a bed. And that Michelle was sitting on another bed not a foot and a half away. He focused on his white-knuckled hands. "I could lose my job."

"If anyone found out."

"I'd know."

"Oh."

"Anyway, it's not in my, um, nature to sleep with someone I just met twelve hours ago."

"Eighteen."

"Huh?"

"We met eighteen hours ago. Remember? When we bumped into each other in the parking lot."

"Oh. Yeah. Eighteen hours ago, then."

She rubbed her cheek against her knee. "Why?"

He grimaced. "Why what?"

"Why is it not in your nature to have sex with someone you just met eighteen hours ago?"

He didn't miss her word usage. He'd described the possibility of their coming together as sleeping together. She'd called it having sex. He cleared his throat. And that's exactly what they would be doing, wasn't it? Having sex? They didn't know each other well enough for the word *love* to enter into the equation. He thought back, trying to remember if he'd ever done it. Had just plain sex. All six of the women he'd been with intimately had been longtime girlfriends, and he'd cared for them to varying degrees. But had he loved them? At the time, he supposed he had, which meant he'd made love to them, not had sex with them.

He gazed at Michelle. With all that wild hair pulled into that neat little twist, she looked different. More presentable. More like the type of woman he would be attracted to. Then why did he have the irrepressible urge to take it down? Watch it cascade down her back in silky, curly strands?

"Do you do that often?"

Her soft, feathery brows drew slightly together. "What? Have sex?"

He averted his gaze.

"Not nearly often enough."

He didn't respond. Couldn't respond.

"I haven't been with a man…well, since before Lili was born."

Over four years.

Jake didn't know why that should make him feel better. The woman had just suggested they climb between the sheets and have at it, and she didn't know him any better than the man in the moon. But he did feel better.

His want of her also shot up a hefty notch.

Michelle's lusty sigh pulled his gaze to her face as she leaned against the pillows and stretched her legs out in front of her. "I thought it couldn't be true. The rumor that Americans are sexually uptight. I guess it's the truth."

The word *sexually* came out sounding like a highly provocative suggestion. Jake fought the desire to stare at her mouth, though she had likely just insulted him. "I don't know that we're sexually uptight. We're just cautious, that's all. These are dangerous times we live in."

She shrugged, the movement making her small breasts jiggle under the cotton of her camisole. "That's what condoms are for."

"There's more than that to be cautious about."

"What? What is there that could possibly be important enough to keep a man and a woman apart when it's apparent they want each other?"

He was unable to tug his gaze away from her openly poignant one. She looked so unimaginably sexy, her eyes alight with fire, her mouth lushly challenging. "Fatal Attraction?"

Her burst of laughter was nearly his undoing. "You're talking about that movie, yes? The one where Michael Douglas's lady friend boiled his daughter's pet rabbit?"

He grinned. "Yes."

"Do you have a rabbit?"

"No."

"Then I can't very well boil it, now, can I?" She rubbed her toes against the arch of her other foot, her expression shifting. "Anyway, I'm returning to France tomorrow. There's no risk there, is there?"

He stared at his hands again. "I guess not."

"So what are you still doing on that bed when you're welcome in this one?"

Jake felt himself on the losing end of this battle. His pulse rate sped up. His throat tightened. And he wanted nothing more than to take her up on her invitation, consequences be damned.

"Respect," he said.

"Respect?"

"Yes. A gentleman never takes advantage of a woman. He…" He couldn't think when he looked at her, so he shifted his gaze to his fingers. "He, um, gets to know her first—her likes, her dislikes, her favorite color, things, um, like that. Gets to know her on an emotional level before moving on to the physical."

Her generous smile caught him off guard. "That's the most I've heard you say all at once. This subject must really bother you."

He shrugged his tense shoulders. "It's the way I was raised."

"But why give a woman what she isn't asking for?"

He didn't answer her. God, she was forthright, wasn't she?

Her head lolled on the pillow. A few strands of dark hair broke free and drifted to lie across her cheek. "Okay, then. Things I like. I like the feel of the sun on my face when it's just risen over the horizon. I like it when I'm in the kitchen cooking, experimenting with new flavors." Her voice dropped an octave. "I like holding my daughter after she's been outside, smelling the fresh air in her hair, on her skin."

Jake's gaze drifted to the picture on the nightstand.

"My dislikes. I don't like when the shower runs out of hot water when I still have shampoo in my hair. I don't like new shoes when they're too tight and need to be broken in." She bit briefly her bottom lip. "I don't like that I can't hear my daughter's deep breathing as she sleeps."

Silence settled over the shadowy room. He'd asked the questions. He didn't know why her answers should affect him so.

"My favorite color is purple."

He looked up to find her smiling. "Purple?"

She nodded. "Now you go."

Jake's stomach tightened. He'd said he wanted to know those things of the women he dated. He hadn't mentioned sharing those answers with them.

"You like...?" Michelle prompted.

"I like..." His words drifted off.

She waited, her head resting against the white pillowcase. "Why don't you start with your dislikes? It might be easier."

"Okay." He paused, thinking. "I dislike..." His mind went completely, totally blank. This was a unique situation for him. Not his reluctance to speak—he'd always been conservative with words. But Michelle's interest in his thoughts threw him for a loop.

"You want me to try for you?"

He nodded slowly, relieved by the reprieve, curious as to what she'd say.

Michelle sat up cross-legged. Jake fought the desire to look at her lap, at the way her panties were likely stretched across her feminine parts. "Okay, Jake McCoy, this is how I see you."

He smiled, wondering just how much she thought she knew about him in such a short period of time, and what he'd say when she was wrong.

"You don't like to step outside your box."

"Box?"

"Yes...your comfort zone. You like things the way you like them, and you don't like change."

He stared at his hands.

"You obey a set of internal rules—"

"What do you know about rules?" he asked a little too abruptly, unaware he'd felt so vehemently about her apparent lack of them, and uncomfortable of her awareness of his truckload full.

She sat silently for a moment, gazing at him. "I know plenty about rules." She rubbed her palm against her leg absently. "It's rules that will cut short my search for my daughter. It's rules that have you on that bed, me on this one." She hopelessly tried to smooth stray tendrils of hair into the twist. "No one actually likes stepping outside their box, Jake."

"You seem to do it easily enough."

"Only because I have to."

He narrowed his eyes. "You have to sleep with me?"

He watched her slender neck contract as she swallowed. "I want to sleep with you."

"So what is it you *have* to do?" he asked.

Her voice was so low it was almost a whisper. "I have to find my daughter so I can go back to my life the way it was."

Jake paused. Interesting. He was just thinking his life had truly yet to begin.

She worried her bottom lip between her teeth, then sighed. "All right. Enough of your dislikes. You obviously dislike anyone guessing anything about you. Why don't we go back to your likes?"

"My likes?"

She nodded.

Well, he'd better get on with it, or she'd likely offer answers for him. And he didn't know if he could bear her guessing so accurately.

"I, um, I like the smell of hay when it's just been cut," he said haltingly.

Her brown eyes warmed. "Good. That's good. I like that, too. You must have been born in the country, like I was."

Too bad those countrysides were in different parts of the world, Jake thought. He caught the errant thought and went on. "I like the taste of roast beef straight from the oven. You know, when it melts on your tongue like gravy." He coughed. He'd be the first to admit, he never went beyond what was absolutely necessary to get his point across. So what was with that gravy bit?

He expected to see amusement in her eyes when he looked

at her. Instead, he saw a simmering heat that caused a responding spark to ignite in his groin.

He didn't quite know what it was about this woman that made him feel different, made him want to act on impulses he might not even have noticed before. He traded the side of his bed for hers, and hesitantly cupped the side of her face. She uncrossed her legs and leaned into his touch, her lashes fanning across her cheeks.

He eyed her mouth, torn between wanting to kiss her and needing to pull away. "I, um, like you."

Like wasn't even the word. He *burned* for her. If he couldn't take her right now, bury himself in her slick, hot flesh, he felt like he'd die. Right then and there. He couldn't remember a time he'd wanted a woman so passionately, so desperately. Above and beyond everything he knew was right and made sense. All he knew was an obsessive need to possess her.

He inexpertly pressed his lips against hers. Testing her. Testing himself. Then all thoughts of right or wrong, awkwardness or skill deserted him, and he branded that lush mouth of hers with a kiss so hot, even she widened her eyes briefly before curling into him, opening to him, moaning in obvious relief and desire.

Maybe she was right. Maybe there were times when just plain sex was called for.

He reached up and tried to take the band from her hair. She made a soft little sound, telling him he must have hurt her. He began to pull away.

"Sorry."

"No, no, it's okay."

Catching his hand, she freed her hair for him. He carefully shook the pins out with his fingers, reveling in the silken feel of her curls as they cascaded around his hands and wrists, teasing the skin there. He tangled his tongue with hers, unable to taste near enough, fast enough for his liking.

There was that word again. Like. He liked her responsiveness. He liked the way she arched against him, the pointed tips of her breasts pressing against his starched white shirt. He liked the sound of her soft moans, her shallow breathing as she pushed and pulled at his jacket, getting it halfway down his arms, essentially pinning him, before moving to the buttons of his shirt.

Oh, how he liked giving himself over to something greater than his internal code of conduct. It felt...indecent. Demanding. Liberating.

He clumsily shrugged the remainder of the way out of his jacket, then his open shirt and bunched-up T-shirt. Michelle immediately pressed her hot palms against his flat nipples, then followed with her tongue, nipping at his sensitive flesh with her teeth, then sucking him deep into her mouth.

Jake groaned, then grasped her upper arms, claiming her mouth once again as his. Delving his tongue deeply into the wet recesses, skimming the smooth enamel of her teeth, pulling her tongue into the depths of his.

She tasted of toothpaste and mouthwash, warm skin and soap. She tasted of things forbidden, things denied. She tasted of hungry female to his needy male.

He wasn't sure how it had happened—whether she had done it or he had done it, or if they had done it together—but he was suddenly undressed. His erection pulsed against the skin of his abdomen, ramrod straight and aching. And Michelle was straddling his lap, staring at him with such incredible longing in her eyes he was afraid it would end before it had even begun.

Hesitantly, Jake ran his hands up the velvety skin of her belly, inching her camisole up and then over her head. He caught his breath at the sight of her, then gently cupped her breasts in his palms. They were the perfect size for her height, with large, upward tilting nipples the color of warm honey. He ran the length of his tongue against one, watching as it tightened into a thick nub. He'd never been so turned on by the mere sight of a woman's breasts before. But Michelle's... They encompassed all that she was: small, saucy, provocative and so very, very sexy.

He thoroughly laved first one, then the other, his motions starting out slow, then growing quick, impatient, until he hungrily pulled at her stiff nipples, his hands restlessly traveling over her molten skin, then down to rest on her outer thighs.

Her voice, when she spoke, was soft and husky, "Yes... yes. Touch me...there."

He closed his eyes and muttered a curse against her temple, then drew back as he slid his fingers inward toward the swollen folds pressing against the soft cotton of her panties. Ever so gently, he skimmed his thumb in the shallow crevice, feeling the dampness of her need and her violent shudder. She tried to squeeze her legs together, but he held them open, then tugged the crotch of her underwear aside, baring her curls to his sight.

She whispered something in French. The sound of the thick, unintelligible words drove him mad with longing as he kissed her again and again. She ground her pelvis against his touch, seeking something he feared for a moment he couldn't give her. Then she reached for his erection, rolled on a condom he vaguely remembered taking out of his wallet, then eagerly guided the hooded tip to her slick opening.

Jake was helpless to do more than watch as she lifted herself up onto her knees, then slowly took him into her, inch by torturous inch.

"Oh, God." She was so exquisitely snug and wet, fitting over him like a too small glove. Sweet, agonizing pleasure broke over him, clenching his muscles, contracting his chest until he could do little more than let her take the lead.

And take the lead she did. Much to his surprise, she took every last millimeter into her compact little body and remained perfectly still, as if allowing her muscles time to adjust to the difference in their sizes. Then she rocked her hips forward.

Jake groaned and grasped her hips. If he…if they…if she continued, he'd be a goner in no time at all.

Michelle hungrily ran the tip of her tongue along the seam of his mouth then drew his lower lip into her mouth. "You, um, never told me what your favorite color is," she murmured, then moaned when he thrust upward into her sweet flesh.

What was she talking about? Oh, yes. His favorite color.

He plucked her from his lap and laid her across the sheets, then covered every inch of her skin with his before lifting her right knee and plunging deeply into her with one long, urgent thrust.

Gone were all the barriers that separated them. He was no longer an INS agent. She was no longer an illegal alien. He was no longer a man who had a difficult time identifying and expressing his emotions. She was no longer a woman with problems he couldn't hope to understand. They were simply a man and woman, giving themselves over to the most fundamental of human needs.

He absorbed her shudder and drank her cry into his mouth as he kissed her. He slowly withdrew, then thrust again…and again, until red colored the backs of his eyelids.

"Red," he said between clenched teeth, sliding his hands under her behind and tilting her hips upward. "My favorite color is red."

Then his world exploded into multifaceted spears of the brilliant, vibrant color.

CHAPTER FIVE

SOMEHOW even the rain looked different. Fantastical.

Fantastical? Jake hated the rain.

But this morning all he could do was sit inside the car and stare out the windshield at it, wearing a silly grin.

Last night was…incredible. Hot. Just thinking about it gave him a hard-on. Maybe all this—his near obsessive attraction to Michelle, his preoccupation with her whereabouts, her tight little body—had been about his need to get laid, and laid properly. Giving in to Michelle's request for just plain sex, without commitment, had been one of the best things he'd ever done. He'd never felt so…free in his life. He wanted to get out of the car and stand in the rain, feel it roll down his face and into his mouth, drench his clothes. And usually, unless it had something to do with a shower, he hated getting wet.

Last night had nothing to do with giving. It had been all about take. He'd touched her breasts not to give her pleasure, but to see if they were as pliant as they looked. He'd plucked at her nipples, not to illicit her moan, but to test the erect peaks. He'd grasped her hips not to guide her, but to grind into her. He'd never done that with a woman before. He'd always been hesitant, more concerned with how the woman would like to be touched than how he would like to touch her.

And Michelle…

His erection grew. He groaned in a mixture of pleasure and pain.

Michelle had to be one of the most uninhibited women he'd ever known. She hadn't cared that the lights were on. Had no interest in pulling the blankets up to her chin to block her skin from view. She'd been gloriously proud in her desire. A powerful aphrodisiac, that, watching a woman throw her head back in abandon and stroke herself up and down on his manhood.

"Cripes."

Jake flicked the fan on high. If he didn't stop this, he'd march right into that motel room and take her all over again. And knowing she'd likely be as open to the proposition as he was made it that much more difficult not to.

He hadn't known what to expect when he woke up that morning. He'd stared at the water-stained ceiling, then nearly hit the ceiling when he realized where he was and what he had done. But then he'd turned his head and found Michelle snoring lightly, her bare behind pressed against his side. She hadn't been in the bathroom getting dressed, putting distance between them. No. And her demeanor had remained the same after she awakened. No morning regrets. No coy remarks or shy smiles. She'd yawned, thrown him a sexy, sleep-softened smile over her shoulder, then burrowed further against him.

Jake had been completely floored.

He hadn't known women like Michelle existed. Well, that wasn't entirely true. What he hadn't known was that everyday normal women like Michelle could be so…sexually generous.

That was normally a man's approach, wasn't it? Not that he had ever experienced casual sex before. Even his first time had been with a girl from town he'd known since kindergarten and had courted his entire life. Both he and Mary Beth had sat in the barn afterward wondering if that's all there was.

Oh, no, baby, that definitely wasn't all there was. There was…there was….

There was Michelle.

He watched the door to Room Twelve open, and his erection popped to life again. She'd changed into a pair of stretchy black slacks and a close-fitting white top. She gave the rain a noting glance, then stepped toward the car without rushing, without using her bag to shield her from the rain. When she climbed in, the scent of shampoo from her damp hair filled the interior. It was all Jake could do not to draw the smell in with a deep breath.

He backed out of the spot and headed for the turnpike.

"Michelle, I…"

She looked at him. "Yes?"

He shrugged, then flicked his gaze to the road. "I just felt…think I need, you know, to say something to you about last night…."

She scooted so that her left knee was curved on the seat and she was half facing him.

He couldn't help his grin. "It was…incredible."

Her husky laugh sent a burning sensation through his veins. "Yes, I'd say last night rates up there on the incredible level." She glanced away.

Jake gestured with his right hand. Catching himself, he snapped it onto the steering wheel. "I mean…what I'm trying to say is… Oh, hell, I don't know what I mean."

And he didn't. He'd just wanted to acknowledge what had passed between them. And her sexy little smile told him he'd not only accomplished that, but that she felt the same. "So you don't regret it?" she asked.

He stared at her wide-eyed. "Regret it? Hell, no, I don't regret it." He grimaced at the vehemence of his words. God, he must sound like a nineteen-year-old who'd just experienced his first blow job. "This morning, though, I thought for a minute that maybe you had. Regretted it, I mean."

She shook her head, her curls bouncing around her shoulders. "Not me."

"Good."

Her smile widened. "Great."

"Yeah, it was great, wasn't it?"

She laughed, and he realized he was pretty much repeating himself at this point. Was he really jabbering? Him? Big, silent Jake McCoy? He couldn't count the number of times his brothers had tried to force him to talk. Often when they were younger, Connor used to pin him down, trying to get him to spill something or other. But he never had. Now he was not only offering stuff up voluntarily, he was repeating himself. Go figure.

After a few moments of silence, Michelle looked at him again. But the serious expression on her face chased every single light, sexually charged thought from Jake's mind.

"Jake, I…"

For the first time, he noticed the slight smudges under her dark eyes. While a current of electricity still crackled between them, it was obvious her mind was on something else. More specifically, the fact that he would be sending her back to France.

Jake mentally ground out a curse. It wasn't that he'd forgotten about that small little detail. Oh, hell, who was he kidding? He had purposely shoved aside the fact that she was officially an illegal alien, and he was an INS agent. Another first for him in this recent slew of firsts. Now the weight of reality pressed in on him from all sides.

Michelle straightened her legs and stared out the passenger window.

"Were you going to say something?" he prompted.

She shook her head. "No...nothing."

He cleared his throat and turned his gaze toward the windshield. The emotional turnaround hit Jake like a two-by-four to the head. So occupied was he with the uniqueness of last night, of Michelle's generous nature, her innate sexuality, he'd completely lost sight of exactly where they were and why.

Not anymore.

He should have gotten out and stood in the rain. Maybe it would have woken him up long before now.

MICHELLE'S MUSCLES felt thoroughly worked out, stretched, pulled and sated. She stared out the window at the passing mountainside and absently touched her slightly swollen lips. She tried to keep reminding herself that this was a solemn occasion. She was being taken back to D.C., where she would be placed on a plane for France, her search for Lili abruptly cut off. But all she could do was think about how she had suggested casual sex with Jake the night before, and how there had been nothing casual about it.

She wasn't sure what it was about this man. He was tall, quiet, wholesome. And she'd loved messing him up. It wasn't so much him that concerned her, but her reaction to him.

She'd had attentive lovers before. Men who knew exactly how and where to touch her to bring her pleasure. Men with far more experience than Jake McCoy. But there had been something substantially different about the way he had responded to her. A hunger in him, a fascinating agility and a capacity for deep emotion that had rocked her down to her toes. When he'd cupped her breasts, she'd nearly climaxed right then and there. Not even when she was younger had she been so easily pleased. There was something about the look in his eyes, the heat of his fingers, the sound of his quiet groans, that had turned her inside out in a way she'd been completely unprepared for.

Never, never had anyone stirred her the way he had.

Michelle leaned her forehead against the steamed glass of the window and tightly closed her eyes. She'd once pondered the difference between sex and genuine lovemaking. But she'd stopped that long ago. She'd come to the conclusion that there was sex and great sex, and that great sex must have been what others called lovemaking.

No longer. As foolish as it was, she knew, deep in her bones, that what she and Jake had done last night was made love.

"Merde."

The sound of the windshield wipers reminded her where she was, as did Jake's question. "Pardon me?"

She turned toward the sound of his voice, goose bumps peppering her skin. "What?"

He lightly shrugged, a sexy grin tugging at the sides of his mouth. "I thought you said something."

"No. No. Nothing."

He fell silent again.

Michelle took the opportunity to study him. Really study him. Wasn't it odd that after knowing the man for only a day she should be so comfortable with him in silence? She was a born talker. At least that's what her father used to say when she would come home from school and tell him moment by moment exactly what had happened to her that day. Why then should she be perfectly content, invigorated even, sitting next to Jake McCoy and feeling no need to say anything?

Oh, God, she was in over her head here.

Which was ridiculous, because tomorrow at this time, she'd be in Paris, half a world away, and Jake and last night would seem even farther away.

And so would Lili.

Guilt, quick and consuming, enveloped her.

Jake made a quick swerve into the right lane, then to the

off-ramp. Michelle had to grab the dashboard to stop herself from colliding with him.

"What is it? What's wrong?" she asked, staring at the approaching tollbooth.

"Change in plans, that's all," he said, looking as shocked as she felt. "We're going to take the scenic route back. Through Ohio."

Her heart skipped a beat. Had she heard him right? Had he just said they were going to Ohio? Ohio was where Lili was. And far from being on their way to D.C., it was completely out of the way.

She didn't dare speak for fear that his response would prove she was imagining things.

He glanced at her as he paid the toll, then headed over the bridge and onto the turnpike going west. "That's where you said Lili was, right?"

She nodded slowly, her entire body trembling.

He shrugged, though there was nothing nonchalant about the move. He appeared determined somehow. Serious.

"Jake, I…" she began again for the second time in as many minutes.

"What is it?"

She bit her bottom lip and sighed. "Look, I don't want you to think that you, you know, need to do this because of what happened last night."

He glanced between her and the road several times, then his eyes widened. He looked so endearingly shocked, she nearly laughed. "You mean like as some sort of…favor for a favor?"

She gestured with her hands, trying to pull the right words out. Instead, she settled for a simple yes.

"No," he said.

"Are you sure?"

"Of course I'm sure." She watched his hands tighten on the steering wheel. The same hands that had given her such pleasure only hours before. She shivered. "Look, Michelle, I don't know what you're used to, but this has nothing to do with…you know, our having had sex."

She couldn't help her smile. "Good."

"Great." He grimaced, then shrugged again. "I just, you know, thought that it wouldn't be that big of a deal to go to Ohio, see if this lead you have pans out, before heading back to D.C., you know?"

She really hated to argue with him. After all, he was doing exactly what she would have wished for, if she had dared to wish. "But won't you get in trouble?"

His grin nearly swallowed his handsome face. "Only if anyone finds out."

THREE HOURS LATER, they rolled over the Ohio line. Jake squeezed the steering wheel. He didn't know quite how to explain this. One minute he'd been driving Michelle to D.C. The next he'd been making a U-turn.

She hadn't had to say a word. Hadn't pleaded with him to give her a little while longer. Hadn't played on his conscience about how important a role a mother had in her young daughter's life. No. He'd been the one to silently say the words. Perhaps that's why he'd made the decision himself.

Or maybe it had more to do with the small, ragged elephant he'd found lying on the bed while Michelle showered that morning.

His knuckles whitened. Or perhaps he was way off with both explanations and he was just looking for an excuse to have her in his bed for another night.

"So many roads," Michelle murmured.

He glanced to find her bent over the map, the sunshine

slanting through the window igniting the blue highlights in her curly black hair. Funny, but no sooner had he turned the car west, than the storm clouds had parted. It was difficult to tell it had rained at all.

Michelle crowded her fingers into all that hair and swept it to the other side of her head. She looked at him. "We want to take route—"

. Her words abruptly broke off, and the shadow of a smile lifted her lips. "What?"

Jake realized he was staring, but was helpless to stop between glances at the road. "Your hair. I like it better down."

"Oh." He noted the slight coloring of her cheeks before she turned toward the map spread across her lap.

Had she just blushed? Jake concentrated his attention on the road. Twenty-four hours ago, he'd have sworn nothing was capable of making a ballsy woman like Michelle Lambert blush. Yet she just had. And he had been the cause of it, or at least his spontaneous compliment had. Out of the corner of his eye, he watched her settle her hair around her face.

"Route forty-three." The rustling of paper sounded as she repositioned the map and following a red line with her index finger. "It should be coming up in a few kilom—miles, I think."

"This PI you hired. How sure was he that Li—your daughter is here?"

Michelle slowly folded the map, the hope momentarily draining from her face. "I don't know. I thought he was sure when we went to Kansas last month, then to North Carolina last week." The map crinkled where she held it too tightly.

Jake was filled with the sudden urge to track down the slimy PI and have at him. Not to mention his desire to get hold of her daughter's father.

Another first. He'd never come to fisticuffs with a man over a woman. Never. Not even with his brothers. When Mitch had decided he wanted Liz way back when, he'd stepped aside and never interfered. When Connor had expressed an interest in one of his dates, he'd found a reason to go home and leave the two alone—though, funnily enough, neither of them had seen her again. He'd never felt the need to dole out his own personal brand of justice. But the desire to have his knuckles cleanly connect with the faces of the men who had done Michelle wrong was nearly overwhelming.

He wanted to tell Michelle not to worry, that he'd help her find her daughter. Then it hit him that he didn't have that kind of power. Not in his job. Not over his own damn sense of right and wrong. And what he was doing was definitely beginning to cross the line over to wrong.

He sighed. This morning, Michelle's case had been passed on to Edgar Mollens. Even now, Edgar was likely studying maps, visiting the motel where she'd been staying, checking the phone records for the room and any messages that might have been left for her. If the PI had called her, Edgar would know about it.

Not only were his actions quickly surging toward the wrong column, but one of his colleagues was probably on his tail as he was doing it.

What was he thinking?

Something touched his thigh, and he nearly jumped. He looked down to find Michelle's small hand resting against his slacks, her gaze curious and concerned as she gazed at him.

He knew what he was thinking. He was thinking that Michelle Lambert was a woman, a mother, looking for her child. And he would be a cad if he didn't help her out at least this much.

He turned to the road. Anyway, Ohio wasn't that much out of their way. What was a few more hours before he took her back to D.C.? Nothing to him. But it could mean the world to Michelle…and to little Lili.

He reached down and covered her cooler hand with his, telling his hormones to take a break and purposefully ending the argument he was having with his conscience.

CHAPTER SIX

"Is THIS IT?"

Jake squinted through the midday sun at the new, trilevel brick house across the street from where they were parked.

"Yes. Yes, this is it." Michelle stuffed the piece of paper she held and the map into his glove compartment, then reached for the door handle.

"Whoa, whoa, where are you going so fast?"

She blinked at him. "To get my daughter, of course."

"Just like that?"

Energy seemed to emanate from her. "What would you have me do?"

"Wait for a few minutes. Maybe scope the place out first. See if you can see any signs of Lili before you go barging in there."

Her gaze dropped to his mouth and lingered there. "Say it again."

Her request caught him up short. Jake swallowed hard, wondering what he had said to make her momentarily forget her mission and stare at him so provocatively. "Say what?" he fairly croaked.

"My daughter's name."

Jake wanted to refuse, then realized how stupid that would be. "Lili," he said, trying to sound matter of fact, though the name came out as soft as a sigh.

"I like the way you say it." She reached for the door handle again. "I'll only be a minute."

Just like that? One second she was eyeing his mouth like she wanted to devour it, the next she was getting out of the car, hell-bent on getting her daughter back?

Jake started to shake his head, then realized she was going up there alone.

"Hey," he said, getting out of the car. "Wait for me."

"No, no. You'll only confuse Lili." What went without saying took form in the shadow that passed over her features—*if Lili was there.* "Please. Wait there."

Jake reluctantly did as she asked. He settled himself behind the steering wheel and closed the door. Only then did a whole new emotion hit him: fear.

He and kids…well, they didn't really get along. He supposed it might have to do with his size, or that as an adult he hadn't spent a great deal of time around children. But on the few occasions when he'd made the effort, the kids had practically gone off running in the other direction. His brother Marc had caught one of the exchanges at the Manchester County Fair one year and dubbed him Jake Von Frankenstein. Jake had not been amused.

Speaking of brothers, David was probably not very amused right now, either. Checking through his pockets, he found and pulled out his cell phone and punched in the number. The line began to ring while he watched Michelle's tiny but firm behind as she walked up the curved drive of Lili's grandparents' house. Nice suburban place. Just around the back, he caught a glimpse of what looked like one of those wood play centers for kids.

Four rings at the McCoy place and David had yet to pick up. Pops would be in D.C. working. Mitch would be doing something or other around his new horse-breeding operation.

He didn't have a clue where his sister-in-law Liz would be. At the diner maybe? Or at the office Mitch had built for her in the barn? They hadn't yet had a phone installed there.

A car passed to his left. Normally, it wouldn't have warranted his attention, except that it slowed. And it was also an exact replica of the one he sat in.

His co-worker, agent Edgar Mollens had tracked Michelle down faster than he'd expected.

Dread, thick and gritty, lined his stomach.

MICHELLE RUBBED her damp palms on her slacks for a third time. She glanced at the large double doors, then at Jake's car, wishing she hadn't asked him to stay behind. Just having him near did wonders for her peace of mind. And if there was one thing she needed right now, it was peace.

Questions, one right after another, swept through her mind. What if the PI had given her a bogus address, just looking for a way to get her out of his office? What if the people who lived here didn't even know Gerald or Lili and called the cops? What if no one was home? Would Jake head for D.C.?

What if she never saw Lili again?

Her heart clogging her throat, she watched her hand rap on the door without any conscious knowledge of having sent the order to her tightly coiled muscles.

Please, please, please…

A full minute later she heard footsteps on tile then a hand touch the doorknob. She realized the occupant must be looking through the peephole. She squared her shoulders and fought the desire to duck to the right. If Lili was there, then Michelle would be the last person Gerald's parents would want to see.

Another minute passed. Michelle's heart beat so loudly, she barely made out a second pair of footsteps on the other side of the door. Finally, it opened.

She stared at the neat, fiftyish woman eyeing her openly. She was wearing a navy and gold silk jogging suit and looked as if she'd just come from the beauty parlor. She resembled any one of the hundreds of older, wealthy tourists that crammed Paris streets in the summer.

This was usually the point where the PI had done the talking. Michelle didn't know how much she'd counted on his presence to break the ice, ask the questions until now. Through Kansas and North Carolina, he'd taken the lead. Now she was on her own.

"Yes? Can I help you?" the woman asked. She gripped the edge of the door with her pink-neon-tipped fingers as if prepared to close it quickly.

Michelle cleared her throat and forced herself to speak loudly enough to be heard. "Yes…hello. I'm Michelle Lambert."

She searched for any sign that the woman recognized her name. There was none.

"Are you Mrs. Evans?"

"Why, yes, I am." The fingers tightened. "Should I know you, Ms. Lambert?"

"I'm looking for my daughter," Michelle blurted.

The door started to close. "I'm not sure I understand."

"Your son…his name is Gerald, yes?"

"Why, yes, it is."

"Is he here?"

"Ms. Lambert, I'm not entirely sure why, but this conversation is making me uncomfortable. Do you mind explaining what it is exactly that you want?"

A man stepped beside Mrs. Evans, and Michelle caught her breath. The resemblance between Gerald and this man was uncanny. She caught a glimpse of exactly what Gerald would look like in twenty or so years. Thinning blond hair, capped teeth, skin the texture of leather from one too many rounds of golf. "Miss, is there something I can help you with?" he asked gruffly. Even his voice was the same.

Michelle opened her mouth, but no sound came out.

The woman looked at the man. "Leland, I can't say as I like this—"

"My daughter, Lili...Elizabeth." Her accent grew heavier, and she fought to enunciate each word clearly. "Do you know where she is?"

The couple looked at each other again, then the man stepped forward, smoothly moving his wife from in front of the door. "The name isn't familiar...Ms. Lambert, isn't it? Neither my wife nor I know anyone with the name Lili. Sorry. Now if you'll excuse us—"

He began closing the door.

"No!" Michelle tried to stop the forward movement.

Footfalls sounded from the sidewalk behind her. Desperately she turned toward Jake. "Please! You must stop—"

Her words died in her throat. Jake wasn't the one behind her. Rather, a man in his mid-forties with dark hair and wearing a pea-green polyester suit stared at her as he pulled something from his jacket pocket. "Ms. Lambert, I'm Immigration Agent Edgar Mollens. I am officially taking you into custody for immediate deportation for the violation of the terms of your visa."

JAKE SCRAMBLED from the car, reflexively reaching for his ID as he strode up the curved drive. Damn, he didn't have his ID. Not that it mattered; Edgar knew who he was. What he should be more concerned with was what Edgar would do once he knew what *he'd* done. Strangely, though, he couldn't bring himself to care. All he knew was an overwhelming desire to protect Michelle from Edgar, who would send her back.

"Let me go, you imbecile." Michelle shouted, tugging her arm from Edgar's grip. "I'm not going anywhere until I get Lili."

Jake came to a stop behind his fellow agent and planted his feet shoulder-width apart. It was all he could do to keep his hands fisted at his sides. What he'd rather do was yank Mollens back by his collar. "Let her go, Edgar," he said evenly.

The agent swung around quickly, his right hand reaching inside his jacket pocket. Jake gave in to the urge to grab him, to prevent him from pulling out the weapon he was surely reaching for.

"Jake."

Edgar settled down and dropped his hands to his sides, a loud sigh indicating his relief. Jake released him, thinking he'd feel better if he had his own firearm. It had taken some effort to leave it in its case yesterday morning. After all, a gun might have come in handy on a hiking trip. A nine millimeter was known to stop all sorts of wild animals.

Jake couldn't say he either liked or disliked the man in front of him. They'd been sent out on a few of the tougher cases together, where backup was required. While he'd disapproved of some of Edgar's personal grooming habits and preferred not to take meals with him, Edgar had scored high on the professional scale. He took his job seriously.

Perhaps too seriously.

He grimaced. *Too* was not a word he would have linked with *seriously* twenty-four hours ago. After all, how could a man be too serious about his job? But standing here looking down the other end of the barrel, so to speak, he gained a perspective he wasn't sure he liked.

Edgar finger-combed the wisps that passed for hair on the top of his head. "Flying monkeys, McCoy, you could have gotten yourself shot. What the hell are you doing here, anyway? Don't tell me. There was a screw-up in D.C. and you were sent out on the same case."

Jake shook his head. "No screw-up."

Edgar's bushy brows drew together. "Then what *are* you doing here?"

"The question is, what are you doing here, Edgar?"

Now that there was no immediate danger, Jake chanced a glance at Michelle. She looked shaken to the bone, her gaze torn between the closed front door and the agent who endangered her freedom to search for Lili. He was filled with a powerful urge to pull her to his side. To block her petite frame from view. To protect her with every ounce of strength he had.

When he returned his attention to Edgar, he found him frowning. "I'm here to deport one Michelle Lambert, illegal alien, back to France." He glanced at Michelle. "Is this her?"

Jake nodded once, curtly.

"Then I'm afraid I have to take her into immediate custody, Jake."

Behind Edgar, he saw Michelle ready to bolt.

The desperate move made his stomach drop down somewhere in the vicinity of his ankles. Where would she go? What could she possibly do? He knew she wouldn't get two feet before Edgar would have cuffs slapped on her wrists.

Edgar's frown deepened. "Are you all right, McCoy? You look a little…odd."

Jake gave a humorless laugh. Odd about covered it. He felt odd. He didn't have a clue what to do with the unfamiliar emotions swirling inside him. He'd always been one to follow his instincts, but they had always led him in the right direction. Now he couldn't be so sure. But he had to follow them anyway.

"You can't take her," he said.

"Okay," Edgar said slowly. "I hear you, Jake."

An image of the ID he'd lost sprinted through his mind, ID he might never see again.

"But you're going to have to give me one good reason why I can't. You know, something for the records."

A reason. Jake searched for one that would stand up to any sort of scrutiny, and somehow he didn't think Edgar would go for the she's-looking-for-her-daughter defense.

His mind finally locked onto one. Without even considering the consequences to his career, he said, "Because she's my wife."

MICHELLE SAT spellbound in the car next to Jake. That agent, Edgar Mollens, motioned for them to drive away first. Jake waved for him to go. Mollens finally drove off, and Jake switched off the engine.

She's my wife.

She didn't know why Jake had said that, but she was mighty glad he had. The agent who had been about to drag her to D.C. had stood in utter shock right along with her for a few moments, then reached out to shake Jake's hand before backing off completely. He'd said something about needing documented proof before the day was out, then got into his car.

She gazed at the man next to her, nearly getting lost in the deep gray of his eyes. She didn't know why he'd done all that he had. Had stopped trying to figure that out since the night before, when instead of driving her to D.C., he'd checked into a motel. Then this morning, did a one-eighty and headed for Ohio. She'd contented herself with being thankful, and thankful only, determined to get the most out of the generous time she could.

Only it appeared that it was all for naught. Yes, the name of the couple in the house across the street may be Evans, but she had no reason to think they knew more than what they had said.

Still, if she had to be taken to D.C., she'd rather Jake do it. Spending any time at all with Edgar Mollens made her insides go cold.

"Why did you do that? I mean—" She caught herself up short, not wanting to push the issue, not wanting to give him an opportunity to change his mind. But she had to know. "Why did you say I was your wife?"

Jake's expression was somber as he probed her face. "I figured it was the only way to get Edgar to take a hike." A hint of a smile played around his mouth. "Hey, there's something to be said for flying straight your entire life. People have a tendency to believe you when you say something."

"Do you think so? Seemed to me you could have knocked Mollens over with a feather."

"I said he believed me, I didn't say he wasn't shocked. That's one of the drawbacks of being predictable." He trained his gaze out the window. She noted the lines of worry drawn between his brows and felt the incredible urge to reach out and smooth them away. A short time ago, he'd said he was doing what he was because he was at no risk so long as no one knew. What happened now that someone did know? Not only someone, but a man he worked with?

She wrapped her arms around herself.

"What did they say?" he asked.

Michelle blinked at him. "Pardon me?"

He gestured toward the large house. "Are they Gerald's parents?"

She nodded.

"And Lili?"

Michelle stared at where she twisted her hands in her lap. "They say they've never heard of me...or her."

He reached for the door handle. "I'll be right back."

For the second time in as many minutes, Michelle sat dumbstruck as Jake strode toward the Evanses' door. Finally gathering her wits, she clambered out after him, catching up as the door opened to reveal Gerald's father.

Jake reached in his jacket pocket, then grimaced and reached into another. He held out a business card exactly like the one he'd given her. "I'm Agent Jake McCoy. I need your son Gerald's most recent address."

The man had to look up to directly address Jake's gaze. "You didn't say which agency you're with, Agent McCoy."

"No, I didn't. It's on the card, sir." Jake met and held his gaze. "The address, Mr. Evans."

Michelle watched in amazement as the older man gave it to him. Relief threatened to sweep her knees right out from underneath her.

CHAPTER SEVEN

JAKE'S HEART pounded in his chest. He tried to tell himself it was because the mere idea of being married, much less to the sexy woman next to him in the car, was terrifying. Then thoughts of night after night in her arms—between her thighs, hearing her soft cries in French—intruded, and he nearly groaned out loud. It didn't matter that any long-term relationship was an improbability. No, an impossibility. His body seemed to have other ideas, and every time he looked at her, trembling from her hair to her feet, he got harder than any man had a right to.

Michelle clutched the piece of paper holding the address for one Gerald Evans in northwest Ohio. "I can't believe this is happening. I don't know what to say...." Her words drifted off, though her lips kept moving.

He'd be willing to bet that her inability to speak was new to her. Chalk up another first.

He couldn't help his foolish grin. Despite the mess he'd just made out of his life with those four simple words back there, "because she's my wife," when Michelle looked at him this way—her eyes liquid milk chocolate, her face practically beaming—he felt a hundred feet tall.

It reminded him of the way he'd felt the first day on the job as an INS agent. He'd been assigned to apprehend an Asian arms dealer who happened to have a taste for a specially ordered type of Chinese herb. He put the only place that sold the herb in New York under surveillance and apprehended the guy. Then he'd watched him go through deportation proceedings and put him on an airplane bound for Peking and the authorities there. It had been one of the most defining moments of his life. He'd felt like he was making a difference, that what he'd accomplished that day not only kept guns off the streets, but told him what he had been put on this earth to do.

What he felt now was a lot like that, only more intense somehow.

"Thank-you should do the trick," he suggested, not sure where the light remark had come from, but glad it had come.

He was rewarded with her smile. "A joke. You just made a joke."

He drove unhindered toward northwest Ohio, toward the address in Toledo where Gerald Evans lived. Two and a half hours, the toll guard had told him. "Yeah. I guess I did, didn't I?"

Michelle slid her hand over his where it rested on the steering wheel. He spread his fingers, and she thread hers through. He gave a tight squeeze. "Thank you," she murmured, her accent thick.

He glanced to find one-hundred-percent pure gratitude lighting her smile. "You're, um, welcome."

She shifted until she was sitting flush next to him, her hip against his, her arm against his side. She sat like that for a long time without saying anything, then slipped her hand from his grip and laid it against his thigh. "Why?" she asked. "I mean, why are you doing all this for me, Jake McCoy? We've, um, already established that it isn't about sex. Anyway, no one's *that* good." Her tiny smile softened her words. "Then you said it was all right so long as no one knew about it, which after what happened at the Evanses' is no longer the case. So...why? Why are you risking so much to help me?"

That was a question he didn't want to examine too closely. He considered telling her it was because it made him feel good, only that had come after he'd done what he had.

He wasn't exactly sure why. One minute he'd been in a pissing contest with Edgar Mollens over who was going to win Michelle's company, the next he was telling his fellow agent he was married to what was now a deportable illegal alien.

"I wanted to give you this chance to find your daughter," he said. Well, it was part of the reason, so he wasn't exactly lying. He just wasn't telling the complete truth, either, though what that truth was, he couldn't say.

She rested her temple against his shoulder. Her gaze caressed him as thoroughly as a touch. "Why?"

He swallowed hard. "I don't know."

Then, suddenly, he did know. He understood all too clearly why it was he was helping this mother find her daughter. What was more puzzling was that he wanted to tell her. He'd never been much for words. He'd learned early on that an expression, a carefully directed look, could accomplish more than any words. And he'd never felt a need to verbally express himself, at least not to the extent that others did.

"I...I was raised without my mother," he said quietly, surprised at the ease with which the words flowed. "She, um, died when I was seven years old." It seemed all his life he had avoided speaking the words aloud, as if afraid openly acknowledging what had been a very tragic point in his life would bring back all the pain. Instead, he felt as if an indescribable weight was shifting in his chest. "I know what it means to grow up without a parent. In my case, it was unavoidable. I couldn't exactly go out and find my mother." He glanced at her, finding her expression warm and curious. "In yours... Well, let's just say that sometime this morning I realized I couldn't take you back to D.C. and put you on a plane without first giving you an opportunity to find Lili." His voice dropped to a near murmur. "A little girl, especially, needs her mother."

She turned, and the look she gave him was direct, so poignant, he felt the strange sensation that she was able to see right through his exterior to what dwelled deep inside.

"So do little boys."

She spoke so quietly, Jake couldn't be sure if she'd said the words or if his subconscious had whispered them.

The first rule he'd learned after his mother's death was that he could never let anyone know how much he mourned her loss. Well, anyone else, anyway. After the funeral, still dressed in their new suits, Pops had dropped him and Connor off at school. He hadn't understood why at the time, but had since assumed that Sean thought it important for them to get back to a sense of normalcy as soon as possible. Only nothing had been normal. And when a bully two years his senior had made it his mission to get dirt on his suit during recess and Jake had found himself pinned to the ground under the older boy's weight, he'd repeatedly cried out for his mother in an agonized way that still echoed through his mind.

He didn't talk to his father for what seemed like weeks afterward. In fact, he rarely spoke to anyone at all. Speaking meant revealing, and revealing meant being stripped of all but his most fundamental defenses.

He realized the car was silent and looked at Michelle. Her brown eyes were moist, as though she'd seen what he'd been thinking. Understood his anguish better than anyone else ever could.

He cleared the emotion clogging his throat. "It was…a long time ago. It's okay. I've adjusted."

"I'm sorry. When I asked you why, I didn't mean to dredge up anything so painful. I guess I've spent too much time around my daughter. Sometimes it seems every other word out of her mouth is *pourquoi*—sorry, why."

Jake thought of the woman next to him and mentally compared her to what he remembered about his mother. He couldn't say whether they were similar, except for the warm smile Michelle wore whenever she spoke of Lili. That look was intensely familiar. If there was one physical thing he remembered clearly, it was his mother's smile. The tremendous emotional impact of her absence was another. A sometimes tangible shadow against his soul. Always there inside him...at least, until now.

Michelle absently traced a circle of heat on his thigh with her fingers. It was all he could do not to scoot farther down so the circle would be encompassing a completely different area indeed.

"Do you know any French?" she asked.

Jake's semiaroused state went up a notch. He found he liked her speaking in French, perhaps a little too much. But now was not the time to ask her to say something in it, not if he hoped to stay on the road. "A bit."

"What? What do you know?"

He'd never used his limited knowledge of foreign languages for conversational purposes and he felt awkward about doing it now. "Okay. *Je m'appelle* Jake McCoy. Agent Jake McCoy. *Votre passeport, s'il vous plait. Par ici, s'il vous plait.*"

Michelle didn't say anything for a long moment, then the hand disappeared from his thigh; her warmth vanished from his side. She moved to the passenger's seat. He didn't think it possible for two people to be in the same car yet be so far apart. The immediate change in temperature made him want to groan.

"What? What is it? Did I mispronounce something?"

She shook her head, keeping her gaze trained out the window. "No. Your pronunciation was good. Very good." Her voice dropped to a whisper. "Too good."

Then it hit him. In French he'd introduced himself as an agent, asked for her passport, then told her to come with him. Cripes, if anything could have underscored the seriousness of their current situation, that did. How stupid could he get?

He cleared his throat. "What other things does Lili say?"

For a long moment, Michelle didn't move, just sat staring out the window. Then her quiet voice filled the interior of the car like a welcome hum. "She's always asking how old she is."

She fell silent again. Well, that attempt at getting things back on an even keel had certainly worked, hadn't it? If his questions would get only one-sentence responses, then this was going to be one hell of a long ride to Toledo.

He chanced a glance in her direction. Rather than finding her sitting stoically ignoring him, she was fingering something she'd taken from inside her backpack, a faraway look on her face. "She was always disappointed when I told her she was the same age today as she had been yesterday, as if she'd expected to have grown at least five years older overnight." Her short-nailed fingers plucked at the elephant's droopy trunk. "She's growing up so fast as it is. Seems like just yesterday she was this toothless imp who cooed at me when she was happy or shrieked at me when she wanted something. It scares me sometimes, her impatience to grow up so quickly, you know?"

She looked at him then. And Jake's stomach did a double dip. The fear she spoke of was there, along with the undeniable fear of never seeing her daughter again.

She tugged her gaze away. "Ironic, really, that after I invested so much time in pointing out the exact date of her birthday she would spend that day away from me."

Jake felt the sudden urge to wrap his fingers around some-thing—more specifically, Gerald's neck.

Michelle had said Lili's birthday was on Saturday, four days away. Maybe she'd see her daughter by then.

"Is she talking much yet?" he asked, then cringed. Of course she was talking much. Just went to show how little he knew about children.

Michelle's bark of laughter eased some of his tension. "Talking? She's a little speechmaker who's motto is 'have soapbox, will travel.' I don't know what they're teaching her in nursery school, or how she remembers everything so clearly, but when I pick her up, I get lectures on the impor-tance of buckling my safety belt or the significance of brush-ing my teeth. Then there are the lessons on how she—and I—shouldn't talk to strangers. That was a big lesson, that one. She memorized our phone number. I'm very proud of her, even if half the time she transposes the last two digits. Just yesterday she was telling me about strangers—"

She abruptly halted. Jake's chest tightened at the stricken look on her face. "What? What's the matter?" he asked, wanting to reach for her hand, but unable to. He cursed at his hesitation.

"I...I just said she told me yesterday." Michelle caught her bottom lip between her teeth and shook her head. "Thank you."

Jake grimaced. "Why should you be thanking me?"

Her smile was weak and watery but inexplicably power-ful. "For a second there, talking to you made me forget that I haven't seen my daughter for eight weeks. I used the present tense when talking about her, rather than the past. I...I haven't felt this close to her in a long, long time."

This time Jake did reach out, before he had a chance to think about it, before he had a chance to hesitate. He cupped her cheek, marveling at the way she instinctively leaned into his touch. He rubbed the pad of his thumb against the dampness of her tears. What she had shared about Lili made the mental picture of her come to life. He could see the blond little girl's mouth going a mile a minute, her expressive face contorting as she realized this fact or that. He could see the fire in the woman next to him residing in Lili.

Jake's gaze was drawn to Michelle's provocative mouth. He'd have given anything to kiss her right then, to taste the salt of her tears, the depth of her anguish.

Instead, he forced his gaze to the road before he ran off it.

AS THE CAR cruised along the I-280 bridge over the Maumee River into Toledo, Michelle stared at the city's landscape, her heart pulsing in her chest. She knew an instant of fear. The city was larger than she expected. She'd assumed it would be a smaller town, like so many she'd seen over the past six weeks in her search for her daughter. Like Canton, where Gerald's parents lived. This city was too large, had too many places where one could hide a four-year-old girl.

"Holy Toledo," Jake murmured next to her.

She glanced at him.

He gave her a small smile. "It's just something Klinger used to say on M.A.S.H. You know, Jamie Farr…" His words drifted off, and he turned to the road. "Sorry. It was an American TV show. It may have played in France?"

She shook her head. "I've never watched much television."

"Oh."

She looked down to find herself clutching her backpack for dear life. She forced herself to relax her grip. "Not much farther now."

"Nope," Jake quietly agreed.

"In a few minutes I'll either have Lili back in my arms, or…"

He reached for her hand, and she gladly gave it to him, familiar with the burst of desire that crept up her skin at his every touch. "We'll deal with the other when—if we come to it, okay?"

She nodded. "Okay."

She glanced at him, memorizing the lines of his profile, the strong jut of his jaw, and envisioned what he must have looked like as a little boy—tall, gangly, probably awkward. And silent, always silent.

There was an intensity about Jake McCoy that both intrigued and scared her. She knew what it was costing him to do this for her—on an emotional as well as a career level. Not that he'd ever really tell her. She got the impression that when he made up his mind about something, he did it. No long explanations. No voicing of possible regrets down the line. His reaction to their lovemaking told her that.

Before she knew it, he'd parked at a curb. A sign a couple of blocks back had announced the neighborhood as the Old West End. Large houses towered over nicely manicured streets. The leaves of some of the larger trees were beginning to turn vibrant oranges and reds. Such a pretty place. Such a dark mission.

She turned toward Jake to find him staring at his rearview mirror. She glanced through the back window, half hoping, half fearing she would find him looking at Gerald. Instead, she saw a car resembling the one they were in parking a block down.

He looked at her. "Are you ready?"

She nodded, completely incapable of speech at that moment.

He climbed from the car, and she followed, meeting him on the brick walkway leading to the large Victorian-style home bearing the address Mr. and Mrs. Evans had given them. Michelle knew a stab of sorrow. Gerald had obviously reached a point where money was of no concern to him, yet he'd never offered any kind of financial support. And she didn't want any, she firmly told herself. His ability to inflict such irreversible pain on Lili by ripping her from everything that was familiar, all that she'd ever known, told her that no amount of money could make up for Gerald Evans's crime.

Jake paused at the multipaned wood door, studying her face. Then he gave a quick nod and rang the doorbell. Michelle's heart nearly stopped right then and there.

Nothing. No sound other than the bell reverberating through the large interior.

He rang the bell again.

"Hello, there!" a female voice called.

Jake tugged his gaze from Michelle and sought the woman working on the lawn next door. She wore flowered Capri pants and a plain yellow T-shirt.

"The Evanses aren't home. Susan has gone to visit her parents in Lansing."

"And Gerald?" Jake asked, sounding amazingly like someone familiar with Lili's father.

"He's on a business trip. California, I think. Due back either late tonight or tomorrow." She pulled off her flowered canvas gloves. "Would you like me to tell him you stopped by?"

"No. No, thank you. We were just in the neighborhood and thought we'd drop in. I'll catch him at…"

Michelle leaned closer and linked her hand with his. "Racquetball. He plays racquetball."

"At the club," Jake finished.

The woman nodded and returned to her gardening.

Jake led the way to the car at a leisurely pace. Michelle had to fight from clinging to his side, to keep her strides regular. She looked up to find him staring again at the car that had parked a block up. It was then she realized the driver hadn't gone into one of the houses. Rather, he sat in the driver's seat staring at them.

Edgar Mollens.

CHAPTER EIGHT

DAMN. Edgar was on their tail, and probably had been since they'd left Canton, Ohio. By now he'd have contacted the main office and have an all-out search going for proof of Jake's marriage to Michelle. And the instant Edgar discovered there was none, Jake had no doubt his peer would pull him over and take Michelle from his custody.

Custody. Now that was an odd choice of words. He felt he had as much control over Michelle's physical nearness as he had over the sun's quick slide to the west. He pressed the gas pedal down as he drove toward the tall buildings of downtown Toledo. He felt more like Michelle held him in an odd sort of custody, an indescribable limbo where he didn't know what was going to happen next, but he knew that he didn't want to be anywhere except where he could be involved.

An idea that had been playing along the fringes of his thoughts since Canton circled, growing closer to the center of his mind—much like the car he drove around Toledo, moving nearer and nearer to downtown.

When all was said and done, the mere concept scared the hell out of him. But it was probably the only option left available to them if they hoped to buy a little more time with Edgar.

He would have to make his fake marriage to Michelle real.

Feeling ill, Jake looked into his rearview mirror. He'd lost Edgar in a snaking trail of traffic, for now. He tightened his hands on the steering wheel and turned a corner, what had to be the county courthouse looming in front of them, a building he'd been keeping an eye out for even before he'd firmly made the decision. Next to him, Michelle had gone silent. He suspected she'd spotted Edgar, as well. Her distance from him was probably better, he argued, despite the itching need to have her smack dab beside him, because given what he was about to do, it was important that his actions not be misconstrued.

Michelle's head turned, not to look at him, but to stare at the courthouse as he pulled into a metered parking space. "What…what are we doing here?"

He switched off the ignition and pocketed the keys. "We're going to get married."

MARRIED?

Michelle stared at him, convinced he had gone completely, utterly nuts.

Sure, she supposed at one point in her life—likely when she was very young and still believed in fairy tales—she had thought marriage romantic. Believed it a union that would bring about a happily-ever-after ending. But with time, she realized there was no pastel-colored world waiting on the other side of the altar. It rained there as surely as it rained here. She'd seen it firsthand, through her parents' marriage, when her mother's death had ruined that happy ending, and her father's second marriage, that ran like a well-organized business powered by convenience and money, rather than thrived as a sacred union through unconditional love.

Then, of course, there was her relationship with Gerald.

All right, as difficult as it was to admit, the morning she'd learned she was pregnant with Lili, she'd idly entertained visions of lacy white dresses, rose-petal-strewn aisles and elaborately iced wedding cakes. But even now she found it odd that she'd never seen her and Gerald forging a life together. Never envisioned them taking Lili on walks through the park. Nor saw him rocking their daughter to sleep in the chair she'd inherited from her mother—the only piece she'd insisted be hers when she'd struck out on her own, no matter what color Jacqueline had painted it. No, just like in the old fairy tales, she had envisioned nothing after the I do part of the ceremony, the cutting of the cake and the opening of the gifts.

Then the marriage proposal had come. Gerald had gotten down on one knee in the middle of the Champs de Mars, held out a ring box to her and asked her to be his wife. And she had looked into his eyes and had seen...nothing. No images of birthdays filled with family and laughter. No Christmases spent together decorating the tree. While their relationship had worked well until that point, it didn't have what it took to take it any further. To have married him...well, to have married him would have been to invite disaster.

So she'd said no. And his obvious relief had only confirmed her thoughts as he'd leaned back on his heels and laughed.

Michelle hadn't realized Jake had rounded the car and stood with her door open until a burst of moist, warm late summer air swept over her. She slowly looked at him, this large, mysterious man who had awakened so much in her, done so much for her. Suddenly she saw wedding dresses and cakes again. She brutally rubbed her eyes to banish the image. And right on the heels of that one she saw Big Jake McCoy standing on a street corner holding Lili's hand in his, waiting for a school bus.

"Merde."

She opened her eyes to find Jake's hand in front of her. "Your presence is required, if this thing is to work," he said.

Michelle sat right where she was, her heart thudding in her chest, her palms slippery and wet.

Jake crouched outside the door, bringing him eye level with her. "There really is no other alternative, Michelle. I think you've figured out that Edgar is on our tail. He's probably waiting right now for proof that we're not married. And the instant he gets it, you can forget about waiting around for Gerald to return later tonight. Edgar wants to see documentation. And it's documentation I have to give him." He glanced toward a couple walking in their direction, the woman dressed in a short white dress holding a tiny bouquet, smiling at the man in the nice suit.

Michelle sank her teeth into her bottom lip, then sighed. "I know."

"You know?" Jake's dark brow rose on his forehead.

She reached out to touch his unshaven cheek. He looked much more real with the stubble on his face, his hair slightly disheveled, his suit a bit wrinkled. "Yes. I know." She smiled. "You are a good man, Jake McCoy. If you promise something, you don't stop until it's done." She rubbed her thumb over the strong planes of his cheek. "And you promised me you would help me find Lili."

His gray eyes darkened to the shade of warm mercury. "This, um, marriage will be in name only, Michelle. You understand that, don't you? If we don't produce a license, Edgar will have you on a plane bound for Paris faster than a flight attendant can say, 'Boarding pass, please.'"

She withdrew her hand and laughed heartily. "Of course I know that. Did you think I intended to make you obey the part about 'until death do us part?'" She shook her head. "This will help you, as well, won't it? I mean, I know you've put your career at great risk by telling that man I was your wife. Producing the proper papers will keep you out of too much trouble, won't it?"

"That's what I'm hoping."

"Good."

His gaze swept her where she sat in the car. "So if we understand each other…why are you hesitating?"

Michelle pretended an interest in her purse, opening it and shuffling through the contents, anything to avoid his direct gaze. "You're going to think this is silly, but…" The couple that had walked by was sitting on a bench under a tree at the side of the courthouse. "I don't know. I think this may be the only time I get married, and…even though it is phony, I at least thought I'd wear white."

Jake skimmed her dark slacks and top, then cast a glance toward the sky and cursed. "Why didn't I think of that?" He glanced at her. "We're going to have to be quick about it. We don't have much time before the license bureau closes. All I can say is it's a good thing we're in Ohio. No residency requirements, no blood test, photo ID is all that's required. Pennsylvania has a three-day waiting period, and you have to have a social security card."

Michelle watched in shock as he closed her door and rounded the car. Within moments they were on the road again. Her heart beat a specific rhythm reserved for this one man who didn't question her foolish, dawdling request, merely acted on it. Within an hour they'd scoured the interior of a local department store and a small florist. Michelle had a white dress and clutched a pretty bouquet of vibrant African violets, and Jake wore a gardenia in his lapel and had two simple rings tucked into one pocket and a disposable camera in another.

As they stood outside the license bureau in the courthouse, license in hand, Michelle was afraid she'd faint flat out.

She glanced at the impossibly tall man standing next to her and smiled. "Jake?"

He looked at her, and she felt that noodle-kneed reaction all over again.

"I just wanted to, you know, say thank you for all this."

His grin was dazzling. "I should be the one thanking you for your quick thinking. Pictures of what looks like a real ceremony will go a long way toward helping us with both Edgar and what will surely be an investigation."

Michelle felt the inexplicable urge to whack him with her violets.

JAKE WASN'T SURE what he'd said, but Michelle had gone from looking like a nervous bride to a woman with murder on her mind within a blink of an eye. He grimaced and looked around the airy courthouse.

Lord, but she looked better than anybody had a right to. He never thought he'd be one to go for the skintight look. In fact, it wasn't all that long ago that he'd openly frowned on such sexy attire. Perhaps it was knowing intimately the treasures clearly outlined beneath the thin, stretchy fabric of Michelle's dress that made him unable to take his eyes off her. He'd be damned if he didn't want to steal her away to some broom closet or supply room and slide his fingers up the hem of that clingy dress and peel her panties down her legs to probe the soft, slick flesh there.

He fought the desire to loosen his tie and led her away from the license bureau door before he overheated.

"So is that it? Are we married?" Michelle asked, following him outside where he dragged in a deep breath.

Jake took in her stricken expression, and an odd tightness gripped his stomach. "No. We, um, have to have someone perform the ceremony, like a judge. No, no, not a judge…"

Around them the lush green of the courthouse lawn looked unnaturally vivid in the afternoon sunlight. Trees dotted the landscape, and curving walkways led to the three other entrances to the stone, domed, four-square building. He caught sight of the couple who had been standing before them in line. Poised in the shade of a tree—the bride in a yellow smock unable to hide that she was well into her third trimester of pregnancy—they were being married by a pastor.

Jake craned his neck to get a closer look at the man of the cloth. His salt-and-pepper hair said he was well into his prime, but his wrinkled, ruddy features made him look far older. He turned slightly away from the couple, opened his timeworn Bible with a flick of a satiny bookmark, then took out a small tin hidden in a cutout hole. He took a quick sip.

Jake nearly burst out laughing.

Michelle backed away from him. "Tell me you're not thinking what I think you're thinking, yes?"

Jake blinked at her. "What?"

"You're not going to ask that…that booze hound to perform the ceremony?"

He grimaced and allowed her to tug her elbow from his grasp. He was struck all over again by how sexy she looked, especially with that pouty frown on her face. "Why not?"

She shifted several times on her towering white heels. "It wouldn't be legal, would it? I mean, the guy can hardly read."

Jake glanced over to catch the old pastor hiccuping. He placed a hand over his mouth and apologized to the young couple, who had eyes only for each other. "Trust me, it's legal enough. Besides, I think it will be fun."

Michelle turned from him, searching the lawn as though another option would pop up at any moment. "There must be someone else."

"We don't have time to find anyone else, Michelle. We've wasted enough time shopping—" He was stopped abruptly by that murderous look in her eyes again. "I know this doesn't look very good, but the sooner we're done with this, the sooner we're back on the road. In the long run, that's all that matters, isn't it?"

The sound of approaching footsteps on the cement walkway pulled Jake's gaze from Michelle. The pastor had finished marrying the other couple and had spotted them. But it wasn't him Jake was concerned about. It was the sight of Edgar bearing down on them from the opposite direction.

"Hidey ho, lovebirds!" the pastor called, fingering his Bible. "Are you looking to get married today?"

"No," Jake said.

At the same time Michelle said, "Yes."

The pastor chuckled. "Seems to me someone's suffering from a mighty case of cold feet."

Michelle stared at Jake, but he didn't have time to explain. Edgar moved closer by the moment. Jake nearly pulled Michelle off those heels as he towed her toward the courthouse, the pastor following right after them.

SAFELY INSTALLED in a judge's outer chambers, Michelle looked at their witness, the drunken pastor, and smiled, hoping the old man would make it through the ceremony still standing. She turned toward the female judge, who was asking her and Jake to join hands.

She was struck once again by how large and strong his hands looked, then noticed how damp they were. Her gaze flicked to his face. While the pastor looked ready to fall over, Jake appeared ready to bolt.

Her smile widened. So big Jake McCoy was afraid of something—namely, matrimony.

Now she understood his desire to be wed by the elderly pastor. The exchanging of vows would have seemed like something out of an American cartoon rather than the real thing. She had convinced him that a judge was the way to go by reminding him that a judge's signature on their wedding certificate would look far better than the pastor's. Practical

Jake would never be able to argue that point. Then he'd told her Edgar was in the building.

"Now repeat after me," the female judge said, eyeing them both openly.

Michelle recited the vows carefully, noticing the way Jake avoided her gaze. She resisted the urge to dig her heel into his foot and instead jerked on his hands, forcing him to look at her. She smiled. He turned a frightening shade of green.

Next came Jake's part. Before following the judge's lead, he cast a forlorn look in the pastor's direction. The pastor had other priorities, though. Turning away from the clerk standing nearby, he opened his Bible and took another hefty swig from the tin. Jake grimaced and solemnly repeated after the judge.

How in the hell did I ever get into this mess? he wondered as he recited his vows.

Jake couldn't exactly define what it was he was feeling. He, more than anyone, knew this was all pretend. The dress Michelle had on, the bouquet she held, the rings he was even now fumbling to get out of his pocket, all of it was show, to prove to Edgar and his superiors at the INS that they were married.

Then why did he bear all the hallmark signs of a man who had stuck his head into a guillotine? Marc had looked like he was going to toss his cookies when he'd married Melanie two months ago. Then again, the thought of facing Mel's tight-lipped mother, Wilhemenia Weber, across a dinner table at holidays… Jake cringed. Hell, that would be enough to make any man think twice.

And then there was Mitch. He could just imagine what had gone through Mitch's mind when his bride was late for the ceremony…again. At least this time Liz Braden had eventually shown up, unlike seven years ago when Jake had silently nursed Mitch back from a subsequent week-long drinking binge that had left them all the worse for wear.

The clerk snapped their picture in front of the judge. Jake winced. His hands shook as he opened the box that held both rings. He took out the smaller of the two simple gold bands. The smile Michelle gave him as she held out her hand nearly knocked him over. He'd noticed how tiny her hands were before, but now, with one lying against his palm, it looked downright childlike. He touched the ring to the tip of her ring finger, then nearly dropped the blasted thing. He slowly budged it up her finger, sunlight glinting off the narrow band. The clerk snapped another picture.

Michelle held her other hand out. He blinked at it, then at her. "Oh." He fumbled for the box again, then handed the other ring to her.

He gritted his teeth, wondering how he'd let her talk him into buying two bands. Sure, they'd been on sale, two for one, of all things. But all they'd needed was the one. His thoughts seemed to manifest themselves in body reaction. Though the band had slid on easily at the store, Michelle now had to twist and turn it to force it up his finger. It was all he could do not to stop her and toss the thing out the open window.

He knew the instant the ring hit home at the base of his finger. He felt a weird sort of heat, as if she'd fused the sucker there. He stared at the symbolic piece of jewelry and nearly hurled.

"You can now kiss the bride," the judge said with a smile.

He stared at the woman. Was she insane? Kiss the bride? The last thing he felt like doing was kissing....

Michelle's silky soft lips met with his. His gaze was riveted to her face as she stood on tiptoe to slant her mouth against his. Everything he was coming to know as her surrounded him: her sweet smell, her lush body, her soft hair.

He groaned and threaded his fingers through the curly hair over her ears, holding her still so he could kiss her more deeply. The heat that began with the ring steamed toward his groin. God, but this woman tasted better than any one woman had a right to—warm, inviting, downright sexy.

The clerk cleared her throat. Jake pulled away, half dazed, and looked toward the sound just as the flash of the camera went off again.

CHAPTER NINE

MICHELLE PRACTICALLY had to jerk him from the judge's chambers after the picture-taking and the paper-signing, for all the control he seemed to have over his body, much less the situation. But as determined and wiry as she was, she was no match for his sheer size. Ten feet down the hall, she gave up and instead pressed him against the cool wall.

Jake blinked at the decidedly wicked smile she gave before slanting her mouth against his and boldly running her tongue across his lips.

"What was that for?" He practically croaked the words afterward.

She shrugged lightly. "You looked like you needed it."

His grin originated in his chest. "Boy, do you ever have that right."

He brought his mouth down on hers.

Ah, if anything could have taken his mind off the past thirty minutes, this was it. He leaned against the wall and hauled her against him. Despite the difference in their sizes, they fit amazingly well together, her mouth on his, his growing erection pressing against the soft flesh of her lower belly. He launched a full-scale assault on her mouth, marveling at the textures there, the smoothness of her teeth, the rasp of her tongue as she gave as good as she got. He pressed his hands harder against the small of her back, drawing her closer still as she hastily undid the top few buttons of his shirt. He shuddered as she pressed the heat of her palms against the bare skin of his chest.

"There," she said, kissing him again and giving his tie a yank. "That's much better."

The sound of approaching footsteps sent reality crashing in on him. What was he thinking? They were in the middle of a county courthouse, for cripe's sake. He dragged his mouth from hers, then closed his eyes and rested his temple against her soft hair, sucking in desperately needed air.

The clearing of a male throat.

Jake grimaced. The pastor must have followed them out, perhaps looking for more compensation than the tenner he'd given him to witness the ceremony. Michelle shifted to look at their company and went stiff in his arms. Jake opened his eyes to stare at Edgar Mollens.

Jake patted his jacket pocket where he'd put the certificate of marriage. He grinned. "Edgar, old buddy, old pal, old friend of mine."

Edgar's fleshy features darkened. "Get off it, McCoy. I knew there was something fishy about this whole thing right from the start. You, married? And to an illegal alien on high alert, at that?" He shook his head. "I knew there was no way in hell. Everyone at the office knows you'd send your own mother back to Kosovo if you found out she was an illegal."

Jake's spine snapped to attention. He reminded himself that his co-worker had no idea his mother had died long ago. Still he couldn't help saying, "My mother's family came over on the *Mayflower,* you idiot."

Edgar's brows budged up on his wrinkled forehead. "So the silent one is capable of anger. I'm sorry to say I've lost a bet."

He folded Michelle's hand in his. "Come on, let's go."

Edgar grabbed her other arm. "You can go wherever you

like, McCoy—at least until you're scheduled to appear before the review board back home. This one…well, she goes back with me and is on the first plane out of here."

"Keep pushing it, Edgar, and I'll show you just how angry I can get," Jake said evenly, his blood steaming through his veins and roaring past his ears.

"Are you threatening me?"

Jake had at least six inches on the other agent, and he used them now to his advantage by stepping closer. Edgar hesitated, then stumbled, but didn't release Michelle. "No, I'm *promising* you that if you don't unhand my wife right this minute, I'm going to break your hands."

Edgar's bark of laughter echoed through the hall. The old pastor turned to look at them where he stood near the stairs. "Get off it, Jake. I just had Pauline check every courthouse between here and D.C. You two are about as married as a goose and a dove. That's a *cooked* goose."

Jake calmly placed his hand on Edgar's right shoulder and squeezed until he released his grip on Michelle, then he slipped the marriage certificate from his pocket. He slapped it against the agent's chest. "Here you go, buddy. Read it and weep." He took Michelle's hand again.

"For crying out loud, you haven't seen the last of me, McCoy!" Edgar called after them.

DESPITE what had just transpired at the courthouse, Jake felt as though a Just Married sign complete with tin cans and streamers was posted to the back of his car, for all the giddiness he felt. Which was ridiculous. Because not even an hour ago, he'd been close to passing out dead cold from nerves. And because while he and Michelle were *legally* married, they weren't *really* married. Theirs was a marriage of convenience. Not for money. Not for prestige. But because Michelle needed a way to stay in the country long enough to find her daughter, and he needed to give it to her. No matter what Edgar and his superiors might think.

The sensation had hit him immediately upon leaving the courthouse. After giving Edgar the certificate. After Michelle had kissed him senseless in the hall. And after she had paused outside the door where prospective jurors were waiting to be called, and tossed her small bouquet over her shoulder. All nervousness had left him. And all he could think about, sitting in the car next to her, heading to the area where Gerald Evans lived, was that he wanted his wedding night. Except in this case it would be his wedding evening. Hell, he didn't care what it was, and he didn't care that last night he'd had Michelle every which way but loose. He wanted to explore every sweet inch of her, thrust into her slick, hot flesh, watch the graceful line of her neck as she tossed her head back and made those soft whimpers that drove him absolutely crazy.

He wanted to do it now.

He gripped the steering wheel tightly and took deep, measured breaths. It was either try to get a grip or pull over to the side of the road and have at her. Haul her over so she straddled him in that clingy little dress. Launch an oral assault on her pointy breasts right through the lacy material of her dress. Thrust his fingers up to touch her panties, then immerse them in her dripping wetness.

He shifted to ease the discomfort of his semiaroused state.

Before he went giving himself over to needs he'd never thought he possessed, he had some business to attend to.

He reached across Michelle's lap to the glove compartment. He had just opened it when she touched his arm.

He glanced into her concerned face. "You...that man..." She took a deep breath, her fingers tightening on his arm. "After all this is done, you're going to be in trouble, aren't you?" She bit her bottom lip. "I mean more than just getting fired. You might be put in…"

"Jail?" He finished her sentence for her, his throat closing around the word.

She stared at him, wide-eyed.

"Yes. It may very well come to that. Edgar may have that wedding certificate, but it's only a matter of time before he gets the proper documentation to haul both of us in for intense scrutiny by immigration review…or even court." But he didn't want to think about any of that. No. He wanted to concentrate on what needed to be done and try to accomplish it in whatever time they had left.

He punched two buttons and placed the cell phone to his ear.

Two rings, then he heard, "McCoy Place, David here."

Jake grimaced. Of all the people to answer the phone. "It's Jake."

"For God's sake, man, where in the hell are you? Pops is this close to putting an APB out on your sorry ass. Mitch has been on the horn with some of his old friends at the FBI, and all the provisions I packed for our hike are rotting in my backpack near the door."

Jake slanted a glance at his pack in the back seat. "Good." He cursed under his breath. "Not about the trip. About Mitch's being on the phone with the FBI. Look, I need a favor."

"No, we haven't seen your blasted ID."

"This is not about my ID, David." He realized that he hadn't absently patted his jacket pocket since sometime last night. At the Evanses' in Canton didn't count, because that had been official…well, somewhat official. He glanced to find Michelle watching him in curiosity. "I need to find out when an individual is due to fly into Toledo, Ohio, and on which flight."

"Holy Toledo?" David said.

"Yeah. Can you do that for me?"

"I'll get Mitch on it right away," his brother promised. "I take it I should cancel my plans, then?"

"Plans?" Jake switched ears. What plans did one need to go hiking through the mountains?

"Yeah, for the cabin I rented. I somehow couldn't envision you roughing it in a tent. That's why the food is rotting in my bag. It was supposed to go into the cabin refrigerator sometime last night."

Jake cracked a smile. The youngest McCoy was capable of a few surprises of his own. "Why didn't you put the food in Pops's fridge?"

"Why didn't I put the food in Pops's fridge?" David repeated sardonically. "Hmm, maybe because we've all spent the past twenty-four worrying about you? And I didn't remember the stuff was in there until I pretty much heard that you were okay by your voice? You know, it would have helped if you'd answered your cellular."

"The battery went dead," Jake lied, cringing.

"Yeah, right." David muttered a mild curse. "Look, forget about it. You don't have to apologize, Jake. Or were you going to apologize?"

Jake cleared his throat and cast another glance in Michelle's direction. Lord, she looked good. "Sorry, little bro."

The silence on the other end of the line was deafening.

"David?"

"Hmm? Oh, yeah, I'm here. Just a little shocked, is all. Did you actually just say you were sorry?"

"Moron."

"No, wait, I want to confirm this, because I don't think that in all my thirty years on God's green earth have I ever heard you say that word."

"Yeah, well, you may be hearing a lot of it in the coming days, so get used to it now."

"What? Why?"

"Mitch off his phone yet?" Jake asked.

Heaving a sigh, David said, "Yeah. Hold on a sec, will ya?"

A moment later, Mitch picked up the phone. He'd listened in on David's end of the conversation, so he didn't waste time with small talk. Of all his brothers, Mitch was the one who understood Jake best. He cut straight to the chase, asking for the name of the individual and the airport he was flying into. Jake asked him if Liz had kept any of her credit cards in her maiden name. Without hesitation, Mitch gave him a number along with an expiration date, then agreed to call and make hotel reservations for him at a downtown Toledo hotel Jake had seen while trying to shake Edgar.

After all this was taken care of, there was a short pause. Jake waited for Mitch's questions.

It was not the sort of question he'd expected. For that, among all the other things Mitch was doing for him, Jake was thankful. "You think you're going to be back by Thursday?" Mitch asked.

"I don't know."

"Good enough. You just make sure you call us if you need anything, you hear? I mean anything."

Jake grinned. "Yeah. Thanks, Mitch. Call me back on the cellular when you get the info."

He pressed the disconnect button, then put the phone on the seat between him and Michelle.

Michelle didn't quite know what to make out of the conversation she'd just heard. She felt that in the past two days, she'd come to know Jake quite well. Certainly not every little detail of his life. She'd be the first to admit she didn't know what the guy ate for breakfast, though she suspected it would be something wholesome and fruity. But he had a brother? And what was it he'd said about the FBI? And just who, exactly, did he know who had the type of power to find out which plane Gerald was on?

She sat back and wrapped her arms around herself, feeling somewhat distanced from the man beside her. But that's not what bothered her most. What disturbed her was that she wanted to know everything about him. Not because it applied to their situation, but because it applied to him. That was disturbing indeed.

She absently turned the simple gold wedding band on her finger. "Your brother?"

Jake nodded and scrubbed his face with his hands.

"He's younger than you?"

He looked at her blankly.

"You said little bro, which I'm assuming means little brother?"

"Oh, yeah. That was David, the youngest. There are five of us, all told."

"Five?" Michelle blinked and looked at him from head to toe. There were four men out there somewhere just like the man next to her? Well, probably not *just* like him. But surely they would be similar in some ways, which led her to wonder which.

He nodded. "There's Connor, the only one older than me. Then Marc, Mitch and David." He gave a lopsided grin. "Shocking, huh?"

"Not shocking, really," she said, lost in thought. "Which one has the connection to the FBI?"

"You heard that, did you?" He flicked on his right blinker and stopped at a red light. "That would be Mitch. He and his new wife have resurrected the old Connor—that's my mother's family name—horse breeding farm, but he used to be with the FBI before he was a PI." He stopped. "Long story. Anyway, if any of the McCoy men can find out which plane Gerald's on, Mitch can."

The McCoy men? The way he said it made them sound like an outlaw gang. Something tingled at the edges of her mind. The Hatfields and McCoys. Weren't they an American legend of some sort? Feuding families?

No, no, the McCoys wouldn't be outlaws, no matter Jake's current circumstances. And now that she knew his brother Mitch was former FBI… She connected the dots of similarity. "Don't tell me. You're all in law enforcement?"

His grin threatened to swallow his handsome face. "Yes. How'd you guess?"

"Even your father?"

"A D.C. police officer. So is David. You didn't answer my question," he pointed out.

It was Michelle's turn to smile. "Call it a lucky guess."

"Anyway, rather than driving around town until Mitch or David gets back to me, I thought we'd check into a hotel, catch something to eat and…"

His words drifted off into a suggestive never-never land that left Michelle hot all over. If only he didn't appear so surprised by his own words. "And?" she prompted.

"And wait until we can go get Lili back."

Michelle's thumb stilled where she played with her ring. *Lili.* Suddenly, inexplicably, she felt pulled into two different directions—and felt instantly guilty for it.

During her time with Jake, she'd felt alive in a way she hadn't for a long, long time. No, alive wasn't the word she was looking for. She felt like a woman. Not someone's mother. Not a great chef. She felt desirable and sexy, and suspected she had merely thrown a stone into a secret well of sensual need deep inside her. And Jake was the willing—well, okay, reluctantly willing—catalyst for that. And finding Lili…

Being reunited with her daughter would end all that.

She bit her bottom lip. Leave it to her to discover the one

man who could make her feel like a woman again, only to find that man lived halfway across the world from her. And was an INS agent to boot. What was it her stepmother always said? If there was trouble, she was sure to stumble across it. Or put her foot in it. One or the other.

She agreed with Jacqueline. She was in *really* bad shape.

She looked at the upscale hotel Jake stopped in front of. It wasn't all that far from the courthouse. She'd guessed some time back that he was traveling in ever widening circles around the downtown area. Whether it was to guarantee they weren't being followed or to gather his thoughts, she couldn't be sure. But she'd gotten a full-scale glimpse of the city. Older stone buildings hunkered alongside newer, modern constructions. The Maumee River bisected the city from its east side, all manner of boats—from paddleboats that had been transformed into floating restaurants to small motorboats—docked on the west side of the river, not far from where they were. Next to the hotel, a tower of metal and glass stretched toward the sky, its blue-tinted panes reflecting the sinking sun.

A valet opened the door for her. Michelle looked at Jake, a funny little tickle starting low in her belly.

"Go ahead."

"Are you sure? Wouldn't it be better if we, um, checked into a motel or something closer to Gerald's?"

He tugged at his tie and glanced in the other direction before saying quietly, "I wanted to treat you to something, you know, a little more special. Seeing as it's our honeymoon and all."

Michelle didn't miss the suggestion laced through his words. The mere prospect of having him lave her breasts with his hot, soft tongue, of cradling him between her thighs, was enough to make her catch her breath.

The valet motioned toward a bellboy. "Howard, take this

lucky couple's bags inside, won't you? We have newlyweds on board tonight."

Michelle felt her cheeks go hot. She took the young man's hand and climbed out of the car, tugging at the hem of her white dress as she did so. She looked at the elegantly lighted exterior of the hotel, the posh lobby visible through the sliding glass doors, the well-dressed, solicitous staff. She'd stayed in the Paris Ritz once. She'd just graduated from culinary school and was in the mood for a celebration. Wanted to be surrounded by the atmosphere in which she hoped one day to work. But while the surroundings were luxurious, the employees impossibly polite and discreet, she hadn't felt quite the same kind of welcome. And while she'd enjoyed the fine appointments of her room, the thrill had lasted for about five minutes, before loneliness had settled in on her. She'd ordered room service, drunk an entire bottle of champagne by herself, then passed out.

This was an entirely different situation, indeed.

She glanced at where Jake spoke to the valet, shivering at his strong profile. For a dangerous second, she allowed herself to believe that she *was* on her honeymoon. That her childhood faceless groom wanted to make sure everything was perfect for their first night together. Then she watched as her simple bag and the backpack and gear on the back seat were loaded onto a cart, and reality pressed in on her from all sides. Still, she wanted to give herself over to the seductive lure of the fantasy, if just for the next hour or so. Until Jake's brother called. Until she could no longer ignore life and reality. She caught herself restlessly caressing her neck and smiled. She and Jake…well, they could fit a lifetime of loving into an hour.

JAKE PLAYED AT trying to give the concierge his credit card, but as he'd instructed, Liz had been emphatic that the charges go on her bill when she called a short time ago. He slid his MasterCard into his wallet, and the overhead light reflected off the bit of gold on his ring finger. His breath froze in his lungs.

Whoa. He was married.

In a strip of mirror behind the desk, he caught a glimpse of Michelle standing behind him looking sexier than ever. He was afraid he'd never draw another normal breath.

"This way, Mr. Braden."

It took a moment for Jake to realize the bellboy had called him by Liz's maiden name. He turned and acknowledged the young man then tucked Michelle's hand into the crook of his arm.

A decided air of expectancy clung to him as they took the river view elevator to the fifth floor. He heard Michelle swallow next to him. All he knew was that if the blasted bellboy wasn't in the enclosure with them, he'd have pressed Michelle against the wall right then and there. Damn, he couldn't breathe. He cleared his throat and ignored the heat that seemed to emanate from Michelle, nearly searing him through his sleeve where her hand rested.

Two more floors. One...

Finally, the doors slid open and the bellboy led the way down the detailed carpeting toward a set of double doors at the end of the hall. The doors were swung inward. He was so relieved that they were going to be alone together, in the privacy of a closed room, he easily swept Michelle into his arms, intoxicated by her surprised gasp, then her nervous laugh. He stepped into the room, barely seeing anything around him. All he could do was gaze at Michelle. Her curly hair was tousled and sexy. Her tongue darted out to moisten very kissable lips. And her eyes had darkened to a seductive shade of whiskey.

Jake turned to slip the bellboy a tip, surprised to find the doors closed, the young man nowhere in sight.

"You know what it means when you carry a bride over the threshold, don't you?" she murmured, pressing her tiny breasts against the wall of his chest.

He realized that's exactly what he'd just done. "Um, no. What does it mean?"

"Good fertility."

Then, suddenly, everything that was Michelle possessed him.

Pulling herself up by her hands around his neck, she claimed his mouth with a hunger and passion that nearly knocked him over backward. He gently slid her down the length of his body until she was standing. He pressed her into his aching erection, thrust his fingers up the back of her dress and cupped her lush little bottom in his hands. She wore no nylons. There was nothing between him and her curved, sweet, hot flesh except her lacy panties. For someone so tiny, she found a way to cradle him just so, making him dizzy with pleasure, urgent with need. Everything around them slipped away. The large room. The river view. The fact that somewhere out there Edgar Mollens was even now trying to figure out a way to get both of them to D.C. and make them the targets of an immediate immigration review. His world narrowed to Michelle Lambert and Michelle Lambert alone.

All at once, he couldn't seem to get enough of her. Her mouth. Her soft flesh. Even as she sought to put distance between them for a moment so she could rip off his jacket, they contorted themselves in order to maintain the connection of their mouths. Oh, and what a great mouth she had, too.

She finally stripped him completely and backed him unceremoniously toward the bed, the soft, needy words in French she murmured driving him wild. He loved it when she spoke French. Down he went. And off went her dress as he pulled it over her head, her pale nipples bare of bra and swaying as she dragged the material down her arms. Jake reached for them, but she grabbed his hands and held them still at his sides.

The first long, lingering flick of her tongue as she dragged it across his abdomen was nearly her last, because he almost lost it right then and there. Around and around, up and down, she dragged her tongue across his skin, watching his reaction until he clamped his eyes closed and gritted his teeth to keep from climaxing prematurely.

Then, abruptly, she was gone.

Jake opened his eyes to find her breasts at eye level. Curving his fingers around a small orb, he hungrily sucked her nipple deep into his mouth, satisfied at her low moan, then pulled the other in, restlessly moving from one to the other until they were wet from his attentions. She worked her thumb between his mouth and her flesh, rubbing the pad along his bottom lip to separate them, then following briefly with her mouth. Then she slid down the length of him, every glorious inch of her stomach rubbing against his straining erection.

He watched in rapt fascination as she slowly, torturously ran her fingertips down his engorged shaft, giving him a thoughtful, thorough squeeze. He thrust his hips upward, impatient to be inside her.

But that evidently wasn't part of her plan. Instead, he nearly came off the bed at the hot feel of her mouth encircling the tip of his erection. If the sensation of her dragging her tongue across his abdomen had been maddening, this…this was downright sinful.

He alternated between clamping his eyes shut and watching her as she slowly slid her lips over the length of him. His hips bucked involuntarily.

She drew away for a moment and shifted to sit at his side, piling her curls on one side of her head as she bent to her task again. Her white lacy panties were plainly visible, as was the springy wedge of her womanhood beneath.

Michelle's mouth went over him again. He fought the need

to thrust upward again, and lost. She cupped him, squeezing ever so gently, and instantly the sensation of imminent climax subsided, leaving only the intense heat of her mouth.

Gritting his teeth, he lifted himself on his elbows and reached for her. She gasped as he lifted her, carefully maneuvering until she was pantyless and her knees rested on either side of his head, so that they could enjoy each other simultaneously.

Jake's throat choked off air as he eyed her engorged womanhood mere inches from his chin. He swallowed the saliva gathering in his mouth. He'd never viewed a woman's intimate parts this close before. The fact that Michelle was allowing him such close contact with her spoke volumes.

There was something inherently beautiful about the way her springy dark hair peppered her skin, enough to protect, but not enough to completely shield the area from view. The way the skin swelled on either side of her distended pink, sensitive flesh. He realized there was a reason writers often referred to a woman's private parts as a split ripe peach. Because right now he was filled with an insatiable urge to devour her.

He tentatively fastened his lips around the enlarged, hooded core of her femininity. She instantly threw her head back and cried out, making all the awkwardness more than worth it.

Wow. A greater aphrodisiac he had never known. He pursed his lips around the tender nub and nibbled, before drawing it into his mouth and swirling his tongue around the tip. If their coming together last night had been all about take, this was all about giving. He wanted to possess Michelle in a way he'd never wanted to possess another woman. He wanted to give her the same type of pleasure she was showing him. He wanted to make her writhe in need, call out his name, cling to him as though her very life depended on it.

The gentle rocking of her hips told him that his inexperience mattered not at all. He tugged his mouth away from her and ran the length of his tongue down her narrow crevice, then thrust it into her tight, hot channel. Instantly, she pulled her mouth away from him and whimpered, her body shuddering in wild abandon, her hips moving in time with his thrusts.

The tips of her breasts teased the muscles of his stomach with her every move. She curled her fingers more tightly around his erection, but while her actions were driving him crazy with desire, he wanted to be inside her *now*.

Grasping her hips, he gently nudged her bottom down his torso until she sat, her back facing him, her hair a sexy, tangled mass around her face as she gazed at him over her shoulder.

Jake admired the long, graceful lines of her back, following her spine with his thumbs until he reached her behind, where he spanned to grasp her hips again. She reached for a condom in the basket on the bedside table, then guided the coated tip of his erection to rest against her slick, hot aperture. He tightened his grasp and thrust upward with every ounce of energy he possessed. Her head snapped back, and she moaned, the sultry, sexy sound winding around him, clutching him as he pulled back and thrust again.

"*Oui, oui, mon chéri,*" she murmured, nearly catapulting him over the edge.

She moved her body in perfect symphony with his until her breathing came in ragged gasps. She leaned forward and rested her hands on the mattress between his legs, her movements becoming slower, more concentrated, her moans deeper. Jake was unable to tear his gaze away from where they were joined. His hard flesh fusing with her soft, her wetness dripping over his erection. He reached down and cupped her bottom in both hands, then spread her a little farther open, allowing for even deeper contact…and completely lost it.

The world exploded into a flash of white hot light.

CHAPTER TEN

MICHELLE HAD NEVER felt so utterly boneless, sated, exhilarated. She fastened the fluffy white hotel robe around her damp skin as she left Jake behind in the shower, a decidedly wicked-feeling smile claiming her lips. Before their first time together, she'd suspected that Jake was an ingenue when it came to matters of sex…well, not an ingenue, exactly, but very definitely conservative and reserved.

Tonight he'd shown *her* a few things she hadn't thought were possible. Just thinking about it made her want to climb into that huge bed to wait for him so they could start all over again.

For the first time, she glanced around the room. Thick white carpeting, monstrous king-size bed, stylish curtains with matching bedspread, gilt-edged mirrors and antique furniture reproductions all combined to make it comfortable and tasteful. But it was the river view from the window covering one full wall that caught her attention. The setting sun slanted bright orange streaks across the Maumee River. It looked magical….which was fitting, because this evening had certainly proved magical to her. She wrapped her arms around herself, then stared at the thin gold band on her finger. Strange that such a simple piece of metal could signify so much. Not unlike Jake. She'd never thought she was attracted to the strong and silent type. But this one man…he'd slipped inside her heart with the simplest of ease.

God help her, she loved him. In an all-consuming way that made her want to forget who she was. Forget who he was. Wipe the slate clean and start all over again. Just him, her and Lili.

The muffled chirp of a cell phone filled the room. She glanced first at the bed, then at the pile of clothes on the floor. Bending over, she fished through the items until she found Jake's jacket. She stepped toward the bathroom as she took the slender receiver from a side pocket.

"Jake?" she called into the bathroom.

She was answered by his tuneless humming. She could have sworn the song was *"You Are My Sunshine,"* but she couldn't be sure. She was more concerned with the ringing instrument in her damp palm.

She stepped into the other room, staring at the phone as it continued to ring. It could very well be Jake's brother bearing news of Gerald's return to Toledo. The possibility both frightened and excited her. Excited her because it meant she might very soon be holding little Lili in her arms again. Frightened her because it would mean the abrupt end to all she and Jake had found in each other's arms.

Biting hard on her bottom lip, she pressed the receive button. "Hello?"

"I'm sorry, I must have dialed wrong," a male voice said.

"No, no, wait!" Michelle quickly interjected.

Too late. The line was dead.

Sighing, she pressed disconnect, then sank onto the mattress. She stared at where steam billowed out from the bathroom. Perhaps she should go in there and climb into the shower with Jake. See if there were any spots she missed on the first go-around. And even if there weren't, she could always start again from the top and make her way down that long, lean body—

The phone rang again, and she nearly dropped it.

This time she didn't hesitate. "Hello? Jake McCoy's... phone."

Silence. Then, "Who's this?"

Michelle closed her eyes. Such a simple question. Such a complicated answer. "Michelle," she said, clearing her throat, aware that her accent had thickened with the heightening of her nerves. "You have information on when Gerald Evans is scheduled to return to Toledo, yes?"

Silence again. "Michelle who?"

She tucked her hair behind her ear and closed her eyes. "Lambert. I'm..." What? Jake's wife? Oh, wouldn't that make this conversation interesting? "You're Jake's brother, yes? David? Or Mitch?"

"Mitch. And you're Jake's... I'm sorry, I think I missed the second half of your statement."

"Friend," she said, instead of any of the other dozen answers that flooded her mind, *lover* topping the list. But still, even that title didn't seem to fit. He was much, much more than her lover.

She looked up to find the man in question watching her from the bathroom doorway. Michelle felt her cheeks go hot. "One moment, please, while I put Jake on the line."

He crossed the room, a towel hung low on his slender hips. Michelle swallowed hard, longing to lick the lingering water droplets from the clean skin of his stomach. She slowly held out the cell phone to him. "It's your brother Mitch."

Jake took the phone and grinned at her. "Bet your conversation with him was interesting."

She couldn't help smiling. "Yes. That it was. He hung up on me." At his raised brow, she explained, "The first time. Then he called back." She motioned nervously toward his hand. "He's waiting with news of Gerald now."

When he raised the phone to his ear to receive the information, in a flash, all good humor left her. Michelle pushed from the bed and strode toward the large picture window, her attention more on Jake's reflection in the tinted glass than the lights beginning to come to life on the nearby suspension-cable bridge.

"Mitch," Jake said, making the one word sound like a greeting and a command for him to speak. Michelle noticed his grimace. "Never mind who Michelle is. What have you got?" A pause. "Uh-huh. Ten o'clock. I see. Yeah, yeah, I know. I owe you big for this." Another pause then Jake glanced at her. "No, you haven't met her before. Yeah, I'll tell her." He turned and slowly paced away from her, but she could still make out what he said. "It's complicated. I can't fill you in on all of the details now, but I'm helping Michelle find her daughter, Lili…. Yes, I suspect this Gerald Evans has her. That's all I can tell you now. What?" A deep-throated chuckle. "Yes, she's…attractive." A pause. "Thanks, Mitch. Yes, I'll keep you posted."

He disconnected, then tossed the phone to the bed. "Mitch asked me to apologize for his abruptness."

She shrugged, pretending nonchalance, when in all honesty, nonchalance was the last thing she felt. Only problem was, she was having a difficult time defining exactly what she did feel. Adrift? Uncertain? On the one hand, she longed to be a part of all that was familiar to Jake, wanted his brothers to know who she was and hoped they accepted her. On the other, she knew it was foolish for her to forge anything that stretched beyond now, this moment, because the next moment might not be hers to decide what to do with.

"So," she began, tucking the robe more tightly around her. "Was your brother able to get the information?"

Jake said nothing for a long moment. He sought and found her gaze in the smooth glass and held it. He looked so solemn.

All the sexy playfulness that characterized the past two hours slipped away, replaced by the stark reality of now.

She'd known this moment would come. But she couldn't say she'd been fully prepared for it. Her heart beat a steady, almost painful staccato in her chest. The current of electricity that had hummed through her muscles only moments before was replaced by an odd numbness.

Jake finally spoke to her reflection. "Yes. Gerald's plane arrives in an hour." He cleared his throat. "Mitch was also able to verify that Evans booked a companion ticket. Looks like Lili is going to be with him."

ADRENALINE RUSHED through Jake's veins, strong and pure. It had been a long time since he'd felt so driven to do something. It was likely he'd never felt it. He forced himself to concentrate on when that last time would have been, but his mind refused to cooperate. All he could think about was that in the next few minutes, everything he'd come to know in the past two days could change.

He glanced at Michelle, who stared at the front of Gerald Evans's house unblinkingly. He'd have given anything to have left her at the hotel, in that posh honeymoon suite wrapped up in that too large terry robe, somehow managing to look as sexy as all get out when any other woman would have been overwhelmed, lost in all that white. In the shower, he had entertained visions of him saving the day, sweeping little Lili from Gerald's custody then returning to the hotel room to reunite Michelle with her daughter.

But Michelle would have none of it. She'd been charmingly furious when he even started to suggest she stay behind. She'd go without him if need be, she'd told him. And nothing short of tying her up would stop her.

He suppressed the urge to touch the end of a curl that impeded his view of her face, the image of her tied to that soft bed tempting him. It would be a mistake to touch her because he needed to be sharp. Needed to forget notions of tangled sheets and soft moans, hot tongues and even hotter other refuges.

He forced a swallow down his tight throat, then looked in his rearview mirror to see a car approaching.

"I think this is it," he said quietly.

Michelle nearly leaped from the car. Jake gently grasped her arm and held her still.

"We need to see if he has Lili with him first."

She bit her lip and nodded. "Of course. Yes, you're right."

The late-model Lincoln all-terrain vehicle slowed, then pulled into the drive to their left. Yes, it was Gerald, all right. But if he was going to do what he thought…

The garage door began to open.

Jake cursed and opened his door. "Wait here."

He knew the instant the words were out of his mouth that Michelle would disobey them. But he couldn't concern himself with that. If little Lili was in that car, then the garage door would impede them from confirming the fact.

As he hurried up the driveway, the clap clap of Michelle's shoes sounding on the pavement behind him, he patted his chest. He realized he was checking for his ID. Of course, his firearm probably would have been equally welcome right about now.

The Lincoln pulled inside the garage. Jake ducked under the closing door. Michelle's ducking under caused the door to reverse direction, leaving them in plain view of passersby.

Jake moved toward the driver's side, Michelle to the passenger's.

"Agent Jake McCoy of the INS," he called. "Get out of the vehicle slowly, Mr. Evans."

The man inside the car opened the door, then cautiously swung his legs out, his eyes watchful, his hands in the air. "What the hell is going on here?"

Jake took no chances. He thrust his forearm against Gerald's collarbone and shoved him against the side of the car. His gaze locked with the other man's.

Gerald barely blinked as he held his hands higher. "I don't know who you are or what you want, but you should know that my wife heard me pull in and is probably this minute on her way out to greet me."

"Your wife is in Lansing."

Gerald Evans's unhesitant smile made Jake grimace. He was obviously a man used to talking himself out of tight spots, no matter the physical disadvantage. "Yes, I guess she is. So why don't you just let me go so we can talk to each other man to man."

It immediately struck Jake that there was no way he and Gerald could have been any more different. Where he was tall and dark, Gerald Evans was blond and of average height. Where he had an economy with words, Gerald was obviously a master of them, instantly measuring what needed to be said and fitting the words to the situation.

Jake had a hard time seeing this man and Michelle together. But he all too easily understood how Evans had talked her into letting him spend time alone with Lili.

"Where's Lili?" Michelle said as she rounded the vehicle, looking in first one window, then the next.

Gerald went rock still. Jake pressed him harder into the cold metal. "Jesus. You're the last person I expected to see here, Michelle."

"I bet she is." Jake ground the words out, itching to rearrange a few of the guy's pretty-boy features. "Answer her question."

Evans rolled his eyes toward the ceiling and sighed. "I don't have her."

"Where is she?" Michelle repeated, giving up her futile search of the empty vehicle. "Did you drop her off somewhere on your way home?" Her anxious gaze found Jake's. "We should have waited at the airport."

Gerald looked momentarily confused. "What do you know about the airport? And why do you think…" His voice trailed off, realization apparently dawning. "You're probably talking about the companion ticket." His irritating grin drove Jake's impatience level up a couple of notches. "My *wife* was scheduled to go with me. But her father fell ill, and she went to her parents' instead. You should have checked your facts a little more thoroughly."

Jake stared at the man he held prisoner. "Where is she?"

Gerald's eyes were suddenly stony, challenging. Jake noticed the malice lurking there, and knew that nothing short of torturing the guy within an inch of his life would make him give up the information. "I don't have her," he said again.

Michelle started rifling through Gerald's jacket pockets, then peeked in the car window. She opened the door and slid the keys from the ignition.

"Don't mind if we have a little look around your place, do you?" Jake asked, thrusting his arm against Gerald's windpipe.

Gerald gasped. Jake removed his hold, and Gerald bent over double, coughing. Across the garage, Michelle's hands shook violently as she found the right key and unlocked the door.

"Why don't you lead our tour?" Jake suggested, hauling Gerald up by the back of his jacket and thrusting him in the direction Michelle had gone.

Ten minutes later, after a thorough search through the large, four-bedroom house, the three ended up in the kitchen near the garage door entrance. There had been no sign that a child of any age had ever been there. Of the three extra bedrooms, two were empty, one a swanky home office. There were no telltale stains on the pale Berber area rug in the living room. Nothing fit for a child was in the kitchen. No milk or juice in the refrigerator or cereal or canned spaghetti in the pantry.

Michelle looked an inch away from hurtling over the edge of an emotional peak. And Gerald looked far too smug for Jake's liking.

"Awfully big house for one man, wouldn't you say?" Jake said.

"My *wife* and I think it's perfect. Children would only muck it up. In fact, we decided before we even married that we didn't want children."

Jake narrowed his eyes. Then why go through all the trouble to snatch Lili away from her mother? And why stand here as though he couldn't care less where Lili was?

"You know, I forgot to ask for a search warrant," Gerald said, smoothing his jacket.

Jake clenched his jaw so tightly, he was afraid it would shatter. "I'd advise you to shut up right about now."

"Why?" Gerald crossed his arms and leaned easily against the counter. "I legally took Lili from France so I could bring her home, here, to the States. I think even a man such as yourself can understand my desire to have my only child brought up properly, in a safe, nurturing environment."

Michelle overtly eyed an assortment of knives protruding from a wooden block on the counter. Jake pulled her to stand slightly behind him, well away from the deadly instruments.

"Legal by whose standards, Mr. Evans?" Jake asked. "Yours?"

"By our government's standards, Agent McCoy. You should know that better than any one of us here. In fact, why is *she* still in the country? Wasn't her visa due to expire yesterday? Shouldn't she be on a plane bound for France even as we speak?"

The knives started looking awfully good to Jake, as well. "What would you know about Michelle's visa status?"

Gerald shrugged. "Let's just say I've been contacted by someone else from the INS...." His words trailed off, his meaning all too clear.

Jake stared at the man responsible for so much heartbreak. He thought about making one last shot at getting the information they needed out of him. But Gerald's smug grin told him it wouldn't get him anywhere.

"You haven't heard the last from me, Mr. Evans." He grasped Michelle's arm and guided her through the front door.

MICHELLE SAT shivering uncontrollably in the passenger's seat, despite the warmth of the night, despite the jacket Jake had draped over her shoulders.

Gerald's coldness was something she had never expected. No, she hadn't thought he'd just hand Lili over to her, not after having gone through so much to take her. But the malevolence in his eyes had chilled her to the bone. For several long, torturous moments, she'd feared for her daughter's life. The shock of that possibility had never dawned on her, and her oversight made it doubly worse. Could Gerald have harmed Lili? For some sick, demented reason had he decided that he didn't want a child with his blood running through her veins in the world?

Jake's warm fingers threaded through the hair over her left ear, making her realize she was rocking slightly back and forth, clutching Lili's elephant as though clutching her daughter.

"We'll find her, Michelle. This, I promise you."

She gazed at him, wanting to believe him. But she couldn't. Not only couldn't they find Lili—even if they did, Gerald

knew perfectly well that there was nothing they could do to
gain immediate custody of her.

A big, hot tear rolled down her cheek, and she violently
wiped it away. After speaking to the man who had fathered her
child, she knew it was even more important to get Lili away from
him. She'd never known him to be so cold, so manipulative.

She didn't realize the car had stopped until she felt Jake's
warm breath on her cheek. He'd turned off the four-lane road
they'd been on onto a narrow, residential street shadowed by
trees, and he'd flipped on the hazard lights.

"Hey?" he murmured, pressing his lips against her cheek,
then rubbing his thumb against the dampness there. "Everything's going to be all right. Do you hear me?"

She nodded and bit on her bottom lip.

"No, I don't think you do hear me, Michelle." He hooked
his finger under her chin and forced her to face him. She
looked everywhere but into his eyes.

Then his mouth brushed hers, once, twice, inviting her to respond. She tightly closed her eyes, a sob gathering in her throat.
Jake thrust his fingers through her hair. "Look at me, baby."

She didn't dare.

"Please," he whispered, running his tongue over her bottom lip then nipping at it. "Please look at me, Michelle."

Her eyelids fluttered opened. She felt as if she were looking at him from the bottom of a shallow stream, his features
blurry, but there was no mistaking the fiery intensity in his eyes.

Slowly, her vision began to focus. On Jake. On his concern
for her. On his closeness. Oh, how she was coming to need
this man.

She slid her arms around his neck, looking at him, drinking him in. She pressed her mouth softly against his. She
pulled back and looked into his face. How dear he was becoming to her, how vital. At that moment, it was difficult to

believe she had survived nearly six whole weeks here without him. Impossible to imagine that she had existed without him for the past twenty-eight years. Worse yet, she couldn't see tomorrow without seeing visions of him coloring the days.

She lifted her hand to his hair, rubbing strands between her fingers, then kissed him again. His quiet groan fed the growing fire within her.

This time when she kissed him, she did so with more urgency. He responded in kind. Then she launched an all-out assault on his mouth, channeling all her churning emotion into the action, pulling at his lips, biting his tongue, unleashing all that swirled within her. He pulled her into his lap, and she shamelessly ground against his erection. She moved her head from left to right, plunging, sucking, gasping for air. And he returned her passion, kiss for kiss, restless caress for caress.

She ripped and pulled at the sweatshirt he wore, and gasped when he slid his fingers under the hem of hers, finding her breasts and plucking at her nipples through the fabric of her bra. Then her bra was loose, and his hot palms covered her. She fumbled for the tie to his drawstring pants and thrust both hands inside his briefs, seeking for and finding his silken erection, sliding her fingers up and down the rock-hard shaft, swallowing his groan. Jake tore at her panties under her short black skirt and shifted so she could straddle him, his mouth never abandoning hers.

Michelle was completely ignorant of the traffic that screamed by on the busy road a mere block away. Didn't want to remember that they were on a residential street, and despite the late hour, passersby could see them. All she knew was an intense desire to have this man inside her *now*.

Jake hauled his mouth from hers, his harsh breathing filling her ear as he rested his forehead against hers. "I...I don't have anything on me."

She kissed the tip of his handsome nose. "We don't need anything," she whispered.

Freeing him from his pants, she thrust her hips forward until her swollen flesh pressed lengthwise along the side of his erection. She shuddered, longing for him to fill her completely but knowing they could give each other pleasure this way. Tilting her hips, she drew her wet heat down the length of him, then back again. Jake groaned against her mouth as she did it again, then again.

The friction of their bodies moving against each other without penetration sent fire racing through Michelle's muscles, chasing the last of the emotional chill away and making her arch her back. Jake immediately took advantage and thrust her shirt over her breasts, then fastened his mouth over one of her jutting nipples. She gripped his shoulders tightly, concentrating on the exquisitely thought-robbing sensation of his velvety shaft resting against her most feminine parts. She slowly, torturously shifted forward, then back.

Jake clutched her hips. "I need to be inside you. Now," he whispered through clenched teeth.

Michelle covered his hands with hers, gasping when he brought the tip of his erection to rest against her opening, his gaze holding hers captive.

She was helpless to stop him. If he was determined to reach penetration.... She moaned, overwhelmed with the need to feel him inside her.

But he didn't enter her. Instead, Jake thrust upward, through her swollen folds, holding her still, holding her hostage as his hips bucked again and again.

Michelle cried out as her body shuddered, the world exploding on the back of her eyelids, even as Jake tensed under her. The feel of the hot evidence of his passion covering her belly sent another round of shock waves rumbling through her.

Restlessly, she reached down and raised his hands to her stomach, guiding him to rub the dampness over her skin, her breasts. Reveling in the feel of his passion covering her, the rough skin of his palms rasping against her aching nipples.

She collapsed bonelessly against him, the sound of their ragged breathing filling the car.

Michelle had never felt so dependent on a man before. She knew what it was to love a man completely, with her entire heart, body and soul. Never had someone been so attuned to her needs, her wants. Respecting her even as he demanded from her. So willingly making her pain his. His pleasure hers. His strength hers. And it was from that strength that she would find what she needed to continue her search for Lili.

She slanted her mouth against his, kissing him deeply, passionately. And in his response she sensed he loved her, too.

CHAPTER ELEVEN

JAKE EMERGED from the bathroom fresh from a shower, fully dressed, his mind swirling with ideas. He opened the curtains, letting in the morning sun. Michelle mumbled something in French then rolled over, pulling a pillow over her tousled head. He grinned, repressing the urge to tug the sheet down over her naked skin, coax her to use her native tongue to drive him wild, then make up for the time they had lost last night after they'd returned to the hotel.

He'd intended his kiss in the car to help clear Michelle's emotion-clouded mind. He couldn't have known it would prove a prelude to much, much more. And the erotic few minutes had also helped clear his mind. Gone was the intense desire to see Gerald Evans take the place of his car hood ornament. In its place was crystal-clear determination, his mind a frighteningly efficient machine as he clicked through every snippet of his and Michelle's conversations over the past few days, and the precious little he'd gained from her file when it had been open on Brad's desk. He ignored the niggling in the back of his brain that reminded him there was still much he didn't know in that file. That didn't apply to the here and now. What did was finding Lili before Edgar found them.

He managed to squeeze in an hour of sleep at some point, but between holding Michelle as she cried in her sleep and murmured words in French he didn't understand, and his need to do something, he'd been awake most of the night.

Suddenly, Michelle bolted upright in bed, the sheet falling from her delectable breasts, her hair sexily tousled around her head. Jake was instantly struck with the desire to kiss her, to finish what they'd begun in the car the night before. He hadn't been able to after returning to the hotel because he'd come out of the shower last night to find her sleeping fitfully.

A knock sounded at the door. Michelle looked at him, the concern on her face evident as she clutched the sheet to her chest. Jake peered through the peephole, then opened the door.

"Thanks for coming so quickly."

The hotel employee glanced from Jake to Michelle, then set up an elaborate, state-of-the-art laptop computer on the table near the phone. Within moments, it was booted up, connected to the phone line and ready to go.

Jake walked him to the door and tipped him generously before closing and bolting the door.

"What's...what's this?" Michelle asked, endearingly confused.

"A laptop computer."

"You can get one of these from the hotel?"

He grinned. "Yes, they allow you to borrow them."

Another knock. This time Michelle bolted into the bathroom. Jake stared after her firm little bottom as she zoomed by, then adjusted himself in his sweatpants. For God's sake, what the woman did to him without even trying. He opened the door again, and this time a cart crammed full of breakfast dishes was rolled in. By the time Michelle came out of the bathroom, freshly showered and wrapped in that silly, sexy robe, Jake was sitting at the computer munching on a piece of toast. She stopped in front of the cart. "This is breakfast?"

"Uh-huh. I didn't know what you liked, so I ordered everything."

She fingered the top of an open champagne bottle in an ice bucket.

He looked away. "Compliments of the hotel."

"Ah."

"I asked them for that latte thing you like."

A sound of deep satisfaction emerged from her throat. She sat cross-legged on the bed behind his chair and picked up the soup-bowl-size cup, doing the human equivalent of purring as she took her first sip.

"What are you going to do?" she asked, lapping cream from her upper lip.

Jake tore his gaze from the painfully erotic flick of her tongue and turned to the computer. He accessed his ISP account with a D.C. carrier then gained access to a special reverse directory only certain government investigators could employ to seek out addresses. Whatever Edgar was up to, it thankfully hadn't affected his ability to access the data. "What's your number in Paris?"

"My number?"

God, but he wanted to touch her. Massage the worried lines from between her expressive brown eyes. Whisper things into her ear that would make her forget the gravity of their search. But while making love to her would work for a little while, afterward they would crash down to earth to find themselves right where they were when they started. Actually, in a worse situation, because an invisible clock was ticking. By now Edgar had likely gotten the documentation needed to pull both him and Michelle in. It was only a matter of time before he found them and pulled the rug from under their feet.

He opened his mouth, prepared to ask Michelle exactly what was hidden in the shadows of her past that made her rate a spot so high on the INS hit list. Then fear forced his question down. It didn't matter, anyway. The information wouldn't change their situation. It would only cloud his judgment, take his mind from the matter at hand.

"You said that Lili knew her home phone number, right? That it was just recently she was taught of the dangers of abduction. It's more than likely she'd been trying to call you, but—"

"But because she doesn't know the correct area code, or understand overseas calling procedures—"

"She probably got a local number instead," Jake confirmed.

Michelle sat straighter, her eyes alight with new hope. God, how he wanted to kiss her.

She clearly repeated her phone number for him. He entered it into the search engine. A moment later, a message popped up informing him there was no such number in that area code. Jake sat back and rubbed his fingers against his eyelids.

"Wait!" Michelle said before he exited the system, her mouth filled with a strawberry. "She always transposed the last two numbers! Try it."

He did. Within moments, a name and number popped up. Jake wrote them down. Michelle wiped her sticky hands on a napkin then picked up the phone and began dialing. Jake reached over and depressed the disconnect button.

"What? We need to call the number, yes? See if Lili has been trying to contact me?"

He tapped the face of his watch. "I don't think you're going to find Ms. Hagan very cooperative right now. It's only eight on a Wednesday morning."

"Oh." Lethargically, Michelle replaced the receiver.

"Anyway, I think it better if we visit in person a little later this morning. It's too easy for someone to give you the brush-off over the phone. Face-to-face, they tend to make a little more effort to help you."

He turned to the computer and checked the listing of area codes in the tri-state area. Noting Lansing's, where Gerald's wife was supposedly staying with her parents, and the surrounding ones, he jotted them down and did a search using the phone number with each of the area codes. Only one came through as a legitimate number. It belonged to an antique shop in Napolean, Ohio. Michelle reached for the phone again.

"It's a business, no? Which means they may be open?"

Jake grinned. "Yes."

She started to dial, hesitated, then handed the phone to him. "I don't think I can handle it."

He accepted the receiver, then folded his fingers over hers. He met her eyes meaningfully, then tugged her until she was sitting on his lap.

He'd done it to allow her to listen in on the conversation. But the instant welcome a certain body part gave to the close proximity of Michelle's hot bottom was something he hadn't anticipated.

Her smile was downright naughty as she dialed the last number. "There."

Jake quickly put the receiver to his ear.

An elderly male answered the phone. Jake spent five minutes on the phone with him, going over all the possibilities. Had a little girl called asking for her *maman* in French? No. Were there other employees who answered the phone? No. Sometimes it helped to keep the person on the line, so Jake asked how the antiques business was going and got an earful on the topic. But when he returned to the subject of Lili, he was told the only strange call the old man had gotten recently was from some fast-talking salesman trying to sell him foreign lottery tickets. Jake advised him to pass on the deal, then hung up the receiver.

Michelle crossed the name off the short list, then got up

and went to sit on the bed. Idly she picked at the food on the cart. "No Lili."

Jake plucked a strawberry from a bowl and held it out to her. She glanced at him from under her thick lashes, her heart so clearly in her eyes it caused his own to constrict. He was about to pull the fruit back when she moved her lips around it, then bit into it with her straight little teeth. He swallowed before she did, watching as juice ran down the side of her mouth and over her chin. She chewed slowly, watching him. He realized he was making the same chewing motion and groaned. God, it was inhuman, the need he felt for this woman.

Glancing at the clock and seeing that they didn't have anything more to do for a couple hours, he grabbed the bowl of strawberries and the bottle of champagne and practically dove on top of her on the bed.

NOTHING. Not a single one of the numbers panned out. Either Lili hadn't been given access to a phone, or she hadn't tried to call.

Michelle sat cradling her coffee cup in concentration. The ticking of a clock in her ears grew louder with each passing minute and with each dead end she and Jake reached. She'd experienced so many highs and lows over the past three days, she didn't quite know where she was. She only knew where she would be soon. In Paris. Without her daughter.

She glanced at Jake, who sat opposite her, his gaze intense on her. She shivered. His want of her physically was lurking in his warm gray eyes, but so was something else. More than curiosity, almost suspicion.

She looked around the small diner near the Ohio Michigan border. Most of the lunch customers had left, leaving her and Jake nearly alone in the corner booth.

"So what do we do now?" she whispered, afraid of his answer.

He didn't answer. It appeared he hadn't heard her.

She put her cup down and pushed her hardly eaten lasagna away.

"There's one other area we have yet to check," he said quietly.

She searched his face, hardly daring to hope that there was another option.

"Gerald's parents' place."

Despite her best efforts, hope ran away with her. "Of course!" Her mind raced. "We have to go through there to get back to…" She allowed her words to trail off, not able to say "back to D.C." "It's only a couple of hours away, yes? That means we can be there before five. A good time to check into strange callers, yes?"

The smile he gave her was decidedly less bright than ones he'd honored her with before. "Yes."

"Then let's go!"

She pulled him up, barely giving him time to put money down for the bill before she tugged him to the car.

The scenery went by more quickly this time. Michelle made herself look at it: the deep greens, the kiss of autumn on some trees. Ignoring the hum of the air conditioner, she pushed the automatic window opener then took a deep breath of the late summer air. Jake shut off the air and rolled down his window, his short hair tousling in the wind. She smiled at him with her entire being.

The landscape was so unlike where she'd grown up in southern France. The land was flat and seemed to stretch out to forever. She noticed a cow farm, and her smile widened. How little Lili would have loved to see the cows. She could envision her daughter making their mooing sound and pointing at the animals several times to make sure Michelle had seen them.

Before too long, they rolled into the small town of Canton, where their search had begun only the day before, but it seemed so very long ago. Jake got out of the car and used a pay phone to call information, then minutes later pulled into a copy center that offered Internet access. Before she knew it, he had the addresses he needed. One number was unlisted. But the number with the last two digits transposed wasn't that far from where they were.

Michelle tried to relax as they drove the short way. She caught herself twisting her wedding band around her finger, then looked at Jake's hand. He still wore his band, as well. The realization made her feel better. Not so alone, despite the unexplained somber expression he wore.

Jake pulled to a stop, staring out the window at a two-apartment dwelling. He referred to the slip of paper he held, then looked at her. "Are you ready?"

For a long moment, she was unable to move. This was it. If the owner hadn't received any unusual calls in the past eight weeks...

She nodded, then reached for the door knocker, fervently praying in her native French. Please let them know something. Please....

A woman answered the door, a cigarette hanging from her fleshy lips, her hair in steel-colored curlers, her flowered housecoat stained and faded. "Whaddaya want?"

Jake held out his business card and introduced himself then explained the situation. Michelle held her breath, afraid to move, afraid to speak for fear that it would result in bad news or the slamming of the door in their faces.

"French?" the woman repeated. "What do I know from French?"

Michelle looked beyond her to where a teenage girl lay across an old sofa, the telephone receiver attached to her ear.

"No, we haven't gotten any unusual calls."

"Are you sure?" Michelle asked. "Maybe your daughter—"

"That's my niece. And I'm sure. Now I've got something cooking on the stove."

She began to turn away. Jake said, "Do you mind if we speak to your niece?"

The woman's expression turned decidedly suspicious. "Yes, I do mind. Now get out of here before I call the police."

"Good Lord, Aunt Bert, can you keep it down to a low roar? I'm on the phone!" The girl got up from the sofa and disappeared from sight.

The woman named Bert slammed the door firmly in their faces.

Michelle stood paralyzed. That was it. No new leads on Lili and her possible whereabouts.

Jake gripped her arms. "Are you all right?"

Michelle realized she had nearly fallen over before he'd steadied her. She slowly nodded, but when the action caused dizziness, shook it instead. "I think I'm going to be sick."

He led her to the side of the house where a stand of bushes hid her from sight as she retched up what little she'd eaten at lunch.

"Aunt Bert's gonna have a heart attack if she finds out."

Michelle ran the back of her hand across her mouth and looked up to find the teenage girl leaning on a window ledge above her. She explained to whomever she was talking to on the phone that some woman had just hurled all over her aunt's front yard. "You drunk or something?" she asked Michelle.

Jake handed Michelle his handkerchief. "No, she's not drunk." He eyed the girl. "That phone have a double line?"

The girl frowned. "Double line? No. But it has call waiting, if that's what you mean."

His smile returned, and Michelle felt her heart give a little jump in her chest.

"You stay here a lot?"

"I live here."

"With your aunt?"

"Yeah, ever since Mom went into detox. Again." She moved the receiver to her mouth. "Hold on a sec, Melinda, can't you hear I'm talking to someone?"

Aunt Bert's loud voice sounded through the window. Michelle jumped, then realized she wasn't anywhere near. She was calling her niece for dinner.

Jake slid his hand in his pocket and took out a small pile of bills in different denominations he pretended an interest in sorting. "What's your name?"

"Stacy," the girl said slowly. "Why?"

"You answer the phone a lot, Stacy?"

The girl's focus was strictly on the money. "All the time."

"Probably because you don't get much by way of allowance so you can go out and...do things that girls your age do."

"So?"

Jake slid a twenty from the small stack. "You get any unusual calls lately?"

"Maybe."

Michelle's throat tightened.

"From whom?" Jake held out the money.

"Who? From these stupid dweebs from school, that's who." The girl tried to take the money, but Jake pulled his hand back.

"I mean from someone you don't know, say in the past eight weeks or so, from a little girl."

Stacy frowned again. "Let me call you back, Melinda." She hung up the receiver then sat with her hands resting against the body of the phone possessively. "You know, it's really weird that you ask that. Do you know her? Because like it really freaked me out, you know? I mean the first time she called, I thought it was one of my friends playing a practical joke, but then she called again, and I got this weird feeling that something was wrong with her, you know? Because she was crying and everything. Then a couple weeks ago, the calls, like, stopped—"

A sob burst from Michelle's throat, and she put her hands over her mouth to quell it.

"She all right, man?"

Jake's grin was one-hundred-percent pure satisfaction. "Yes, she's all right. Thanks, Stacy. Thank you very much." He handed her the twenty, then carefully led Michelle to the car.

JAKE GLANCED to where Michelle had her fist over her mouth to stop sobbing. He suppressed his desire to celebrate. Knowing Gerald's parents had had the girl was a long way from his and Michelle's chances of recovering her. Besides, Stacy had said the calls had stopped a couple of weeks back. It could have been because her grandparents had caught on to what Lili was doing. Or because she'd assimilated and no longer felt the need to call her mother. Or, worse, had given up any hope of her mother finding her. Or, worst of all, she could have moved somewhere else.

Jake turned the corner onto the Evanses' street and immediately jammed on the brakes. He didn't have to explain to Michelle. She was also staring at the dark blue sedan parked two blocks up. *Edgar.*

"Damn," he muttered.

He put the car in reverse and he backed up until the car was completely blocked from sight.

"What's he doing here?" Michelle whispered.

He could have responded in any number of ways. Told her that since they'd lost him in Toledo, Edgar's best chance of finding them was by camping out here because it was likely Gerald had told Edgar of Lili's whereabouts. He could have said he didn't know. He could have told her not to worry.

But he did none of them. Instead, he put the car in Park and started to get out.

"Listen to me carefully, Michelle. I want you to drive two blocks up then turn left. Park between two cars if you can, preferably under some trees. Wait there for me."

She reached out and grabbed his arm desperately. "Do you think Lili's there?"

"That's what I'm going to find out."

He gently pried her fingers from his arm, but before he closed the door, he curved his hand over the side of her face. She instantly closed her eyes and leaned into his touch, making him want to groan.

There were so many conflicting emotions crowding his chest, he didn't know what to do. He withdrew his hand then closed the door, motioning for her to go. She did so, slowing after she cleared the cross street, likely watching him in the rearview mirror. He turned the corner and shoved his hands deep into the pockets of his sweats.

The feel of the unfamiliar material reminded him that he should be somewhere in the backwoods of the Blue Ridge Mountains right now, devising ways to make David pay for dragging him out there. Instead, he was falling head over heels in love with a woman who was turning his life upside down. Searching for her daughter with only this one hope of finding her. And it was eating his gut not knowing what secret lurked in Michelle's past, a secret serious enough to have Edgar tailing her for two straight days.

He didn't bother pretending he didn't see his fellow

agent. He strode to the side of the car and rapped on the closed window.

Edgar jumped, having been slumped over catching a nap. Then he scrambled to get out of the car. "For God's sake, McCoy, you could have given me a freakin' heart attack."

"Yeah, well, consider it down payment on the large debt I owe you."

Edgar frowned at him. "Did you just crack a joke, McCoy?"

Jake ignored him and looked at the house across the street. "How long have you known the little girl's been here?"

"Since last night." Edgar straightened his suit coat. "Only she's not there anymore. Grandparents took off with her yesterday morning, right after you and the Frenchwoman left."

"It's Michelle." Jake stared at him. "Any idea where they went?"

He shrugged. "Could be just about anywhere, considering the resources these guys have. East coast, west coast. Seeing as the girl has a legal American passport, they might even have left the country. And seeing as the old man is retired…"

Jake ran his hand over his face, suppressing the desire to hit Edgar. But coldcocking Edgar wouldn't get him anywhere, because his fellow agent was completely right. There was no telling where they'd gone, or when, if ever, they'd be back.

Not that it mattered. If the agent next to him had a say, Michelle would be heading to France soon anyway.

"So where's the French…Ms. Lambert?" Edgar asked, scanning the street.

Jake shrugged. "Could be anywhere. East coast. West."

Edgar squinted at him in the setting sun. "That would be funny except I know you never joke, and this is no laughing matter."

"Yeah."

"You know your ass is in trouble, don't you? I mean, she's told you why we refused her extension request?"

Jake narrowed his gaze on the other man, his chest tightening in apprehension.

He'd wanted to ask Michelle directly about what marred her record. Wanted her to be the one to tell him, help him understand. But if the past day was any indication of how long it would take him to get around to it, he'd never find out.

"Yeah, I know," he lied.

Edgar's burst of laughter surprised him. "Sure you do, old boy. Sure you do."

Jake was caught between needing to go and needing to stay. He glanced up the street. His car, of course, was nowhere in sight. Michelle would be sitting where he'd instructed her to, scared spitless, waiting for him to return.

"So you going to arrest me?" he asked.

"Naw, you know I wouldn't do that. Not without the woman here, anyway."

Jake figured as much. He nodded and began walking away.

"Hey, McCoy, during time-outs, you know, from all that hot and heavy sex you're probably having with her, why don't you try asking her about Blue Earth and a bunch of highly classified naval documents that came up missing in San Francisco about ten years ago?"

Jake forced himself to keep moving. To act as if what Edgar said didn't hit him like a blow to the gut. To pretend it didn't matter that what hid in Michelle's past was probably worse than anything he'd imagined.

The problem was, it did matter to him, deeply.

CHAPTER TWELVE

IT WAS the following morning when Jake finally pulled into the driveway of the old McCoy place. His eyelids felt leaden, his body anesthetized as he switched the ignition off and sat staring at the transformed house. As they said they would, Mitch and Liz had erected an ornate iron archway at the end of the driveway, supported by foundations of new red brick. Spelled out at the top was Red Shoe Ranch.

He looked to where Michelle slept fitfully next to him, her cheeks paler than ever, her curled-up position both defensive and defenseless. She'd said Lili's name several times during the night and startled herself awake, only to find that nothing had changed; they were still heading to D.C.

Only Jake hadn't taken her to D.C. He'd brought her here.

He looked at the house. He really didn't know why he'd driven here or what he hoped to accomplish by bringing Michelle. If he had a brain in his head, he'd take her to the airport and put her on the first airplane out. Then again, if he had a brain in his head, he would have found out why the INS wanted her out of the country so badly.

If his three-year stretch in the Marines so long ago had taught him anything, it was the importance of protecting one's borders. Not just from the enemies without, but also from the enemies within. Posted for fifteen long months in a war-torn Third World country, one experience stood out starkly from the others: the day he'd watched an old lady try to cross the border. She needed the help of a cane to walk, each of her wrinkles telling a different story of hardship and pain, and appeared to pose a danger to no one. Then a search found that she carried bricks of plastic explosives strapped to her body, hidden by oversize housecoats and a shawl—explosives that would have killed people of her own country had they gotten through, all because of a difference in theologies.

The experience had twisted Jake's gut. It had also made that much easier his decision about which law enforcement branch to work in when he got home.

Knowing he had not only failed in his job, but had wittingly allowed someone who possibly posed a threat to his country, his home—no matter how he felt about her—to remain there for a prolonged length of time, sat like acid in his stomach.

A voice in the back of his mind told him that he was overreacting, that the hurting woman next to him who was murmuring her daughter's name in her sleep couldn't possibly pose a threat to anybody, much less the big, bad United States of America. But he refused to lie to himself anymore, refused to continue to play the fool as he had so willingly the past few days.

"Then what the hell are you doing here, McCoy?" he muttered, realizing that he'd brought that same threat home, straight to his family's doorstep. He should have taken her to his apartment in Woodley Park—where Edgar probably would have knocked on the door quicker than they could have closed it.

Michelle stirred at the sound of his voice at the same time that Mitch's old dog, Goliath, spotted the car and issued a short but loud series of barks.

"Where...where are we?" Michelle asked, her accent thick, her heavy-lidded eyes sultry. Jake tried to ignore how sexy she looked. That was what had gotten him into trouble in the first place.

Yeah, like he had put up a fight. Not only had he given in, he'd given in over and over and over again. He didn't think there was a time in his life when he'd made love to a woman so often in such a short span of time and so…thoroughly. Not that it mattered. He was filled with the urge to press her back against the seat and have at her all over again. It was time he started thinking with his brain rather than other parts of his anatomy.

"The house I grew up in," he said. "Come on, get your stuff. I'll take you inside so you can get some sleep."

He felt her gaze on him, much as he'd periodically felt it on him during the long drive home. He sensed that she knew something was wrong, but she hadn't asked him what—which was just as well, because he likely wouldn't have told her. He needed time to get his thoughts together, time to get used to the idea that the woman he thought he knew so well was in fact very different. He reached for the door handle, inexplicably relieved when she did the same on the other side.

Goliath began to jump, but one look from Jake sent his mammoth paws to the ground. He really didn't know why everyone else had a discipline problem with the pooch. Goliath always behaved well around Jake.

Spotting Michelle, the slobber puss sprang for her, stamping paw prints over the front of her shirt, his furry butt waggling back and forth wildly along with his bushy tail.

"*Merde*," Michelle said, though the smile on her face revealed her true feelings. Jake ordered the dog down, and Goliath immediately obeyed, sitting at Michelle's feet and whining.

"Come on, let's go inside." Jake turned toward the door then stopped. It was just after dawn, and he'd hoped they could sneak in without notice. No such luck. The front steps were jammed full of McCoy males and two McCoy females.

Jake grimaced and rubbed his forehead as he led the way toward the silent group. He really wasn't up for this. There would be questions. There would be answers. Then there would be more questions. And if he wasn't careful, his sisters-in-law Melanie and Liz would be planning a wedding for him and Michelle in no time.

He slowly moved his hand from his forehead, realizing he already was married. Worse, he was still wearing the wedding ring. Damn. The last thing he wanted was for these guys to know what was going on straight from the start. There were things he needed to do, calls that needed to be made.

He and Michelle finally stopped near the foot of the stairs. Jake cleared his throat as seven pairs of eyes looked back and forth between them. "This is, um, Michelle," he said. "My wife."

Holy mother of God, Jesus and Joseph! Had he just said what he thought he had? Judging by the wide eyes, dropped jaws and a couple of groans he got, yes, he very much indeed had said it. Even Michelle stared at him in openmouthed shock.

"Hi...good morning," Michelle said from next to him, pushing her purse strap on her shoulder, looking about ready to bolt.

Not that he could blame her. If he'd been given a second, he would have been leading the way.

"Oh, she is French!" Liz was the first to regain her composure as she jostled her way through the crowd to approach Michelle. "Hi, I'm Liz. And the other lone female over there is Melanie. It's a—" her gaze strayed to Jake, a knowing twinkle in her eyes "—pleasure to meet you, Michelle. Welcome to the family."

Behind her, Sean cleared his throat. Jake berated himself again for having brought Michelle home, but for entirely different reasons than before. He hadn't even thought of how his family might interpret his actions. Okay, so he had never brought a woman home before, but this was different. Michelle wasn't a woman. He cringed. Of course she was a woman, but not just any woman. And now that he had introduced her as his wife…

Ah, hell, who was he trying to kid? It was one thing being on the road with her, just the two of them. Quite another to be here, being judged by the only people who had ever really mattered in his life. Truth was, he didn't quite know what he was feeling. A part of him wanted to step in front of Michelle, protect her from curious McCoy eyes. Another wanted to take his words back, explain exactly what he meant by *wife*. But when it came down to it, he was completely incapable of doing either.

Liz looked at him meaningfully, then took Michelle by the arm. "Come on. Let me introduce you to the rest of the McCoy clan. Oh, and don't let all that testosterone scare you. They may be all rough and tough when it comes to the law, but they're all just a bunch of softies when it comes to the fairer sex."

"Softies?" Connor echoed, grimacing.

Liz smiled at him, then leaned closer to Michelle. "Okay, most of them are. Connor and David here still like to think themselves immune, but Mel and I are working on it."

Jake didn't miss how easy it was for her to exclude him from that dwindling group of bachelor McCoys. He opened his mouth to correct her, to tell her that he was still very much a bachelor, then he caught Pops staring at the ring on his finger. Judging by the heat of his face, Jake suspected he turned fifty kinds of red. His father lifted his gaze. The grin Sean gave him nearly knocked him over.

Liz continued with her introductions. "This here is the family patriarch, Sean. But none of us call him that. He's Pops to us." She motioned to where Connor stood at the top of the stairs, his arms crossed over his denim-clad chest. "The old hardie up there is Connor, the oldest. Next to him, that cutie is Mitch, my guy." Her smile nearly spread across the whole of her face. "Where was I? Oh, yes. See the one next to Mel? That's her husband, Marc." She leaned closer to Michelle to add in a lower voice, "They've been arguing, so don't pay them any mind—something about Marc being assigned to protect one of the presidential candidates. He's Secret Service. Oh, and the blond one over there with the Brad Pitt good looks? That's David, the baby of the family." David snorted even as he grinned his hello. "Never mind him. He's not too happy right now, either, because Jake was supposed to go hiking with him this week." Liz turned her smile on Michelle. "Looks like Jake had more interesting things on his agenda, though."

Jake grimaced. If Liz only knew the half of it.

Aggravated, he waved toward the house. "Why don't you take Michelle inside and show her to my old room. I..." What? Need to get as far from here as humanly possible? "Um, I need to go get something out of the car."

Michelle looked at him as Liz led her through the throng of bone and muscle on the stairs, Mel instantly taking her other arm when they reached the top. Jake didn't miss the shadow of grief in Michelle's brown eyes when she saw Mel's girth, the baby she carried grown larger every time he saw her. He also didn't miss his wash of guilt at having abandoned her to the well-wishing but overwhelming attentions of his sisters-in-law.

He cleared his throat then turned toward the car. As soon as he'd moved a couple of feet, he pulled and twisted at his wedding band, covertly trying to work it from his finger. The sucker wouldn't budge. Goliath caught up with him, his tongue lolling from the side of his mouth as Jake frowned at him.

"Quite a looker, your Michelle," Pops said, coming up on the other side of Goliath.

"A little on the short side, isn't she?" Connor said, coming up on Jake's other side.

David popped up next to him. "They've always said dynamite comes in small packages."

"Yeah, and if it's one thing Pops always tried to drill into you, it's to stay away from explosives. You'd best remember that," Connor said.

Jake curled his fingers into fists. He wanted to tell them all to leave him alone so he could sort everything out, figure out where to go from here. But he knew better. The moment he asked them to leave, they'd only stay longer. "Anyway, it's nothing like that," he said. *Liar.* It was exactly like that. Michelle's combustible response to him was exactly the reason he was in this mess.

Jake looked at Mitch as they neared the car. He couldn't quite make out what his younger brother was thinking. It wasn't too long ago that Jake had called Mitch's relationship with Liz into question. While Mitch had never been the vengeful type, it didn't make sense that he wouldn't say something, anything, now.

They reached the car. Jake made a show of opening the trunk.

"So tell us what it is like, then," Connor said, leaning against the side of the car and crossing his arms.

Jake rifled through his backpack, not really looking for anything but not wanting to look at the only brother who was older than him, either. Connor had always been what his high-school English teacher had called a Nosey Parker. Jake couldn't count the scrapes he and Connor had gotten into over the span of their lifetimes. From something as simple as what to fix for breakfast to what they should do about Marc, who was always getting into some sort of trouble or other when they were younger, anything was capable of setting them off. Ultimately, though, Jake had usually conceded. Not because he thought Connor was right, but because it wasn't worth more than a couple of jabs.

"It's complicated," Jake muttered.

David poked around inside the trunk and spotted the backpack. "Hey, you really were going to come hiking, weren't you? Are those Timberland? Good Lord, Jake, you really went top of the line, didn't you?" David absently tugged the backpack from Jake's grip. His chuckle somehow lightened the atmosphere. "Look at this. All the things a guy needs for survival in the wilderness." He quirked a brow at Jake, holding up a book. "Did you really think I'd make you eat moss?"

Jake snatched the book. "It was a possibility."

"I'm crushed."

"You'll get over it."

Pops cleared his throat. "She seems like a nice enough girl."

Jake stuffed the book into his pack then looked at his father. "She's a woman, Pops, through and through. And yes, she is nice—straightforward, fresh, um, nice." He felt his face go hot again. "When she talks, I know where she's coming from, you know? And she…gets me. Most of the women I date…um, dated, thought something was wrong if I wasn't talking a mile a minute. Not Michelle. We can sit for hours without a word passing between us—"

Connor barked a laugh. "Probably because she doesn't know English well enough to carry on a—"

"Her English is better than yours, Con of the Jungle."

His four brothers and father went silent. Judging by their open-eyed expressions, Jake pretty much figured he'd shocked the hell out of them.

Sean squeezed his shoulder. "I don't think I've ever heard you say so many words before in one breath."

David laughed. "Yeah, and I wouldn't exactly say wit is one of your stronger suits, but what you just said to Connor…

Well, let's just say that since your jaw's still attached, he must not have expected it, either."

The six of them laughed, Jake included.

Marc shrugged. "Hey, whatever trips your trigger, you know? And after getting a look at her…well, I can certainly see where she'd be capable of doing that."

Mitch frowned at Marc. Jake was reminded again that Mitch had yet to say anything about the situation. He'd yet to do anything more than smile when it was expected. Jake didn't know why, but he had the feeling his brother had something to share that wasn't along the lines of, "You did what?"

Sean sighed and looked at the house. "Yeah, well, I think we've busted poor Jake's chops enough, guys. What say we leave him to his business and get in to that, um, breakfast the McCoy women have scared up for us?"

"Scared being the operative word," Connor grumbled, stuffing his hands deep in his jeans pockets. He gave Jake a sidelong look, shrugged, then started toward the house.

David hefted the backpack out of the trunk. "Mind if I look through this stuff?"

Jake waved him off. "Go ahead. Just know I have an inventory of everything in there."

Marc chuckled then put a headlock on their youngest brother as they sauntered away.

Only Pops and Mitch remained. Pops gave Mitch a long glance, but Mitch ignored him and pretended an interest in the old barn that stood hulking in the right front corner of the property.

Pops sighed. "Okay, obviously you two have something to discuss. Just don't be too long, or else Liz'll have both your butts in a sling." He started to step away, then stopped. "You do remember what day it is, Jake?"

Jake stared at his father, searching his memory. Then it hit him. It was the anniversary of their mother's death. He nodded solemnly.

"We thought we'd head over to the site around eleven. That okay with you?"

"Yeah."

Finally, he and Mitch were alone. Jake closed the trunk and looked at his younger brother curiously.

"Come on, let's go see how the horses are doing," Mitch said, draping an arm around his shoulders.

Jake ground his teeth together. Why the dramatics? He had the sinking sensation that he was being led to the slaughter. Then he realized that Mitch must know what he'd found out from Edgar, which shouldn't have surprised him. When he'd called Mitch the day before, he should have known he'd do some checking around on his own. And considering the nature of the information, the FBI would be the perfect place to do that checking.

Jake sighed. Normally, he would wait for Mitch to do the talking. But he couldn't stand the silence a moment longer. "Look, Mitch, I know what you're going to say. And while I appreciate your concern, this is really something I have to work out by myself."

The wide-eyed look was something Jake should be growing accustomed to by now, but the truth was, it wasn't an expression he was used to inspiring. He didn't think it ever would be. "Fair enough," his brother said, finally.

They entered the new barn, the sharp and subtle odors assaulting Jake's nose as fresh straw crunched underfoot. One of the stallions nickered, and Mitch reached into a pail near the door for a cube of sugar to feed him.

"So you know all you have riding on the line here, then, huh?"

Jake nodded, wishing he had his brother's touch with animals. Just like with children, animals tended to be wary of him, afraid. Why, he wasn't sure. Maybe it was because he never fawned over them the way his brother did. Hesitantly, he reached out for a few cubes of sugar, the grainy feel a new one against his skin. He held his hand out to the sleek black stallion whose nameplate read Seti.

"Lower your hand a little and bring it in a little closer," Mitch said quietly.

Jake did so. The horse smelled it first with his cool nose, then lapped the cube up with infinite skill. Jake frowned at the wet mess he left behind. Mitch laughed and handed him a towel. "Never were much for getting dirty, were you, Jake?"

"That's not dirt, that's slime."

Mitch slapped him on the back and led him down the aisle.

"So…how's married life treating you?" Jake asked, hoping to encourage their conversation away from himself and Michelle.

"Liz and I are doing just fine." Mitch shrugged. "She insists the color I painted the office is not the color she requested. Hell, I tell her, what's the difference between magenta and eggplant, anyway? Then there's this discussion about kids. I want them now, she thinks it's too soon. Says I should content myself with being an uncle to Marc and Mel's baby for the time being." His grin was infectious. "She also won't even consider going above two kids."

Jake hiked a brow. "You want more?"

Mitch nodded, looking a little gob-smacked. "Yeah, I do. Funny, isn't it? I never really gave it a great deal of thought until after I finally roped Liz in. Now I want to pop as many out as we can. I don't think there's anything more exciting than the thought of ten or twelve little Lizzes running around the place."

Jake nearly choked.

"Okay, maybe four or five."

"You know, you're just as likely to get another batch of stubborn McCoy males."

"Yeah, I know." He tightened his grip on Jake's shoulder. "That wouldn't be so bad, would it? The place could do with a few more strapping males. Of course, my first choice would be a little girl, one who preferably would wear those cute little pink dresses and shriek if she so much as got her black patent leather shoes dirty."

Jake smiled at the image, only in his mind he superimposed little Lili's face on the girl in question.

He cleared his throat, realizing he didn't have a clue what Lili was like. Was she like her mother? Was she affectionate, playful, able to tell a joke as well as get one? Was she sweet and feminine, leaning toward all things frilly?

"Gotta tell you something, though, Jake," Mitch said as he led them out the other side of the new construction. "I never thought you would beat us all to the fatherhood bit."

"Fatherhood?" Jake nearly croaked.

Mitch smiled at him. "Of course. You realize that you are officially a stepfather now, right? That Elizabeth—"

"Lili," he automatically corrected.

"Okay then, Lili. You know that the moment you married her mother, you essentially took on the role of her father. Well, a father once removed, but from what I saw listed on her real father… Well, let's just say you're her father."

"Father?" Jake felt like an idiot for repeating Mitch so often, but he couldn't think of anything else to say. Yes, while he'd married Michelle to help her stay in the country long enough to find Lili, he'd never stopped to consider what that meant for her daughter…his daughter.

He suddenly felt light-headed.

"What's the matter, Jake? You all right?"

"Yeah." He grinned stupidly. He was all right. More than all right, he felt proud, somehow. Which was even dumber, given their circumstances. But just the thought of a little girl out there needing a father, and him being legally in line for the job… "Wonder if this is the way Marc feels. You're right, of course. Lili is now my daughter, even though I've never met her."

Mitch chuckled quietly. "Difference is, you're going to get to skip all those slimy diapers."

Jake laughed. Then laughed again. Then laughed so damned hard he nearly bent over double.

Good Lord, he was a daddy….

MICHELLE WALKED around Jake's room, then walked around it again. Most might think the room revealed little about the boy who had once inhabited it. She smiled. She thought it revealed everything.

The narrow bed in the middle of the room was covered by a blue broad plaid patterned spread, the curtains at the windows made from the same fabric. The old desk in the corner was completely clean, likely everything tucked away in the drawers, a place for everything and everything in its place. The bookshelves were neat, the books lined up by size rather than by author. She stepped closer. *Tom Sawyer* sat right alongside Clancy. She fingered a small, tarnished statue of a cowboy, strong and silent. She ran her thumb over the somber features then put it down.

She told herself she should feel out of place here, in this strange room, in this foreign place, but she didn't. Jake was everywhere. In every corner. In every crease in the curtains. Surrounding her. Filling her.

She moved to the window. Jake was coming out of a low building with his brother…Mitch, she recalled. Her heart did an immediate somersault in her chest. Oh, how she loved this man. And the thought that she soon wouldn't be able to see him…

She wouldn't think about that, refused to think about that.

She hugged her arms around herself and listened to the sound of laughter coming from downstairs. His family was just as she imagined. Cohesive. The type that gathered on Sundays, like today, for dinner. Breakfast was a rarity, Liz had told her when she'd brought her upstairs, but what with everything that was happening with Jake... Well, last night found them all gathered at the house waiting for word.

She couldn't imagine growing up in such an environment. While her mother was alive, it had been just her father, mother and her. Then there had been Dad and Jacqueline, then later, three more children. But there was never the closeness so evident in the family downstairs. Everyone in her family had always had their own agendas. Her step siblings had school activities, Jacqueline was busy with her interests, and while Michelle and her father occasionally managed to grab a meal out together, it wasn't the same thing. The ghost of her mother always seemed to be hovering somewhere nearby.

She remembered that Jake, as well, had lost his mother. But rather than rip the family apart, it appeared to have drawn them closer together.

A brief knock sounded at the door. Thinking it was Jake, she told him to enter.

"Hi," Liz said. "I didn't know if you'd still be up. Jake said you two were on the road pretty much all night. But I just wanted to bring you up a plate of food, you know, in case you were hungry." She set a tray on the clean desktop, then turned and smiled. "If you're not tired, you can always come down and join us."

"Thanks. Maybe I will."

Liz held out a small bag. "I'm sure you probably have everything you need, but I gathered some things you might want. There's a toothbrush, toothpaste, nightgown." Her smile was decidedly wicked. "If you're anything like me, you never wore much to bed before. In this place, though, you never know who'll be walking through the door."

Michelle laughed, deciding she liked this Liz McCoy, wife of Mitch. "Thanks."

Liz looked around the room. "Okay. I guess I'll leave you alone then. Just give me a yell if you need anything, all right?"

"All right. And—" she smiled, "—thank you."

"No need for thanks. You're family now, Michelle."

She closed the door quietly. Michelle stared after her for a long moment. How she wished that Liz's words were true. That she really was a part of this large and warm family. That she and her daughter could be included in these meals, the inside jokes, a part of the intricate support system so evident in their closeness.

She startled herself with the direction of her thoughts. She'd never before considered living outside France, residing in another country where the customs, the language, were so different. Never considered raising her daughter anywhere else. And it was dangerous to be considering it now, because it wasn't an option.

Jake had been acting strangely ever since his run-in with Edgar outside the Evanses' last night. He'd been quiet, thoughtful, almost sad, even. She'd wanted to ask him what was wrong, but hadn't dared. She was afraid of what his answer would be. Had he given up all hope of finding Lili? Had the prospect of coming home, of returning to his normal life, made him realize the mistake he'd made by helping her by marrying her?

She nearly jumped when the door opened again. This time it *was* Jake.

Her heart skipped a beat. If she thought she felt him in the room before, it was nearly overwhelming now. He seemed to fill every inch with his height, his presence.

"Everything okay?" he asked, his eyes dark and watchful.

She nodded. "Yes." She tried for a smile, but couldn't quite conjure one up. Her mind swirled with questions she could no longer ignore, no matter the answers. "No. Everything is not okay." She sank down on the bed and tucked her hair behind her ear. "I think we need to talk."

He nodded slowly. "Yes, I think we do."

She studied his face as she had so often over the past twelve hours, finding nothing there that hadn't been there before, which was precious little. She forced a swallow past her thick throat. "You first."

His small smile surprised her. "You started it."

She closed her eyes, then opened them to stare at the ceiling. "Ever since…after you… I don't know. You've been acting a little strange since last night." She sighed. "I know, everything about this whole thing is—" she gestured helplessly with her hands, "—is strange. But you seem more…distant somehow, not really with me." She searched his eyes. "Is something wrong?"

He didn't say anything. Merely stood looking at her unblinkingly. Then he moved to the bed and sat down stiffly next to her. "Yes, Michelle, something is wrong."

She bit on her bottom lip. She'd known something was wrong, but his admitting it made it all the more real. He was going to tell her he didn't care for her, she knew it. Tell her that he'd been carried away in the heat of passion and that now it was time for them to talk about sending her back to France. If the concept of returning to her home without Lili wasn't bad enough, the thought of going back without hope of ever seeing Jake made her heart break.

"You're sending me back, aren't you?" she said when he didn't speak.

The shocked expression on his face made her heart dip low in her stomach. "What?"

She didn't dare believe that's not what he'd been about to tell her.

"I… Last night, outside Gerald's parents, Edgar…" He looked toward the window. "Is that really what you were worried about?"

She nodded, filled with the urge to touch him, to kiss his endearing mouth. "Edgar what?"

"Edgar told me exactly why you rated such a high priority on the INS hit list."

"Hit list?"

"Those they deem important to get out of the country as soon as humanly possible."

She raised her brows. "I rate that?"

"Uh-huh."

"Why?"

He looked at her again, his gaze probing her face and eyes. God help her, but despite everything going on, she wanted to push him against the mattress and straddle him. "Because of what you did ten years ago in San Francisco."

Every muscle in her body instantly relaxed. She was filled with the sudden, uncontrollable urge to laugh.

CHAPTER THIRTEEN

MICHELLE STOPPED LAUGHING, then her smile quickly faded. Jake's stony expression told her he didn't find the situation the least bit amusing. He was right, of course, considering that Edgar Mollens was still out there somewhere looking for them. Lack of sleep might have been to blame for her foray into hysterics, or the sheer absurdity of the circumstances.

She looked at him a little more closely. "San Francisco? That's the reason I was denied an extension? Why Mollens has been trying to deport me? Because of something I did ten years ago? Something that's hardly worth mentioning?"

His eyes darkened. Apparently he felt differently about the situation, as did his government.

"You're serious, aren't you?"

"Yes, Michelle, I am. Tell me about it."

It took her a minute to call forward the memories in question. It had been so very long since she'd thought, really thought about that time in her life. Yes, right after she'd left the INS office on Monday, she'd considered what had happened in San Francisco a likely reason her extension had been denied. But surely it couldn't have been serious enough to warrant her being placed at the top of the INS hit list.

"What? What should I tell you, Jake?" she asked. "About how I was involved in Blue Earth? That we were against America's underwater testing of nuclear weapons? A group

400 FOR HER EYES ONLY

comprised of eighty percent Americans? My God, every college student does the same thing." She looked into her lap.
"Okay, maybe they all didn't join Blue Earth, but most of them
wanted to."

"Important papers came up missing while you guys were
protesting."

She eyed him. "From where?"

The shadow of suspicion on his face made her cringe. Perhaps this was more serious than she knew. "From the Navy."

"And that's what this is about?"

He didn't answer her.

She pushed from the mattress. She walked from one side
of the room to the other, chewing on her fingernail. "That
wasn't our mission. We simply went there to stop the U.S.S.
Admiral nuclear warship from leaving port. Block San Francisco Bay. Focus public attention on their practices via newspaper and television media coverage. At no time was anything
said about going on a covert mission to filch any top-secret
documents." She began pacing again, trying to think back to
that time so long ago. She remembered the salt air, the chilly
mornings, though it was the height of summer. The youthful
righteousness she'd felt. She remembered also thinking at
that time that nothing in her life would be able to equal that
moment. A vision of Lili filled her heart and mind as she
looked at Jake. Oh, how wrong she had been. That time
seemed very long ago, indeed. "The only one I think capable
of doing something like that would have been Enrique. The
morning of the protest, he disappeared."

"Enrique?"

She recalled the cocky Spaniard in all his arrogant glory.
"Enrique Del Jose. He was our second in command, so to
speak. He pushed off the boat sometime before dawn. I was
the only one on deck, freezing my butt off and wrapped in two

wool blankets at the time, waiting to watch the sun rise on the other side of the Golden Gate bridge. He didn't see me, and he seemed startled when I asked him where he was going. He told me he had some sort of business to look after." She stared at Jake. "Wait! It could have been Julie Cochran. She left the boat the night before, claiming she had family in the area, and never made it back until the following day." She looked him squarely in the face. "Or have you ever considered that it wasn't any of us at all, but someone inside who actually stole the documents? I mean, it was a military installation, yes? Wouldn't there have been security up the wazoo?" She leaned her head back and closed her eyes. That argument was neither here nor there. "Anyway, in the impending melee, I never thought about who was missing."

"By melee, you mean the hosing down of the boat, the arrest of nearly everyone on board—"

"Yes." She came to sit next to him, searching his profile. "If the deed was in fact so important, if I was personally suspected of any crime—big or small—because of the group I belonged to, or who I was involved with, why wasn't I detained longer than the others? Tried? Given a jail sentence? Isn't that usually what happens?"

"Involved with?"

Michelle cringed. She had said that, hadn't she? She looked at her hands and the ring on her finger. "Yes. Enrique and I...well, that doesn't matter now, does it?" Never before had she been ashamed of her past, sexual or otherwise. But for some inexplicable reason, she felt reticent to share this information with Jake. Perhaps because she was afraid he'd judge her. Or maybe because none of it mattered anymore. Everything she'd experienced before had been a prelude to meeting him. She forced herself to look at him. "Anyway, wouldn't I have been detained in San Francisco? Taken to trial?"

He stared straight ahead and rubbed the bridge of his nose. "Not normally. If the arrested is a foreign national, procedure usually dictates we send them back home, with a warning to the government in question to keep an eye out for the person. In some cases, the foreign government will actually detain the individual."

Michelle widened her eyes. "You mean France has this on my record, as well?"

He slowly nodded. "Most likely."

"Oh."

"Then you have to combine that information with the fact that when you came this time you flew into Dulles airport, right near the nation's capital."

She stared at him. "You mean it was suspected I'd tried to steal national secrets from D.C.?"

He shrugged, making her hope he found the prospect as stupid as she did.

"I flew into D.C. because this is where Gerald's trip ended. I thought…I thought he had Lili here somewhere."

Finally, his eyes softened. She was filled with the urge to reach out and touch his stalwart face, to trace the ridge of his nose with her thumbs, to drag her fingers along the well-defined lines of his mouth.

"How long were you a member of Blue Earth?"

She sighed and dragged her gaze away from dangerous territory. This is what was keeping her from finding her daughter? "Three months, maybe?" She tucked her hair behind her ear. "Long enough to figure out that for all the philanthropic deeds the group was involved in, the simple fact of it was, to belong, you needed to have money. I…" She bit her bottom lip. "Once I drained the trust fund my mother set up for me, my services were no longer needed." She shrugged. "Not that it mattered to the group. For every poor member they lose, three more wealthy students pop up to take his place." She stared at where a light breeze ruffled the plaid drapes at the window. "God, I haven't thought about that time in my life for a long time."

"Unfortunately it's a fact the U.S. government, or any other government, won't soon forget."

Jake didn't know what to think. He clasped his hands tightly in his lap, mostly to occupy them. He was having a hard time being alone with Michelle in a room with a bed without wanting to climb on top of her, without wanting to forget everything and everyone and claim her all over again. "I've been with the INS for fourteen years, Michelle. Before that, I was in the Marines and I saw... Well, I served overseas. My life has been all about protecting borders, and the importance of doing so. One person. That's all it takes. One zealot who wants a shot at eternal glory, and this entire government could come toppling down. And with it, the world economy." Didn't she understand that? Didn't she understand that her past made her a risk the United States or any other country couldn't afford to take? They didn't care that her daughter had been taken from her, that her intentions were purely noble. All they saw was that she'd been involved in highly questionable activity in the past. One strike and you're out. Given the sheer numbers of foreign nationals applying for visas and green cards from abroad, and the country's vulnerability once a risky individual was within her borders, his job had been to guarantee that those who were out of the game stayed out.

God, his head pounded as though a thousand little hammers were busy building a skyscraper inside his head. What would he have done had he learned this information three days ago, when he'd pumped Brad for information at the INS? Would he have put Michelle on a plane? Would he have seen her as the same risk Edgar did and hunted her down with only one intention?

He didn't know, because the fact remained that he hadn't known then. He knew she posed no risk at all to the federal government. Her being here didn't jeopardize anyone's life or freedom. The well-being of one particular individual, Lili, his daughter—his stomach dipped—was at risk if Michelle was forced to return to France.

"I see," she said quietly. Her dark eyes held supreme sadness. His throat thickened. What was it about her that made him want to protect her from the world? What magic did she wield over him?

He watched her twist her wedding band around and around. He crooked his index finger under her chin and tilted her head toward him. "No, Michelle, I don't think you do see." She searched his eyes, a spark of hope lighting the depths of hers. "I'm telling you that the situation you're facing is serious. But I'm not bowing out of my promise to you. I told you I'd help you find Lili. And, damn it, I'm going to do that. Because the truth is, when I married you, no matter what the reasons, Lili became just as much my responsibility as yours."

"But—"

"Shh," he said and claimed her mouth with his, not wanting to hear any more questions. Not willing to face the reality that he might have to see through his promise without her here. It all depended on what he could accomplish in the next day or so. And how much time Edgar and the INS were willing to let them have.

He closed his eyes and groaned as he plunged his tongue deep into her mouth.

"SO WHAT, exactly, were you two doing up in your room all morning, Jake?" Connor asked.

Jake stared at his older brother as he, Marc, Mitch, David and Pops all made their way toward their mother's grave- site. The day was warm, the sun nearly at its zenith, dappling the lush grass through thick tree branches.

"It's called none of your damned business," Sean said, and David threw a faux punch in the eldest brother's direction.

Marc snickered. "You'd be amazed how much one can do with the door locked."

"After vows are exchanged," Sean corrected.

Marc's grin widened. "Yeah, well, that's what you think."

Mitch groaned. "Would you guys stop? You'd think we were heading for a bar rather than visiting Mom."

A hush fell over the group as all six came to stand around the simple stone that marked Kathryn Connor McCoy's grave.

"Hard to believe it's been twenty-eight years," Connor said.

Jake didn't respond. Found that he couldn't.

It felt strange being here, honoring a tradition Pops had begun the year following the loss of his wife. He didn't feel as he usually felt. Yes, he supposed he missed her. Rather, he missed the presence of a mother figure in his life. But he no longer mourned her absence as he once had. Other emotions crowded his chest. Additional priorities vied for his attention.

"Wish I could remember more about her," David said, as he did every year.

"Yeah, well, you have trouble remembering the name of the girl you spent last night with. Why should you be expected to remember something from when you were two years old?" Mitch said.

Pops rolled his eyes heavenward, then laid the simple red rose he held across the top of the stone. The rest of them followed suit, until six different types and colors of flowers decorated the top.

"I wasn't with a girl last night," David whispered to Mitch.

"So how am I supposed to remember a name that doesn't exist?"

Mitch narrowed his gaze on the youngest. "Okay, then, the night before."

David's grin nearly swallowed the whole of his face.

"You guys won't be happy until we're all weighed down with a ball and chain," Connor groaned.

"Speaking of ball and chain," Mitch said, "Liz asked to come along today."

Silence fell.

The annual visit had always included only the six of them. It didn't matter where they were, what assignment they were on or what they were doing, they always pulled together for this one day to remember the woman responsible for their walking the earth. Others might overhear their irreverent conversation and question their affection, but it was enough for them to know that this day meant a lot to each of them in their own different ways.

Of course, now that the family had been added to, it was only natural the newer members would want to be included in the visits. Jake didn't find it surprising that Liz had asked to come. And he imagined Mel might want to come, too. He just didn't know how he felt about the concept right about now. Oh, hell, he didn't know how he felt about a whole host of things right about now.

Sean coughed. "I think it's a good idea if we include the girls—"

"Women," Marc and Mitch corrected.

Sean grinned. "Okay, I think it's a good idea if we include the women from here on out." He reached out and touched the top of the stone. "I think your mother would enjoy meeting them. And what with Mel being pregnant, and—" his gaze trailed to Jake "—and with Jake being a dad and all, I think your mother would be glad to see we're all finally moving on."

Was it his imagination, or had his father put a special emphasis on *all?* He glanced at his brothers to find they were all looking at Pops, as well. And Pops was doing his best to keep focused on the headstone.

"So what are you trying to say, Pops?" Connor asked. "What's this 'all' stuff?"

Marc shifted uneasily.

Mitch said, "Come on, we all knew he was involved with someone."

"Correction, we all suspected," Connor said. "You were the only who knew anything."

Mitch shrugged. "That's splitting hairs, isn't it? The fact is, Pops *has* been seeing someone." He glanced at his father. "And it's my guess that it's moved to serious territory." He stuffed his hands in his pockets. "Is that what you're trying to tell us, Pops?"

Sean McCoy seem to turn twenty different shades of red. Jake grimaced. He'd never, ever seen his father blush before. "I wasn't intending to tell you anything." He rubbed the back of his neck, then looked at each one of them in turn. "I mean I was, but not here, not in front of your mother."

"Mom's not really here, Pops," Mitch pointed out.

"And you yourself said she'd probably be glad we were finally moving on," David prompted.

Sean's cheeks expanded as he drew in a long breath. Then he slowly let it out. His gaze seemed especially drawn to Marc, Jake noticed, though he couldn't figure out why. Of the five of them, Marc was the least likely to understand the ins and outs of personal relationships. Okay, maybe Melanie was right, and all the McCoy men were a little deficient in that area, but Marc especially seemed to be lacking.

"The woman I'm seeing...she's... What I mean is..."

Jake grimaced. "I'm coming to learn it's best if you just come out with it."

That roused a laugh from the group. Jake's grimace deepened.

Connor stopped laughing first. "Yeah, Pops, why don't you take your cue from Dr. Spock here and get on with it already?"

"Dr. Spock was a children's specialist," Marc pointed out. "You mean Mr. Spock."

They all stared at Connor.

"So I got it wrong," Connor grumbled.

Sean held up his hands. "Jake's right. There's really no way to say this except to say it." He turned to look squarely at Marc. The middle McCoy appeared shocked at the undivided attention and took a step back. "I've been dating, quite seriously, for a while now." He ran his fingers through his thick, silvery hair. "Aw, hell, Marc, I'm seeing your mother-in-law, Melanie's mom, Wilhemenia Weber."

"What?" Connor asked, his voice a croak.

Jake was surprised, too. But only because he'd thought Pops was going to tell him he was dating someone they all knew from town. In the light of his situation, the information didn't hit him as hard as it seemed to hit his brothers.

He slowly looked them over. From Connor, who pointedly avoided Sean's gaze, to Marc, who stepped backward, then forward again, completely speechless.

Marc finally appeared to gain control over his tongue. "So what you're telling us... What you're saying... Do you mean my mother-in-law may become my stepmother?" he said.

Connor finally looked at Sean as he appeared to work the kinks out of his neck. "Well, you're just going to have to end it."

Jake hiked his brows and watched as Connor turned on his heel and stalked silently away.

MICHELLE SAT at the kitchen table, her fingers wrapped around her mug of black coffee, as Jake's sisters-in-law combined their talents to make dinner. She'd tried to tell them tactfully they'd added far too much salt to the huge roast they'd put into the oven over an hour ago at a temperature sure to char it while leaving the insides raw. But the two women had consulted with each other and decided they'd done the right thing.

She gazed through the back window at the green, green meadows that stretched as far as the eye could see behind the house. Two sleek black stallions—at least, she thought they were stallions—leisurely nibbled at the grass in a nice sized pen while Goliath ran the length of the newly erected wooden fence, barking at the two other males.

Unlike Ohio, this land reminded her somewhat of home. While there were no neat rows of grape vines, there were rolling hills in a shade of green she once thought was only possible in the south of France.

Home.

She supposed she should feel relieved that she still thought of France as home. Because that's exactly what she needed to be thinking about right now. Despite the past few hours spent losing herself in Jake's strong arms, their conversation had made several things very clear. That she had put him at far more risk than she'd thought. And that she needed to go home as soon as possible…for his sake. But before she did so, she had to make sure nothing would happen to him. And, ironically, that meant seeking out the man they had expended so much effort avoiding.

Her heart thudded so hard it hurt.

"What do you think? Should I let them boil for another five minutes?"

Startled from her thoughts, Michelle nearly choked on her

coffee when Liz posed the question to a frowning Melanie. Both women were looking into a large pot they'd filled with potatoes and water, their heads together, emphasizing the difference in their shades of blond. Michelle's gaze drifted to where Mel absently rubbed the small mound that was her stomach. She tried to remember how she'd felt when she'd been six months pregnant with Lili. Her lips twitched in a smile as she remembered all the hopes and dreams that had filled her. All the plans she had made…

Melanie turned from the stove, wiping her hands on a dish towel. "So, Mitch tells us you have a little girl?"

Michelle shouldn't have been surprised by the question, but she was. Of course this family would talk to each other. Just because she thought herself and her problems closed off from the world didn't mean that was the case. She nodded and managed a polite smile. "Yes. Lili. She's…four," she said, keeping things simple. She didn't trust herself to go into detail about how Lili's birthday was this Saturday, and that she would be spending that day away from her. She was afraid she'd end up a blubbering mess.

"That's nice," Mel said, smiling. "You don't mind if I ask you for some advice, do you? I mean, this being my first and all…well, sometimes it gets a little overwhelming, you know?"

Michelle smiled. "Yes. I know."

Fingers of smoke began to billow from the oven door. She'd never seen such an oven before. She suspected the door to the left was for firewood, of all things.

"Oh, no!" Melanie cried, thrusting open the oven door.

The room instantly filled with acrid black smoke.

Michelle got up and pushed open the window. Liz propped open the door. Mel turned first one way, then another, then grabbed a pair of oven mitts and ran the charred meat out the back door. For long minutes, all of them coughed as they grabbed what they could to fan the smoke out. To top everything off, a smoke alarm sounded in the other room.

"Great! Just great!" Melanie said, tossing her oven mitts onto the counter. "You have no idea the big deal Marc is going to make out of this. He's constantly humiliating me in front of our friends—not to mention his family—about my lack of culinary skills. This…well, this one just takes the cake."

"I wouldn't use any food adages right now, Mel." Liz gave a short burst of laughter. Mel glared at her. Liz instantly tried to look contrite, though amusement shone in her bright hazel eyes. "Sorry."

Michelle cleared her throat. "Well, you can always look at it this way. At least they won't ever find out how much salt you put on the meat."

The two women stared at her. Afraid she had said completely the wrong thing, she searched for an excuse to leave the room. Then Mel followed Liz's lead, and laughter chased the last of the smoke from the room.

"Oh, God," Liz said, clutching her side. "That smoke alarm is going to pierce my eardrums."

Mel sighed. "The battery's got to run out sooner or later, right?"

Michelle retrieved the broom from the corner, then led the way into the other room. She positioned the blunt end just so below the alarm. With one calculated whack, the blaring alarm was immediately cut off. She smiled at the two women.

Mel rested both hands against her protruding stomach, her lips twisted in thought. "What is it you said you did for a living again?"

Michelle grasped the broom tightly. They hadn't exactly gotten around to sharing information such as what each of them did in their daily lives. "I'm, um, a chef."

Liz smacked her hand against her forehead. "God, do I ever feel dense."

Mel linked her arm with Michelle's. "Well, why didn't you say something before?" she asked as she led the way to the kitchen.

Liz took her other arm. "Maybe because we were too busy acting like Southern know-it-alls."

Michelle had spent the past hour reviewing ways she might be able to put together a meal with the salvageable remains of the other women's attempts. She smiled as Mel and Liz released her.

"Just tell us what you want us to do," Mel said.

And Michelle did.

JAKE STARED at his plate in barely disguised shock. This couldn't be dinner. Where was the thick slab of meat? The mountain of potatoes dripping with butter and gravy? He turned again to see the bread on a small plate at his left elbow, then looked at Michelle. She seemed to be purposely avoiding his gaze. He frowned, then looked around the table, seeing that everyone had the same thing he had.

In the center of the large plates that usually held piles of food was one perfect, silver-dollar-sized circle of what appeared to be beef—though he couldn't be sure because some sort of white sauce covered it—with what looked like a boiled potato decorated with—were those parsley leaves?—next to it. A small helping of cut green beans tossed with some sort of sliced nuts was to the right. And some sort of brown sauce had been dribbled over the plate in a kind of zigzag design.

If he thought the McCoy men had been quiet before, they were downright silent now. Nobody messed with their meat and potatoes.

"It's bourguignonne and *pomme de terre,*" Michelle said quietly. "I hope you like it."

Jake heard what sounded like a snicker from Liz. He caught Michelle biting her bottom lip to keep from laughing, as well. What were they up to?

"This the first course?" Marc said, looking hopefully at the stove and countertops. Both were empty of a solitary pan. "I hope this is the first course." He forked his potato. "This had better be the first course. Oww!"

Mel lifted her fork, then smiled at everyone.

Sean cleared his throat. "Well, Michelle, this looks…pretty enough to frame."

"You're supposed to eat food, not frame it," Connor grumbled from the other end of the table.

Jake looked back and forth between the two men. He'd hoped that during the drive from the cemetery to the house, things would have cooled down enough for them to have reached some sort of truce. But the interior of Mitch's new four-door truck had remained awfully quiet. Not even David's half-assed attempts at humor had been able to crack the silence.

Mitch was the first to try the mystery meat. At the sound of his silverware against the plate, the occupants of the table watched as he carefully cut off a small bite, then slowly put it into his mouth. One chew. Two. Then he closed his eyes and made a humming sound Jake had never heard from him before. "Oh, Michelle. This is… What I mean is…wow. That's the best piece of meat I've ever tasted."

"Piece of meat? Scrap is more like it," Connor said under his breath as David and Jake tried the food.

The explosion of flavor on his tongue was unlike anything Jake had ever experienced. He reluctantly swallowed the bite, then looked at Michelle. She was concentrating a little too fully on her plate.

414 FOR HER EYES ONLY

Mitch leaned closer to his wife and lowered his voice, though everyone in the room heard him anyway. "Liz, what happened to that big roast I saw in the refrigerator this morning?"

Liz smiled a little too widely. "This is it."

Sean coughed and reached for his glass of milk. "You cook much, Michelle?"

Jake wiped his mouth with his napkin. "Actually, Michelle's a chef."

David brightened. "I knew this food looked familiar. I went to this frou—um, this French place in D.C. last spring. The stuff they served looked just like this. Huge plate… Anyway, I've gotta tell you the cost of the meal would have been enough for me to eat off for a month. So I guess we should feel honored to have a chef of Michelle's caliber in our midst."

This time Michelle tittered in a way that shocked Jake. She lifted her napkin to her mouth but didn't look at him. "Um, pardon me."

The go-ahead on the food having been given, it took a whole two minutes for the contents of the plates to vanish, not even leaving the decorative design as the men sopped it up with their bread. Thank God there was at least a lot of that.

"Well," Marc said, "I think I speak for everyone when I say that was certainly a meal to remember." He began to push from the table.

"I second that." David followed suit.

Mitch cleared his throat. "Um, Michelle? While I enjoyed the meal and everything, the next time around…you may want to double, no, quadruple, the portion size. We McCoy men really cut loose come meal time. And meat—a lot of it—and mashed potatoes hits the spot unlike anything else."

Jake could have sworn that was a smile Michelle hid behind her napkin. "I'll keep that in mind, Mitch. Thank you."

Liz sat up straighter. "I, for one, thoroughly enjoyed the meal, Michelle. Feel free to cook for us any time you want."

Jake couldn't figure out what was going on, but the way the three women eyed each other, then quickly looked away told him something certainly was.

Near the door to the living room, he caught David whispering to Marc, "You put up the money for the pizza, and I'll run into Culpepper to get it."

"Make it two pizzas with the works, and you've got yourself a deal," Marc said.

A moment later, the sound of a football game filled the interior of the house, another tradition now that autumn was just around the corner.

Michelle began to clear the plates with Liz and Mel, leaving Jake, Connor and Pops at the table.

"We'll get those," Pops said, taking the small stack Michelle had gathered. "It's only fair seeing as you gals took care of the food."

Connor snorted. Jake glared at him and took the glasses to the sink. Connor pushed from the table then stalked through the back door.

"What's that all about?" Mel asked, putting a fresh pot of coffee on to brew.

Liz emptied a bag of store-bought cookies onto a plate, stuck one in her mouth, then placed the plate on the table along with clean glasses and a gallon of milk. "You know, now that you mention it, all you guys were a little quiet during dinner. Did something happen?"

Sean met Jake's gaze. "Nothing that won't blow over in a day or two."

The phone rang. Pops snatched the receiver up in the middle of the second ring. He glanced at Jake, then rounded the corner, apparently in a bid to speak in private. To Mel's mom,

Wilhemenia? Jake didn't know. But one thing was for sure—
nothing would blow over if Sean didn't let things lie for a bit.
Connor was more upset than Jake had ever seen him. It was
a good sign that he'd stuck around for dinner, but Jake guessed
that was more to see how their father would ultimately respond to what he'd said than an indication that Connor's
mood had improved.

He glanced at Melanie, wondering what she'd have to say
when she found out what had really gone down at the cemetery that morning.

"Coming through!" Jake moved out of the way as David
zipped through the room, undoubtedly on his way to pick up
the pizza.

In the chaos of his family's constantly industrious lives,
Jake almost forgot how Michelle had avoided looking directly
at him during dinner. Almost. He sought her out, only to find
her stacking dishes in the dishwasher, her back firmly to him.
He didn't know what had happened while he was gone, but
he was sure it was more than the dinner they'd just eaten.

CHAPTER FOURTEEN

MICHELLE CLOSED the bedroom door with a soft click. She'd told Jake she really needed to get some sleep. She did, but that's not the reason she wanted to be alone. Dinner may have been all fun and games for her, Mel and Liz, but there was nothing fun about what she needed to do now.

She sank down on the single bed and wrapped her arms around herself to gather warmth, despite the heat of the day. What would Jake's family say if they knew about her past? Jake had seemed more upset by the news than she would have thought possible. And he knew her better than the others. Cared for her more.

She stared at the cell phone on the bed in front of her. She reached for it, then pulled her hand back.

Coward, she told herself.

Yes, she admitted, she was a coward and a fool. A grade-A fool for thinking that this thing with Jake could have ended any other way than it had to.

She rubbed her forehead. How easy it was when enfolded in Jake's strong arms to believe everything would be all right. That somehow he could move the mountains that separated her from her daughter, and protect her from his government, who wanted to send her back to France.

She wasn't sure when this had all happened. She suspected way back in the beginning after the purse snatching, when he'd played knight in shining armor to her damsel in distress. She'd taken one look at those sober gray eyes, those large hands, and all that deeply suppressed need for someone to share the burden with had bubbled to the surface. She rolled her eyes to stare at the ceiling. Who was she kidding? She'd wanted to shift the leaden weight on her shoulders completely over to him. Trouble was, he'd been more than willing to accept the load. Some new millennium woman she was.

Still, it baffled her how, after spending twenty-eight years on her own, having and raising her daughter, forging a career and a life for herself, how she'd managed to get sucked into visions of a fairy-tale life she'd stopped believing in long ago.

But none of that changed that all possibility of finding Lili was exhausted. And that by staying here, without taking any action, she was only delaying the inevitable. While that had appealed to her a mere hour before...well, now she recognized the unfairness of it.

Already, she'd begun to make her niche in his family. Liz and Mel—they were the sisters she'd always hoped her stepsisters would be but never were. They were happy and witty and incredibly smart, and she knew that it wouldn't take very long to come to care for them—and the rest of the McCoy bunch—very much. Just as she'd come to care immeasurably for Jake. By allowing those bonds to grow stronger, she'd be hurting more than just Jake. And the pain she would feel would only deepen.

God, when had the world gotten so damned complicated? Since when was it a sin to play the role of rebellious college student? To want her daughter back with her mother where she belonged? When had it become a bad thing to love someone so much you would sacrifice even your own heart for them?

She reached into her backpack and rustled around. Frowning, she began taking the things out one by one. After a thorough search, it became apparent she was short one small stuffed elephant.

She closed her eyes. Lili would have a fit.

Oh, dear, sweet Lili…

She didn't know how she would possibly live without her daughter for one more day, much less the years that yawned before her. One thing was plain, though. She would never give up looking for her. Never. She would have to do it from France. She didn't care where she'd find the money for it. She'd beg, borrow and steal, work three jobs, borrow from her father, to get it. Whatever it took. But she would never stop looking, no matter how old she or her daughter got. She only hoped that one day Lili would forgive her for not having been a better mother.

Her fingers circled the cold plastic of the cell phone. After spreading out her visa papers, she carefully punched in the contact number, then lifted the phone to her ear. "Agent Edgar Mollens, please."

THE STUFFED ELEPHANT looked ridiculously fragile in his large hands. Jake ran his thumbs down the length of the rounded belly, then fixed the lopsided trunk. He'd never been much for toys when he was a kid. That this one could hold so much significance baffled him. But it did.

He slid a glance toward the stairs Michelle had disappeared up a half hour ago, claiming a need for some major shut-eye, then he looked at his brothers. Two large pizza boxes sporting nothing but goo littered the coffee table, and every other available piece of furniture sported McCoy males in various stages of repose. The football game was at half time, Liz and Mel sat in the kitchen discussing recipes Michelle had passed on to them, Pops was in the hall on the phone again and Connor's absence was obvious but not mentioned.

He still didn't know exactly what had happened at dinner, but he was sure the acrid smell of something burned had more to do with the lack of meat than Michelle's cooking skills. What had warmed him was the way Michelle was getting along so well with his sisters-in-law. Hell, he wasn't as comfortable around them, and he'd had months to adjust, while all she had needed was a couple hours. He shook his head, deciding it was a woman thing.

He wasn't sure when it had happened, or why. But an overwhelming urge to make her his wife for real, for always, filled him to the point of pain. The impulse could have begun as early as the day they met, when he'd sat across that café table from her, watching her lick foam from her upper lip. Or when he'd brought her home, mingling reality with the surreal quality of the past few days until he could no longer discern one from the other. He couldn't imagine his life without her in it. Tucking her tumble of dark hair behind her ear. Smiling her sexy little smile. Getting him to bare his deepest emotions in a way that scared the hell out of him, yet made him feel…real.

The memory of the quick ceremony in Toledo, Ohio, emerged. He cringed. She deserved better than a few hastily exchanged vows before a judge with a drunken pastor as their witness. As cutting edge as Michelle appeared to be, she'd wanted a traditional wedding with all the trappings, and he found he wanted to give it to her. The whole nine yards. The wedding dress with a train that would stretch all the way to France, if that's what she wanted. A full bridal court. A huge rock that could try but fail to match the light that seemed to make her glow from within.

He glanced longingly at the stairs. What he wouldn't give to go up to his room and climb into that bed next to Michelle. And then propose to her properly.

But he couldn't, not yet. This time he intended to do it right, but he had some things to do first.

Jake stuck the elephant on the chair behind him then cleared his throat. "Guys, this is, um, a little difficult for me, but…"

Marc was practically one with the sofa, his long legs stretched out next to the pizza boxes. He regarded Jake with a long look, then crossed his arms. "Gotta tell you, Jake, we were wondering when you were going to get around to asking."

Mitch cleared his throat from Pops's arm chair. Jake blinked at him, not missing the grin he threw his way. "Anyone time it?"

David made a production of looking at his watch. "Nine hours, twenty minutes and thirty seconds." He grimaced. "Shoot. That means Pops won."

Jake rubbed his palms on his sweats. Sweats. He still couldn't believe he was wearing them. Truth was, the suckers were mighty comfortable. "Anyone feel like catching me up to speed? Ask what? And what did Pops win?"

David sat forward, resting his forearms on his jeans-clad knees. "Well, ask us to help you find little Lili, of course."

Marc took his feet off the table. "We all bet how long it would take for you to finally speak up. Pops won."

Jake rubbed his chin, realizing he needed a shave. "What?"

David grinned. "Truth is, while you were upstairs this morning, doing whatever it is you were doing with Michelle, we all took turns with the phone and started pulling strings and yanking chains. We would have filled you in before, but we were waiting for any real news. Besides, we figured you'd ask for help eventually, and we didn't want you to think we were interfering by bringing up the idea first."

Jake frowned, trying to take in what his brothers were saying but feeling as though he was missing a few of the finer points.

Mitch's face sobered. "Granted, during our phone conversations two days ago, you didn't give me a whole hell of a lot to go on. But it was enough to piece together the situation. And with that slime puppy Mollens calling here—"

Jake nearly choked. "Edgar Mollens called here?"

"Yeah. Got Pops first. It wasn't pretty," Marc answered. "He tried back again yesterday, but didn't get much farther with Mitch."

Mitch shrugged. "Shoot me, but I don't like people threatening me or any of my brothers."

"What did he say?"

"Nothing that matters now." Mitch waved him off. "What I'm trying to say is that about an hour ago, Gerald Evans, Lili's father, was pulled in by authorities in his area, and we're awaiting further word. Pops's doing, if you want to know. While I still have some contacts at the FBI, no one was willing to do anything quite this shady."

David spoke. "Hey, I have some pull with the DCPD, too, you know. It wasn't just Pops."

Three McCoy brothers stared at him.

Marc shrugged. "Unfortunately, I wasn't able to do much with the Secret Service, either—"

Jake held his hands up. "Whoa, whoa, whoa. What are you guys telling me here? That you went ahead and worked on finding Lili on your own? Without being asked? Without…" His voice trailed off, the explosion of gratitude he felt for these brothers of his overwhelming in its intensity. For the first time in a day, hope surged through his veins, joining his increasing determination to find Michelle's…their daughter.

"Yes, that's exactly what we're saying." The perpetual grin that split David's face vanished, replaced by a weightier expression, one Jake had never seen him wear before.

Pops came into the room from the kitchen, apparently having finished his telephone conversation. Liz and Mel were on either side of him, their confusion evident. The recliner creaked as Mitch got up. "In fact, I'm betting Pops has some news to share."

Jake practically leaped from his chair. He looked toward the stairs to find Michelle standing near the bottom, leaning against the wall, listening. Myriad emotions flickered across her features, her eyes large in her pale face. He wanted to go to her, but he could do little more than stand there and stare at her, then Pops, his heart thudding in his chest.

"I've found her," Sean announced.

The expectant hush that filled the room was nearly suffocating. Jake stepped forward. Michelle rushed to Sean. "Where? How? Can I see her?"

Pops's grin was all-consuming. "She's at a downtown D.C. hotel with her grandparents. How? Well, that's a little more complicated." He reached out and touched Michelle's arm. "And, yes, you can go see her. In fact, you can pick her up as soon as you're ready."

The floor shifted beneath Jake's feet. It seemed impossible that after everything they'd done, everywhere he and Michelle had gone, his father had accomplished in a few hours what they couldn't in several days. "Uncomplicate things, Pops. Explain to me how...how you found her."

Sean's grin melted into a simple smile. "I'd really like to take all the credit for this, but I can't. You'll see what I mean." He cleared his throat. "This morning I had a few of my buddies at the station call a few of their buddies, until someone found someone who worked in the Lucas County sheriff's office in northwest Ohio. It didn't take much convincing to have them pick up one Gerald Evans and take him to the local station. It was there under pressure of questioning that he revealed where his parents were." He crossed his arms. "The funny thing is, Lili's grandparents had already come to the conclusion that what they were doing was wrong, no matter that the law was on their side, technically speaking. They were already on their way to D.C. from where they were staying in New Hampshire—" his gaze scanned Michelle's ashen face "—to bring little Lili back to you, Michelle. They checked into a hotel a short time ago and are waiting for you to come."

Michelle looked ready to rush out the door. Sean gently grasped her shoulders.

"One more thing. They, the Evanses, asked me to pass on their apologies—"

"You've seen them?" Jake interjected.

"No. I spoke with them on the phone. I wanted to make sure everything was on the up-and-up before I said anything." He looked at Michelle. "Anyway, once everything is settled, they said they'd like to be in contact with you, you know, to keep them posted on how Lili is doing. And while they'd understand if you said no, they'd like you to consider allowing Lili to come visit every now and again."

He handed Michelle a slip of paper. "That's their number. Sometime down the line, you might want to give them a call, you know, when you're ready. Or—" he shrugged "—don't. I figure after what they've done, I wouldn't blame you if you didn't want your daughter to see them again, even if they do gain some points for bringing her back to you."

"Which hotel?" Jake asked, grasping the item he'd left on the chair and checking for his car keys.

Sean told him.

Jake took Michelle's arm and led her toward the kitchen.

"Hey, wait up!" Marc called, following.

"You're not going anywhere without me," David said.

Liz dabbed at her eyes. "Mitch, warm up the truck. We're going to need the room."

MICHELLE COULDN'T quite bring herself to trust that her daughter had really been found. She stood in the hotel lobby shaking like a hand mixer, expecting any moment to hear that the Evanses had changed their minds and checked out, no forwarding address provided. Or to be told that she could see Lili, but Sean had misunderstood and that her daughter was going to remain with her grandparents.

Jake's presence next to her meant more than she could express, but she didn't dare turn to him for support or seek warmth in his arms. No matter what happened in the next few minutes, she'd made her decision. There was no going back now.

The elevator doors dinged then slowly slid open. Michelle's heart nearly burst straight through her chest.

Lili!

Inside the cubicle, her daughter held the hands of Gerald's parents and had her little chin tilted up, rattling on about something or other, so she didn't see Michelle right away. Then she shifted to look into the lobby. She stopped speaking mid-sentence, then catapulted herself toward Michelle.

"Maman! Maman!"

Michelle's sob seemed to fill every corner of the lobby…and seep through every crack in Jake's heart.

He stood silently and watched as Lili flew into her mother's arms, speaking in a combination of rapid-fire English and French, her small arms squeezing Michelle's neck, her short skirt hiking up to reveal cartoon-laden undies.

"I know you tried to call, baby," Michelle murmured, covering her daughter's face with kisses and tears. She must have realized she'd spoken in English, because she immediately started speaking in French.

Pops came to stand next to Jake while the rest of the McCoy bunch hung back. It had taken three cars to get them all there, but Jake was glad they had come. "Pretty little thing, isn't she?" Pops said.

Jake nodded, completely incapable of speech. Not because he didn't have anything to say, which had always been the case not long ago. But because he couldn't possibly push anything past his throat if he tried.

"I always thought French was one of the more interesting languages," Mitch said from the other side of Jake. "Do you know what they're saying?"

Jake shook his head.

Behind him, Marc loudly blew his nose into a tissue. Right on the heels was David's voice "For cripe's sakes, are you crying? Jaysus, Marc! What is it with you married guys, anyway? Before you know it, you're going to be crying at those TV commercials like Mel and Liz do."

"Stuff a sock in it, David," Mel said, taking the tissue from Marc and sopping the tears from her cheeks.

Jake listened to the arguments with half an ear. His focus was on the woman he loved, who was being reunited with her daughter. And he was standing across the room completely paralyzed, without a clue as to what he should do, if he should be doing anything at all.

He was also aware of the prickle of exclusion. As much as he hated to admit it, he recognized the sensation too well to ignore it. It was the same way he'd felt growing up. He'd always been a part of the McCoy family. Participated in the Sunday dinners. Visited at least twice, if not three times a week. But he'd never really felt…included. That is, until today, when his brothers and father had pitched in without even being asked to do something for him. Just because he was one of them. He'd realized then that he didn't have to tow it alone any longer. That he'd never had to.

He also stumbled onto the true, mind-boggling extent of his feelings for Michelle.

When had he stopped being a silent loner? When had he trusted himself and those he talked to with things he had to say—without fear that they'd ridicule him or that he'd embarrass himself?

He knew exactly when that moment had happened. The instant he met and fell in love with Michelle Lambert. Opened his heart and let her in, not just partially, but all the way.

He noticed that Connor had joined the group at some point in the chaos of leaving the house and had come along. He stood to the side, his arms crossed, his gaze hooded as he watched the reunion. Of all of them, he seemed the least impressed with what was going on.

Michelle finally disentangled her arms from around her daughter, though she kept a grip on her, as if afraid the girl would vanish again if she completely let her go. She turned her daughter so that they faced Jake. She looked at him and said something into Lili's ear in French. Then she smiled and repeated it in English. "Lili, honey, say hello to Jake."

Lili hesitated. Her gaze seemed locked on his knees as she put one of her shoes on top of the other. Then she looked into Jake's face.

Jake swallowed so hard, he could swear it echoed through the room. "Hello, Lili," he managed to say.

She gazed at him intently a moment, and in that instant Jake realized how very much she resembled her mother. "Hello."

Jake's heart did a funny little somersault in his chest. His gaze flicked to Michelle. But rather than looking at him, she was saying something to Lili in French, her face serious. "Nice to meet you, Mr. McCoy," Lili said slowly.

"It's…nice to meet you, too, Lili," he said, trying to keep emotion from his voice. "I, um, have someone here who's been looking forward to seeing you." He produced the stuffed elephant from behind his back.

"Julianne!" Lili practically flew to him.

Jake crouched, holding the toy out to her. His gaze swept her from the tip of her blond head to her toes. She was so small. So fragile. He wanted to reach out and touch her, but didn't dare. He contented himself with a smile. A smile she returned before she stepped back to her mother, murmuring in French to her inanimate friend.

"Thank you," Michelle said quietly, though she could have been talking to anyone given the way she looked strictly at Lili.

Jake wasn't sure what was happening. Why had Michelle instructed Lili to call him Mr. McCoy rather than Jake? But now that he had put a name to the feeling he'd grown to know too well, the rejection he felt cut deeper than it had.

Michelle rose to her full height, clasping Lili's hand in both of hers. "I…I don't know what to say," she said to the group, biting her lip as her eyes filled with tears anew. She included the Evanses, who stood just outside the elevator, in her sweep. "Thank you…thank you all so very much."

A couple of Jake's brothers coughed, and behind him, Marc blew his nose again.

Lili tugged on Michelle's hand. Michelle bent to let her daughter say something in her ear. The stage whisper ended up being louder than regular conversation. "I love Nana and Grandpa, *Maman*. And they love me."

Michelle seemed to choke on her reply as she smoothed wisps of Lili's white-blond hair from her face. "I know, baby. I know."

Her gaze lifted again to Pops and the rest of them. Jake tried to tell himself it was the emotion of the moment, that with all that was going on Michelle was preoccupied, but again he got the distinct impression she was purposely avoiding his gaze. "I don't know how I'm ever going to repay you.

But I will." She finally looked at him, and the finality he saw there nearly booted his heart straight from his chest. "I will."

TWO HOURS LATER, Jake stood outside his bedroom door, his eyes tightly closed, his hand a hairbreadth away from knocking on the hard wood. He released his breath.

The long drive to the McCoy place from D.C. had been bad enough, what with Liz, Melanie and Pops riding with him and Michelle and a very chatty Lili, who seemed to bask in all the attention, none the worse for wear after her ordeal. But as soon as they were inside the house, Michelle had all but swept little Lili up and disappeared into his bedroom, where they'd been for the past half hour.

"English, *Maman*. I want to talk English," he heard Lili say through the door.

There was a pause, then Michelle said, "All right, baby. We'll speak English, if that's what you'd like. Come here." The sound of clothes rustling. Jake envisioned her pulling Lili onto her lap. "I'm so very, very proud of you, do you know that? So very proud."

The girl giggled.

"And I missed you so very, very much."

"How much?"

Jake smiled where he stood on the other side of the door. It appeared Lili shared more in common with her mother than her knockout good looks.

"More than the whole wide world, baby," Michelle said and loudly kissed her. "More than the whole wide world."

Jake opened his hand from where it was rolled into a fist, debating whether he should interrupt. Truth was, he didn't know where things stood between him and Michelle. Now that she had her daughter back, was there room in her heart for him?

The door opened. Jake started, looking guiltily at Michelle, who appeared to be just as surprised to find him there.

He cleared his throat. "I'm sorry…I just wanted to make sure that…you know, everything is okay."

The smile she gave him was tremulous, at best. "Yes. Everything is more than okay, Jake."

He scanned her rosy features, thinking he would never tire of looking at her. Drinking in her energy. Her innate sensuality.

Then her gaze slid to the floor, and she opened the door a little farther. "Come in. I was just coming to get you."

Uh-oh. Jake stood frozen for a long moment, not liking the sound of her voice, the way she had said the words. He reluctantly followed her in and closed the door behind him.

Lili sat at his desk, her thumb firmly in her mouth, her elephant sitting in front of her. "Hi, Mr. McCoy," she said around her thumb.

There was that funny little weightlessness again mixed with grim apprehension. He smiled. "Hi again, Lili."

Michelle crossed her arms and nodded toward the bed. "Please…sit down."

Jake slowly did as she requested, his gaze glued to the little girl playing with her toy.

"I…I really don't know where to start, Jake."

"The beginning is as good a place as any," he said quietly, finally dragging his attention away from the little girl to her mother.

"Okay…" She sat on the bed, too, well away from him. "I can't tell you how very grateful I am for all you've done for me…and for Lili…."

What was she saying? She didn't have to thank him. They were a family. His chest tightened. Weren't they?

"I know how much you've put on the line to help me. To help

us. I…" She sucked her bottom lip into her mouth. "I just want you to know that I won't be causing you problems anymore."

He sat there for a long moment, feeling as if the room were spinning out of control. His entire line of sight narrowed in on her. Only her.

"What…what are you saying?"

"I…what I mean to say is, Lili…we'll be going into the city today. Catching a flight back to France tomorrow morning."

Her words didn't sink in on the first go-round. He stared at her mouth, trying to verify that it had indeed moved…had really said what he thought it had. Michelle's unwavering sober expression told him it had.

He sprung from the bed so quickly, he nearly catapulted her off the other side. "What?"

"Please," she said quickly, rising from the bed and rounding it to face him. Her fingers felt warm and dry where she caressed the side of his face. "Please, don't make this any harder than it already is. I've caused enough trouble for you, Jake. You said yourself that your government will never be able to overlook my past. They'll never let me stay here." She blinked away the wetness filling her soft brown eyes. "And you…" Her smile was sweetly sad. "I can't see you anywhere else but here." She shrugged in a gesture of frustration. "Can't you see this is the only way? That my leaving is the only possible outcome? We've been fooling ourselves if we thought it could work out differently. It can't—"

"It can," he said vehemently, gently grasping her upper arms and hauling her closer. "Michelle, please listen to me. I…" He hesitated at the slight shaking of her head. "Look, I've never been great with words. Lord knows I'm far from a poet, but we can work this out, together. We can go before the immigration review board, hell, court if we have to. My clean record can cancel out yours if it comes down to it."

The shaking of her head grew more decisive. "I can't... won't let you do that, Jake."

"Isn't that my decision to make?"

"That's just it, isn't it? Every decision that's been made since I met you has been your decision. This one has to be mine."

He found it nearly impossible to draw a breath. His heart thudded like a bass drum in his chest; fear threaded through his bloodstream like a poison. "Early on, before we...before we became a couple, you said something to me that really hit home. You said all you wanted was to find Lili—" he motioned toward the little girl who had laid her head against the desktop and was drifting to sleep "—and go home. Go back to the way your life was before all this started." His throat grew unbearably tight. "I remember sitting there looking at you, marveling over the feelings starting to grow even then, thinking that I was just waiting for my life to begin." He searched her eyes. "Don't you see, up until that point, I didn't know my life was missing anything. Not until I met you. I..." His throat made a clicking sound as he swallowed. "I love you, Michelle. And I want you and Lili to stay. To be my family."

He stood there for long moments, frozen. He'd never told anyone before that he loved them. Never bared his soul the way he had just bared it to Michelle. Hell, he hadn't even known he possessed a soul until she had touched it. But there it was. And he'd never felt so naked in his life.

She averted her gaze. "I love you, too, Jake."

Her voice was so low it was almost a whisper. But far from being the happy proclamation he might have wished it to be, it seemed a sad punctuation point. He watched her bite her lip, presumably to keep the tears welling in her eyes from trickling down her cheeks. "But it's too late."

There was a brief knock at the door. Jake moved to tell

whoever it was to go the hell away, but Michelle placed a finger over his lips. "Yes?"

The door opened a couple of inches. "I'm sorry to interrupt," Liz said quietly, her gaze darting everywhere but to their faces. "But if we're going to make it...well, we're going to have to leave in the next few minutes."

"Okay," Michelle whispered.

Liz hesitated. "You want me to take Lili downstairs to wait with me?"

Michelle nodded, her gaze steadfastly on Jake's.

A sleepy Lili easily took Liz's hand and was led from the room. The click of the door catch was unusually loud in the quiet room.

Jake opened his mouth, trying to work it around words that made sense.

"Shh," Michelle whispered, sliding into his embrace.

Jake stood, not daring to touch her, groaning when he felt the hard thud of her heart beating through her rib cage.

"I just want you to know that I..." Her words trailed off, her voice catching.

Jake pulled back to look into her face.

"I want you to know that our time together...it was the best of my life. The love I feel for you...it will never go away. I will carry it with me always." She let him go.

Jake felt as if the very ground had been snatched out from under his feet.

Michelle twisted the simple gold band on her finger. She opened his hand and slowly placed the hot band of metal in his palm, then closed his fingers over it.

Then she was gone.

CHAPTER FIFTEEN

JAKE FELT LIKE breaking something. He wanted to take a baseball bat and pound something, anything into a pulp. Make it resemble the mess that was his life as he watched Liz back out of the drive with Michelle, little Lili waving at him through the back window.

He didn't understand a thing. Despite all Michelle's explaining, a thousand and one questions remained. *She loved him.* His heart skipped a beat. *She didn't want to stay.* His heart dropped to the ground where surely someone would come by and stomp on it any second.

The first person who came up was Pops.

"Did they decide some shopping was in order?"

The fact that someone had spoken took forever to register as Jake watched Liz's car disappear from view. It took a few moments longer for the words to make any sense.

"What?"

He turned to find Pops standing next to him. "I asked if the girls decided some shopping was in order, you know, for little Lili."

"Shopping?"

Pops's grin faded from his lined face. "Jake? Where are they going?"

Jake turned and went into the house, stalking the length of it, then pacing back. When he came to a stop, Pops was just where he'd left him.

"You know, I thought finding Lili…by reuniting Michelle with her daughter, that the three of you could start being a family."

"Family? There's not going to be any family, Pops. Liz is taking Michelle and Lili into town so they can catch a flight out to France."

"What?" It was Pops's turn to look as though someone had just sucker punched him.

"I said—"

"I heard what you just said, Jake. I'm just having trouble believing it." His chest puffed out as he took a deep breath. "You know, I thought this day couldn't possibly get any worse. First, the thing at your mom's gravesite, with Connor saying what he did, then my having to decide to break things off with Billie—"

Jake held up his hand. "Whoa. Wait a minute. You're going a little too fast for me here." This communicating stuff was going to take a little longer to get used to. Then again, he was tempted to never speak again. Look at where his opening up had gotten him.

He squinted at his father. "Did you just say you broke things off with Mel's mother?"

Sean looked over his shoulder, relief washing over his face, apparently because Melanie wasn't anywhere near. "Yeah. She wasn't too happy about it, either. I mean, she didn't say anything—which is how I knew she wasn't happy. Just kind of made this *oh* sound. You know the kind. That small word that says so much yet so little?"

Jake frowned. No, he didn't know.

"Anyway, I just want to ask you one thing, Jacob William McCoy… Are you *crazy?* I mean, have you completely lost your mind?" He pointed a finger in the direction the car had gone. "Your brothers and I didn't go to all that trouble just so you could blithely wave as those two women leave your life. And I sure as hell know that *you* didn't go through what you have over the past few days toward that end, either."

Jake stared at him mutely.

Sean paced a short way, then stalked back, his eyes blazing. "What is it with you boys, anyway? I mean, I know I haven't always been a good father, that my parenting skills were pretty much nonexistent while you guys were growing up. But, good Lord, you all couldn't be any dumber had I purposely set out to make you that way."

Jake blinked at him, completely dumbstruck.

"Well, don't just stand there, you idiot! Go and bring them back!"

He couldn't move. Then, finally, he found himself shaking his head. "You don't understand, Pops. I didn't let them go anywhere. Michelle just…well, she just up and left. Going after her isn't going to accomplish anything."

"How can you be so sure?"

"Because she made me that way."

Sean looked at him long and hard, then turned and walked into the house, the screen door slapping closed behind him.

"MEET ME at the diner in downtown Manchester."

Edgar Mollens's final words echoed through Michelle's mind as she slowly slid into the red booth and anxiously glanced around the retro-style diner called Bo and Ruth's Paradise Diner.

"Look, *Maman!* An angel." She absently watched as Lili plucked a candied cherub from a perch in the middle of the table.

"Yes, *ma chérie,* an angel," she said, not having the energy to correct her. She feared the image of Jake's crushed expression was burned into her mind forever. She saw the haunted shadow in his eyes whenever she closed her own. She felt her heart break all over again at the memory of his speechless countenance, his obvious pain.

Liz slid in across from her, her eyes watchful, her posture unsure. A wiry-haired waitress sashayed up to the booth and regarded Liz with a wide smile. "Well, if it isn't the little newlywed come to town for a visit."

Michelle's gaze was riveted to the woman's face. She wondered how many people knew of her and Jake's...arrangement. She didn't dare call it a marriage. Not now. It was too dangerous to her mental health to think of their time together as anything more than an almost was.

Liz coughed. "Mitch and I have been married a whole two months now, Myra. I hardly think that qualifies as newlyweds."

Michelle felt her cheeks go hot. Of course. The woman Liz had called Myra wasn't referring to her; she was talking about Liz.

"And who do we have here?" Myra asked.

"I'm Lili," Michelle's daughter announced.

"Well, hello there, little Lili. I'm Myra. And do I ever have just the thing for you."

"Ice cream!" Lili exclaimed.

Michelle watched her daughter as if from a distance. While much remained the same, in the two hours since they had been reunited, she'd come to notice certain changes, both subtle and obvious. The closest she could come to describing it was that her daughter had undergone a certain type of Americanization in the two months since Gerald had taken her from France. Her English, while accented, was clear. Her behavior was decidedly more outgoing. And she bore no obvious emotional scars from her ordeal.

Tears welled in her eyes as she counted her blessings.

She reached out to touch her daughter's hair, but Lili

pushed her hand away as she introduced the angel to her stuffed elephant, Julianne.

Michelle's gaze trailed through the window to the street. Was Edgar already there somewhere, watching them?

Myra served Lili a child-size portion of cherry pie complete with ice cream, then poured coffee for Michelle and Liz. After a few failed attempts at striking up a conversation with what must have seemed to her a morose pair, the waitress shrugged her skinny shoulders and sashayed behind the main counter, where Michelle noticed two beefy men holding coffee cups and openly watching them from their stools. Through the window that looked into the kitchen, a man wearing a white knit cap and another woman also looked on.

Liz took a long pull from her cup. "Look, Michelle…I know I promised I wouldn't ask any unwelcome questions, but…" She sighed, then sat back in the booth. "I'm going to have to break that promise. Are you sure you know what you're doing?"

Michelle stared into her cup, trying not to compare her romantic future to the murky black liquid. She slowly nodded. "Yes. It is the only way to guarantee Jake won't get into trouble."

Liz's laugh surprised her. "Did you explain this to Jake that way? Believe me, the last thing any of the McCoys are afraid of is a little trouble."

Michelle managed a small smile. If she knew anything, she knew that. But she wouldn't, couldn't ask Jake to sacrifice any more for her than he already had. This was the only way she could guarantee he would remained untouched.

As Edgar had explained it to her, Jake was facing prison time for his part in this "whole charade." She smoothed her daughter's hair from her face, Lili's interest in her treat making her forget to push her away. If she gave herself up with no further fight, Edgar had agreed to leave Jake and his involvement in the entire matter out of it. But she, of course, would effectively be barred from ever entering the States again.

"He doesn't even know me," she found herself whispering.

Liz frowned, saying nothing for a long moment. "I'd bet you two know each other far better than either of you will admit to." She crossed her legs under the table. "Knowing someone sometimes has very little to do with knowing the minute details about each other's lives. If you're lucky, like Mitch and I are, it has to do with your *knowing* each other. Know what I mean?"

Michelle squinted at her. "In the…biblical sense?" she said, remembering the company of an impressionable four-year-old.

"Then there's that," Liz said, color warming her cheeks. "But no. What I mean is, without your having to say it, you know and he knows that what you share goes beyond the details. Details that were important before you met, but take on a whole new meaning afterward."

Michelle searched her face, trying to figure out what she was saying.

Liz sighed. "Okay, look, I'm still pretty new at all this love stuff myself. It took me most of my life to figure out that home isn't a place, but a person." She waved her hand. "But that's neither here nor there. What I want to tell you is that I've known all the McCoys for…well, for far longer than I'd like to admit to." Her smile told Michelle otherwise. "And Jake…well, Jake is never one to impulsively jump into anything. He's the type of guy who has his routines and never, I mean never, veers from them. Never, that is, until you."

Michelle averted her gaze, feeling her cheeks heat again. Liz's words made her remember her and Jake's first night together. Their long conversation about sex and his truckload of inhibitions…and her lack of them. She appreciated the irony of the situation. His argument that a couple should know each other better, that sex should be more than just a physical coming together, but that it had as much to do with respect and a general liking of the person you were sleeping with. Then there had been her counterargument that things like respect and liking had nothing to do with physical attraction.

Oh, how all that had changed, and quickly.

Liz was looking out the window as she continued. "I guess what I'm trying to say, Michelle, is this." She met her gaze. "Jake had more than the reasons you think to do what he did. He might have said he was marrying you to help you, but I suspect even he's coming to see what a lie that was." Her sudden smile seemed completely out of place. "As a matter of fact, I think he's already figured it out."

Michelle sensed his presence before she saw him. She turned her head to where he stood just inside the door, his gaze glued to her face.

Liz laid her hand on top of Michelle's where it lay on the table. "I can't tell you how much it must have taken him to come down here. Promise me one thing—that you'll hear him out."

Michelle nodded slowly.

Liz slipped from the booth. Lili had finished her pie and easily gave her hand to Liz when the woman offered to show her exactly how those little angels were made in the kitchen.

Michelle felt as though her heart had leaped up and was firmly lodged in her throat. But before she could say anything, the clang of a cowbell announced the arrival of another man.

Edgar Mollens.

Michelle bit on her lip as much to keep from crying out as to keep the tears from falling. Telling Jake once that she must leave had practically ripped her in two. To tell him goodbye again…

Her gaze fastened on his dear, dear face as he looked first

at Edgar, then at her, his confused expression endearing him to her further. But the last thing she expected was the slow shaking of his head. No words. No protests. No declarations. Merely a simple gesture that said too much.

Edgar cleared his throat. "McCoy."

It seemed to take a moment for Jake to realize Edgar had spoken. "Mollens."

Edgar looked at Michelle meaningfully. "Your decision was the best possible one, Miss Lambert. You may not see that now, but rest assured, you will. And so will Jake."

"McCoy," Jake said quietly.

"What?" Edgar regarded Jake with a frown.

"I said McCoy. Her name's Mrs. McCoy." Jake didn't budge his gaze from Michelle's face as he said the words. "No matter what, we are married, Michelle. Your leaving won't change that. Not for me." He lifted his hand where his wedding band glinted in the afternoon light. "I'm married to you no matter where you are physically." His voice lowered to a gravelly roar. "I'd prefer it if you were here."

Edgar quickly stepped closer to Michelle. "Remember everything we talked about…Michelle. No matter if you leave now or two months from now, after all the legal red tape is out of the way, you will be leaving. The difference is whether Jake will go to prison or not. There's no way your marriage will stand up in a court of law. It'll fall apart like the house of cards it is within an hour of questioning."

Michelle looked from Jake to Edgar, her heart thudding painfully in her chest. *You're wrong,* she wanted to tell the INS agent. Hers and Jake's marriage was not a house of cards to be blown over with the lightest wind. While their union hadn't initially been based on love and permanent commitment, it had grown into that. And she suspected that rare were the times when young marriages could weather what hers and

Jake's had in such a short period of time and manage to come out the stronger for it.

She glanced at her ringless finger. The absence of the simple wedding band meant little. Her bond to Jake transcended what a piece of jewelry could symbolize. She loved him, above and beyond nearly everything else in her life. She'd never thought herself capable of loving anyone other than her daughter for a long, long time, but from somewhere within, Jake had coaxed out a love that brimmed generously from her heart, filling it, filling her…bonding them.

Slowly, Jake began to lift his arms, inviting her into his embrace. With barely a hesitation, she slid from the booth and ràn to him, burrowing into the soft folds of his sweatshirt, clutching him as if he were the four elements combined, everything in this world that she needed to survive.

"God forgive me for hurting you," she murmured, tilting her head to receive the kiss he pressed to the top of her head. "God forgive me for putting you through what you're going to face because of me. But I can't help myself. I love you, Jake McCoy."

Edgar muttered an especially crude curse. "You've just signed your death warrant, McCoy. Trust me on this. The company will never recognize your marriage."

Jake tucked Michelle tightly against his side and faced his co-worker. "You just go ahead and try to make this marriage look like anything less than a real marriage. You won't succeed. This is as solid as it gets. You're the one who's going to come away with something on the bottom of his shoes, Edgar."

The cowbell rang. Michelle looked up to see Melanie leading every last member of the McCoy family through the door like some sort of ragtag brigade. They were joined by the two men at the counter and the man with the cap in the kitchen.

Liz rushed out on the cook's heels along with the other woman, then out came Lili. She bulleted to Michelle, tunneling her way between her and Jake, curving her thin arms around each of their legs.

Jake freed a hand and hesitantly reached down to touch Lili's blond curls. "You chose the wrong family to screw with, Edgar. No one ever crosses the McCoys."

EPILOGUE

JAKE SNEAKED UP on his wife—*his wife;* how he loved calling Michelle that, with no reservations, no fears that their relationship didn't qualify—where she talked to his sisters-in-law, Liz and Melanie. He put his hands on her narrow waist and swiveled her to face him, the rustle of her wedding dress filling his ears, her flushed features and twinkling eyes filling his gaze. He'd never seen a woman look so beautiful. He wanted to tug her into the mammoth white tent set up in case of inclement weather, hoist her on top of one of the linen-covered tables and have at her right then and there.

But there were a hundred or so guests milling about the McCoy farm so he limited himself to a chaste taste of her sexy mouth.

He'd planned to ask her if she was happy but no longer felt the need to. The way she glowed in the setting sunlight that kissed her profile, practically floated over the neatly trimmed lawn in her puffy white dress, her laughter tinkling above the sound of silverware clinking against china, told him she *was* happy. And it made him feel proud to know he was partially responsible.

It was difficult to believe it had been just three weeks ago that Michelle and Lili had been a heartbeat away from vanishing from his life. That the woman wriggling in his embrace had called Edgar Mollens and struck a deal that would get him off the hook with the INS.

So much had changed since then. Michelle and Lili had already transformed his apartment in Woodley Park into a home. Frilly curtains, colorful pillows, full cupboards and hoards of toys made it difficult to recognize the place when he came home at night. And he couldn't have been happier. Although he did have to talk to Michelle about the scruffy little cat Lili had brought home the day before.

"Hey, Jake, you know the rules," Melanie warned him. "No monopolizing the bride until after the reception."

Liz agreed. "That's right. You two are going to have plenty of time on your honeymoon."

The women fell silent, looking at a spot somewhere over his left shoulder. A man cleared his throat. Jake glanced to find Edgar standing awkwardly behind him and Michelle. His first instinct was to run, though running was no longer a concern.

Instead, he grinned, and he and Michelle turned to greet him. He extended his hand to his fellow agent. "Glad you could make it, Edgar."

"Yeah. Me, too." He glanced at Michelle. "Mrs. McCoy. Congratulations. You're a fetching bride."

Michelle's smile widened. "Thank you, Edgar."

Edgar's discomfort level seemed to grow the longer he stood there. He lifted a hand to his head and smoothed the little hair remaining there. "Look, I just wanted to, you know, apologize again for everything. And to give you this. Think of it as a wedding gift of sorts—except, of course, that you've earned it."

Michelle accepted the envelope.

"No need for apologies, Edgar. Funny thing is, you may be partially responsible for Michelle and me being where we are right now."

His wife's tiny gasp drew his attention. She slid out a brand-spanking-new green card. She looked at Jake, fresh tears making her eyes look that much brighter. Then she threw her arms around Edgar. "Thank you. Thank you so very much."

Edgar's face turned beet red. "It's nothing, really. Your coming in and explaining everything that happened in California ten years ago helped enormously. The review board unanimously decided you were no threat. From there, I didn't have any problem expediting things to get you this."

Jake pressed his lips against Michelle's ear. "Shall we forget Hawaii and make Paris our honeymoon destination, instead?"

Her answer was the closing of her eyes and a squeeze of his arm where it encircled her waist.

"Well…congratulations," Edgar said, ungracefully backing away and nearly tripping over a tent stake.

Liz and Mel immediately descended, wanting to see the new card that identified Michelle as a resident alien—though Jake didn't plan to stop until she was a full-fledged citizen. He caught a glimpse of Pops some distance behind his sisters-in-law, staring after the setting sun. The old man had been quieter than usual lately. And now, in the midst of the celebration, he couldn't have looked more melancholy.

Jake scanned the guests comprised of family, townsfolk and co-workers, until he spotted Mel's mother, Wilhemenia, straightening the hill of gifts on a nearby table.

Mel elbowed him in the ribs. "So are you going to leave us alone so we can indulge in some more girl talk or what, McCoy?"

Jake tore his gaze from Wilhemenia and held his hands up in surrender. "Okay, okay."

Michelle smiled. "Lili's in the barn, I think. Why don't you make sure she's not getting into any trouble."

Jake lifted her left hand and kissed the back, then reluctantly left his wife to continue her post-ceremony gossiping session. He caught Melanie saying something about Michelle's wedding ring, and his grin widened. He waved at David and Connor where they stood to the side clutching their long-neck beer bottles for dear life. The last two single McCoy brothers were obviously uncomfortable attending the third wedding reception for a McCoy in the past half year. Jake rounded the bandstand and navigated around one of several gas lamps. Ah, there she was.

Near the new barn, Mitch and Lili were feeding the livestock. His heart skipped a beat when Billy the Kid Goat licked Lili's palm, and she threw back her blond head and shrieked with laughter. Absently, Jake rubbed his leg.

In the past twenty-one days, he and Michelle and Lili had spent nearly every moment they could together as family. Except, of course, when he was at work, or when Lili took her afternoon naps and went to bed at night. It was then, when the little munchkin was otherwise occupied, that he and Michelle took advantage of every moment alone....

He looked at his monkey suit, longing for the jeans and oxford shirt he'd been wearing earlier in the day. Jeans. He couldn't remember the last time he'd worn a pair. But, as Michelle insisted, he looked damned good in them. He grinned. Well, he couldn't deny that they were more appropriate for a life that included a playful, messy four-year-old.

For the first few days after Michelle's decision to stay and fight the INS with him, he'd been torn as what to do. Quit his job? Or stay until everything was settled? He'd already pretty much guessed they wouldn't terminate his employment. Their reasons would have been shaky, at best. After all, the job of deporting Michelle had not been assigned to him, so conflict never entered the equation.

Now that she had her green card, he had to decide what he

wanted to do. Something that helped potential immigrants, he thought. He and Mitch were already discussing the possibility of his buying into his P.I. partnership and including immigration and naturalization aid to their list of services.

And Michelle... Well, she had already been snapped up by a French restaurant within walking distance of their D.C. home, and her plans to open her own restaurant were already in the works.

"Jake!" Lili called, snapping him from his reverie.

He smiled and continued to the barn as she ran toward him. Even now, he acknowledged a tiny pang of awkwardness around the little girl. She was so...tiny. He, so large. But the pang instantly disappeared as she catapulted herself into his arms, giggling as he compensated for her weight by swinging her around. He crouched and straightened the skirt of her frilly dress. He couldn't be sure how much she understood of everything that had happened in the past three months. He planned to make the rest of her life as carefree and happy as possible.

"Did *Maman* tell you I talked to Nana and Grandpa this morning?" Lili said, speaking so quickly the words emerged as a single very long, breathy one.

Jake nodded, watching as Mitch gave him a wave then disappeared into the barn. "Yes, in fact, she did."

"They may be coming to visit me next month, did you know that?"

"Really?" He feigned ignorance, though he and Michelle had discussed the possible ramifications of their visit for the past three days. "That's great."

She hooked a finger inside the buttoned flap of his shirt and tugged. "Uh-huh." Her face screwed up into an expression that was becoming as familiar as her smile. It meant she was chewing something over. That she would share the thought was a forgone conclusion—another one of the qualities she'd inherited from her mother. "Since you and *Maman* are married, does that make you my papa?"

Jake tried not to cough at the sudden tickle in his throat. "That depends."

She frowned at him. "On what?"

He swept her bangs from her forehead with a brush of a finger. "On whether or not you want me to be."

She appeared to consider it long and hard. "Okay."

His chuckle vibrated straight down to his feet. "That easy, huh? 'Okay'?"

He hadn't heard Michelle approach, but her words were impossible to ignore. "She knows a good find when she comes across one." She came to stand between them. "Just like her mother."

Jake stood up, hiking a giggling Lili with him. Michelle locked her arms around them both and kissed Jake soundly on the cheek. Lili did the same on the other.

Jake closed his eyes and tightened his hold on both of them. He wasn't sure what he'd done, but it must have been something very good indeed to deserve the love of both of these special women.

Life just didn't get any better than this….

"So, shall we fly this joint?" Michelle whispered into his ear.

He chuckled, knowing she meant "blow this joint," but not caring. "Don't we have a couple of things to take care of first?"

He put Lili down, then took Michelle's hand as Lili tugged them to their guests. Liz clinked her glass several times until everyone settled down, then directed all the single men to gather for the tossing of the garter.

Jake eyed Michelle. He'd been aching to get under those yards of white material for hours. He only wished his family and most of Manchester weren't gathered to watch as he finally did so. To hoots and calls, he knelt and slowly slid her skirt up. He grinned at her surprised giggle and attempts to keep him from lifting it too far. But all laughter left him when he slipped a finger under the red and white garter, the flesh of her bare leg unbearably hot, air suddenly a rare commodity. It didn't matter how often he made love with this woman, every time was like the first time. Awkwardly, he drew the scrap of material down her leg. Once he finally had it free, he turned, twirling it around his index finger.

"Throw it, Papa!" Lili shouted from where Pops held her nearby. His throat tightened as he faced the small crowd of single men.

He chuckled when Marc and Mitch forced Connor and David to join the group, then stood as crossed-armed, smiling sentinels when the two bachelors tried to bolt. Turning, Jake gave the garter a squeeze, then flung it over his shoulder. A roar of laughter rippled through the gathering, and he turned to find the naughty bit of silk and lace sitting on top of the youngest McCoy's fair head. David dragged the garter from his hair and nearly tripped over his own feet when Connor punched him good-naturedly on the arm.

"The bouquet!" the waitress from the town's diner shouted. Bulleting her way through the throng of men, Myra waved her hands. "Do it just as we practiced, Michelle!"

Jake chuckled as he helped his wife to her feet.

But whatever the two women may or may not have practiced, the bouquet went far wide of the target of ten or so women gathered…and landed straight in Wilhemenia Weber's lap.

*Everything you love about romance...**and more!***

*Please turn the page for Signature Select™
Bonus Features.*

Bonus Features:

FROM McCOY, WITH LOVE

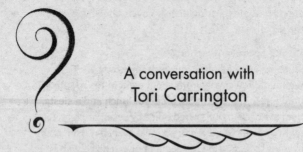

A conversation with
Tori Carrington

4

When interviewed for this book, Tony and Lori were on holiday in Tony's native Greece. Maybe it was the warm morning air, the chance to relax or the laid-back vibe of the country but whatever combination of elements were at play, we think you'll find these personal reflections as inspiring as we did.

How did you begin your writing career?

Our career began with reading and love of a great story. I (Lori) have always been a voracious reader, beginning with Goldilocks and every printed page I could lay my hands on. Tony has always been an avid movie fan, starting with the likes of the old spaghetti Westerns and continuing with every genre available. So it was only natural that when a book or a movie moved either or both of us, we'd spend sometimes hours discussing it, what came after the words *The End,* how we might have changed the direction of the story—essentially not wanting the experience to end. When in 1984 Tony suggested we try our hand at writing a story of our own, everything clicked perfectly into place. Here we are now, some thirty published novels later, happier for the experience.

Do you have a writing routine?
Since we write full-time, our days are pretty regimented. We write from about eight in the morning until one in the afternoon, break for lunch and a siesta, then are back in our shared office by seven or eight at night until about eleven or so most every day. Half our evenings are devoted to keeping our extensive Web site (www.toricarrington.com) updated and chatting online with fellow romance lovers and fans. It's said that technology and the Web serve to further isolate people. We disagree. We've met some of our best friends online. And there's something uniquely beautiful about meeting someone you've talked to for sometimes years online in the real world. We have fans we call friends in faraway places such as Pakistan, Bulgaria and Australia we probably would not have connected with outside our books. That would be a shame, indeed!

When you're not writing, what do you love to do?
Everything! Well, short of jumping out of airplanes and rock climbing. We love to travel and explore different cultures and towns and cities. And since Tony's originally from Greece, we spend a great deal of time there, as well, soaking up all things Greek. We attend at least six major writing and fan conferences a year and have no problem putting work aside to schmooze with fellow writers and friends and to refill the creative well. We also try to carve out time either before or after a conference to get out and explore the local environs. Recently in Dallas after the Romance Writers of

America's annual writer's conference, we spent the afternoon with a couple of longtime friends searching a nearby cemetery for Bonnie Parker's—of Bonnie and Clyde fame—grave marker. We never did find it, but we had a hell of an interesting time looking. And it certainly isn't an experience we'll soon forget.

Reading, of course, is also a favorite pastime. Wherever we are, you'll find newspapers, magazines and all sorts of books littering the place. A hotel room? Brochures and travel books and local papers will be stacked on the floor and tables along with biographies of local interest. At home our to-be-read piles pose a direct threat to our health because they constantly seem at risk of toppling over on us. And, of course, it only stands to reason that the book we want is always near the bottom of those piles.

Kayaking is a newly acquired hobby. We were turned on to it by our Harlequin editor, Brenda Chin, and love everything about the feel of gliding on top of a body of water, taking in nature and just enjoying feeling connected to everything around us.

The McCoys have a large fan base. What is it about these guys that keep readers wanting more?
If we knew the answer to that, all our books and the characters that inhabit them would be equally as compelling. Honestly, we don't know why others feel the way they do. We can say how we feel about this family, however. And it begins with them being a family. They're adorably dysfunctional and strong and each individual doesn't think twice about coming together as a whole for the good of the family.

We will say that we're endlessly flattered by the interest in these magnificent men and women. We're incapable of writing a single, stand-alone book. Good characters always seem attached to other good characters, whether they be brothers and sisters or friends or the neighbor that lives up the way. Our stories are colored with people that often demand stories of their own.

In the case of the McCoys, we began with Marc McCoy. We hadn't planned for a series of books. We'd merely been searching for his identity, and part of that included his being the often-overlooked middle son of five. It was our Harlequin editor who called us up after reading *License To Thrill* to say, "You know Marc has four brothers, don't you?" And thus our first miniseries was born. We so thoroughly enjoyed writing the books and exploring the minds and hearts of each of these stubbornly irresistible men that when we finished the fifth and what was then the final book, we were already thinking of ways we could continue the miniseries, if just for the sake of our own imaginations, you know, to keep these men very much alive in *our* minds and hearts. And so was born Kathryn Buckingham McCoy, the complete opposite of these men careerwise, but no less strong and stubborn. It was wonderful visiting with this remarkable, salt-of-the-earth family again. And, dare I say, our minds are alive with ideas on how we still might continue the saga.

Circling back to what keeps readers wanting more, since our own reluctance to let go of certain stories was what inspired us to load our first sheet of fresh typewriter paper in an old manual IBM we bought for twenty dollars at a garage sale, we're proud that our stories are now finding a special place in others' hearts.

What or who inspires you?
For Tony, his first source for inspiration was his parents. His father, Evaggelos Karayianni, passed away in 1987 at 102 and was the quintessential Greek philosopher, imparting sage advice much like the Oracle of Delphi. If at first you didn't understand what he was saying, you could be sure that one day you would. We're still awed by advice he gave us long ago that we're only now beginning to grasp. Philosophy for him wasn't a handful of archaic words in a book to study for an exam; it was a way of life. And his mother, Kostoula Kaloyeropoulou Karayianni, found strength in hard work and her family. Salt of the earth. We miss them both enormously and we feel their presence always.

Also, everything and everyone we cross paths with inspires us. We hate to be so vague, but it's true. Since we're in Greece as we write this, I can tell you how just this morning we walked to the beach to pick up some fresh fish for dinner and on our way back we stopped to get some greens to fix along with them. The supermarket was just opening and it's then you get a feel for how such a business operates by watching employees work together to get things up and running. There was a synchronicity that's fascinating. A way of coming together to make something so large and complicated look simple and accessible. There was also an easy camaraderie between the employees that spoke of having worked together for some time, giving them a family feel (hmm, I'm seeing a theme here). As we watched from outside, the whole began to break off into separate entities and characters began emerging along with endless questions. The elderly man who handles the tomatoes with such care with gnarled fingers and smile grooves around his deep-set eyes— what has he done all his life? Does he have family? Live nearby? What does he do with his time when he knocks off work for the day? The pretty cashier—is she hit on by male customers? Does it bother or flatter her? Does she have a boyfriend who picks her up when her shift ends, and do they go for a ride along the nearby beach before going home? Linger over baklava at a café? Who do they all love? What do they hate? Do they have dreams of possibly reaching out beyond the supermarket? Or are they happy there, working together as a family?

Sometimes we ask these questions when we have a chance. (The elderly man is a widower from an island in the southern Aegean and used to sponge dive. He has five children, two of whom now make their lives in the States with families and children of their own. He enjoys going for long walks by himself and passing the time in a nearby *cafeneio* with his friends, drinking Greek coffee and contemplating politics and the world at large. The pretty cashier just broke up with her longtime boyfriend and is mostly flattered with the attention she gets. She dreams of designing her own line of clothes and takes night classes toward that goal. Both are happy with their present jobs.) Sometimes we allow our imaginations to answer the questions.

Will the supermarket idea ever make it to paper? Maybe. Maybe not. But for us the time was well spent. Because for a little while we shared the lives of these people we all overlook as we move through our own lives.

So, simply, life inspires us.

How did you meet?
At a Greek diner, of course. In the East Side of Toledo, Ohio, over coffee and baklava, no less. It was a clearly defining moment—until then I believed "love at first sight" were words reserved solely for romance novels. Not anymore. The instant I met Tony's rich brown eyes, I saw my future stretched out in front of me like a strand of polished, precious pearls. I glimpsed breathless joy and happy years spent together. Of us sitting on a front porch swing enjoying the weather and each other well into old age. Neither of us could have imagined that now, twenty-two years after that first meeting, we would be where we are, doing what we're doing. Sometimes it seems like a dream. Like we're still standing in that diner seeing all this in each other's eyes.

I like to joke that ever since learning about Greece, I wished I were Greek. Since that wasn't possible, I did the next best thing: I married a Greek.

What book do you wish you had written?
We could write another book just talking about the books we wish we had written. While not every book we read qualifies—or perhaps they do because even when books disappoint they inspire conversation on how we might have written them differently—there are enough of them that to try to pick a handful would be difficult to contemplate. Every book, whether it be fiction or nonfiction, a classic or a postmodern feminist day-in-the-life comedy, evokes myriad responses in us. When

either of us reads a particularly good book by a natural talent, we may walk around in a reflective daze for days pondering what it was that made us think we could write. And ultimately we're moved to reach further, work harder, write better. A bad book also teaches us what not to do. But all books hold some message, some meaning that adds something to our lives.

What keeps you real?
Each other. Reality. Life. Whenever we start to feel a little full of ourselves, experience the desire to puff out our chests in self-satisfaction, something will happen to provide a much-needed reality check. Recently, our niece Matina had major surgery, and three months after the procedure, when we all thought she was experiencing a difficult recovery, she fell deathly ill. It was eventually determined that the surgeon had accidentally nicked her pancreas during the original surgery, sending her entire system off balance and into jeopardy. Following an additional three months in the hospital in intensive care, she's thankfully well on the road to recovery, but her struggle reminds us of how very fleeting life is. And how very lucky we are to be healthy and happy. And in the end, that's really what it's all about, isn't it?

Marsha Zinberg, Executive Editor, Signature Select Program, spoke with Tony and Lori in the spring.

McCOY

A Family Tree

McCOY FAMILY TREE

Sean McCoy (Kathryn Connor McCoy—deceased) m. Wilhemenia Weber
D.C. Metro Police Officer
Family Patriarch

Marc McCoy Secret Service Agent m. Melanie Weber	Mitch McCoy Ex-FBI/ Ex-P.I./Rancher m. Liz Braden	Jake McCoy INS Agent m. Michelle Lambert	David McCoy D.C. Metro Police Officer m. Kelli Hatfield	Connor McCoy U.S. Marshal m. Bronte O'Brien	Kathryn (Kat) Buckingham McCoy Criminal Defense Attorney
July 1999 **License To Thrill**	March 2000 **The P.I. Who Loved Her**	July 2000 **For Her Eyes Only**	March 2001 **You Only Love Once**	July 2001 **Never Say Never Again**	**A Real McCoy**

McCOY FAMILY TREE BONUS FEATURE

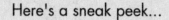

Here's a sneak peek...

A Real McCoy

by
Tori Carrington

Has she got what it takes to be a real McCoy? In the next twenty-four hours defense attorney Kat Buckingham will discover she's adopted, that her biological father is very much alive and that she has five very protective older brothers. Oh, yeah, and she'll be wrongfully arrested...for the murder of her fiancé.

CHAPTER 1

A GREAT MAN is measured not by his assets or his failings but rather by how he can deliver a kiss while his target is walking on a treadmill, listening to a taped deposition and leafing through legal briefs.

Kat Buckingham smiled as her fiancé, James Smith, managed not only to plant a kiss on her cheek without breaking her stride, but did so without smacking her chin or making her feel like she was putting him out.

He held up Chinese takeout. "I got your favorite."

Kat tugged the right muff of the headphones away from her ear. "I'll meet you in the kitchen in twenty."

She watched as James walked away from her in the historic Georgetown town house she'd bought last year. He disappeared through the foyer on his way to the back of the first floor. She refastened the headphones then pressed the button for rewind to listen to the part she'd missed again.

Somehow in law school Kat had never imagined herself being this busy and twenty-seven. As a junior criminal defense attorney at the law offices of Kennedy, Salizar and Jewison, her calendar easily eclipsed the grueling schedule she'd kept at GWU. Multitasking had always been the name of the game, but now… Now she found herself running circles around her own circles. She caught on something on the tape she was listening to.

"…the patient displays all the classic signs of post-traumatic stress disorder. If caught in time, he would never have committed the crimes…."

Kat pressed the rewind button and listened to the passage again while jotting a reference note on her pad. The pen slipped from her hand. She reached to catch it, pulling her earphones from the player and catching the edge of her Skechers on the moving treadmill. She was mildly surprised the abrupt spurt of bad luck didn't end up with her butt first on the floor. Instead she stood next to the whirring treadmill, silent earphones still attached to her head, the pen she'd dropped lying at her feet.

That's all right. It was nearly nine o'clock on a Sunday night and she hadn't had a minute to herself all weekend. Maybe this was fate's way of giving her a proverbial kick in the behind.

She switched off the exercise equipment and the cassette player then gathered her notes and legal briefs together and dumped them unceremoniously into her briefcase. The scent of something sharp filled her nose as she rubbed the towel around her neck against her damp face. It smelled like something burning.

That's odd. James had brought takeout. Why would he be cooking anything?

She longingly eyed the stairs to the second floor, desperately wanting a shower, and instead headed for the kitchen. "James? What's that smell?"

The crystalline sound of breaking glass made her pick up her pace, then a loud thump drew her up short. What was that?

She pushed the swinging door open and stood staring at James's bloodied, inert body on the otherwise spotless yellow kitchen tile. She rushed to his side and dropped to her knees. "James? James? Oh, God, what's happened...?"

Blood covered his face and the front of his crisp white shirt as movement caught her attention from the corner of her eye. She gasped as a shadow darted out the open back door.

Kat pressed her shaking fingertips to James's carotid artery. No pulse.

Oh, God...

She scrambled for the cordless telephone on the wall barely aware she was kneeling on broken glass as the sharp shards tore through her leggings. "Help! He's dead. My husband's dead!"

U.S. MARSHAL HARRY KINCAID sat in his plain sedan down the block from James Smith's fiancée's Georgetown town house and glanced at his watch. He might as well go home. Routine dictated that Smith would probably stay the night at Kat Buckingham's house.

Hell, truth be told, he shouldn't even be there. He'd filed his quarterly report on Smith's status yesterday. Still, something kept him there even though he had another report due on another protected witness later next week. Something that might or might not have to do with

Smith's pretty fiancée, criminal defense attorney Kathryn Buckingham.

Pretty. The woman was drop-dead gorgeous. And probably didn't have a clue that her tall, slender frame, natural, almost-white-blond hair and green eyes turned heads, both male and female, when she walked down a street.

But what got him were those moments when her thoughts appeared to wander—usually when she was doing three things at once—and she'd get a wistful, almost lonely look on her strikingly beautiful face as if staring at something she wanted but knew she'd never have.

Of course, it didn't help that he'd come across some very interesting information on Kathryn Jane Buckingham last week while trying to verify that she wasn't involved in her fiancé's extracurricular activities. Information that not only proved how small the world was, but how strange and curious. He'd grappled with the newly acquired knowledge for the past five days, trying to decide what, if anything, he should do with it. Not on a professional level. No. This information was very personal indeed and could have a tremendous impact on his fellow marshal and best friend Connor McCoy's life.

Harry rubbed his face. What did it say about his own life that he was sitting outside a witness's house on a Sunday night in May watching other people living their lives rather than living his own? Worse, he was infatuated with the fiancée of a relocated witness who should, by all rights, be behind bars along with the people he'd helped convict three years ago. If not for his past crimes, then for his present.

But that wasn't for Harry to judge. He'd filed his report on James Smith's questionable activities. Now it was up to his superior to decide what to do with the file. Either turn the other cheek or forward it on to the proper authorities for further investigation.

He adjusted his rearview mirror and reached to switch on his ignition when he spotted a DCPD car speeding up on the street behind him, sirens blaring. It screeched to a stop in front of Buckingham's place.

Harry reached for the door handle and started to climb out as an EMS vehicle roared up from the opposite end of the street drawing to a halt mere inches away from the front bumper of the cruiser.

Oh, hell.

Remembering the uneasy feeling he'd had over the past week, Harry rushed for the town house, his badge in hand.

AN HOUR LATER Kat sat perched on the edge of the couch in the living room, the blanket someone had draped over her shoulders doing little to combat her uncontrollable shivering.

James was dead....

The three words wound around and around her numbed brain like an unbroken chain, becoming one long sentence rather than countless separate ones.

It seemed impossible that she should lose someone so close to her again in such a violent manner. Wasn't it only a few years ago that she'd lost her parents in a car crash? Wasn't it her they had been visiting when they'd driven home in that freak ice storm?

Her shivers coalesced into a long, bone-racking shudder.

A silent, watchful policewoman sat opposite her while voices sounded in the foyer, closer than the kitchen where James's body lay. Kat looked up, staring almost sightlessly at a man who looked vaguely familiar. She might not have registered him at all but for the intense way he was looking at her.

"Mrs. Buckingham?"

She looked up into the face of another man dressed in a plain brown suit that had seen better days. "It's Miss…"

Her gaze made it as far as the palm-size notepad he held. "My information shows that you told the 911 operator that, quote, 'He's dead. My husband is dead.'"

Kat swallowed, hardly remembering the exchange. "We're…we were engaged. The wedding is…was scheduled for this August."

He flipped through the notepad again and made a note with one of those pens you picked up at the dry cleaners. "And the deceased's name?"

Kat pushed her hair back with a shaking hand. "Smith. James." She finally looked up into his face. "Who did you say you were again?"

"Detective Leary."

She glanced around. "I've already told one of your associates the information."

"Actually, Miss Buckingham, I was the one you told it to."

She squinted at him. "Then why are you asking me again?"

"Just to make sure I have the information straight."

More flipping. Kat discovered it was easier to look at the pad than at him. "Did you and Mr. Smith have an argument tonight?"

"No...I told you no." This wasn't happening. The blanket slipped from her shoulder and she repositioned it with little success. Her own hand caught her attention and she stared at the blood smeared there. James's blood.

"I...I was on the treadmill going over a deposition when James came in with dinner...."

"The Chinese food carton that started the fire in the microwave."

Kat nodded. "Yes. I had just finished and was going to join him in the kitchen when I smelled something burning and heard breaking glass."

Her voice caught and her trembling increased twofold.

"And this?"

She stared at a Ziploc bag that held what looked like a savings passbook.

"We found this near the body, Miss Buckingham. Your name is listed in the front. Were you and the deceased arguing over finances?"

Why would she and James argue about money? While they weren't wealthy by any stretch, they were doing well.

She caught the present tense of her thoughts and felt a fresh bout of tears threaten.

It didn't make any sense. Nothing made any sense.

"Miss Buckingham? Why was this next to the body?"

"I don't know," she said, her voice catching. "I have no idea why my savings passbook was in the kitchen."

"Detective, can you pursue this line of questioning

once Miss Buckingham has had a chance to compose herself?"

Kat felt the urge to laugh hysterically. She didn't think she'd ever feel composed again.

She glanced at the man who had asked the question to find the familiar one who had been watching her from the foyer.

"I'm the detective conducting this investigation, Kincaid, so if you'd be good enough to stay to the side."

Emotion welled up in Kat's throat. "Please…please. My fiancé's dead. Can I have a few moments alone?"

The pad flipped closed.

"Actually, I have all the information I need, Miss Buckingham." He looked to the policewoman across from her. "Officer, please place Miss Buckingham under arrest for the murder of one James Smith."

...NOT THE END...

Look for A REAL McCOY, in stores April 2005.

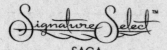
SAGA

The five McCoy brothers are about to meet the
newest member of the family…their sister!

National bestselling author

Tori Carrington

A brand-new, longer-length story from the
miniseries The Magnificent McCoy Men.

A REAL McCOY

In the next twenty-four hours, defense attorney
Kat Buckingham will discover she's adopted, that her
biological father is very much alive and that she has five
very protective older brothers—all working in law
enforcement. Oh, yeah, and she'll be wrongfully
arrested…for the murder of her fiancé!

Available April 2005.

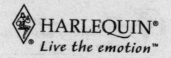
HARLEQUIN®
Live the emotion™

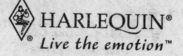